Maria Louisa Charlesworth

Ministering Children

A Tale Dedicated to Childhood

Maria Louisa Charlesworth

Ministering Children
A Tale Dedicated to Childhood

ISBN/EAN: 9783337077839

Printed in Europe, USA, Canada, Australia, Japan

Cover: Foto ©Andreas Hilbeck / pixelio.de

More available books at **www.hansebooks.com**

MINISTERING CHILDREN:

A Tale

DEDICATED TO CHILDHOOD.

BY

MARIA LOUISA CHARLESWORTH,

AUTHOR OF

"ENGLAND'S YEOMEN," "MINISTRY OF LIFE," "SUNDAY AFTERNOONS IN
THE NURSERY," "COTTAGE AND ITS VISITOR," "AFRICA'S MOUN-
TAIN VALLEY," "THE BEAUTIFUL HOME," ETC.

"Even a child is known by his doings, whether his work be pure, and whether it
be right."—PROVERBS xx. 11.

"Doctrines are the pillars of a discourse.—Illustrations are the windows that let in
the light."

NEW YORK:
ROBERT CARTER AND BROTHERS,
No. 530 BROADWAY.
1867.

PREFACE.

DIFFICULTY being sometimes felt in training children to the exercise of those kindly feelings which have
the Poor for their object, it was thought that an illus-
trative tale might prove a help toward this important
end. It must be allowed by all, that the present is a
day of increased exertion in behalf of those who are in
need ; but much care is necessary that the temporal
aid extended may prove, not a moral injury, but a
moral benefit, to both the receiver and the communi-
cator of that aid. May it not be worthy of consideration, whether the most generally effective way to
insure this moral benefit on both sides, would not be
the early calling forth and training the sympathies of
children by personal intercourse with want and sorrow,
while as yet those sympathies flow spontaneously. Let
the truth be borne in mind, that the influence of the giver
far exceeds that of the gift on the receiver of it ; and it
must surely then be admitted, that in all aid rendered

to others, the calling into exercise the best feelings of the heart, in both the giver and the receiver, is the most important object to be kept in view. To this end it is necessary that the talent of money be not suffered assume any undue supremacy in the service of benevolence. Let children be trained, and taught, and led aright, and they will not be slow to learn that they possess a personal influence every where ; that the first principles of Divine Truth acquired by them, are a means of communicating to others present comfort and eternal happiness ; and that the heart of Love is the only spring that can effectually govern and direct the hand of Charity.

MINISTERING CHILDREN

CHAPTER I.

"Oh! say not, dream not heavenly notes
To childish ears are vain;
That the young mind at random floats
And can not catch the strain.

Dim or unheard the words may fall,
And yet the heaven-taught mind
May learn the sacred air, and all
The harmony unwind."

"And this is the confidence that we have in Him, that, if we ask any thing according to His **will,** He heareth us."—1 John, **v. 14.**

THE chimes of the great church clock in a large old town were playing a quarter to nine, on a bright September morning, when a little school-girl, shutting her mother's door, came stepping down the long dark flight of stairs at the top of which she lived; she wore no shawl, or cloak, or bonnet; a frock of dark brown stuff, a little white linen apron tied round her waist, a white linen tippet, and a little fine linen cap with a single border crimped close round her face; this was the little school-girl's dress. Her name was Ruth: **and on her** arm she had hung **her** green baize bag with her Bible and school-books.

1

"Good-by, mother," she said : and shutting the door, stepped slowly down the dark stair-case, while her little white figure lighted up its gloom. When she reached the ground-floor of the house, she heard a low faint moan, as of some child in pain ; she stopped a minute to listen, and heard it again. The door at the bottom of the stair-case stood a little way open, and Ruth had sometimes seen the widow woman and her child who had come to live in that room ; and when she heard the moan again, she looked into the room, and there she saw the child in bed.

"Are you ill?" asked Ruth.

"Yes," said the child ; "and my pain is so bad! and I have nobody to be with me."

"Won't your mother come?" asked Ruth.

"No, mother 's got a day's work ; she won't be home all day ; and my pain is so bad! I wish you would stay with me."

"I must go to school," said Ruth, "but I will ask mother when I come home, to let me stay with you a little."

"O do! and make haste, do make haste! I don't like to be left alone."

Ruth went on her way to school. The sun was shining bright, and its warm rays beamed on her face, which was almost as white as the little crimped linen cap that pressed closely round it. Merry children, boys and girls, ran shouting and playing past her ; but she walked slowly on her way to school, and went up the high steps, and in at the school door, as the great church clock was striking nine. A good mark was set down in the book against her name, and she went to her place on the form.

Lessons went on for an hour, and the great church clock struck ten. Lessons went on for another hour, and the great

church clock struck eleven. **Then a** lady came into the school, and called the second class to come to her. The children gathered round her, and Ruth was one of them; **they** got their Bibles and stood before her, and little Ruth had the place that was always hers, close by that lady's side. **Ruth** did not answer so many questions as some **of the** other children; she never spoke unless she was asked, and then **she** answered so softly, that no one but the lady heard; but **the** lady always seemed to smile at Ruth when **she** did answer, as if she had **answered right.** When the great church clock struck twelve, the lady went away; and the children put up their books into their bags, and went to their homes. Ruth could not stay with the sick child till she had asked her mother; but she thought she would just look in, and tell **her** she was come back. Ruth looked in, and the child was lying quite still in bed; she did not speak, so Ruth went **up and stood beside her.**

"Oh! I am so glad you are come!" **said the poor child;** "what a long time it was you kept at school! Oh! I **want** something so bad! I can't eat this bread mother left me, it's so hard, it hurts me when **I try.**"

"I have not had any food to-day," said little Ruth.

"O dear," said the sick child, "how bad it is! what do you do when you have no food?"

"I tell Jesus," said little Ruth.

"**Who do** you tell?" asked the poor child.

"Jesus," said little Ruth.

"Who is Jesus?" asked the poor child.

"What! don't you know who Jesus **is?**" said little Ruth. "I thought every body knew that except the poor heathen. He is our Saviour?"

"**Does He** give you some food?" asked the poor child.

"O yes, He often sends us some food when mother has nothing: but I must go to mother now, or she will scold."

"Do ask her to let you come and stay with me," said the poor child.

"Yes, I will," replied little Ruth; and she went up the high stair-case to her mother's room; she did not run with light quick steps, like children generally; but she went up slow and faint; for it was not one day alone, but many days, that little Ruth went to school without food. She had lost her own father: the father she now had was not her own father, and he thought only of himself and his own wicked pleasures, and left his wife and her children without food. But little Ruth had learned to pray; the lady who came to the school taught her from the Bible; and she had learned to know the love of God her Saviour; she loved and trusted Him, and, as she said in her own words, when they had no food "she told Jesus."

When Ruth went into her mother's room, she saw on the table a can of steaming soup. "O mother! is that for us?" she asked.

"Yes, to be sure it is, Miss Wilson sent it in this minute."

Miss Wilson was the lady who came to the school. Ruth had not told Miss Wilson about their having no food that day; so when she saw this can of hot soup she knew it was Jesus her Saviour who had put it into Miss Wilson's heart to send it to them. The poor babe was asleep on the bed; but Mary, Ruth's little sister, was standing at the table crying to be fed. Then the mother got a bason, and poured it full for Mary There was meat, and rice, and potatoes in the nice hot soup; and poor little Mary left off crying directly she had her spoon and began to eat. Then the mother poured out a larger bason for Ruth, who stood quite patient by the table. Ruth waited a minute with her food before her.

"What are you waiting for now?" asked her mother; "I have nothing more for you."

"No mother; but that widow's child is laid in bed; she says her pain is so bad, and her mother 's out working, and she wants me to sit with her."

"Poor thing!" said Ruth's mother; "well, take your dinner, and then you may go a little while if you like."

"She has no food, mother, but a hard **bit** of bread, and **she** says she can't eat it, because it hurts her."

"Oh! and so you want to be after giving her some of yours, **do** you? here, give me yonr bason then, and you take this jug." And Ruth's mother, pouring some more soup into the broken jug she had taken for herself, gave it to Ruth. "There, take care how you go, that you don't lose it now you have got it!" said the mother. And Ruth, holding the jug in both hands, went slowly **and** carefully down stairs. How **happy was she** now—in her **hands** she held the food she so much wanted; **and** the poor **sick** child, left all alone, **was to** share it with her **and** be happy also! As she got near the bottom **of** the stair-case she stepped quicker in her eager haste; then, pushing open the door, she went in saying, **"See here,** Miss Wilson sent us this beautiful soup, and **mother** 's given me some for you!"

"O dear, how nice! how glad I am!" said the poor child.

"Have you got a bason?" asked Ruth.

"Yes, there 's one in that closet, and a spoon too," said the child.

Ruth found a small yellow bason and a spoon: she broke up the child's dry bit of bread in the bason; poured some of the hot soup over it; folded her hands, and **asked a** blessing in the name of Jesus; and then the **two children** dined together. The warm nourishment brought the color **to** the white cheeks of little Ruth, and soothed the poor, faint, weary child. "How good you are to me!" she said to Ruth. "I feel better now; I think I shall go to sleep." Ruth put away the bason in the closet again; the sick child had closed her eyes, already almost slumbering; and the little ministering girl went back to her mother.

A day or two after, as Ruth came in from school, the sick child's mother was going out, and she stopped and said to Ruth, "My Lucy told me how good you were to her: the God above bless you for it! She is always calling out for you; I wish you would stay a bit with her when you can, just to pacify her."

Ruth's mother gave her leave to take the babe down and nurse it in the poor child's room—where she still lay on her wretched bed, covered with a torn counterpane. Ruth walked up and down to quiet the babe and get it to sleep; she hushed and hushed it, but that would not do; so at last she began to sing one of her school hymns in a low voice,

> "Jesus, refuge of my soul,
> Let me to Thy bosom fly."

The sick child listened; the low sweet singing soothed the infant to sleep, and the sick child into quiet feeling. "Is that Jesus you sing about, who you ask for food?" said the poor child.

"Yes," replied Ruth, "that's Jesus our Saviour! I can sing you something else about our Saviour, if you like."

"Yes, do," said the poor child. And Ruth sang—

> "We read within the Holy Word
> Of how our Saviour died;
> And those great drops of blood,
> He shed at eventide."

Over and over again, while she rocked the sleeping baby, she sang the same soft words. When she stopped, the sick child said, "I can't read; I never went to school long enough to learn."

"What, can't you read the Bible?" said Ruth.

"No, I can't read any thing; I don't know any thing about it."

"I can tell you all about it," said Ruth. "I know such a number of stories out of the Bible! Miss Wilson tells them to us, and sometimes we tell them to her. And I know a great many verses, and some chapters and Psalms.'

"I like stories best," said the poor child.

"Well, then, I will tell you one. Let me see, which shall I tell you? Oh! I know, I will tell you about the little lamb! Once there was a good man, his name was David; he was not at all old, he was quite young; and he didn't live in a town like this, but he lived in beautiful green fields, and on great high hills, where the flowers grow, and the trees, and where the birds sing. He was quite young, but he loved God, and Jesus our Saviour. And he prayed to God. And when he saw the stars come out in the sky, he thought about Jesus our Saviour, who lives up above the stars in Heaven, and he wrote about Him in the Bible. He lived alone on the great high hills; and God took care of him; and he had a great many sheep and lambs, and they all ate the grass and were so happy! and he took care of them all. But one day there came a great roaring lion; he came so quiet; he did not make any noise! and he took a little lamb in his great mouth and ran so fast away! but the little lamb cried out, and David heard the little lamb, and he ran so fast that the great lion could not get away! and he caught the great lion and killed him; and he took the little lamb in his arms, and carried it quite safe back to its mother. Is not that a pretty story? And I know what Miss Wilson tells us about it!"

"What does she tell you?" asked the poor child.

"She tells us, that it is just like Jesus our Saviour; when Satan the great roaring lion tries to take us away, if we pray to Jesus, Jesus won't let him have us; but Jesus will take us up safe in His arms, and carry us to Heaven when we die, and then we shall be so happy there!"

"Will he carry me?" asked the poor child.

"Yes, He will if you pray to Him," said little Ruth.

"I don't know how to pray," the poor child replied.

"I will teach you my prayer," said little Ruth.

"O God, my Heavenly Father, give me Thy Holy Spirit to teach me to know and love Thee. Wash me from all my sins in my Saviour's precious blood. Keep me from all evil, and make me ready to live with Thee for ever in Heaven. For the sake of Jesus my Saviour. Amen."

"That is one of my prayers, and I can teach it to you. I have taught it to our Mary, and she can't read yet."

The poor child tried to learn it, but she could not remember the words; still it seemed to soothe her, to hear Ruth repeating them; at last the poor child said, "Wash me from all my sins! What are sins?"

"That is when we do wrong," said little Ruth; "we can't go with our bad ways to Heaven, but Jesus can wash them all away in His blood."

As little Ruth was coming home from school one of those bright September days, she saw a poor woman sitting on a door step with a basket full of small penny nosegays of autumn flowers. Ruth stood still before the basket to look and admire. She had never known what it was to hunt over the meadow banks in spring for violets and primroses, or gather the yellow daffodil and beautiful anemone from the woods, or the sweet and frail wild rose from its thorny stem in the hedge; she had sometimes plucked a daisy from the grass, but this was the only flower that Ruth had ever gathered. And now she stood to look **upon** the woman's basket full of nosegays of garden flowers. While she stood looking, a mother and her little girl passed by.

"Oh! mamma," said the little girl, "look at those flowers!"

"A penny a nosegay, ma'am; only a penny a nosegay!" said the poor woman, holding out some of her flowers.

"Do you wish for a nosegay, Jane?" **asked the mother of her** little girl.

"Yes, if you please, mamma."

Ruth thought how happy that little girl was to have a nosegay of her own! she watched her take it; and then the mother and her little girl went on, and Ruth went slowly the other way to her home. But as soon as the little girl had left **the** basket of flowers, she said, "Mamma, did you **see that** poor child who looked so at the flowers?"

"**Yes, Jane**, do you think she wanted a nosegay?"

"**O**, mamma, will you buy her one?"

"I have not another penny **with me, or** I would."

"**Do** you think she would like me **to give** her mine, then, mamma?"

"Yes, suppose you do; I dare say she very seldom has a flower."

"Then I will; mamma, shall we go back?" The little girl looked back, and saw Ruth walking slowly away.

"O, mamma, she will be gone!"

The little girl did not like to leave her mother's side, **so** they walked quickly back together, till they overtook Ruth, and then the little girl gave her the flowers; the bright color came into the cheeks **of** little Ruth as she curtsied and took the flowers; and then she set off to run with them home; she could not run far, but she walked fast, **and looked** at them all the way she

1*

went. " Mamma, did you see how fast that little girl ran with her flowers ?" asked Jane.

" I dare say she wanted to take them home," said her mother.

And so that ministering child parted with her nosegay for the little girl, who had never gathered any flower but a daisy. Ruth soon reached home with her flowers; and first she went to the poor sick child, and she said, " See what beautiful flowers I have got ! A lady bought them in the street, and her little girl gave them all to me ! I will give you that beauty !" And Ruth pulled out the only rose from the nosegay, and put it into the little thin hand of the dying child. " O how sweet it smells !" said the poor sick child ; and she lay on her hard pillow and the rose in her hand—the only gift she had had to gladden her, except food, since she had lain ill in her bed.

" Jesus, our Saviour, made the flowers !" said Ruth. " Miss Wilson says it was Jesus made every flower to grow out of the ground."

" How kind He must be !" said the dying child.

Then Ruth took the rest of her flowers up to her mother, and they were put in water to live many days.

Ruth used to go in often to see the poor sick child, and tell her stories from the Bible, and sing her hymns when she had the baby with her. But one cold November day, when she came into the house from school, the poor child's mother came crying from her room, and said to her, " O ! I am so glad you are come ! I thought I must have come after you ; my poor child's dying, and she keeps asking for you." Ruth went in and stood by the bed, and the dying child said, " Dear Ruth, I am quite happy. I love you very much ; and I want you to sing that about ' Those great drops of blood Jesus shed at even-tide.' " Ruth sang it as well as she could, but she was ready to cry

"I want you to sing it over and over, as you do to the babe," said the dying child.

Ruth sang it two or three times, and then she stopped; the poor child had shut her eyes, and seemed asleep, but she soon opened them again, and said, "O do sing about 'Jesus let me to Thy bosom fly;'" and while Ruth sang, and the mother stood weeping by, the little child fell asleep, and died. Ruth cried for her little friend, and missed her very much. But now the child's poor mother said she wanted Ruth to comfort her up, as she had done her poor child; and she begged Ruth to read to her, and tell her those beautiful stories, for she could not read herself. And so Ruth became the poor widow's little comforter.

When we see a child dressed neat and warm in her school dress, we often think she is well taken care of; but it is not always so; and sometimes the little school girl or boy is much more hungry and faint, than the child who begs his food in the streets. We cannot tell how it really is with poor children, or poor men and women, unless we visit them in their homes. Miss Wilson had often been to see little Ruth, so she knew all her sorrows, and she comforted and often fed the little girl, and loved her very much. But there was another child who went to the same school, and wore the same neat dress, and stood in the same class as Ruth, but she had no comforter; her name was Patience. She lived like Ruth, in one room, up a dark staircase; but she had no mother, like Ruth; her mother died when she was an infant; and poor Patience had never had any one to love or comfort her. Her father was a bad and cruel man; Patience had been taken care of by an elder sister, but her sister was gone quite away from her home, and she lived alone with her father. She came to school every day, but she generally came late; she had earned to read there, but she hardly ever knew her lessons; and she never answered when asked the reason. She was very small, and very thin; and the lady who came to the school never saw her laugh, or smile, or cry; she always looked upon the ground, her lips were pressed together, and she seldom answered when spoken to. Miss Wilson, the lady at the school, thought she did not care about any thing; she had never been to see her in her home, she thought it was no use to go and see a child who seemed not to care for any thing; so she did not know the sorrows of the little girl, and therefore she did not try to comfort her: nothing seemed to amuse or interest her, she looked with the same dull eyes on all. Poor Patience had no comforter, no blessed ministering child had been yet to her. One day as Patience was walking to school, a little companion came and walked by her side—a rosy-faced child, eating bread and butter, finishing her breakfast on the way to school. Poor Patience had had no food that morning, she would have been so thankful for part of the child's bread and butter; but she did not ask for any, and when they reached the school, the child threw all she had left of it to a fat black goat who lived at a stable close by. The black goat tossed his head, and eat it up. Then poor Patience said, "O Nancy, how glad I should be of the food you waste!" and she stood watching the black goat eating up the bread and butter. But Nancy was not like little Ruth, she was not a ministering child, and she ran up the steps into the school, and thought no more of her bread and butter, and her little hungry school-fellow.

CHAPTER II.

"And if there be any other commandment, it is briefly comprehended in this say-ing, namely, Thou shalt love thy neighbor as thyself."—Rom. xiii. 9.

IT was a large old town in which little Ruth and Patience dwelt; there were streets broad and narrow, long winding streets, and short ones that cut across from one long one to another; old churches stood about the town, and new ones were built among the new-built houses; there was a busy market, a town-hall, and shops large and small; to which the country people came from far and near. In one of the broad streets, at the corner of a short and narrow one, there stood a large grocer's shop. Tea and coffee, white sugar and brown, dried fruits and spices, candles and sugar-candy—all sorts of things that grocers sell, were sold at that cor-ner-shop. Mr. Mansfield was the grocer's name; and many a step passed in at that shop-door when no purchase was to be made, for there was no good cause in all the town that had not some interest in Mr. Mansfield's heart—and, for the most part, in his shop also, where gold and silver found a ready way out as well as in. The rule of weight in that shop seemed to be, "Good measure, pressed down, and shaken to-gether, and running over." The poor people from far and near, had all a fancy for that corner-shop; no one ever asked why; perhaps there was no need, where every one felt the same.

Behind the shop there was a parlor, where **Mrs.** Mansfield usually sat, because it was **easy for** Mr. Mansfield to step in there, and rest himself a little when opportunity offered. It was Mrs. Mansfield **and her** little daughter **Jane who** passed **by,** when Ruth **was looking at the** flowers. **Jane was the** ministering **child who** had made little Ruth so **happy with** her nosegay. Little **Jane had** several brothers and a baby sister. Their nurse was a tall, grave woman ; she never played with them, never sang **to** the baby, and yet they were all as merry **and** happy **as children could wish** to be ; their happiness was her happiness, and **their** infant troubles her care to soothe ; and just at the right time she could always **think** of and say the right **thing.** The nurse did **not** undertake to teach the children in **her charge** any **lessons out of books ;** her **own** reading was **not of the most perfect kind ; but they** learnt some lessons from **her heart** and life, no after-time **could efface.** One lesson **that** they learned from **their** nurse was, reverence for old age. How quick those little children **were to see** an old man or **an** old woman coming down the street, when they were walking out ; **to step off** the narrow pavement to leave **them room,** while they **would** look up at them with kindness **and interest, and be** sure to see in a moment if any thing could **be** done **to help them.** Another lesson these little children learned **from their nurse, was truth** ; their nurse had never any **thing** to conceal ; **she always** did and said the same in their mother's **absence as in her** presence, so that the children always believed their **mother and** their nurse to have **one way in** every thing. **And** the children **were all** familiar **with the** sight of the large Bible with its buckram cover, from **which** their nurse **sat** to read—learning, with earnest care, the way to **heaven.**

Some hours of every day little Jane passed with her mother, learning to read and work. One day, when the reading was done, before the work-box was opened, Mrs. Mansfield said to Jane, "I must go out to attend a penny-club meeting; would you like to go with me?" Jane was delighted to go, and ran up to nurse to put on her things. "I don't know where mamma is going," said Jane; "I could not understand." "I know," replied nurse; "it's the penny-club meeting to-day; that's where your mamma is going." "What is that?" asked Jane. "It's for the poor," replied nurse. Now little Jane **had** so often heard her parents speaking of the **poor, and seen** her mother working hard; and when she asked her, "Why do you work so long, mamma?" she would say, "For the poor;" that Jane had no doubt the poor belonged to her parents; and, therefore, that they belonged also to her; and she always listened with interest to all that was said about them.

"Are you going for the poor, mamma?" asked little **Jane, as she set** out with her **hand in** her mother's. "Yes, my dear," replied Mrs. Mansfield; **" your parents** can buy you all the clothes you want, **but** there are **a** great many poor people who can hardly **tell** how to feed their children, and they can not possibly buy them warm clothing; so some richer people said, **that if** these poor people would lay by one penny a **week, for a** whole year, they would put another penny to it; and then, at the end of the year, these poor people would have all these pennies put together, which would make many shillings for them to take to the shop and buy warm clothes for their poor little children. But this is the Town Hall, where we are going, and you must try and listen to what is said."

Jane sat on a step at the top of the room, by the bench where her mother was seated, and she looked up at the speaker, and listened to all he said. Before the speaker had done, he looked down to where little Jane was sitting, and said, "Perhaps there are some children here who could lay by one penny a week, to clothe some poor little boy or girl, who has no warm dress like their **own.** Would it not give them more pleasure than spending their money on themselves?" Jane heard and understood what the speaker was saying, and she thought it was exactly what she could do, because she received from her mother a penny every Saturday to spend as she liked best; but she did not say any thing then to her mother, because she had been told at other meetings, that she must sit still and not speak.

After the meeting, Mrs. Mansfield talked long with the ladies **present;** little Jane held fast by her mother's hand, which she **tried** to draw **with** secret impatience towards the door; at last **Mrs.** Mansfield said, "Good morning," to the ladies, and went down the Town **Hall** steps alone with **her** little **girl.**

"O mamma! mamma! would not my penny do for the poor?" asked Jane.

"Not one penny, dear; one penny would not do much in clothing a child."

"**No,** mamma, not one penny; but one penny every week for **a whole** year, like what you told me as we came."

"**Yes,** that would meet some poor mother's penny, and clothe her child."

"May I give it then, mamma?"

"I am afraid you would wish for it, after a little while;—you could buy no ribbons for your doll, or sweatmeats and cakes for **a** feast; nor could you go to the toy-shop for a whole year, and **a** year is a long time."

"**No,** mamma; but the little child who has no warm clothes!"

"Yes, you would make the poor child warm and happy; you **would** be able to help buy new flannel, and white calico, and pretty blue print with white spots upon it, and the poor mother would see her child run about warm and neat, as I see you."

" O, mamma, I wish Saturday was come !"

" But what if you grow tired, Jane, and begin to want the things you have been used to buy for play? I can not help you ; your father and I have taken all the penny tickets we can afford ; if you begin you must go on, or you must disappoint the child !"

" I do not want any more toys or sweetmeats, mamma, I will **not disappoint the child ;** may I **try** ?"

" Yes ; indeed you shall if you wish. I hoped to have found some lady at the Town Hall who would have been able to help a poor old woman who came to me yesterday to ask for her little grand-daughter, when all my tickets were promised, but now it seems my own little girl will be her friend !"

" O yes, mamma, how glad I am, shall I see the little **girl,** does she live in the town ?"

" No, she lives in a village seven miles off; she is a little orphan, her father and mother are both dead, **and** her poor old grandmother has taken her home to live with **her.** Her grandmother said she was coming into the town to-morrow, and I told her to call on me, for I hoped to get her a ticket, so you **can** see her ; I do not know whether the little girl will be with her."

" Do you know what the little girl's name is, mamma ?"

" No, but we can ask her grandmother to-morrow. Now I am going into this shop to buy you some winter stockings :" Six pair of lamb's-wool stockings—how warm they looked !

" Mamma," said little Jane, when they left **the** shop, " may I give my old socks to the little girl ?"

" I am afraid they would not be large enough," replied Mrs. Mansfield, " but I have some worsted stockings of your brother

Edward's that would be sure to fit her : if you like to spend a
little of your play-time every day in mending them neatly
enough to be worn, then you shall have them to give to the
little girl."

"Do you not think her grandmother could mend them,
mamma, as you do **for us ?**"

" Yes, I dare say she could, but she is sure to have plenty of
other things to do, and I could not let you give to the poor that
which you had taken no pains to have ready for use and comfort."

" But I do not know how to mend stockings, mamma."

" It is not very difficult ; you could soon learn how to do it,
and **I think** you would be very happy working for the poor little
orphan girl."

" **Yes,** I should, is **it as hard** as stitching, **do** you think ?"

" No, the threads are not so fine."

" Shall I begin to-day, mamma ?"

" Yes, if you like, I will find the stockings for you as soon **as**
I go home."

" Nurse ! nurse !" said little Jane, running in, " I am going to
help buy warm clothes for a poor little girl with my penny every
week ; and mamma is going to give me all Edward's old warm
stockings, if I mend them up quite neat."

" **Well, that's a good beginning,"** said nurse, " **if you** do but
hold fast to it."

And so, in one short hour, little Jane had stepped into a world
of thought and feeling that seemed at first to hide from sight
much that before had power to please ; it was but at first—the
lighter tones of childhood's merriment **soon** blended with **the
deeper** echoes of the heart's responsive sympathy—and her life
yielded their mingled harmony.

That afternoon little Jane began the stocking-mending in her play hours, seated at her mother's side. After a while she sighed and said, " It is rather hard at first, mamma."

" So are many good things at first, my child ; would you like to give up doing them, and learn when you are a little older to mend stockings for yourself, instead of learning now for the poor ?"

" O no, mamma! how nice it will be when I have done one pair! May I keep them in my own box ?"

" Yes, you may have each pair as you finish them. You shall fold them up and keep them yourself; but if you get tired and wish to give up doing them, you have only to tell me ; I could not let you give up if I were teaching you for yourself, but no one should work unwillingly for the poor."

" I shall never like to give it up, mamma ; I do not mind if it is a little hard."

And Jane worked busily, on, till her mother said, " Now you have done quite enough for one day, and quite as well as I could expect ; you can go to the nursery and play with your brother till tea." And merry were the shouts of the happy child as she ran, fresh from her self-chosen service of love, across the nursery-floor with her little brother at play.

At tea Mr. Mansfield heard what Jane intended to do with her pennies—he quite approved ; but when she climbed upon his knee, before her mother took her to bed, he smiled and said, " Perhaps my little daughter thinks her father can find her candies without pennies to buy them ?"

" O no, papa, I don't want any more ; I shall be so happy when I have made the little girl quite warm !"

" So you will, my Jane, and so is every one happy who tries from the heart to help the poor and needy ;" and with his blessing he sent her to her rest. Jane went to her pillow full of thoughts of her little unknown friend. Already she loved the orphan her hand was helping to clothe ; she longed for the next day, that she might get on with the warm stockings for her feet, and then she remembered she was to see the old grandmother who would put the penny to meet her penny ; her happy thoughts blended in bright confusion, till, like folded flowers at night, they closed their leaves, and all were lost in **deep and** gentle slumber.

The next morning Jane gave many a look from the nursery window on the street below, and nurse was often called to see whether any one of those who came in sight could be the grandmother. At last a knock at the street-door, then her mother's call to her, and Jane came down, stopping a minute at the parlor-door, it stood open a little way, and Jane could see the old woman and the little girl. **Jane** ventured slowly in and **stood** close by her mother's side.

" Well, Jane," said her mother, " this is your little friend. **It** is my little daughter, Mrs. Jones, who wishes to **put** her penny to meet yours. What is your grand-daughter's name ?"

" Mercy, ma'am, Mercy Jones. Make a curtsey, Mercy, to the young lady, and say, Thank you."

Jane hid her face behind her mother, and hoped nobody **would** say any more to her ; till after a time her mother said, **" Now** you may go back to the nursery, Jane." Jane stole a look at **little Mercy,** as she went slowly out, and she felt as if she cared more about that poor little girl than all her play ; and, going back to the nursery, she watched till they went away—the tall old woman and the little girl. Then the sound of her brother at his play broke again upon her ear, and she ran to join him.

In two days more the first pair of stockings were mended. Jane learned how to fold them up ; then she carried them safely to her own little trunk—all her treasures were taken out, and the stockings put in first, safe on one side of the box, plenty of room was left for the other five pair near them, and then the other contents of the box were piled on its other side ; and when at last Jane had shut the lid and turned away, she came back once more to see again how nice they looked—all ready for the orphan child ! It was the first labor of her hands for the poor and needy ; a child's large feeling on so small occasion may win a smile ; but the occasion had, for the first time, touched the deep chord of human sympathy within her heart, and the vibration was long and full.

Weeks passed away, and when the snow of New Year's day lay thick upon the ground, the stockings were all done—six folded pairs of mended stockings in Jane's own trunk, all ready for the orphan child. Then came another visit from the old grandmother, but not from the little Mercy. " Bless you, Miss," said the old grandmother, as she took the piled-up stockings from Jane's trembling hands, " would not Mercy have liked **to come** ! but her poor feet are **so** bad with the chilblains, **she can** 't put them to the ground ; but won 't they soon be **well** when she has run about a bit in these warm stockings ! why, they are the most beautiful stockings that ever I saw, and enough of them to last her almost till she grows an old woman !"

" They would not **fit her** then," said little Jane.

" **No,** dear, no more they would, but I can biggen them a bit **when** they get too small ; I understand all that sort of thing ; I was always brought up to it."

" Will they really make her feet well ?" asked Jane, remembering the old woman's words to that effect.

" Yes, dear, that they will, the sight of **them** almost I think, for she has hardly had a bit of stocking under her boots all this hard winter ; and the boots are got stiff, and her feet are tender, for when her poor father was alive she was well clothed. I do . all I can for her, and she never complains, but I am often afraid she feels the difference."

"They are all mended," said Jane; "Mamma says they will do quite well; I did not know how to mend stockings before."

"Well, dear, it will be none the worse for you that you learned it for the poor and fatherless. I think I see the look of my Mercy when I show them to her! I know her first word will be, 'O grandmother, now I can soon go to the Sunday school again!' She is wonderfully fond of her school since Miss Clifford came to teach in it, and Miss Clifford takes a wonderful deal of notice of her, and has been to see her; she did not know the poor dear had not a stocking to her foot, or that would soon have been there."

"Could you not have told her?" asked Jane.

"Why, no, Miss, I never tell; I say always, if it comes it comes, and I know where it comes from; but if I asked, why it might be another thing!"

Mrs. Mansfield, who had left little Jane alone with the old woman, came back just in time to hear this last sentence, and to see the earnest inquiring look Jane fixed on the old woman, whose reply she had not been able to understand. Mrs. Jones shortly after took her leave, and Jane was left alone with her mother.

"Did you understand what Mrs. Jones was saying when I came in, Jane?"

"No, mamma, what did she mean? why did she not tell the lady about her little grand-daughter having no stockings?"

"I think you will understand her meaning if I put it in my words. Poor Mrs. Jones meant that she told her wants only to God, and then if help came to relieve those wants, she knew that it was God who sent it to her, by some earthly friend.

The honest and industrious poor, who have been accustomed to earn all they receive, do not often like to ask of any one but God."

"But, mamma, if they do not tell, how can it be known?"

"We must ask God to teach us to know the wants of the poor. And if we really wish to help and comfort them, God will put it into our hearts to supply the wants He knows they have. You did not know that little Mercy Jones had no stockings, but you wished to help and comfort her, and you were led to prepare the very thing she wanted most. God knows all the wants of the poor, and He can put the thought into our hearts of that which He knows will be best for them."

Little Jane was silent, lost in the thrilling awe of one who felt herself to have been chosen and taught of God to supply the want she had not known. Her mother knew the power such first impressions have to train the heart's young faith, and with her arm round little Jane, she sat in silence too.

"Then, mamma," at last said Jane, "I can never know unless God teaches me?"

"God is your heavenly Father, Jane, and He will teach you all He wishes you to know if you love to learn of Him."

"But how will He teach me to help the poor, mamma?"

"God will teach you sometimes by putting the thought in your heart; but He will also teach you in other ways: has He not given you an eye and an ear?"

"Yes, mamma."

"Then He meant you to use them; do you not often find out what I want without my having to tell you?"

"Yes, mamma, because I live with you."

"I am afraid I might get many little girls, and grown up people also, to live with me, and they would not find out the things I often want, without my asking, as you do. Is it only because you live with me?"

"O, no, mamma, it is because I love you as wel. !"

"Yes, dear Jane, this is the secret: you love me, and therefore you find out my wishes and wants as far as your power permits; and if you love God, you will quickly learn how to serve Him, according to His holy will; and if you love the poor, you will be sure to find out their wants and how to comfort them."

The clock struck eleven. "O mamma," exclaimed Jane, "I have not done my lessons, and it is eleven o'clock!"

"Never mind that to-day, my dear; perhaps we have been learning what lesson-books could not teach us; you can do your writing now." And well it was for that young mind not at once to be pressed with lessons. It had felt and thought enough for one morning of its early years, and writing was mental rest.

CHAPTER III.

If ye love Me, keep my commandments."—JOHN xiv. 15.

THE village where Mercy lived with her grandmother was seven miles distant from the town where Mr. Mansfield lived and little Jane, where also lived Patience and little Ruth. The village church stood on a hill, and close beside it the clergyman's dwelling, hid among trees. There was a large and beautiful house in the village, called the Hall, where the Squire lived ; and Miss Clifford, little Mercy's friend, was the Squire's daughter. Miss Clifford loved the poor who lived around her house ; she had known and loved them from the time when she was but a little child, and they loved her ; for the heart of the poor can give as pure a response to hallowed interest and love as the heart of the rich. Miss Clifford had a white pony named Snowflake ; when a little child, she often rode out with her father, and called with him at the farms, and sometimes at the cottages. And when she grew older, she had a groom of her own to ride out with her every day, and then she often went alone to the houses of the poor. She used to carry her little Bible with her, and read to the poor old people who could not read for themselves : the very sound of her voice seemed to comfort them, and still more the blessed words that she read ; and feeble old people, and little children just able to run alone, would learn from her lips the holy words of the Bible—those precious words which lead all who love them to heaven. It was not Mrs.

2

Clifford who had taught her little daughter to visit the poor. Mrs. Clifford felt for the poor, and sent them gifts at Christmas; but she did not know what it was to love the poor and be loved by them, for she had never been among them herself; but Mrs. Clifford loved the word of God, and she knew what was written there; so she was happy that her child should early tread the blessed path that leads amongst the homes of the poor, though she felt unable to visit them herself. The visits, when a child, to the farm-houses, and sometimes to the cottages, with her father, might have been one means of leading Miss Clifford to think about and love the poor; but that could not have been the only or the chief reason. The poor people, who had no one else to teach them as she did, believed that God had put it into her heart to be their comforter; and this reason for her visits to them, and her care and love for them, no doubt was the true one. Miss Clifford had no sister, but she had a brother some few years younger than herself; he was a wild, high-spirited boy, with a generous disposition; but a long habit of pleasing himself had made him selfish and too often disobedient. Mr Clifford was a very indulgent father; he allowed Herbert—for Herbert was the boy's name—to amuse himself just as he pleased, to spend his money as he liked, and he provided for him every gratification suitable to his age and circumstances. But, with all this indulgence, Herbert was never allowed in a single act of disobedience, nor was he ever allowed to break through any rule or principle of justice toward others. Herbert knew that if the lessons that his tutor required him to prepare were neglected, his father would never admit any idle excuse. The rules to which Herbert was subjected by his father were but few; but, such as they were, they might never be broken; this Herbert knew; but his wild spirits, and his haste after amusement, led him sometimes to forget; and then he would fancy *that* not to be disobedience which proved to be so, when tried by the rule of his **kind but** firm parent. Herbert had never yet known what it was to be a ministering **child.**

Mr. Clifford was a great favorite among **his tenants.** He was no less firm as a landlord than he **was as a father;** but then he was as kind and considerate **as he was firm.** No rule he made was allowed to be **trifled with;** but his **rules were simple** and few, and known by **all who dwelt** on his estate; and **his** tenants, both **farmers and laborers, learned** at last **to know** that he made **their interest one** with his own. His feeling was **strong** of the common brotherhood uniting the **whole** human family, and made itself manifest, whether occasion led him **to** speak to the stone-breaker on the road, or the poorest **cottage-**child. Even with the lowest and most **debased, he never lost** the feeling of a common manhood, with all that **it involved and** demanded. It is ever those who best **know, and best fill their** own position, who can most readily and effectually keep **all with** whom they have intercourse, each **one** in his **own** place. In retaining ourselves, and regarding in others the **simple** standing that God has given, there is a native dignity, a moral elevation, which, while it tends to set aside the false assumptions of pride, makes a constant demand on the effort to maintain that integrity, both in ourselves and others, without which none **can** fill he earthly position to which God has called them.

All the farms in **the** village were the property of Mr. **Clifford,** except one occupied by a farmer named Smith, whose father and grandfather had **rented** the same farm before him. **Farmer** Smith's fields were **kept** like a garden for neatness; **and** every **ear of** the wheat that waved on **them in the** golden harvest **time was** sown by the hands of **the village** children. When brown and soft October came **to** mellow earth and sky, when the plow had turned the fields' rich mold, and the heavy roll

had pressed the long ridges flat, and the wide-spreading rake
had broken the hard clods, then went the sowers forth—fathers
with their merry children, girls and boys, all whose little feet
could pace the fields backward and forward, and not grow
weary, whose fingers could drop the precious grain from the
little wooden basket held on their left arm, three grains into
each hole, all these might go ; two lines following their fathers,
who, walking backward, made two holes at every step with iron
rods in their hands : following as fast as they could their father's fast steps, and stooping low as they followed, they dropped
in the grain with their little fingers—thus the bread that was to
feed thousands, was sown by the hands of little children. While
the robin sung beside them on the yellow branches of the faded
maple-tree, and, as the children passed it by, flew on higher up
in the hedge-row, and perched again beside them, as if to cheer
their work with its song, or to win the ear of childhood for its
strain of gentle mirth. But wheat-sowing, like all other things
on earth, has its wintry days ; and when November proves damp
and cold, the wet land gets heavy, and the children suffer.
This had been little Mercy's first year of dropping wheat. When
her parents were living, Mercy never thought of being among
the little droppers; but they had both died of fever in one
year, and left their orphan child to earn her bread under the
care of her kind old grandmother, and her uncle Jem—her
grandmother's only son, who lived with his mother. Mercy had
lived three years with her grandmother, and now she thought
it a pleasant thing to go and work under the blue sky in the
fresh-plowed fields ; and so it was ; but when the wintry rains
came, the work grew heavy for her slight strength ; her boots
became stiff with the wet land, the chilblains settled in her feet,
and when the dropping-time was over, little Mercy was laid up,
unable to walk ; her greatest sorrow being, as her grandmother

had stated, that she could not get to the Sunday-schoc where Miss Clifford now taught.

The eldest of Farmer Smith's family was a son named William. William seemed to know and love every foot of land on the farm, every tree and every living creature there; but the chief favorites were a dog called Rover, and a young horse named Black Beauty. Black Beauty was born and reared on the farm; when a foal he followed William like a dog, and now he was committed to William's care, and, though only lately broken in and full of spirit, William could manage him, without whip or rein, by the sound of his voice. The horse was a beautiful creature, and Farmer Smith would say sometimes that if the children had not all been so fond of the horse, he must have taken one of the many high offers he had had for him; but, as it was, he made his children's affection for the creature a cover for his own, and a fair excuse for keeping him. Besides which, Farmer Smith knew that the last thing Mrs. Smith would approve, would be to see the horse led away; and so, in consequence of all these reasons taken together, Black Beauty led an easy life, with none but familiar and kindly voices falling on his sensitive ears. Mr. Smith's next son, Joseph, called by the family Joe, was very quick at his books; therefore, his father kept him a year longer than he would otherwise have done, as a boarder at a school in the town; but it was considered that he had now learned sufficient, and he was put to work on the farm. The younger boys were Samson and Ted. Rose, the only girl, was the treasure of her father's heart, and the light of his life; he had her named Rose, for that had been his mother's name, and he said, "May be, if she has the name, she may take after the nature too, and my mother was one of the best of women—ask the poor if that is n't true, and I will always trust them for knowing what any body is!" Little Rose grew up among the corr., and the barley, and the sweet-scented beans—for her hand was mostly in her father's, and her feet trotting by his side; she hunted the red-cup moss in the muddy ditch, her little feet at the top, while her father stood at the bottom; hers were the first rosy nuts gathered from the hazel-tree, when glowing autumn came to ripen the fruits; she called the wild birds all her own, and her displeasure fell on any one who dared to take the warm, soft nest from tree or hedge. Rose went, when very young, to the village day-school; there she formed a friendship with little Mercy, and was learning quite enough to satisfy her father; but Mrs. Smith was not so easily satisfied. Mrs. Smith said they had but one girl, and she should always consider that they had been very much to blame if they did not give her a good education, and a boarding-school was the place to which she ought to be sent; that if she were willing to part with the child, she did not see why Mr. Smith should object. Mr. Smith felt as if the sunbeam would pass from every thing, if his little Rose were taken from his home; but he never opposed any thing on which his wife was resolved; so Mrs. Smith made all the arrangements, and William drove Rose with Chestnut, the gig-horse, to her boarding-school.

The strange faces and stiff ways of the towns-people, and the long streets, instead of wild lanes and trees, were very dull to the country child; but she learned her lessons, worked a sampler which was put in a frame, and came home at midsummer like a bird free from its cage. On reaching her home, Rose sprung from the gig into her father's arms,—her young brothers, Samson and Ted, came out with their welcome; Rose kissed them, rushed up the staircase to her mother, who had not expected her so soon; then down again to speak to Molly; then into the farm-yard, where she stroked Rover, and all the cows, who were reposing in the straw till the cow-house door should be opened ; then into the stable, where she threw her arms round Black Beauty's neck ; and, finally, was attempting to count the fowls, which baffled her skill, by running one among another, when out came her mother at the back-door, saying, " Why, child ! you run about like wild ; come in to tea, do." And Rose was soon in her old place by her father's side at tea.

But this Christmas time, her second holidays, Rose had come with graver thoughts. A little school-fellow had died, and the sense of separation and death had passed, for the first time, over her heart. Rose did not say any thing about it, she did not know very well what to say ; her mother was a person of but few words, and these few were mostly quick ones ; and Rose hardly knew that a change had passed over her which others might observe. Her mother saw that she had lost her wild spirits, but still she was often merry, and she ran about and made snow-balls with her brothers ; but at other times she would sit thinking alone in the chimney-corner, watching the burning wood and the flame creeping up the great logs. She wondered where her little school-fellow might be ; she knew that she was somewhere—not where her body was laid, in the dark grave—where then was she ? Rose knew there were two worlds beyond the grave, one the only heaven, and another the dreadful hell ; to which then was her little school-fellow gone ? Rose cou l not tell. And then came the thought—If I should die like he , where should I go ? Rose felt she did not know ; and then sl e thought upon the words their minister had said, whose serm(ns she heard at school—sermons which even a child could unc erstand and remember ; and she wished that she could think of all he had preached about, and do as he had said that all who had God for their Heavenly Father should do ; and all these thoughts made her grave.

On the last day of the year Mrs. Smith was busy ironing :

Rose had finished the little things her mother had given her to do, and was seated on the stool by the fire, where she remained for some time, quite silent.

" What are you thinking of, child ?" at last said her mother

" Why, I was thinking, mother, that I wished our ministe. here preached like the one where I go to school. I can't understand any thing here."

" How does your minister preach ?"

" He preaches about our Saviour, and he speaks it so plain, I am never tired of listening. I wish he were here."

" And if he were here, you would not hear him half so often ; you have three times as many Sundays at school as you have at home ; I am sure I would not trouble about that."

" No, mother ; but if he were here, then you and father would hear him too."

" And I suppose it 's that you always sit thinking of ?"

" No, mother, not of that."

" What is it, then ?"

" Why, the last Sunday before I came away from school, our minister preached about, ' Feed my sheep,' and ' Feed my lambs ; he said that our Saviour had told us to do so, and that it meant doing all we could for others—to help them for this world, and that good place where good people go ; and I have been thinking that I don't do any thing to help others."

" Well, child, I am sure I don't know, for I never heard that plain way of preaching that one could understand ; but I can't see that it can belong to the like of you to be after doing for others. I think if you mind your lessons at school, and do what I set you to do at home, you may very well play between whiles, and take it easy too."

" But, mother, so many people do think about helping others, it 's only I that do nothing !"

"So many people, child! what do you mean? I think every body is for self—that is the beginning and the end, with most that I see."

"That's how it is with me, mother, but it is not so with all! When I went to spend the day with aunt Mackenzie at the Hall, she put up the prettiest little apple-pudding in a basin with a cloth over it, and sent it up to Miss Clifford; and I asked her if Miss Clifford was not well, for I thought that must be her dinner sent up to her; and aunt Mackenzie laughed and said, that was not the way to serve up ladies' dinners; and then she told me that there was a poor old woman near, dying of old age, and that Miss Clifford went to carry her a little pudding, which the old woman liked better than meat. I said, I wondered Miss Clifford did not send it, when she had so many servants! and aunt Mackenzie said, It was Miss Clifford's taking it that made the best part of it. She feeds herself! and she said, none could think what her hand and her voice could do · for sickness, that had not known it as she had."

"Well, child, but you don't think you could do like Miss Clifford, I suppose?"

"No, mother, but you know you often do send something to sick people; and I thought if I took it to them, perhaps they might like it all the better, and then I should be trying to do as our minister said."

"Well, I don't know but what they would, if you are bent on being like Miss Clifford!"

"No, mother, I could never be like Miss Clifford; but I do sometimes think if Miss Clifford did but teach me, as she teaches Mercy, I might learn more of what our minister at school says."

"Well, child, it's all very well for Miss Clifford to be thinking about every body else, but, as I say, Miss Clifford is no rule for you, that I can see."

2*

" No, mother, but there is Miss Mansfield in the town ; neighbor Jones says that she has put Mercy into the penny club this year, and Miss Mansfield is younger than I am."

" I dare say that was her mother's doing ; and selling tea no doubt is better than sowing wheat, for it was not much of it that was likely to come up if the weather had held so wet as it was !"

" But then, mother, there is Mercy herself—when I was at home last midsummer, and you sent me to ask how dame Clark was—there was Mercy, upon the table by the window, all alone, with the Bible on her knee ; and I asked her why she was there ? and she said, dame Clark had just fallen asleep, and she had come down to watch, for the people made such a knocking on the door when they wanted any thing, she was afraid they would wake her. And I asked her who set her to nurse dame Clark ? and she said, nobody set her, but that she liked to do it. And I asked her if it was not very dull ? and she said, that it was not dull at all ; that dame Clark liked her to read chapters and verses to her, and to hear her sing ; and she said dame Clark called her Comfort !"

" I always did say that Mercy was the best child in the parish," replied Mrs. Smith ; " I never look twice after her, let her be doing what she will up here."

" But, mother, I don't do any thing for others."

" Well, child, what would you do ?"

" Why, yesterday, widow Lambert told me that little Johnnie could not leave his bed, with the chilblains in his feet ; she said he had quite outgrown and worn up his socks, and she could not make the money to buy him any more ; and I thought if I might but have a little of our worsted, I could knit him a pair of socks in my play-time."

" Well, I have no objection, I am sure," replied Mrs. Smith, " but what's the use of one pair ?"

" O, mother, I could make him two pair, if I might !"

" Well, to be sure, two is better than **one any day** !"

" May I begin to-day, **then**, mother ?"

" I thought your pins were set fast with your father's **stock-ings**, and you won't do much more than finish them of evenings, these short holidays ; but if you wish to be after the **socks in** the day, I will lend you mine, when I **have** finished the **pair I** am after now for Ted—but I am only in the first sock yet."

A cloud passed **over the** joyous look that **had kindled on** the **face of little** Rose, **at her** mother's **leave to** make two pair of socks—when she found that she must wait days for pins ! but still her heart felt lighter—she had talked with her mother about it, and it was not so bad as she expected.

When Rose was gone to her pillow that night, Mrs. Smith said, " I have found out what ails the child—she wants to be after the poor, doing for them !"

" Don 't say a word against it," replied Mr. Smith ; " let the child have her way, it's just like my mother ! she took to read-ing her Bible and caring for the poor, when she was quite young ; I have heard my grandfather say so ; **and** she made one of the best of women ; I hoped the child would take after her grandmother, when I named her Rose."

CHAPTER IV.

EVERY one was up early who had any thing to do on Mr. Smith's farm. Mr. Smith set all his men to work, and then was ready for breakfast by seven o'clock. It was the last day of the year on which Rose had talked to her mother about making the socks for little Johnnie, and on the new year's morning, while setting the breakfast table by candle-light, she heard widow Jones speaking to her mother at the back-door. Rose guessed that widow Jones was going off to the town; and she was right, it was the very day on which widow Jones received the stockings for Mercy from little Jane. O, thought Rose, if I had but two pence, neighbor Jones would buy me a set of pins! but I dare not ask mother, she would think it all waste to have two sets, when I can not use both at once. O, if father would but come, he would give me two pence, and then mother would not mind, if father had given me the money for my own! Rose looked from the front door out into the snowy morning; far into the darkness her bright eyes searched, but no father was in sight. Could she ask her mother? No; she dare not. Yet perhaps her mother would for once let her have another set, as she was going so soon back to school? but while she stood full of doubt between hope and fear, she heard her mother's quick voice say, "Well, good day, neighbor;" and the back door shut, and poor Rose's hope was gone. William, and Rover, William's dog, had just come in, both were white with the falling snow, but Rose stooped down and threw her arms round Rover to hide her tears. William's quick eye saw that his little sister was in trouble. "What are you telling Rover about, hey, Rose? Come, look up and tell me, there's no good in hiding it all in Rover's snowy ears; and there's nobody by but me." "Oh, it's nothing now, William," replied Rose. "What was it then?" asked the kind brother. "It was only that I did so want a set of pins, and neighbor Jones has just gone to the town, but they cost two pence, and I was afraid to ask mother, because I have one set, but they are fast with father's stockings, and mother said she would lend me her's when Ted's socks are done; but I am afraid that won't be in time for what I want before I go to school; and father did n't come in sight, though I looked for him all the time that neighbor Jones stood at the door! "I should like to know why you could not have asked me," said William. "I should think I might have done as well as father for once, and better than Rover, but never mind now, I dare say it will all come right in the end." And Rose had wiped away her tears with William's red pocket-handkerchief, just as she heard her father shaking the snow from his feet outside the door.

While Rose was sitting between her father and William at breakfast, a thought came into her mind; she knew that Mercy had a set of pins, and that it was very seldom that poor widow Jones could buy any worsted to put them in use; perhaps she might not have any use for them now, and if not, she knew that Mercy would lend them to her; so after dinner that day, Rose said, "Mother, it's fine now, may I go and call on Mercy, I have not seen her for a whole week?" "Yes," replied her mother, "if you have a mind, only take care and keep out of

the snow-drifts." So off set Rose, with the eager step of hope
and expectation; the sky was cloudless blue, and all the snow
looked sparkling diamonds: Rose liked to feel it under her little
feet, and the ministering child left the track of her footsteps in
that pure untrodden snow.

Rose knocked at widow Jones's door, and Mercy said, "Come
in." Rose opened the door, and there sat little Mercy in her
grandmother's old arm-chair, with her feet in another chair
wrapped up in a thin old blanket; a few coals were left close
by her side to keep the little fire in, a table with a cup and plate
from which she had taken her dinner stood near her; on the
table lay her little Bible; her hymn-book was in her hand.

"Why! Mercy, are you ill?" asked Rose, going up to her.

"No, only my feet got worse with the chilblains. I have
kept my bed nearly a week; but grandmother's gone to the
town to-day, so uncle Jem carried me down before she went,
that I might not feel so lonesome with no one in the house."

"I wish I had known it," said Rose; "are they very bad?"

"No, they are getting better now, and since I have been kept
in-doors, I have learned a whole chapter out of the Bible, and
three short Psalms, and two hymns, and Miss Clifford came to
see me, and then I said some of them to her; and grandmother
said that was as good as going to school. I have been thinking,
perhaps Miss Clifford will come to-day, it's almost a week
since she was here, and the weather has broken out so fine!"

"Do you really think Miss Clifford will come to-day?" asked
Rose.

"I seem to think she will," replied little Mercy, "only I don't
know; but I have learnt another Psalm, perfect every word—
and a hymn too."

"Do you like going to the Sunday-school very much?" asked
Rose.

"Yes, that I do! and so would any one if they did but once get into Miss Clifford's class," replied Mercy.

"I should like it, I am sure," said Rose.

Just then they caught a sight of the black pony of Miss Clifford's groom passing the window, and the hearts of both the little girls beat quick as the lady entered. Miss Clifford spoke kindly to Rose as well as to Mercy, saying as she made Rose sit down beside her, "I am afraid I have stopped some pleasant talk."

"No, ma'am," replied Mercy, "Rose was only saying how she would like to go to the Sunday-school."

"Do you really wish to come to the Sunday-school?" asked Miss Clifford looking at Rose.

"I go to a boarding-school, ma'am and I am afraid mother would not let me," replied Rose.

"What made you wish it?" asked Miss Clifford; "Come and tell me."

Rose came within the arm so kindly opened to receive her, but she did not speak.

"If you could tell me why you wished it," said Miss Clifford, "perhaps I could find some other way to help you, if your mother objects to your coming to the Sunday-school."

Rose answered in a low voice, "Because I want to do as our Minister at school tells every body they must; and I don't know how."

"What is it that your Minister tells you to do?" asked Miss Clifford.

"He says, Every body must come to Jesus—and I don't know how," Rose answered; and the child's large tear fell upon the hand that held her, and the tears of answering feeling gathered in Miss Clifford's eyes. When Mercy saw the tears in Miss Clifford's eyes, and on the cheek of Rose, she cried too, she knew not why, except because she saw the tears of those she loved—and that alone is often cause enough for childhood's weeping; a purer, higher cause than some that after years too often offer.

"Does not your Minister tell you how to come to Jesus?" asked Miss Clifford.

"I don't know," replied Rose, "because I can't remember only a little of what he says."

"Will you listen to me, then, and try and understand, if I tell you?" Miss Clifford asked.

Rose looked up in the lady's face, and that look was assurance enough.

"Who have you come to now, while you are standing here?" asked Miss Clifford.

"To you!" answered Rose.

"Yes, you have come to me; and you have been telling me what you want; and I am going to give you, if I can, the knowledge that you tell me you want. Now, just as you have come close to me, and told me what you want, so you must come to the Lord Jesus and tell Him. I hear you now, because I am near you; but Jesus is always near to you. He hears every word; and whenever you speak to Him, He stoops down and listens to ? . you say; and He can teach you all you want to know, and give you all you ask Him for. Do you pray to Him?"

"I say, 'Our Father which art in Heaven,'" replied Rose: "our governess said I ought: and sometimes I say other things, when I want them very much. Our Minister said we might ask for all we wanted when we pray, only governess does not know when I do that."

"Do you tell our Saviour that you want to come to him?"

"No, I don't know how."

"If I write you a short prayer, do you think you could read it?"

"O yes; I can read writing a little."

"Then go to the door, and ask the groom for my basket; I have ink and paper there."

Rose brought the basket, and Miss Clifford wrote in a plain hand :—

"O God, my Heavenly Father, I ask Thee to bow down thine ear and listen to my prayer. I am a little, sinful, helpless child; and I want to come to Jesus, that I may be safe and happy for ever. O lead me to Jesus my Saviour! Let me come to Him, that I may know and love Him and keep His commandments. Let me be washed from all my sins in the precious blood of Jesus my Saviour. And give me the Spirit of Jesus to dwell in my heart, that I may be Thy child, and live with Thee for ever. Thou hast said Thou wilt do this, if we ask; and I ask Thee to do it for me, O my Heavenly Father, for the sake of my Saviour, the Lord Jesus Christ. Amen."

Miss Clifford heard Rose read the paper, then folded it up and gave it to her; making her sit down by her, while she talked to Mercy. After a little conversation, Miss Clifford heard Mercy repeat her Psalm, which was said without one mistake; then Mercy repeated her hymn, and Rose thought, as she listened, that certainly the hymn would please her father. After this, Miss Clifford took leave of the children, saying to Rose, "I have a class of farmers' daughters every Monday afternoon, at three o'clock, in my house. You are younger than any here, but if you would like to come, and your mother has no objections, I shall be very happy to receive you; do you think you would like to come?"

"Oh, yes, ma'am, very much," said Rose with brightening color.

" Perhaps you would like me best to ask your mother about
it ?"

" Yes, if you please, ma'am."

" Then I will ride round that way to-day, so you will not be
kept long in suspense," said Miss Clifford, smiling at the eager
look on the face of Rose; and then, with her kind " Good-
by !" to both children, the lady mounted her white pony, and
was soon far away.

" How glad I am that Miss Clifford did come," said Mercy, " I
thought she would !"

" How very kind she is," said Rose.   " If mother will but let
me go, how glad I shall be !   How I wish I knew that piece
of poetry you said, Mercy."

" It's a hymn," replied Mercy ; " have you got a book
like mine ?"

" No, I wish I had ; I learnt some pieces of poetry at our
school ; but father says they are too fine for him, and I dare
not try mother ; but I think father would like what you said.
Is it very hard to learn ?"

" No, it is not hard at all ; shall I lend you my book for a
little while ?   Only I must learn another before Miss Clifford
comes again."

" If you will let me have it," said Rose, " I will try and learn
it to-morrow, and then you shall be sure to have it back again."
So Mercy lent her little treasure hymn-book ; Rose put it safe
in her pocket ; then tucking the folded prayer down deep into
her bosom, she remembered how long she had stayed.   She
had quite forgotten the pins, and no wonder—there had been
enough in that call on Mercy to fill her young heart ; and now
seeing the fire almost out, she stooped down to put on the
shovel of coals that stood beside it ; Mercy guessed her inten-
tion, and exclaimed, " Oh, no, not all those, only one or two,

just to keep it in till grandmother comes ; that is all the coal there is, and there won't be any warmth left for grandmother !"

" But, Mercy, you will be froze ; you look as cold as the snow now."

" That is only because the door stands open ; it goes so bad, it won't shut from outside, except by those that know **how to** humor it."

" Not shut from outside !" **said** Rose ; " why don't you **have a** new one ?"

" That is the new door," replied Mercy : " the old one was all to pieces ; grandmother went backward and forward to steward Jacobs about it till she gave up hope ; and then she dreaded the winter so bad, with only that old door to keep it out, that she went **all** that way **to** Squire Lofft himself ; she only **saw** the ladies, but they came over in their carriage, and looked **at** the door ; and then they went to steward Jacobs and gave the **order ;** and steward Jacobs was angered to think grandmother should **have** been to Squire Lofft, and the door was made of green wood, and it shrank all **round,** and now there is no keeping warm any how ; but Miss Clifford has found it out, and she says there are more ways than **one of** setting that **right."**

" What will she do ?" asked Rose.

" I don't know," replied Mercy ; " but grandmother says that **now** it 's once in **Miss** Clifford's hands it 's sure to come out right."

" Then **you won't be cold** long ?" said Rose earnestly—forgetting **all** but the slight shiver of little Mercy. " I 'll **see** if I can't **make** the door shut outside for me ! Only I **wish I** had some **of our** logs, just to make up the fire fit **to be seen.** But I must go now, or mother will scold. **Come** now, door, you shall shut for me !" Rose **gave a** hard pull, but back again went the door ;

then a gentle pull, but the moment she had let go, it flew open.
" Was there ever such a door ?" said Rose in despair.

" Never mind !" said little **Mercy** from **within**, " never mind
trying it any more : there 's nobody but grandmother and uncle
Jem can shut it from outside." But in the heat of her **dis-**
pleasure with the door, and the man who had made it, and distress at leaving the helpless little Mercy exposed to the cold
evening **air, Rose pulled** and shook the door, but pulled and
shook in vain. Horse's feet came down the lane, but Rose
was **still** contending **with the door, and did not** hear them.
It was William on Black Beauty.

" Hey day, little **miss !** are **you** breaking into neighbor
Jones's **while she is away ? She will soon be home** to find
you out."

" Oh, William !" said **Rose,** ready to cry with her vain efforts ;
"I am so glad it is you ! There is poor Mercy—she can't put
her feet to the ground with the chilblains, and not a bit of
warmth in the fire, and I can't shut the door !"

" It 's no more use to lose patience with a door, than it is with
a donkey," said William, getting down from his horse.

" Oh, do try to shut it !" said Rose ; " and speak to **poor
Mercy first.**"

" **Well, Mercy,**" said William, going **in ;** " why I guess you
could not **go dropping now. Poor thing !** and is that all the
fire you can give New-year's **day ?**"

" **No, I have some coals, but I am** keeping **them** till grandmother comes in."

" Let me see them. Well, to be sure—they would about fill
the sugar-basin ! I left Jem riving wood hard enough to-day,
and he shall feel a little of the weight of it home before long ;
so don't save up that poor handful ; there—it is all gone ! That's
the first coal I have **put** on neighbor **Jones's** fire ; and **I** think

I have known her years enough to have done it sooner. Now for the door. Well, 'tis a fashion of flitting, to be sure! I fancy he that made it would learn to work better, if he had just one night behind it this January weather! A bit of string is the only thing that will do it." William took from his pocket a ball of string; slipping the string round the latch within, he drew the door quite close, and tied the string tight round the hook that fastened back the shutter without. Then, lifting Rose on Black Beauty, he gave her the rein; the little maiden, seated sideways on her brother's saddle, well at ease, pondered on past events, and felt to see her folded paper was quite safe, while William kept even pace by her side.

Rose was soon seated before the warm wood-fire, making the toast for tea, and wondering how William could manage about getting some logs for Mercy's fire, when William came into the kitchen, and said, " Rose, look here !"

Rose ran to his side at the window; there, over the cold snow, which lay white beneath the darkness, Jem was making his way home from the farm, with one of the deep farm-baskets on his shoulder, piled up with logs of wood.

" Is all that for neighbor Jones?" asked Rose, her face beaming with delight.

" Yes, that it is," replied William, " it was father piled it up like that; I found him, and I told him how the poor thing sat shivering there, and he said he should never forgive himself if that orphan child perished with cold. I will say it is a pleasant thing to see father give! I told him about the state of things I had found, and he went at once to Jem and said, ' I suppose you would not be much against carrying half-a-dozen of these logs home with you to-night?' Jem shook his head with a smile; he never took it the least that father was in earnest, but father had piled up the basket with his own hands in no time, and then he set it the next minute on Jem's shoulder, and said, 'There, now make the best of your way home, and tell your good mother I would give any **lad** on my farm such a load as that is, if I could find any to trust as I can her son!' and then father was off, as he always is when he thinks he **has** done." Rose listened, and as she listened she slipped her **hand** into her brother's. William felt this silent expression of the new-formed link between them; he had met his little sister in her heart's young sympathy, she felt she could turn to and depend on his aid, and it seemed to her he stood the nearest to **her** in the new world of feeling and effort her trembling steps had **entered. Jem was out of** sight, but Rose still watched from the window—as if she thought to see the dying embers on Mercy's cold hearth blaze up around the new-year's logs; William still stood by his little sister, and felt and shared her joy; the flickering fire-light showed **the** elder and the younger face—both beaming with the glow of blessed charity.

" Where's Jem?" asked Mrs. Smith, in a loud voice; " **le'** him know I want him before he's off to-night."

" He **is** off already, mother," said William; " what did you want?"

" **How vexing !**" **exclaimed** Mrs. Smith; " that is always the way—people are off just when you want them most! Here **I** had a bottle of beer put up all ready for him to take home to his mother; for how she will toil **through** the lanes in this deep snow, **I can't** think."

" Never mind, mother," said William, " I'll run after him; don't wait tea for me if father comes in." William's hat was **on, and** away he ran, and Rose still stood at the window, watching her brother through the darkness, **by the** light of the snow.

" Tell Mercy to have a little heated right not, and let her **grandmother go warm to rest,**" shouted Mrs. Smith after William "Yes, mother," William shouted back as he ran. "Ah!" thought little Rose, "what would have been the use of mother sending that message, if William and I had not seen to the fire!" William overtook Jem almost at the cottage-door, and delivering the bottle of beer and the 'message, he returned to the farm. Jem, with a thankful heart, stowed away the wood, made up the fire, set little Mercy carefully in another chair, that his mother's might look ready for her to sit down in at once ; set out the frugal meal, put the tin mug in readiness to heat the beer, and then, sitting down upon the stool, which was his usual seat, took little Mercy's feet carefully on his knees ; that, as he said, they might feel a bit of comfort from the fire too.

Meanwhile poor widow Jones was toiling along the snowy lanes ; turning at last the longed-for corner, she suddenly caught sight of the ruddy glow, cast by the blazing wood-fire through the large casement on the snow. "And what's the matter now?" said widow Jones to herself, as she hastened on with quicker steps and beating heart; "sure the child has not set herself afire and the old place too!"—the thought of a warm glowing hearth having been kindled up was too great an improbability to enter widow Jones's mind. At last her hand was on the latch, and in a moment more she saw the picture of comfort— the two she loved more than life, the logs of burning wood, the arm-chair waiting for her, the little supper-table set ready !

"There's mother!" said Jem, and starting up, he laid little Mercy's feet gently upon the stool where he had been nursing them, and took his mother's old umbrella and basket from her hand. Widow Jones, overcome with fatigue, exhaustion, and surprise, sank down into her arm-chair, while Jem poured some beer from the black bottle into the tin mug, and set it on the side of the burning log to heat, and cutting off a piece of bread, he knelt down before the fire to make some toast to put into it.

" Well, I never thought to find the like of this," said widow
Jones, at last. " Where in the world did you manage to get
firewood and beer ?"

" That's all master's and mistress' goodness," replied Jem ;
" but never mind that, mother, till you have taken a sip of beer,
and got a little life into you."

But widow Jones could not wait. " Bless them for it !" she
said, fervently ; and then, taking up her basket from the table
where Jem had set it down, she went on to say, in a livelier
tone, " Here, Mercy, child, I have a rare surprise for you ; if you
are not to run about with warm feet at last, I don't know who
is ; look you here !" And pair after pair of warm stockings, all
mended and folded, and given by the hand of little Jane, were
piled up on widow Jones's knee.

" Oh, granny ! what, all for me ?" said Mercy, as she stretched
out both hands to receive one pair, and feel its warmth. And
then, while she unfolded pair after pair, widow Jones told the
history of all : Jem opened both his eyes and mouth to listen,
saying, as his mother ended, " Why ! the world is warm all over
to-day, out here in the country, and down there in the town !"

But the beer in the tin mug began to boil, and the toast to
put into it had long been made ; so widow Jones and her son
Jem and her little grand-daughter began, with thankful hearts
and hungry appetites, to partake of their simple fare.

At the farm, Mr. Smith had come in by the back door, and
William returned by the front, and they all sat down to tea.

" What 's this ?" asked Rose, as she took a long, thin parcel
from under her plate.

" You had better look and see," said William ; " it seems you
have the best right to it."

" There is no direction upon it," said Rose. " Mother, shall
I open it ?"

" Well, I suppose there is not much use in keeping it shut,"
replied Mrs. Smith.

Rose opened it slowly and carefully; " O my pins! my pins!"
she exclaimed, "mother, was it you? Did you tell neighbor
Jones?"

" Tell neighbor Jones—no; what should I have to tell her?"

" You had better ask Rover," whispered William, " he knows
more about it than mother." Rose laughed at this: " O, William, how glad I am! did you tell neighbor Jones?"

" No, not I. You seem to think no one has the sense to buy
a set of pins but neighbor Jones?"

" You did not go after them yourself, did you?" asked Rose.

" You had better ask Rover about it," replied William, " he
has the most right to answer, seeing you told him first in the
morning." So Rose was provided with her set of pins—four
bright steel pins—and to-morrow she could begin little
Johnnie's socks.

Rose had now only one anxiety, and that one was, to know
whether her mother had given leave for her to go up to Miss
Clifford's class of farmers' daughters at the Hall ; but she could
not venture to ask ; so she took the long stocking she was
knitting for her father, and sat down on her stool in the chimney
corner to her evening's work ; William went out to see after the
cattle, Mr. Smith sat down to rest by the fire in his old-fashioned
arm-chair, Mrs. Smith took her knitting at the table, Joe sat by
the same table deeply occupied with a book of travels he had
lately met with, and Samson sat down in the opposite chimney-
corner to Rose; little Ted was gone to rest for the night.

At last Mr. Smith said, "Did I see Miss Clifford cross the
drift this afternoon?"

" She was there," replied Mrs. Smith, " whether you saw her
or not."

"She did not call, I suppose, did she?" again inquired Mr. Smith. Rose looked up, unable to **knit** another stitch from anxiety.

"Yes, that she did," replied Mrs. Smith, "she came to **ask** Rose to a class of farmers' daughters held at the Hall. I told her that I thanked her all the same, but I always had kept myself to myself, and I meant that Rose should do the same."

"**Must** not I go then, mother?" asked Rose."

"**No,** child; I told Miss Clifford so, and she does not expect it now."

Rose **laid down** her knitting, and hiding her face in her pinafore, cried and sobbed.

Mr. Smith did not **say a word, but** he **got up, took** his hat, **and went out for his last round in the farm-yard,** unable to bear **the sight** of the child's grief which he felt he **could** not comfort. **Mrs.** Smith knitted on, and Rose went on crying, while **Samson** spread out **both** his hands nearer and nearer over the **fire,** as if he did not quite know what **he** was **doing.**

"There, child, leave off crying, do!" **at** last said Mrs. Smith. "What's the use of taking on so because you can not go up to **the Hall?** What's the use of a boarding-school, I should like **to know, if** you have not lessons enough there, without going up to **the Hall after** them?" But poor Rose was in no readiness to **explain any feeling just** then to her mother, she only cried **on.**

"**Now,** Rose, leave off crying directly!" said her mother. Rose tried to keep back her tears, and went on slowly with her knitting; meanwhile, Samson had slipped out, **and** in a few minutes William **came in** and took Samson's place in the opposite chimney-corner to Rose. He stretched out his wet feet and cold hands to the fire, and said in a low tone, "Rose I have a secret to **tell you,**" but poor Rose did not look **up.**

"O, I see how it is," said William, "there is nobody but Rover will do, you began with him this morning, and by what I can see you mean to end the same. Here, Rover, go to Rose, she has something to tell you, I guess she is for sending poor neighbor Jones off for some worsted to the town, but she will tell you all about it; go, sir, go." Rover looked up at his master, wagging his tail, and then went and looked up at Rose—as if by way of inquiry. "O, William, how can you talk so!" said Rose, too full of sorrow still to laugh, "I don't want you, Rover, go away."

Poor little Rose! her day had begun with tears, and for awhile it seemed likely to end with the same; and so it often is, that when we try to walk in the narrow way that leadeth to everlasting life, we find that tears are there as well as smiles—but the tears in that narrow way water its fair flowers, and make them grow the faster. After awhile, Mr. Smith came in again, Rose knew it was almost her bed-time, and she thought it would be pleasant just to hear what William's secret was, so she went nearer to him and said, "What secret do you know William?" "Why," said William, "I have thought of a way to keep up the fire on neighbor Jones's hearth all this whole winter!"

"O, Will, have you? what is it?"

"Why, it was only this morning that father was asking me who he should give a job of hedging and ditching to. I said then, 'We had better think who we can best spare to take it;' but I have been thinking this evening, that it would be as well to consider who stands most in need of it, and I am pretty sure that will be Jem; and then he will have all the wood he cuts away, and that will go far to keep a fire on their hearth all the winter."

"Do you think father is sure to let him have it?" asked Rose.

"Yes, I am **sure he** will, if I say only two words about it. Jem has **not** been put to it before, but I never saw the thing **yet that** he did not finish **off as well as a man,** and better than many men, because his mind is always in the thing he is after."

So little Rose went to her pillow with thoughts of Jem hedging and ditching, and the blazing fire kept up on widow Jones's hearth, and sympathy's warm light drank up the mist of sadness, and, having offered up the lady's prayer, she laid down **her** head and was soon **asleep.**

CHAPTER V.

*"So then faith cometh by hearing, and hearing by the word of God."—Rom. x. 17.

THE next morning, Rose thought again of Miss Clifford, and her lost hope of going to the class at the Hall; she sighed once or twice while she was dressing; but she had her little treasured prayer, and that comforted her; she had also her pins, and Mercy's hymn-book, from which to learn the hymn that she thought would please her father; so she ran down stairs with a cheerful step, and was soon engaged preparing the breakfast. After breakfast, the boys helped clear the table; Mrs. Smith went off to the dairy; and Rose began her morning's work. First, she made up the fire; then she washed the cups and saucers, mugs and plates, from the breakfast-table, and put them away; after this, she swept up the farm-house kitchen, the room they always occupied; and then, with her little can of wheat, went out to feed the fowls;—quite unconcerned at snow or freezing wind, she stood in the stone-yard, which was always swept early, and scattered the grain round her, while the hungry fowls came flying over the low wall at the sound of her voice to pick it up; and the little birds peeped down from the bare branches of the old ash-tree that stood beside the low wall, watching till Rose should throw them a distant handful, which she never failed to do, looking up with a special call meant only for them—and then down flew on lighter wing the little birds of the air, while Rose stood a watcher between them and the fowls of the farm, guarding the rights of both. After this, Rose went with her mother to set the upper rooms in order; and then, for the most part, her household work was done; but, on churning days, and baking days, and washing days, and ironing days, there was more to be accomplished, and sometimes Rose was busy with her mother nearly the whole day; but this was neither churning, nor baking, nor washing, nor ironing day, and Rose had done all, and put on her clean pinafore, by a little after eleven o'clock.

And now her time was her own, to employ as she liked; and she might begin her socks; but she must ask her mother for the promised worsted; and, she thought, perhaps her mother might be angry with her still, for crying the night before; but if she did not ask, she could not begin poor little Johnnie's socks. Had she not better learn her hymn out of Mercy's book, and then she need not ask her mother at present? Yes, but Rose knew that when she had set her sock on, and counted the stitches, she could knit and learn too; and poor Johnnie had no socks to his feet; so she went to her mother, and asked, "Mother, may I have that worsted for Johnnie Lambert's socks now?" Mrs. Smith had looked many times at her little daughter; she had seen her pale with the last night's crying, yet busy all the morning, a little grave, but pleasant still in all she did or said; she remembered how the child had wished she could learn of Miss Clifford, and she began to think whether she had done right in refusing; but Mrs. Smith never liked to give up her own way, and she had yet to learn that "a man's pride shall bring him low, while honor shall uphold the humble in spirit;" but when her little girl asked in fear and trembling for the worsted, Mrs. Smith replied, "Yes, child, to be sure, did n't I tell you you might? It 's in the drawer; you may take what you want, and wind it at once"

" May I make two pair then, mother ?" asked Rose, **gathering courage.**

" **Yes, to** be sure, if you make one ; one pair is n't much **use** alone."

So Rose ran off for her worsted ; she knew exactly the right size, and how many stitches to set on ; she opened Mercy's little hymn-book on the chimney-corner, hung the skein on the back of her father's arm-chair, **and** was just beginning to wind her worsted and learn her hymn, when her father passed the window **and came in at the front door ;** he took off his great coat and **hat,** all white with the fresh-falling snow, and came in for a rest **and a** warm.

" Well, little girl, busy **as possible** ; that 's all right ; never mind being tired with work, so long as you are never tired with idleness ; work well, and rest well, that 's my maxim ; but idle work, and idle rest, I should like to know what 's the **good they** ever did to any body ?   What are you after now ?"

" O, father, you can hold my worsted, while I wind ; **it gets** tangled up **on the** chair.   I am going to **make** some socks for poor little Johnnie Lambert ; he has **not a** bit of sock to his feet ; mother says I may make **him two pair."**

" That won't do you, nor **mother, nor** Johnnie Lambert any harm, I guess !   What **book have you got** open there ?   Are you so hard put **to** it for time that you must do two things at once ?   That is **not,** for the **most** part, the best way."

" **No,** father, **but** that **is** Mercy's book ; she lent it to **me to** learn a hymn, **and she** wants the book ; so I told her **I would** learn it to-day, **if I** could, and take it back to **her."**

" And have you not books enough without **Mercy's !**   I should have thought you might ; I know **I paid eleven** shillings down this last half-year for books and **such like** things, and yet it seems you have to come to Mercy after all—whose schooling never cost a single bit of gold; that is what comes of boarding-school expenses, **I see.**"

"No, father, but what I learn **at school** are pieces of poetry that are not any use at **home,** because you say they are too fine for you; so I thought I would just learn such a beautiful hymn, that Mercy said out of her book to Miss Clifford, and see if you did not like that; only you hear it, father!" Rose took up the book, and, standing at her father's knee, she read :—

"By cool Siloam's shady rill,
    How sweet the lily grows!
How sweet **the** breath beneath the hill
    Of Sharon's dewy rose !

"Lo ! such the child whose early feet
    The paths of peace have trod;
Whose secret heart, with influence sweet,
    Is upward drawn **to God !**

"By cool Siloam's shady rill,
    The lily **must** decay;
The rose **that blooms** beneath **the hill**
    Must shortly **fade** away.

"**O** Thou, whose early feet **were found**
    Within **Thy** Father's **shrine—**
Whose years with **changeless** virtue crowned
    Were all alike **divine ;—**

"**Dependent on Thy** bounteous breath—
    We seek Thy grace alone;
In childhood, manhood, age, and **death,**
    To keep us still Thine own."

The father listened, then took the book and said, "Let me see it ;" and, looking at the first verse, read aloud the words, "'Of Sharon's dewy rose !'—that was what your grandmother would often speak about when any one took notice of her name."

"I know, father, for our Minister preached about that, and governess always makes us learn the text when we come home; it's in the Bible, 'I am the rose of Sharon, and the lily of the valley;' and our Minister said it meant our Saviour."

"Oh, child, how like you are to my mother! I never knew that was in the Bible, though I have heard her speak about it so often! I suppose I did not take so much notice then; she would have been pleased enough **if I had** thought about some of her words then as I do now; but I can not remember many **of them** now, only I would give any thing to have you like her. Do you think you could find where that is in the Bible about the rose of Sharon?"

"No, father, I can't tell where to find any thing in the Bible, because I have not got one. Mercy has one of her own."

"What then did I pay down that eleven shillings for, if **you** have not so much as got a Bible?"

"I did ask our governess, father, but she said that **it was not her** business to get me a **Bible**;—that if I **wanted** one, I must ask you for that, and I thought **I would before** I went to school again."

"Sure enough you shall have **one**! ·I don't know that my mother ever had any books **except** her Bible and her prayer-book, and she had learning enough to make her one of the best of women, and how should you ever be like her if you have not so much as a Bible to look into! I will see to it next market-day, you may rest sure of that, and now I must be off **again.**"

And the happy child sat down to her knitting, and her hymn; **but how** often did she cease to murmur **the sweet words,** while her thoughts were gone to her promised Bible.

"There, child," said her mother, coming in with a couple of

pair of old socks in her hand, " if you take my advice, you will
mend up those old soft socks first for widow Lambert's boy,
they won't be so stiff to his feet ; if they are as bad as you say,
he would hardly bear the new ones for a time yet."

" O yes, mother ; and then if I mend them on this snowy day I
can take them to-morrow !" So when dinner was over, and cleared
away, Rose still went on darning, and learning, till the light of
the short day began to fade, and it was time to set the tea.

Rose whispered to William in the evening, " What did father
say about Jem ?"

" O, it's all right enough," replied William ; " Jem's to begin
to-morrow, and he looks as great as a prince about it.   I called
in this morning to hear how neighbor Jones was, after her
walk in the snow ; Mercy was on her feet ; Miss Mansfield had
sent her some warm stockings that had set her up again.   Jem
had been in to tell his mother the news about his getting the
hedging and ditching, and she said she was thankful enough,
but she knew it was all that blessed child's doing, who would
not rest while the widow and the orphan were cold !"

" Who did she mean, Will ?"

" Why, you, to be sure !"

" But it was not I ; it was you, Will, that did that."

" No, Rose, I am afraid I should never have thought of it, had
it not been for your taking on so about Mercy's fire ; but now
we have begun 'tis likely to go on well for them, I hope."

The next was a bright winter's day, the heavens were clear,
and all the earth looked white and beautiful ; within the house
Rose was as busy as a bee among the flowers of spring.   This
was baking-morning ; Rose peeled apples for pies and turnovers,
filled little round tartlets with jam, and washed over the tops
of the loaves with a feather dipped in beer, to make them brown
and shining.   No play-time, no work for Johnnie Lambert that

morning, but Rose had finished darning the soft socks the day before. When baking was over, her mother gave her two large rosy apples, but she slipped them both into her pocket—one for Mercy, and one for little Johnnie Lambert.

After dinner, Rose had her mother's leave to take the **socks** she had mended to Johnnie Lambert. " Are you going any where else, child ?" asked her mother.

" Only to take Mercy back her hymn-book, mother."

" I thought it was likely you were going there ; you may take her one of those **apple turnovers** you made this morning, if you **have a mind ;** I dare say she gets little more than bread, and not too much of that ; it must be a hard matter for the old woman to make out this winter time." Rose lifted her beaming face to her mother, who stuffed turnover and socks into a basket ; and off set the ministering child, pressing with light step the soft and sparkling snow.

First to Johnnie Lambert's, under the hill. His mother was seated at work, patching up Johnnie's frock, while the poor little **fellow was** wrapped up in her cloak by the **fire.** Rose found ready entrance. " Look, Johnnie, **see !** I have brought you two pair of soft warm socks ; **won 't you soon run** about now ?"

" Well, I am sure ! who would **have thought of** seeing socks on you, Johnnie ?" said his **mother.**

" I am knitting him new **ones,** and they will be done before I go to school," said **Rose.** " And there 's an apple for you, Johnnie !"

" Look, mother, look !" **said** little Johnnie, who understood the pleasure of an apple, more than the comfort of warm socks —to which his little feet had been strangers quite long enough for him to forget them. Many a sweet golden apple had Rose gathered from their orchard-trees, **but** never one before had given her so much pleasure as this—while she looked **at the**

little chilblain prisoner, wrapped up in his mother's cloak his
face all one glad smile at this autumn treasure come in winter's
depth to cheer him.

Then on went the happy child—lightly along the snowy lanes
as the bird that glides over the summer lawn, her basket in her
hand, her little shawl pinned round her, and her face glowing
with the healthful breath of the frosty air; up the hill side, then
along the winding lane, to widow Jones's door. At the door she
stood still in amazement; it was new all over, and fitted so close
that not one cold blast of wind could possibly make its way in,
to get itself a warm at the winter fire. At last Rose knocked
with some hesitation, but the new door was quickly opened, and
Mercy stood before her.

"Why, Mercy, how quick you have got a new door! Did
Miss Clifford do that?"

"Yes, that she did; it's hardly been up an hour yet, and it
goes as well as a door can go; and grandmother's out, and she
does not know a word about it, and I have had nobody to tell.
I am so glad you're come! Grandmother will be so surprised,
she won't know the place; just you come and feel how warm it
is by the fire now; and look here, only look!" and Mercy's little
hand drew out to view a dark crimson curtain, hung by rings
on a strong cord, behind widow Jones' old arm-chair, between
the fire and the back door. Rose looked in silent admiration
from the new door to the thick sheltering curtain, then back
again to the new door.

"But Miss Clifford could not bring the door?" said Rose, unable still to take the mystery in.

"O no, I will tell you all about it. I was sitting here all
alone, so warm on one side by the fire you made us; and so
cold the other, for the wind drove in piercing; and I heard a
great lumbering outside, so I went to look, and there was car-

M. C.   p. 60.

penter Mason with his man and cart, and this new door. He said he heard that there was some little fault about the other, and so he brought a new one; and while he was doing **it Miss** Clifford came, and carpenter Mason took great notice of the least word she said; and she asked him to drive those two big hooks into the wall; and he took a deal of pains, and said **he** had made them both fast in a beam; and that beautiful curtain was rolled **up on the** groom's saddle, and carpenter Mason hung it up, and drew it himself behind grandmother's chair; and when he was gone, Miss Clifford said that I might tell grandmother that the curtain came from her room—where some new ones had been put up. **I am sure I can't** think what grandmother and uncle Jem will say when they come home? The draught from that back-door used to blow the candle-flame all on one side, so that it was no use to try and burn one on windy evenings; but now, what with the new door, and the curtain, and the warm fire, **we** shall not know how to be comfortable enough!"

After a little more admiration and conversation, Rose opened her basket, and said, "See what mother has **sent you!** We baked to-day, and I made that turnover, and I **brought you that** big apple! Shall we set the table together?"

Mercy willingly agreed and the **small round** table was set out to the best effect, the turnover in the middle; then Mercy also agreed that Rose should put on another log, to make a real good fire for once; and Rose **filled the** kettle, and hung it over **the** fire to boil—for little Mercy was still lame; and then the children looked round on all with entire satisfaction, and, saying "Good by" to each other, Mercy waited within, in glad expectation of the happy surprise of her grandmother, and **uncle** Jem; while Rose ran swiftly home to tell them **all the** welcome tidings of the new door and the warm curtain.

The next day farmer Smith and his son William went off to

the market; and all day long Rose thought upon the promised Bible; the **hour for her** father's return came, but Rose could not watch, she must prepare the tea and make the toast; but presently she heard his cheerful voice **in the** back kitchen, saying, " Well, wife, it 's cold enough !" and then his hat was hung on the peg in the passage, and the whip set down in the corner by the hat, and his next step was in at the kitchen door; down went the toast, and Rose was at her father's side.

" Well, my little girl," said her father, with his kindest smile, " **all** safe and right—Chestnut, and William, and father, and Bible, and all !" and he drew the precious book from his inside-**pocket,** and placed it in the hands **of his** child. Rose took it with trembling joy, the gilt edges **of its** leaves all sparkled in the fire-light blaze. " Oh father, is this mine ?" she asked.

" Yes, to be sure it is," said her father; and then, laying his hand upon her head, **he** said in the solemn tone **of prayer,** " My mother's God give thee **his** blessing with **it** !"

The past excitement of hope and expectation through the day, and now her hope fulfilled, and the voice of prayer—heard for the first time by Rose from her father's lips—prayer of which her Minister at school had said so much ! all these mingled feelings overcame the little girl; she threw her arms round her father's neck and sobbed : he pressed her to his heart, and the first tear **he** had shed since he had wept for **his** mother, fell on the head **of** his child.

Rose heard her mother's step, and at the sound her arms un-clasped from her father's neck, she folded up her precious Bible, and sat down again to finish the toast. William smiled a knowing smile at her when he came in, and whispered, " It was I who helped father to choose **you** such a beauty of a book !" But **it was not** its purple cover, **it** was not its gilt edges, that **had made** the hand of little Rose tremble with joy. No, it was that she held at last her own Bible—the Book from which she had heard the Minister preach such 'sweet words—words that had already taught her to know and love her Saviour. Before tea, Rose showed her treasure to her mother, who said, she hoped Rose was not going to take such a book as that to be worn shabby at school! But her father replied, that he bought it for her to have always with her; for that, he believed, was the use of a Bible! So Mrs. Smith said no more, and Rose, relieved from all apprehension of separation, carried her treasure up with her that night to bed.

The next day was Sunday, and after breakfast, while Mrs. Smith was still busy in the back-kitchen, Rose sat down on her father's knee by the fire. She had been thinking of how her father had said, when he gave her the Bible, " My MOTHER's God give thee His blessing !" and now, putting her arm round his neck, she asked, " Father, why did you say, My MOTHER'S God—is not God your God !"

" I don't know, Rose," replied her **father.**

" Then, father, won't you ask God to be your God? Our Minister says, that God will do all good things **that** we ask Him **for ;** and I know it is so, because **I asked Him** that mother might let me do something to help others, as our Minister said we should, and then mother **did. And I** asked that I might have a Bible of my own, and now I have. So, won't you ask, father ?"

" Yes, Rose, I hope **I shall.** I don't feel comfortable never reading the Bible with you children. I should like to **have** family prayers as my mother used, but I don't know what **has** become of the book of prayers she used ; I am afraid it's altogether lost: and our Minister here is **not one that** you can speak to about that sort of thing, for he has never spoken a word **to** me about it himself !"

" Oh, but father, our Minister at school says that we may pray to God in words from our own hearts; and I tried, and I found it was right !"

" Well, Rose, I don't know, for I have not tried it yet; but I do know it's the thing that ought to be done, and I will talk to your mother; for there is nothing like to-day. My mother used to say, ' To-day, William, not to-morrow !' I have found it a good rule for this world, and it is not likely to be worse for the next."

" No, father, to-day must be right, for that is what we say every Sunday in the Psalm at church, ' To-day if ye will hear His voice, harden not your hearts !' "

As they walked to church that morning, their children being on before, Mr. Smith said to his wife, " Do you know where my mother's Bible is ?"

" Yes, to be sure, I locked it up to keep it safe from the children."

" I wish you would look it out then ; for I feel I have been very wrong to neglect it so : a locked-up Bible is a bad witness against me. I should wish we should read it every day with the children—have family prayers I mean, morning and evening, as they do at the Hall, for I know there is but one Way alike for all."

" Well, I think it was a pity you did not consider of it from the first; I never can see the use of changes—it's nothing more than saying, We have been wrong all along before !"

" And so we have, wife, and all the shame lies in the wrong thing—not in trying to do the right : and are we not always telling our people that they must make a change, and do better by us? And if they never see us take a step in the good way they may well think what's the need for them to change ? for you may be sure they are well aware we are not all we ought to be yet ; but if they see us doing better than before, may **be they** will think it time to begin to consider their **own ways,** before it be too late."

" Well, I am sure I don't understand it, so you must do as you please ; that is all I have to say."

That afternoon when Mr. Smith went into his little parlor, his mother's Bible had been laid, by his wife, on the table : he took it in his hand—the lamp that had lighted his steps to the kingdom of Heaven !—**he** opened it—he saw the well-worn **leaves**—**he** could not read the words, for his eyes were dim with **tears ;** but kneeling down, he **took it** for his own—his lamp in life—his guide to Heaven.

That evening, when they were all assembled, farmer Smith sent Rose to the parlor to fetch her grandmother's Bible ; he took it from her hands and said, " My boys, you don't know this Bible, but I know it well ; it was your grandmother's, and it has been my sin that you have not known it as long **as you have** known any thing. It guided your grandmother to Heaven ; she never looked on any thing as she looked on this book. I have heard her talk to it and say, " My blessed Bible, my comforter, my guide to Heaven's gate—how **I** thank God **for** you !" and then she would say to me, ' My **son, bind the** words of this book as chains about thy neck, write **them on** thine heart.' Ah ! my mother, I have not done so **! but I** trust, by God's help, I shall **;** and see to it, **my boys, that** you lay up its words in your hearts, that it may lead you **to a** better world than this."

Then Molly **was called** in, and took her seat, and farmer Smith read the first Psalm. " Let us pray," then said the father, and all knelt down, while, with a trembling voice, he offered up his prayer.

" O God, pardon our manifold **sins.** Pardon, O God, our neg· lect of Thy Word. May ᵗhe Bible be from this time our de light. We thank Thee for Thy mercy; we thank Thee for Thy patience; we thank Thee for Thy goodness. O God, bless our children; **bless our servants**; and **take care of** us this night, for the love of Thine only Son our Saviour Jesus Christ. Amen."

The next morning, when farmer **Smith** came in to breakfast, Mrs. Smith had laid the Bible ready for him. Molly was called in; the yard-boy was set in the back kitchen, that no one might **make a** disturbance, and Mrs. Smith failed not to say to him, "**You may** keep near the passage here; you will be none the **worse for hearing!**" **The father** read the second Psalm, and prayed again.

"**O God, we thank Thee for the** night: we thank Thee for **safety and rest. O God,** take care of us this day; keep us from all evil; **teach** us to please Thee. **O God,** bless us all; **and** make us to remember and love Thy **Word, through Jesus Christ our Saviour.** Amen."

From that day, morning and evening prayers **were always** heard in farmer Smith's dwelling.

Rose could not finish the socks for little Johnnie Lambert till the day before that on which she was **to return** to school; she could not hope to be **spared to** take them, because it was time **for her things to be** packed up; so after dinner she said, "Mother, **I have finished** little Johnnie's **last** sock; will you please give them **to widow** Lambert when you see her?"

" And **why not take them yourself, child?**"

" I thought you **would** want me, mother, **for** packing my clothes."

" O, I can see to that; **it** is n't likely **when** you have worked up all your playtime into socks for a barefoot child, that I should hinder you from the sight **of them on his** feet. I have found **you** up an old pair of Ted's boots, **for I dare** say the child's are **as much** to pieces as they are together, and there 's no use in his wearing out your work as soon as you have done it, for want of a pair of boots to cover it."

So away went the ministering child, with her own hand to draw on the socks of the fatherless boy, and to see him stoop down and feel them with his little fingers, while the tear of thankfulness glistened in his mother's eye. Rose took a farewell of Mercy, and then hastened home. And when she turned the corner of the road, there, on the top of the green slope at the garden-gate of the farm, was Miss Clifford on her white pony, and David her groom holding his black pony at her side. Rose longed to run home for fear Miss Clifford should be gone ; but she did not like Miss Clifford to see her running, so she walked down the hill to the bridge, and then began as fast as she could to climb the green slope. Miss Clifford was talking to Mrs. Smith, but she saw Rose coming, and wishing Mrs. Smith " Good day," she rode down the slope and met the child.

" I heard from Mercy that you were going back to school," said Miss Clifford, " so I called to wish you good-by, and to bring you a little hymn-book like Mercy's, for she tells me that you have no hymn-book, and were pleased with her's ; there it is, I have written your name and mine in it ; so now there will be no fear of forgetting each other—will there ?" Rose took the book from Miss Clifford's hand, and curtsied to the very ground, while her eyes told her young heart's gladness. Then with a parting smile on the little girl, Miss Clifford raised Snowflake's rein, and in a moment more she was cantering up the opposite hill, while Rose ran with her treasure to her mother. Mrs. Smith was greatly pleased at Miss Clifford's call and present to Rose, after her refusal about the class ; and the last evening of the little girl's holidays was soothed by the tenderness of all in her home, and so went the ministering child back again to her school in the town.

CHAPTER VI.

"How much better is it to get wisdom than gold? and to get understanding rather to be chosen than silver."—PROVERBS xvi. 16.

"WHERE is Herbert?" asked Mr. Clifford, on sitting down to the dinner-table one day, as the month of January was drawing to a close. "Mr. Herbert came in late, sir, and will soon be down," said a servant in waiting. Herbert quickly entered, with glowing cheeks, "I am very sorry to be late, mamma, but papa will not mind when I tell him what has hindered me! I know, papa, you thought I never should be charitable, but I shall; I have taken up with it at last, and capital fun it is!" "Indeed," replied Mr. Clifford, "Charity, having to do with the wants, and often with the sorrows of others, is not generally associated with fun; but it is always pleasant to hear of charity, so after dinner we shall call on you for an account."

"O, papa! you take things in such a serious way, it puts out all the fun in no time! but I will tell you, papa, and I am sure you will say I could not but do as I did." So when the dessert was on the table, Herbert began. "Now, papa, for my story. I had been skating, and I thought I should be late home, so to save myself the corner of the road, I just cut across old Willy Green's garden. I leaped the ditch, and as I stopped a minute to recover breath, I saw Willy Green sitting on a trunk of a tree, on the edge of his garden ditch, a little lower down. I thought, as he had seen me come in, in that sort of way, I must stop and speak to him; so I said, well, Willy, you won't take me up for trespassing, you know at least I am an honest lad! but he **did** not speak a word, he only shook his head, and sat panting for breath. I was frightened enough then, for I believed he was going to die, and I alone with him there! **So I** said, Do you feel ill, Willy? After a minute he managed **to** speak, and then he said, ' O, master, I **been after** riving a bit of firewood, and I thought my **breath would never** come again !' And there was his hatchet wedged **in** the old tree, and he had not had the strength to get it **out again.** I soon pulled it out for him, and then I asked him how he could think of trying at **what** he had no strength for ? and he said he had been perished with cold the last night, and laid shivering for hours; so he thought he would try after a few chips, just to make a blaze and get a little warmth into him, but that it had almost **cost** him his life's end." **Herbert saw the** tears fill his sister's **eyes,** so he made haste to what he thought the best part of the story. " Well, papa, I had spent the last of my **money on a new-** fashioned riding-whip, but I remembered that **my** next **month's** allowance would be mine in a week, **and a** week would be quite soon enough to pay for some coals, if **I had** them sent in to old Willy to-morrow; and I thought, papa, you would not mind my giving a promise in such a **case**; so I said to old Willy, who was standing by me, Never mind, Willy; you shall not be tempted to kill yourself **over an** old log; and I gave a desperate push, and sent the old **tree down** into the ditch, for, being hollow, it was not so heavy as it looked; but the poor old fellow called out as if it had been his barn of a cottage blown down. It was such fun, because I knew how I meant to surprise him ! **So** I said, Don't break your heart after the old log; you shall see plenty of shining black coal at your stile to-morrow ! I thought he would be as pleased as possible at this; but I suppose it seemed to him too good to be true, for he only shook his head, and said, 'I thank you, master, but I fear there's no good comes of casting away the least of God's creatures.' But I shall show him what I mean when to-morrow comes. I could not have done better; could I, papa?"

"Indeed, Herbert, I am afraid you will find yourself in a serious difficulty: you seem to have thrown my rule, as to your monthly allowance, overboard, with old Willy's log. It can be hardly necessary for me to remind you of what I have repeated to you year by year, that I never allow you to anticipate your allowance by any debt or promise. I give you what is amply sufficient for you, month by month, and while I am spared to watch over you, I never will allow you to acquire the habit of making the expenditure of the present a debt upon the future."

"But, papa, it was only one week beforehand, and it was for charity!"

"Whatever the length of time, or whatever the object, your father's rule, my boy, was the same, and you can not break the rule without incurring the penalty. Your next month's allowance is forfeited, as I always told you it would be if my rule was broken by you."

"But, papa, I promised!"

"You promised what you had no right to engage for, and have no power to perform: if you learn by this lesson to avoid a too hasty promise through life, it will be well for you; and this was a promise made in direct infringement of my rule, and therefore the sorrow of recalling the promise must be yours. If you had not wasted your money, you would not have found yourself without any, when a real want came before you."

"Then, papa, I must leave old Willy to perish with cold, and the only bit of firewood he has, in the ditch!"

"God forbid, Herbert, that you should have a heart, and I a son, capable of such an act! If you can render no aid to the needy without your purse, then you put your money before your powers of heart, and mind, and body ; and this is a base substitution, and proves that, for your own sake, you have **need, in-** deed, to be separated from your purse for a time."

Herbert said no more ; he saw his father was resolved, and that all appeal was hopeless : he tried to restrain **his** feelings while his father was present, but when **Mr.** Clifford retired **to** his study after dinner, **poor Herbert's** despair broke forth.

" Oh, mamma, **you will help** me, will you not ?"

" **What can I do** for you, Herbert ?"

" **Will** you send as much coal as would last out that old log ?"

" No, dear Herbert, I can not do that ; the work is yours, and I must not take it out of your hands. Try to look at it calmly, it is your first real difficulty in life, and all your future **will** be influenced by it."

" It is not any use to think about it, mamma ; **if you will not** help me, I shall never get out of it. And perhaps **old Willy will die with the** cold, and the whole village will say **it was** I who robbed him **of** his firewood ; they will think I did it for mischief, and never meant to give him **any thing** better ; and then, mamma, I shall hate the place, **and never be** able to bear it !" And Herbert hid his face **in his** hands in a passion of tears. Mrs. Clifford remained silent ; and his sister's face grew pale, **but she** did not speak. Looking up at last, Herbert said, " Mamma, do you think **that if** I asked papa, he would let **me** have a man to get **the log out** of the ditch ? If **I** could **but** once right old Willy, I would never meddle with charity again !"

" You can ask your papa, if you think it likely," replied Mrs. Clifford, sorrowfully, without looking at her son.

" But, mamma, if papa does not, what am **I to** do ? Is it not dreadful to be in such a state ? **It seems the** worst thing in the world—to have gone and robbed that **poor** old fellow of his log, and then leave him to perish with cold; that is what he will think, and all the village will think—it drives me wild! will you not give me a word of advice, mamma?"

"I will tell you something, dear Herbert, if you will listen to me."

"Yes, mamma, I will listen to any thing; I seem to have no thoughts, only one dreadful blank of dead hopeless cold in me." And Herbert came and stood by his mother's chair, and put his arm around her neck; the storm of his passion had spent itself, but it was with a face expressive of utter hopelessness that he stood prepared to listen.

"When you were a little child, Herbert, and when you loved the Bible you so seldom look at now, you were standing one day at my knee, having tried long and patiently to learn that beautiful verse, 'Unto us a Child is born, unto us a Son is given, and the government shall be upon His shoulder; and His name shall be called Wonderful, Counselor, The mighty God, The Everlasting Father, the Prince of Peace.' When I had explained it a little to you, I said, 'Herbert, will you make that blessed Saviour, God's beloved Son, your Counselor?' You looked very thoughtful, and said, 'I don't know, mamma.' I replied, 'He is your papa's Counselor, Herbert; your papa goes to ask Him in every difficulty, to teach him what to do; and so do I: if you do not, you can not walk with us in the narrow way to heaven—for none can walk in that way without His help.' Then you looked up, and said, 'I will, mamma; I will do as you and papa do, and go to heaven with you.' Oh! Herbert, how earnestly your mother prayed for you, that your infant words might not fall to the ground, but might be fulfilled from your early years. And now comes the trial, whether you will forsake Him whom you chose as the Guide of your youth, or whether you will turn to that Heavenly Counselor, and seek for direction in your present trouble where none ever sought it aright and in vain."

"But, mamma, it is so long since I have really prayed—if I ever did."

"Perhaps it is to lead you back to prayer, dear Herbert, that you have been suffered to fall into this difficulty."

"But, mamma, what use is it to pray, when, if papa will not let me have any money, it is not possible to get out of this trouble ?"

"Do you think, Herbert, that God who made you, made you to be dependent upon money ? or that if you truly turn to Him, acknowledging your fault, and asking His forgiveness and help, He could not aid, and would not pity you ?"

"Well, mamma, I will try, but indeed it is very hard to look out into the dark where I can not see as if any light could come."

"Only try, dear Herbert, and it may be your glad surprise will prove the first beginning in your heart of a blessed life of prayer and praise."

"My head aches, mamma, and I have not begun to prepare for my tutor, to-morrow, and he never will hear of an excuse unless papa speaks for me, and I am sure papa will not do that now ; so I shall not have time to come down again this evening."

Herbert wished his mother good night; and then went to the sofa where his sister had been silently listening to all, and as he stooped to kiss her, she said, "Have you never watched till you have seen the first bright star shine through the dark cloud at night ?"

"Yes, I have seen that," replied Herbert.

"There is no darkness upon earth, dear Herbert," said his sister, "that God can not lighten. Prayer is sure at last to

4

bring a star in the dark cloud, if you do not give it up;" and Herbert looked at her **sweet** smile, and the first ray of peaceful hope seemed to steal into his heart.

Herbert **went round by his** father's study, and **on** being admitted, he went up to his parent and said, "Will you forgive me, papa, **for** my disobedience? I am very sorry for it."

"Yes, my dear boy, you have my full forgiveness. I suffer as **well as you,** while I leave you unaided in what looks to you so hard a **lesson; and** it is a hard one if you try i in any way but the **right way;** do you know that one right way, Herbert?"

"**Yes,** papa, I think I do."

"If so, my boy, it may prove the best lesson you have ever learned, **and sad** would **be the act** that should deprive you of the need to acquire a knowledge so blessed!"

"But, papa, if I get out **of this, I** can never try charity again!"

"**I think** that **depends upon** whether **you get out** of this trouble on the right side or the wrong. The after-effect of all our troubles depends upon whether we scramble out of them as **best** we can on this world's side, and by its way; or whether we ask our Saviour to give us His hand in the deep waters, and help us out on the side nearest heaven, on which none can get out without Him. Suppose I ask you to give me back that many-bladed knife I gave you on your last birth-day, because, the first time **you opened it** you cut your fingers with it? Do you wish for that reason to part with it?"

"O no, **papa, that was only the** first time, and I am sure any one might have done **the** same! I **soon** learned to know the different springs."

"And even **so with blessed** charity, my boy—it is a finely-**tempered** instrument, and many there are who wound both **themselves and** others for want of skill in using it. None but the God who creates it in man can ever teach us to manage it aright. You have wounded yourself, and risked the injuring another, by a mistaken use of it ; but if you once learn **how** to use it, you will be willing to part with your purse, yes, with every earthly possession, rather than with it. And now, good night, and God bless you, my child, and pour into your heart that most excellent gift of charity, the very **bond** of peace and of all virtues, without which, whosoever liveth is counted dead before Him—even true love **to God and man."**

Herbert went slowly and sorrowfully **to** his room to take his **mother's** counsel ; the hope that for a moment had soothed him, **reflected from** his sister's smile and words of assurance, was gone again ; his head was heavy and his prayer was heavy, it did not seem to rise to heaven or bring him any light. He sat down to prepare his lessons ; but all attempts at study were vain, his thoughts still wandered to that shivering old man and his wasted log in the ditch ; he was learning a deeper lesson, in **which** his books of human learning could not aid him, and his mind refused to turn to studies which yielded no sympathy in his pressing need. Weary with the vain struggle of feeling, he thought he would lie down on his pillow and try to lose himself and his trouble in sleep—but he could only wake to find all the same as he had left it. Then his sister's words came back upon his heart—" Prayer is sure at last to bring a star in the dark cloud—if you do **not** give it up," so kneeling down again he tried to lift the same heavy heart and heavy prayer to heaven. He rose and drew back his curtain, and standing within it looked up to the sunless sky ; the heavy clouds were chasing each other across the low horizon, and not a star was visible. Yet, thought Herbert, the stars are still the same, and perhaps to-morrow night the sky will be cloudless ; but I shall have no comfort, for no stars lie for me behind my trouble! He **turned** back again into his room ; he had placed his lamp in a

further corner when he went to the window, and now as he
looked toward it, its light fell on **the crimson cover of his**
Bible, and **he** remembered his mother's words, **" that** Bible,
Herbert, you so seldom look **at now !"** He went and took **it**
sorrowfully **and hopelessly down, but** still he took it—he **took
the Book** whose words are spirit and life—he took the Book
whose words can **wake the dead,** can turn darkness **into** light,
and warm the heart, and **nerve the** spirit, with **a** living energy
that **death** itself has **no power to** destroy—Herbert took his
Bible, and sitting down, he opened it at the first chapter of the
book of James, and there alone beside **his** lamp, his **elbow resting on the** table, and **his heavy head upon** his hand, he looked
upon the sacred page and read till **he came to the** words—" If
any of you lack wisdom, let **him** ask of God, that **giveth to all**
men liberally, and upbraideth **not** ; and it shall be given him ;
but let him ask **in** faith, nothing **wavering." He read no** fur-
ther ; the sacred word had spoken to him, it knew **his** need,
and answered to that need, with a voice that searched far deep-
er than any other words had done. His mother had told him
to pray ; but his Bible **had** told him how, even with "faith"—
believing that God would **hear and** answer ; his sister had told
him that whatever our dark trouble might be, prayer could
bring **a bright star shining** through it ; but his Bible mentioned **the very star he wanted,** even " wisdom"—the light of
wisdom to show **him** what to do. And **now once** more he
knelt to ask with **hope** in **God,** whose word **of** promise his
heart had found **in his** time of need. He asked again that he
might be able to find **some** right way out **of his** trouble. And
then his thoughts wandered over the **village.** Always bent on
his own amusement, he had taken no interest in the wants or
the comforts of any one there, no eye **had looked** in grateful
love upon him, no voice **had blessed** him. **He** knew not how

.o ask the aid of those of whose comfort he had proved him-self regardless. Then the rich boy felt his true position, not allowed now to fall back on the aid of any in his father's ser-vice, he did not know one to whom he could turn for help in his trouble—it was as a lightning-flash that pierced through the tinsel of wealth and showed him his personal poverty, **in all** save that which a hasty word had the power **to** deprive him of. But while thinking **on all who dwelt around** him, among whom he could not **see one whose love he** had won, one on whose **willing aid he** had any right to depend; suddenly he saw again **in** memory **the son of widow Jones,** " honest Jem," as he had seen him in reality a few days before, feeding farmer Smith's sheep, the sheep all gathering round him, eating sometimes from the turnips at his feet, and when they failed there, looking up to his hand which reached them out a supply, while one little weakly lamb, **held** safe under his arm, nibbled a **turnip held** for it in his left hand. The scene on the snowy field was **so pretty that old** Jenks the coachman had driven slowly by, saying to Herbert, who was on the coach-box at his side, " I would trust that lad, if I were in want of a friend, as soon as I would any **man** in the parish !" **And** the thought came into Herbert's mind, that if Jenks **would** trust the shepherd-lad to **be** his friend, **he** might trust **him** too. The remembrance of the young shepherd brought so much relief to Herbert, that he gave thanks, **and said** his evening prayer with a more cheerful heart, and then lay down on **his** pillow and fell asleep.

His anxious mother came into his room, and thought, **as she** looked at her sleeping child, " Has then sleep **such** power to restore peace **to** the troubled brow ? how deep the repose of his expression now ! Alas, poor boy, will he **awake to** the same distress ? O that some light may break upon him, some true thought guide him !" While still his mother lingered, Herbert opened his eyes, his mother stooped down to him, and he threw his arms round her neck.

" O ! mamma, you were quite right, quite right ! I thought it was all no use, but then that young shepherd **of** farmer Smith's came into my mind; you know who I mean, mamma ; they **call** him in the village ' honest Jem ;'—he is the only person I could ask to do a kindness for me now that I have no money to pay them. I think **every one** else would expect me to pay them, but I don't **think** that he would, from what Jenks said the other day. **Do you** think that would do, mamma ? **Do** you think papa would mind my asking him ?"

" No, I think you have fixed upon quite **the** right person. I **have heard** your sister speak in his praise, **and your** father only feels it right not to furnish you with help from any resources **of his own ;** he wishes you to find a remedy of yourself and independent of your home ; that you may both learn and remember the lesson he hopes that this trial may teach you."

" But, then, mamma, I have no doubt he is off by six o'clock to the sheep, and he would say he could not give his master's time **to** me, so I must be up and off by five o'clock, or sooner than that, **to** give time to drag the old log up again. O, I do think I shall **have** it up by to-morrow night, and it makes me so thankful !"

" **And** does nothing else make you thankful, my child ?"

" Yes, mamma, because I know where the thought came from ! **and it was my** Bible **that first** seemed really to comfort me, and help me **to pray."**

" And then, Herbert, when you have taken this first step in the narrow way—that way which is only entered by prayer, shall you **wish** to leave it again, and forget all that has helped you now ?"

" **No,** I hope I should not **wish to** leave it, mamma, but I don't know whether I shall be able to walk in it : do you think **it** would all be so hard as this has been ?"

" What was it that made this hard, can you tell me that ?"

" Why, it was my own fault, mamma, I suppose."

" Yes, God does not willingly afflict or grieve : His ways are pleasantness, and His paths peace."

" But then, mamma, I am always getting into trouble, so that I should soon be in another, I am afraid !"

" And if you are, dear Herbert, would it be no comfort to you to have the same Heavenly Father, who has answered you now, to go to as your Guide in every difficulty ? and might you not hope to cleanse your way from its present so frequent faults, by taking heed thereto according to His Word ?"

" Yes, mamma, perhaps I might ; I do hope I shall try, for I feel very different to-night to what I did before."

And so the mother blessed her child and left him to his rest.

Left to himself, Herbert's thoughts turned again to old Willy. Was the old man then shivering in his bed ? he had not had the little fire of chips he had hoped for, to warm him with, before he slept ! Herbert had not remembered this before, and saddened again with this fresh recollection he fell asleep ; he slept and dreamed. Herbert thought in his dreams, that, unable to rest, he rose from his bed, and went by night to see whether old Willy were indeed lying shivering with cold. He walked along the well-known road, crossed the little stile into old Willy's garden, and gently opened the cottage-door : all was still within the cottage, and there at the further corner of the room lay old Willy sleeping in his bed ; and, leaning where the low bed-post rose—bending over and watching old Willy, a radiant angel stood. The old man was asleep ; he looked full of peace, and drew his breath as gently as an infant, and smiled as if he dreamed of holy things. Herbert thought that he did not feel at all afraid of the angel, and the bright angel turned his face of love and looked on Herbert, and said to him

"My child, what brings you here by night?"

"I came," replied Herbert, "to see whether old Willy slept, or whether he was lying shivering with the cold, as he told me he did last night."

"He did shiver long," said the bright angel, "before he fell asleep, but he has slept some hours now; I count the moments while he sleeps, for when he wakes he must feel the cold of this house and shiver again."

"Can not you keep old Willy from feeling the cold when he wakes?" asked Herbert.

"No," replied the angel gravely, "I can not do that; that work of love is yours. You could not do my work, and I can not do yours."

"What is your work?" asked Herbert.

"You could not understand my work if I were to tell you, because it is only an angel's work; but you can understand your own, because your God and our God has taught you in His Word.

"I did mean to have made old Willy warm," said Herbert, "but I have no money now."

"Poor child! can you do nothing without money?" asked the radiant angel. "Do you wish to help any—pray for them, and you will soon find you are taught how to help them. You must hearken to the voice of God's Word—that is how holy angels learned their work in Heaven, and that is how you must learn yours on earth."

Then the bright angel turned and looked again on old Willy, and Herbert awoke from his sleep. At first he wondered where he was, but he heard the ticking of his watch, and starting up he lit his candle and looked at the time; it was nearly five o'clock; so having dressed, and offered up his morning prayer, he crept softly down stairs, let himself out, and went forth into the darkness.

CHAPTER VII.

"Pleasant words are as a honey-comb, sweet to the soul, and health to the bones."—PROVERBS xvi. 24.

"I HAVE no doubt Jem is used to logs, and knows how to manage them," thought Herbert, as he walked along. " I did not bring a cord with me, but he is sure, I should think, to have cords at his cottage ; people who have to do with work must always be wanting such things." The road was longer than Herbert had supposed, and though he ran and walked by turns, yet the time went on apace, and Jem's cottage was still distant At last he saw the dim beginning of the lane, and a figure come up it and turn the corner of another road. "Hallo! stop there!" cried Herbert, and running on, he found the figure, now standing still, to be none other than Jem himself, with his bill-hook hanging from his hand, and his hatchet over his shoulder. Jem knew the young Squire by sight, and exclaimed, " Why, Mr. Clifford, sir ! I hope there's nothing happened !"

" Nothing, I hope, but what you can set right," replied Herbert, " if you will have the kindness to come to my help."

" If you please, sir, I am ready right away," said Jem, still in a maze of astonishment at what could have befallen the young Squire at such an hour in the morning.

" I'm afraid it's later than I thought, or you are earlier; how are you off for time?" asked Herbert.

" Why, as to that, sir, I am my own master now for a bit, as the saying is."

4*

" How is that ? I thought you kept the **sheep on** Farmer Smith's farm ?"

" So **I do, sir** ; but just as **this year came in,** master gave me a job of hedging and **ditching** ; **and now he has been** so good as to let me have another turn of it ; and master **has set** the man Billy **Warren** for the time to look after my sheep ; so you see, sir, the hour is nothing particular, because, as I take it by **the** job, master don't mind an hour one way or the other—so there 's no need to be looking after that."

Herbert felt the light of hope. that had led him to Jem, brighten, at the words of the kind-hearted lad, and was about to turn round for old Willy's, when he remembered the cord.

" I am afraid we shall want a cord," said Herbert, " and I did not bring one. I suppose you keep such things always at hand in your house ?"

" Dear me, no, sir ! it is not much we have to turn to, save a pair of hands and feet, thanks be to Heaven for them, and the notion how to use them ; but if a cord be the want, **I** can soon fetch one down from master's at **the farm.**"

" There is nothing can be done in this job without it," replied Herbert, who felt that now he must come to a confession. " The mischief is, that yesterday I found old Willy Green killing himself almost, over **an old trunk of** a tree, and I hoped to have been able **to send him in some** coals to-day, so I tumbled the old log down into his **ditch ; but I had** forgotten **myself** when I promised the coal, and now I find I can not keep my word, and I have been almost distracted about it ; and I want to get the **old** log up again, and I did not know who to ask to stand my friend and help me, but I thought perhaps you would ; but if **you** take a look at it first, you will **better know what** we shall want to get **it up with.**"

" **As you please, sir,**" said Jem, **and** he turned and followed at Herbert's side. The two walked in silence on, the print of Herbert's light foot fell **side** by side in the snow with the impress of the heavy tread of Jem's step of toil and strength. Herbert thought to himself, " Jem does not like the job, I am sure, or he would have said something more than, ' As you please, sir.' I wish I could find out what he feels about helping me in it ; it is so wretched not to know ! I must make him say something." **" I am afraid, Jem,"** said Herbert, " you **are** thinking **you don't** like the business ; but if you could **just help** me through with it, I should always feel grateful to **you !"**

Now, Jem understood that he was expected to speak, and when once he understood that, he was always ready, and his words were sure, when they did come, to come warm with the glow of his kind, true heart : he replied, " Well, master, I was just thinking I ought to have been at it alone, **instead of** your being waked up before so much as a mouse has oped its eye ; and if I had but known, sure enough I would, and I might have known, if I had had half a thought—as the saying is."

" You could not have known," replied Herbert ; " it was only yesterday I did it."

" Well, sir, that may be, but I might have known that poor old man would come to the want of firewood, such weather as this has been ; instead of leaving him, who has no more strength than a child, nor yet so much, to be hacking at that old stump ; and then it was I set it down so near the ditch, I thought to leave it out of the way ; but may be it 's all for the best, as mother is so often saying." And, with Jem's last word, they stopped at the stile. Herbert sprang over, with a heart almost as light as his step, for its heavy weight had melted away under the sunshine of Jem's kind words. Jem followed after him, and they were soon at the **edge of** the ditch, both looking down **in the** dim gray twilight of morning on the old stump below.

There stood the poor boy, with hatchet over his shoulder, and bill-hook in his hand, surveying the log from above—his was the strength to aid, his the skill to devise how, his the willing mind ; and there stood Herbert by his side in helpless dependence, with eyes of hope and fear now fixed on Jem— **then on** the log below. Jem stood in silence a few moments, then down he laid his bill-hook, and, springing into the ditch, planted his feet upon the log, and, raising his hatchet with both hands above **his head,** fetched a stroke which clave a slit, where it entered the wood, about twice the length of the blade. "That's the job, sir," said Jem, looking **up** to Herbert from below ; " it's not a bit of use for us to be thinking we could haul the old log up again ; why, a horse could not do it ! But a few such strokes as that will bring it up in a right sort of **a** way—all ready for use !" A second time the ponderous hatchet, raised by those strong arms and firm and honest hands, fell with unerring aim, splitting the **wood** beside **one of** the hard **knots of the old trunk.** "That's kind, now," said Jem, in a conciliating tone, to **the old** log ; " that's just doing as you should, and splitting right away as I meant !" Herbert laughed **at** Jem's soliloquy to the **log ;** a happy laugh, for bright thoughts **were** breaking in on his heart—thoughts of raising the log all ready for old Willy's use, and seeing it raised by hands that **seemed to** love the labor—thoughts that broke on Herbert's trouble like the gleams of the sun now shining across **the** darkened sky of night. Stroke followed stroke, without an **other** pause, till the first log, severed **from the** parent trunk, lay at the feet of honest Jem ; **down** sprang Herbert into mud **and** mire, seized it in his hands, and, scrambling up again,

lifted the log above his head, and **gave a** loud "Hurrah!" Never did shout of triumph ring more joyfully after the past trial of despair, than this from Herbert's lips: he shouted it with voice as loud and clear as if he thought to reach the ears of love within his home, with this his first glad utterance since his trouble had begun: but his parents heard it not—for joy, in our obstructed atmosphere, heavy with sin and with sorrow, still pauses on the wing, and waits a messenger to bear her on her way—not so **in Heaven, where sin** and where sorrow are not! But though the note of triumph reached not the hearts that would have echoed back its gladness, it did fall on old Willy's ear, and roused him from his slumber—to him it was a signal of surprise and fear. He opened the little casement above his bed, and looked in terror from it, expecting to see a company of thieves stealing his early vegetables. Herbert heard the little window open, and saw the **old man's** troubled face—" It 's no thief, Willy, we will keep watch !" **but** old Willy still looked out into the dim light, anxious **and fear-**ful. "Never fear, daddy, it 's I !" said Jem. **And Herbert saw** the change that passed across the face of the old **man at that** true-hearted voice, as he shut his little window **to lie** down again and sleep; while Herbert turned **gravely** back, log in hand, to Jem. "Old Willy is not your father, is he?" asked Herbert. " No, sir, I can't say he is, **but** I got in the way of calling him so when I was a child, and so I keep to it, **and** may be it cheers him now, for he has none belonging to **him** that have a care to see after him; not but what he is worth **a** dozen and more of them that neglect him! but, by what I can see, **it 's** the way of this world—as the saying is—to slight them that are **old** and feeble." **All the time of this** reply, Jem had been arranging his plan for a second attack upon the log, and now away again went the hatchet, stroke after stroke, but

the wood was hard, and Jem began his pacific discourse again.
"Well now, you had best give in at once, for I can tell you 'tis
your master upon you, and there's no use in standing out, 'tis
only wasting your time and mine!"   Whether the log took the
hint, or whether the hatchet took the exact grain of the wood,
we need not ascertain, but so it was that a capital cleft was the
result of the next stroke, and Jem pursued his advantage so
vigorously, that Herbert soon laid a second log by the side of
the first.

"Do you always talk to yourself in that way?" asked Herbert.

"It's not so much to myself I talk, sir, as to the thing I am
after; it makes it seem more company-like, and gets me into a
better humor with it; and I am so in the way of it now I don't
always know how to get on without it, when may be I ought.
I took to it young, and that's why it hangs to me so, I suppose:
for you see, sir, my mother was left a widow when I was but a
few months old, and she has often said how she missed the kind
word of my poor father more than the money he earned her,
though she had to labor hard enough; and then people spoke
short to her in her trouble; and took it as a burden laid on
them; as you know, sir, the widow and the fatherless are always taken to be when they come on a parish; and as long
back as I can remember, I have seen her fret for a rough word,
and then I have seen her wholly cheered up by a kind one; so
it came to me young enough, that good words must be among
the best of good things, if they do but come from the heart—
as the saying is, and so I tried at them myself; and I have
found, times and often, that a good word will do it when a bad
one won't, and by reason of that I have got in the way, and
now I don't know as that I could get out of it; but it's not
words will do all," added Jem, as he prepared himself for
a fresh onset upon the log.   Stroke after stroke, stroke after

stroke, with good words in between, till a third and larger log was separated from the trunk. Herbert laid his treasures side by side, as he would have laid fox or hare from the hunt a few days before.

" Now, Jem," said Herbert, " you have given me one of the best gifts, I declare, that I ever had in my life, and you must not be kept here any longer. If I could but find old Willy's hatchet, I would try at it myself before I go back."

" Well, sir, as for that, my time is my own ; master won't be against an hour or so either way."

" No, Jem, but it 's the strength it costs you, and you must not spend all you have upon me."

" Well, sir, I won't go against your word, but as for strength, I 'm only getting it up by those few strokes ; there 's no fear of being the weaker for a stroke for them that can't strike for themselves." Herbert looked inquiringly at Jem, uncertain whether he meant him or old Willy by " them that can 't strike for themselves ;" but Jem in his honest simplicity understood not the awakened start of the young spirit's independence ; but he did understand that he was to retire, when, in a moment more, Herbert flung off his coat as Jem had done, laying down his hat upon it, and springing on the log, seized Jem's hatchet, and raised it above his head in the act to strike. " Have a care, sir, for Heaven's sake, have a care !"·cried Jem, entreatingly—as having sprung on the brow of the ditch he looked down on Herbert, "That old hatchet is as sharp as any thing, and if it slips the wood, it may take your feet as like as not." Herbert paused a minute while Jem gave full instructions how to place his feet, now to avoid the knots of the old trunk, and to take it in the grain of the wood. At last the stroke was given, a little way —some poor half-inch the hatchet condescended to enter—and no more. " That could not have been done better for the first !"

said Jem; " but I am thinking, sir, there are as many logs as
old Willy will burn in a day : but if you **have a** mind to work
in right earnest, why he will **be** in want of **a** few chips to help
make the old logs burn, **and it will** be best to begin with them,
till the strength gets up a bit, and the knack of the other gets
known ; it 's not learned in an hour to cut up an old log, and you
were **not** born to it, you see, sir ; so it don't come natural."

" **I** suppose I was born to help the poor !" said Herbert, looking **up** gravely into Jem's pleading face above him—his own
glowing with the **effort** of the recent stroke, and the rays **of the**
morning sun falling like Heaven's blessing on his young un-
covered head. " I was born, I suppose, to help the poor !" again
repeated Herbert, looking thoughtfully down on the old log at
his feet; " but if you think **old** Willy **will** want chips, I **will
not** be against trying at them first."

" That he will, sir, and daddy's bill-hook is **not so** heavy as
mine by half; I can find it up in his old log-house." The bill-
hook was found, and springing down on the log, Jem gave Herbert a lesson in cutting chips ; and then away went honest Jem
to his work for the day, the risen sun gilding the sky.

Herbert toiled away at the log to his great satisfaction, till he
suddenly remembered the time ; then, without further delay, he
carried the chips that lay scattered around him, and piled them
up by the precious logs at old Willy's door, when sudde   the
door opened, and the old man looked out.

" **Bless you,** master, what are you after now ?" said o' Willy,
in a wonderment at sight of the young Squire, soiled, · J laden
with chips. Herbert looked up, his healthful effort shedding
as bright a crimson **on** his cheeks **as** the risen sun hau **but now**
shed upon the morning sky, and **laying down his** b .rden close
beside **the** door, he replied, " Why, Willy, I am very sorry, but
I promised what I could not perform. I am very sorry, Wi'ly,

but I can not buy so much as a shovel-full of coals. I don't mind telling you, Willy, but I have forfeited my money that I have to spend for my own, and so I got Jem to help me get up your log again, but it was too heavy, and so he cut those logs off, and I cut the chips! Won't you be warm now, Willy?"

" Yes, bless you!" said the old man, and his voice trembled with feeling; " warm outside and in too! And it's a deal better than casting away one of God's good creatures, to make room for another. I had wholly a dread to see the coals come in, and my old log left at the bottom of the ditch. And then, master, it was the hand of kindness that gave it me, and I thought it seemed hard to cast it away like that."

" Who gave it you?" asked Herbert, with a quick idea that it perhaps had been Jem himself.

" Why, you see, sir, Farmer Smith has set Jem—my Jem, as I call him—to a job of hedging and ditching, and so one day he came here with his barrow and that old log in it, and he said, ' Here, daddy, I have made mother a fire for many a day o come, and this old log is for you; now, don't you be after 'hacking on it; I'll set it right away against the ditch here, and then, when I get a little further on in my job, I'll take an hour at it as I can, and soon have it in pieces for you.' And so it just eases me that it's not all gone for nothing, after his taking that care after me. But you will catch cold, master, out in this freezing air."

" O no, Willy, I am not afraid of that," replied Herbert, who had been listening with anxious attention to the discovery that the log had been Jem's gift at the beginning; " but," added he, " I am off to breakfast now; and be sure you get up a blaze with those chips; I shall come to look after it, so be sure you do!" And Herbert was off, while the old man, leaning on his stick with one hand, and shading his eyes with the other from the radiance of the eastern sky, watched him out of sight; then turning back into his cottage, began to light up his fire and prepare his frugal meal.

"Well, Herbert, my boy, is all right?" said his father, as he gave him his morning embrace.

"Yes, papa, getting right, I hope. I am sure, mamma, that thought of Jem was right enough, for he is the best fellow I ever saw; he was just all that I wanted! And we are not going to drag up the old log, but cut it all to pieces down there in the ditch, and get it up ready for use—is not that capital, papa? And I cut the chips, and I am to cut some logs another time; and I made up such a pile at old Willy's door! I mean to go down after my lessons, and see what sort of a fire he has. And only think, mamma! it was Jem himself who had carried the log for old Willy's fire, and meant to cut it up for him; old Willy told me so. But, O if you had seen old Willy, papa, when he opened his bit of a window at the end of his cottage, and took us for thieves! He did not look the least more satisfied when he found it was me, than if I had been a downright thief; but the moment Jem spoke, he looked as if he thought no harm could come to him. I wonder what all the village think of me?"

"It is not what people think of us, my boy, but what we really are, that we have need to inquire. Suppose you take that question as an exercise for your own heart to-day, WHAT AM I? Answer it faithfully in writing, and put the date of the month and year to it, and let me have it with a seal on, to lock up for you in my private desk till a year has passed away, if you should live to see it."

"I will, papa, if you wish me; but I am afraid it will be a poor account."

"Better to face the truth at once; then we may hope to begin to reflect its likeness," replied Mr. Clifford. Then, with a smile of assurance, Herbert whispered to his sister, "The star did come in a cloud, and the cloud is gone now!" and hastened off to prepare for encountering his tutor.

"I am very sorry, Mr. Merton, that I am not ready with my lessons," said Herbert.. "I got into trouble, and it 's taken more than my best thoughts to find a way out of it." Herbert's tutor saw at once that it was no excuse of idleness; and placing confidence in his young pupil, such confidence as, if oftener used, might yield its pleasant fruit, he replied, "Perhaps you have been learning a better lesson than any I set you. Shall we sit down to your books now, and see what we can do together?" The look of surprise, gratitude, and pleasure that instantly lighted up Herbert's face was assurance enough to his tutor that he had not erred in his confidence; and that morning's study was equally pleasant to teacher and pupil.

At last Herbert was free to set off once more to the aged Willy's broken-down cottage; a wreath of smoke was curling up from it to heaven—the happy witness of his morning's effort; he knocked with his stick upon the door; then, opening it, peeped in. There sat old Willy, while, in the open fireplace beside him, burned red and hot the logs that morning saw prepared for use; behind him a thick crimson curtain shut out the draught, and shut in the warmth of the fire; a table was drawn close to him, and on it lay his open Bible.

"Well, Willy," said Herbert, "here I am, come to see how the old logs burn! What a capital fire they have made! Did you use my chips?"

"Yes, master, and they were greatly needed to get a heat up under the logs; but I found a sprinkling of coals, and after a time I got up such a fire as I have not had for long, and the other big log is drying at the back."

Herbert drew out a little stool from the open chimney, and sat down close by the fire, in front of old Willy. Now Herbert had by no means forgotten his dream, and **he looked** round old Willy's room with a feeling of awe. On the **further** side of **the** room he saw a low bedstead, not unlike the one he had **seen in** his dream : he wondered whether old Willy knew any thing about the angels ; he thought the best way would be to talk to him a little on that subject, but he hardly knew how **to begin,** till, remembering the open Bible which lay on the **table, he** said—

"If you read the Bible, Willy, I suppose you know about the angels ?"

"Yes, master, I read about them there, and what they do for the like of me."

"Do you think that they really watch over you, Willy ?"

"Don't I know it, master ! for does it **not say the very same** in my Book? And is it not the like thoughts to that, that keep me happy and praising God at night times, when the wind blows my old place about as if it were ready to come down and bury me !"

"Do you think the **angels** will keep it from falling, Willy ?"

"No, I never read the like of that ; **but** I know they are **watching over me** ; **and I think** that, if it **fell,** they would carry **me, as** they did that poor beggar that I read of, straight up to the **blessed heaven above.**"

"But **are you** not afraid to sleep in this old house for fear it should fall."

"No, master ; why should I be afraid ? It 's not death I am afraid of ! **I say,** why should I be afraid ? It would only be a going home ; and, somehow, I think about the bright side ; and **for** the dark side, why should not I be leaving that all behind— **for why** then should I think about it ? And don't I know

He that keeps me together soul and body can keep the place that's over my head till He takes me up to a better? Is not that just what he spoke to poor men that looked to him for comfort as I do? 'Let not your heart be troubled : ye believe in God, believe also in me. In my Father's house are many mansions : if it were not so, I would have told you. I go to prepare a place for you. And if I go and prepare a place for you, I will come **again and receive you** unto myself; that where I am, there ye may be also.' My blessed angel taught me those **words,** before ever I could read them in my book !"

" Did the angels teach you that ?" asked Herbert, leaning forward.

" Not them that live up above, master, but that one that's a sister of yours. I always call her so, because, to my thinking, she seemed sent right away from the holy Heaven to teach me, a poor old dark sinner as I was."

" Do you know my sister ?" asked Herbert.

" Why, I knew her before I knew myself," replied old Willy, with a smile.

" Now, Willy, I know you are joking, my sister is not half so old as you."

" No, bless her !" said old Willy, " she is but an infant of days by the side of an old sinner like me. **But** I mean, that I never **knew** myself, till she taught me what I was."

" **How do you** mean that she taught you, Willy ?"

" **Why, you see, sir,** I was a poor old ignorant sinner, **that** had lived all my days only for this world. Well, I used to sit on that settle by my door for hours in the summer-time, **when** I had nothing to be after, and she saw me many **a** time as she went riding by on her white pony. Well, **one** day she stopped and I saw her come stepping over the stile, so I rose up and made my obedience to her, and she said, ' Sit down again, I am come to sit a little while with you on this pleasant seat.'   Well, she talked to me ; and asked me if I thought about Heaven all the long hours I sat by myself on that seat at my door ; and I told her I could not say that I had much understanding about that.   Then she asked me if I did not think about God's blessed Word, that showed us the way to Heaven ; and I told her I could not say that I ever had any knowledge of that.   Then she said, would I like to have her read to me out of her Book, that I might get a knowledge and understanding of those things ; so I said, if she pleased, I should take it a great favor. Then she took a little book from her bag that hung on her arm, and she **said, 'This is the** Bible, God has given it to us to show us the way to Heaven.'   So I bended my attention to listen ; and she read me about the beggar Lazarus, and the angels that bore him to Heaven.   I thought that was not like the ways of **this** world, but I did not say a word ; so when she had done, she asked me whether I could tell her why it was that the angels above came down to carry up that poor beggar, that had not so much as a bed to die in, to Heaven ?   **So** I said, I had no understanding in such things ; then she said, that the beg- gar loved the good God who **made** Heaven and earth, and the good God loved that poor beggar, and so He sent His angels for him to take him to be with Him in Heaven.   Well, I thought it was wonderful, and not much like to the ways of men, but I did not say a word.   Then she asked me if I loved the good Lord as that poor beggar did ?   So I said, I did not seem to know ; then she said, if I did not know, that showed I did not love Him, for if I loved Him, I must have a knowledge that I did : and she asked me if I should like to know and love the good Lord who sent His angels for the poor beggar ?   And I said, Yes, for certain I should if I could come at it ; and she said, the poor beggar came at that knowledge, and therefore I

might if I tried to gain it ; and she said she would come and
read to me about it from her Book. Well, I sat and thought
on that poor beggar—carried right away up to Heaven by the
angels as soon as the breath was out of his poor body. I
thought, if I could be done for as he was, that would seem
wonderful comfort to think upon. And I sat and watched for
her to come again, for I saw she had got it all, and I seemed to
think she would bring **it to me, though I** could not tell how.
Well, she came again, just as she did before, many times ; I
can't mind the words she read to me now, only those first, but
somehow it all seemed as if it came to me."

"What came to you ?" asked Herbert.

"Why, the understanding to know it all ! I seemed to get
light in me to see it—I got a sight of what a dark, bad life I
had led, without a bit of love in my evil heart for the good
Lord, who died for me : and then I saw Him still waiting for
me, still calling to me, a poor lost sinner, to come to Him : **it**
broke my old heart quite up, but then I got comfort—looking
up to Him. Well, then, she said to me, ' Willy, God gave
the Bible for you to look into as well as for me ; would you not
like to have one, and try to read **it ?**' **I have** clean lost all my
learning, said I. ' But, Willy,' **said** she, ' I think it would
come back again ; suppose we try ?' So the very next time
she came carrying this blessed Book in her own hands ; and
the first word she made me read was our Saviour's name,
JESUS. ' There, Willy,' said she, ' now you can read the
name of your Saviour—who loved you, and died for you, **and**
sent me to teach you ! Now see how many places in the New
Testament you can find that name in, against I come again.'
How I did study, to be sure, and without a bit of spectacles,
for my eyes are wonderful ! She left me many bits of marks,
and I tucked them in where I found that name : and I looked,

till to be sure I seemed to have nothing day or night in my
mind but that name JESUS! And when she came again, how
pleased she was to be sure! Then she said, ' Now, Willy, you
have learned your Saviour's blessed name, now you shall look
after the Holy name of GOD, that is a terrible name, Willy,
for those who do not love the name of JESUS, but I hope you
do, so you don't need to be afraid to look upon the Holy name
of GOD?' Well, I thought it seemed a serious thing as she
spoke it, but I kept hold of that first name JESUS in my mind,
when I looked after the other, and to be sure I seemed to find
GOD every where! And so I always kept those two together,
and so I do now, for when I get upon that great name of GOD,
then I think of JESUS, and it lifts me on. And, after a time,
my learning did seem to come to me again, and now there is
scarce a part of the Book but what I can get comfort out of—
thanks be to God that sent her to teach me to know Him that
loved me, and gave Himself for me !"

Herbert had listened with breathless attention, for he loved
his sister with all the affection of his heart, and now he replied,
" You have not seen my sister, Willy, for some weeks now ; she
has been ill."

" No, master, not since the beginning of January ; she came
here then, and the groom carried a big bundle, and if it was
not all for me ! just this fine curtain as you see it hung across
here ; and there was that little curtain for the window, instead
of the old thing that was rotted to pieces there before ; and
that one she brought—it is wonderful the wind and rain it
keeps out, from the thickness of it ! that was the last time I saw
her come in : but, to my thinking, she is never out of my sight,
for I seem to see her in that light that shows me my Saviour—
for she don't seem of this world, to my thinking."

" Well, good-by, Willy," said Herbert, gravely, " it won't be

long before I am near you again!" and he shook hands with
the old man, and hastened home. He was soon in his sister's
boudoir ; she was lying on her sofa, and Herbert laid his head
upon her shoulder, and the pent-up feelings of his heart broke
forth in tears.

"What is the matter, my darling Herbert ? what has happened ? where have you been ? You must not cry so—tell me
all about it."

"O, **Mary,** why are you so long **ill ? When** will you be
well again ?"

"When the spring-time comes, then I shall be well again,
and we will walk and ride again together as we used to do."

"Are you sure you will be quite well then ?" asked Herbert.

"We can never be quite sure about any thing upon earth ;
but I do not feel any doubt about it, and the doctor thinks so,
too."

"O ! **then** I shall be happy again !" said Herbert ; "and shall
we go and see old Willy together ?"

"Yes, dear, we will do any thing you like. Should you like
to go and see him with me ?"

"Yes, I should like it very much. **I am just** come away
from him."

"And had he a warm fire with **the** logs which you and Jem
prepared ?" asked his sister.

"Yes, that **he** had ; **and he** looked so comfortable ! **Not**
the least cold, and he said **my** chips were the greatest use in
making the old logs burn ; and to-morrow morning **I** mean
to go all alone ; I know, if I try, I can do it with **old Willy's**
hatchet ; and then I shall feel of some use in the world. Only
think, if I could make old Willy's fire with **logs I** had chopped
for it !"

"Yes, it would be very pleasant **to** make his fire ; but I

5

hope there will soon be other ways to do that without your
chopping wood, because I don't think you are strong enough
for that, and I don't think papa thought of your doing that."

" O, Mary, you don't know what nice work it is ! If you could
but have seen how many chips I got off the side of that old
tree, where Jem had chopped the logs, you would have known
I could do it ! I will not hurt myself, indeed ; it does every bit
as well as skating, and then it makes old Willy's fire !"

" Yes, but if you hurt yourself, I am afraid it would make
me ill."

" You need not be afraid, indeed, Mary. I will think of you
—and then I am sure to take care. You see Jem taught me
just how to do it, and old Willy's hatchet is very light."

That evening, when Herbert had prepared his lessons for his
tutor, he remembered the question his father had given him to
answer, and, sitting down again to his desk, he took a sheet
of paper and wrote at the top—

" *Question.* What am I ?

" *Answer.* An Englishman—a gentleman."

But then Herbert paused, and thought to himself, " That will
do so far, but what next ? Why, I may as well say I have two
ponies and a groom : no, that will not do, the question is not
what I HAVE, but what I AM. Well, then, let me see, what else
am I ? I am sure I don't know. I could say I am a huntsman,
but that would not look well alone. I can not say I am any
thing in the way of study ; nor yet in the way of nature—for
I am not a naturalist, nor a botanist, nor a gardener. Let
me see—what should a gentleman be ? Why, he should be
polite, but papa says I am too forgetful of other people's comfort to be polite, though I try at it sometimes. Am I generous ?
I am afraid not ; because my thoughts, and my time, and money,
have all been spent on myself. O dear, what am I ? If I am

not polite, and not generous, perhaps I am not a gentleman yet, but only a boy? I will write that: but then, what am I besides? I am sure I don't know; I am just nothing—I have been no use to any one, and no comfort to any body! I will write that down; but no, that is only what I am NOT; and papa said I was to write what I AM. Well, then, I see it is no use looking on the bright side, I can not find myself there, so I may as well come to the dark side at once, I shall have no difficulty then!" So Herbert took a fresh sheet.

"*Question.* What am I?

"*Answer.* An English boy.

" Passionate, selfish, sinful. ·

" I have forsaken the Guide **of** my youth, and forgotten the Word of God: but I hope I have found the Heavenly Counselor—and that he will lead me in a better way.

" HERBERT CLIFFORD."

Herbert folded it up, and took it to his father's study; he found his father there, and said, "I don't want to disturb you, papa, I have only brought you what you wished—it's dreadful, but it's true! You can read it, **papa,** for you know it all." His father took the paper, and looked upon it; then, taking the conscience-stricken child to his embrace, **said,** " My precious boy! you have found the Truth—or, **rather, the** Truth has found you; ' take fast hold of her, let her not go, keep her, for she is thy life' —then shall your path be ' **as the** shining light, that shineth more and more unto the perfect day!'"

Again that night Herbert turned to the Book that his heart, and not his head alone, remembered now: and from the second chapter of St. James, he read, " Hearken, my beloved brethren, hath not God chosen the poor of this world, rich in faith, and heirs of the kingdom which He hath promised to them that love Him?" Could he help thinking of old Willy!—not now as a poor helpless old man, shivering with cold, but as rich in faith—had not Herbert found **him to be** so? and an heir to a kingdom—eternal in the heavens—and, thinking on these things, Herbert fell asleep on his pillow, while a radiant angel, like the one which watched over old Willy, kept guard through the night over the sleeping boy; and bright dreams of warm hearths, and glad faces, and open Bibles, and love around him every where, made sweet the slumbers of the happy child.

CHAPTER VIII.

" The rich and poor meet together : the Lord is the Maker of them all."—Proverbs xxii. 2.

HERBERT woke ; he looked at his watch—it was half-past
five o'clock; so, rising with the vigor of a resolved will,
he set forth again in the darkness, his thoughts busy with his
work, and how he should manage it all without Jem ; till, silent
and dim in the distance, he saw the cottage where old Willy
dwelt.   He quickened his steps, and, as he drew near, he heard
the sound of a heavy stroke ; he listened, and heard it again,
and then an encouraging voice saying, " Well, there, to be sure,
'tis as well to give in, when it must come to that in the end !"
and the sound of a log falling, as if thrown up, fell on Herbert's
ear.   There was no mistaking the tone or words of the speaker.
"It is Jem, I declare !" said Herbert to himself, as, without waiting to reach the stile, he scrambled over the hedge.

" Why, Jem ! I meant to have cut you out this morning, and
shown what I could make of the old log by myself."

" Well, sir, I thought as much ; but there 's none the worse
for it as it is, and may be there 's some will be the better ; for
'tis as knotted an old tree as ever was, and stands out against a
stroke wonderful !"

" Why, you have not cut away these three logs this morning,
Jem, have you ?"

" No, sir ; I got a stroke or two last evening in my way home.

for this time of the year the sun lingers a-bed till I often wish he
was up a bit earlier; but I suppose he comes right to his time,
for all that—for our Mercy is often singing before 'tis light—

> " ' My God, who makes the sun to know
>   His proper hour to rise.' "

"**Yes,**" replied Herbert; and he tried to remember a little as-
tronomy, to establish himself in Jem's simple belief of the sun
coming right to its time; but it would not just then occur to
his mind, so he gave all his thoughts to the log.

"**Why,** Jem, I declare you have split the tree half its length!"

"**Yes, sir,** that's what I had in my mind—to split it if I
could, and then we might hoist it up, for it gets the mastery
down here in the mud, by being a bit unsteady; but I found I
could not get it to halve as it was, so I am set to work again
till it thinks better of it."

When three more logs were off the split was effected, a large-
sized piece was separated, which Jem raised up to Herbert from
below, and then fastened two cords he had brought from the
farm, one at each end of the log, and by dint of pulling, and groan-
ing, and pleasant speaking, the remainder was drawn up sideways
and lodged on the solid ground. Herbert sprang upon the con-
quered tree, and, with hat in hand, was again preparing for a
loud " Hurra !" when he suddenly remembered old Willy fast
asleep, and, springing down, seized up Jem's hatchet, to carry on
a practical warfare, instead of his suspended note of triumph.
Herbert could now plant his foot firmly on the tree; the sun having risen, its light fell full upon his work, unshaded by the sides
of the dark ditch, and with old Willy's light hatchet, and Jem
directing, cautioning, encouraging, and praising him by turns, he
succeeded at last, and severed a considerable log from the old
stem. His triumph and independence were now at the hight

and Jem was dispatched to his work with a warm shake of his rough honest hand, for the help he had given him.

" Well, sir," said Jem, " the pleasure is none the less to give than to receive, as the saying is ;" and then he packed himself up with hatchet and bill-hook, and, with his bow of respectful reverence to the young Squire—not less esteemed by honest Jem because he had turned in confidence to ask his aid—he again departed to his day's work. Another log was separated, and Herbert pulled out his watch, to see if he might venture on a third, when he suddenly remembered the useful chips ; so, exchanging the hatchet for the bill-hook, he set to work in a different fashion, till a supply of chips lay scattered around him. Never did woodman with more thankful heart survey his work than the youthful Herbert, that cold winter morning ; and who shall tell the heartfelt satisfaction with which he piled up logs and chips at old Willy's still closed door—while mingling thoughts of the poor old man, so rich in faith, an heir of the kingdom of heaven, watched over by angels, taught by his sister, and now warmed by his hand, glowed in Herbert's young heart and beamed in his eye ! With what care did he arrange and re-arrange the pile, that it might look to the best effect when ol Willy opened his door. And then, putting hatchet and bill hook safely away in the shed, he made haste to leave old Willy alone to his surprise ; and, turning round to take one more look, he got over the stile to set forth on his way home.

" O, papa, I really feel a man at last ! Only think ! I have chopped off two logs, and one alone by myself, and now I quite understand it ; I know how it can be done, and how it can not. I wonder whether you know all about the grain of the wood, papa, and getting the hatchet right for a split, and keeping clear of the terrible old knots ?"

" I know a little about it in theory, my boy, but not, like you, in practice. But I begin to feel a rich man, seeing I have a son who can do one useful thing without his purse! And now, if we should have to go to the backwoods of America, you can build us all a log-house."

"I do believe I could, with Jem to help; he is such a capital fellow! I wish he worked for you, papa."

"We must not covet our neighbor's servant; and you see Jem can be of no great use to us without being in our employ: if he had been my man he would not have been your helper in this difficulty. I only think it is a pity that Jem can not come and teach you Latin and Greek; then you might yet hope to take a good degree at college, which I am afraid Mr. Merton does not consider there is likely to be much hope of at present."

"O, papa, Jem would be a great deal worse at Latin and Greek than I am! and then, you see, papa, I can not get the same spirit into my lessons, because I can not see why we should learn things that we don't the least care about, and that are of no use to any one, and that only to take up a great deal of pleasant time!"

"And suppose the young tree was to say that it could not see the use of the wind that blew it from side to side, fatiguing it every rough day; nor of the rain that drenched its leaves, and yet still battered down; nor of the sun that chose out the hottest time to come scorching upon it.—I suppose you could set the young tree right on that subject and could assure it that though it might find the boisterous wind, and the battering rain, and the scorching sun, all a little inconvenient at times, yet that it would prove very unfit for its place in the forest or the grove if it got rid of those troublesome influences—what do you say to that?"

"Yes, papa, of course every one knows what a tree wants."

"And so, my boy, every one who watches over you may

know what you want, and yet you may be at present unable **to** judge. **You** must take it on trust a little while ; **and rest as-** sured that if your powers of mind are unexercised, and **your** thoughts uncultivated by the study of the lives and writings of other men, you would never be fitted to fill **your** Heaven-ap- pointed position in life. You **see the use now of making a fire** for old Willy ; but by and by **you will, I** trust, see still greater use in being able to acquire an **influence over the** minds of those who will meet you **in your own** station **in life,** and by this means you may, through your influence **over the** men of your own rank, make **many an old** Willy **warm** and prosperous, who might otherwise have **been suffering from neglect** and indiffer- ence : but this you can never hope to do if you fail to culti- vate those powers of your heart, or mind, or head, which God has bestowed on you, as needful to the right fulfilment of the duties of the station in which He has placed you."

" Well, papa, I don't think that I shall do worse at my lessons for making up old Willy's fire ; I am sure I did better **yesterday."**

" **No, my** boy, the **poor** man's blessing is **a drop of** Heavenly dew descending to invigorate the heart, **and mind, and head, of** him on whom it falls. I have not the **least expectation of** hear- ing that old Willy's bright fire leaves **your** understanding burning dimmer than before. So long **as you** observe your tutor's rules and requirements, you **may** find as much pleasure as you can in ministering to the **old man's comfort ; and** may the poor man's God make your work **and service of** love acceptable to himself."

This conversation passed during the cheerful morning meal ; and after breakfast Herbert lingered with his sister as he often did a little while, and she said, " Is this useful woodcutting for old Willy the only thing you have **learned in these** last few days to value the knowledge of ?"

" No, Mary, **not the only** thing. I know what you mean, and it is a better knowledge than wood-cutting—you mean that I have learnt that God hears **and answers prayer ?**"

" Yes, **dear** Herbert, **and you have learned it** not in word only, but in deed **and in** truth ; **as only** those can learn **it who** make trial **of it, as you have** done, in the way the Bible teaches."

"I hope, Mary, whatever I forget, I may remember that knowledge, for it is wonderful to think of the comfort **that has** come out of my trouble ! and I feel now as if I knew to whom to go whatever difficulty I might be in."

" That blessed confidence, dear Herbert, nothing but our own **experience** can teach us ; how happy for you to have learned it **so early !"**

After that day's **lessons, Herbert rode** with his father ; they talked of pleasant things, and Herbert felt as if he had been more of a companion to his father in his ride than **he had ever** been before. The evening **was** given to preparation for his tutor, and the next morning **he** was off again between **six** and seven for **old** Willy's. " I should not wonder if I were to find Jem there again !" thought Herbert, as he pursued his **way**— and truly enough there stood the faithful Jem, hewing and hacking the remnant of the old tree ; while several logs **lay round it,** the fruit of the past evening's labor—Jem seeming to **consider** that Herbert had the exclusive right to bear off in person **to the** cottage every portion of the log **that** had become so great **an object of interest** to him. Herbert insisted on his own acquired capabilities, and Jem was **sent off** to his hedging and ditching. Meanwhile, as soon as daylight dawned, old Willy rose, determined not to let the young Squire be off again without an old man's thanks : and he stood **by,** beneath the risen sun, when Herbert **clave in twain the** last fragment of the hard **old tree ;** and **now** Herbert might safely shout, so standing with **one** foot on each of the last severed logs, he gave three loud

" hurrahs !" and then, **with** old Willy's smiling help, piled up the precious store of wood within the little shed, and so pursued his homeward way beneath the old man's blessing.

As Herbert walked home, he felt that great things had **been** done—the logs all prepared for use, and yet old Willy had **not** struck another stroke, nor lost another breath **upon them. Jem** had become his friend ; and that **because he had asked and re-** ceived the kindness **of the shepherd-lad ; for so it** was, the way **in** which Herbert **had turned to Jem had won the** heart of the widow's **son, and he had said in his** cottage-home, " There is not **a thing I would not be after doing for my** young **master at** the **Hall** there, **if I knew that he** wanted **it."** Jem then had **become** his friend ; and who that knows the value of the poor **man's** love, but would have rejoiced in this ! Then also Herbert **felt** as if his parents had never seemed so well pleased with him ; his sister **so** happy, or his tutor so kind. Well might **his step** be swift, and **his** heart light. How many stars might **he count** now, **where** all was once so dark before him !

That morning, as **he** lingered again with **his** sister, **he** said, **" I have** such a capital plan in my head ! **Do** you **not** know how often papa has wished I could be **down stairs of an** evening ? Well, now I have no more wood-**chopping to** do before break- fast, I don't mean to give **up getting up early ; I** mean still to get up, **and do** my lessons before breakfast-time, and then I can be down **a great part of the evening.** Is not that a capital plan ?"

" Yes, indeed it is ; **only** you won't let this early **study rob you of** the time you want to seek a Heavenly blessing ?"

" **No,** I think I should be afraid nothing would **go** right, if I could neglect that. I will tell you **what I mean to** do, Mary : I mean to learn the Epistle of **St. James all** through ; three verses every morning ; it will **be the** only lesson I shall not have to give an account of to any one ; I shall learn it alone with God and myself !"

Herbert kept his resolution ; he was up morning by morning to his lessons, and by this means secured the happy evenings with his parents and his sister. He kept watch over old Willy, and, as the days went on, he began to think what next must be done to keep up the fire on old Willy's hearth ? One thing alone was certain, and that was, that he could not let old Willy be cold, though no log now lay in the ditch. All his thoughts were unsuccessful ; he could devise no plan. But those who, like Herbert, think upon the wants of others and pray for their relief, are sure to find there is a Hand unseen working for those on whom they think and for whom they pray. Herbert seemed to himself to get no nearer to any further aid for old Willy : but sometimes that which we think far off is close before us ; and our next step shows it plain. Old Willy's fire-wood was getting low, and Herbert knew not what to do: sometimes he thought that his mother or his sister, who knew he had no money, might some day surprise him by supplying old Willy's want ; but Herbert's father had secretly requested that they would not do so ; he wished to see Herbert make his own way alone—and though he was quite ready now to aid him, if really necessary—he did not wish to do so until he found that it was necessary. Herbert said nothing, but he became more silent and thoughtful ; care for the poor and needy was pressing on his heart. O happy they who bear the burden of the wants of others, before they know the weight of personal calamity themselves ! Jem was keeping his sheep again ; it was not to Jem that Herbert must now look : and once more things began to seem dark, and Herbert felt his own comfort was bound up with the comfort of that feeble old man, who had already been warmed by the labor of his hands; yet still he knew not what to do.

While in this difficulty, as Herbert was coming from the stables one morning, he was met by the gamekeeper's eldest boy—a child about his own age—who, coming up to him, said, " If you please, Mr. Herbert, we have gathered a heap of sticks out of the park; father said he thought you might be wishing for dry wood, and that he might as well have it ready as not."

" What a capital thought!" exclaimed Herbert, "it's the very thing! but how came you to know I wanted wood?"

" Well, sir, father saw you riving up old Willy Green's log before it was light, and he said he never felt so ashamed in his life—to have all us boys abed, and you working like that. So we were all up the next morning; father called us before it was light, and he said you were off for all that! so we scrambled up the Park in the dark, and rare good fun we had, and we got such a heap before school! and the next morning we were up and out before you passed by—for father watched; so then we thought that was something! And I asked father if I might not tell you what we were after; and he said, not till we had something to show: but if you will please to come and see, there's something to speak for us now—father said I might ask." This overflow of cheerful words was poured out as the poor boy by the side of the rich hastened back to look at the gathered wood: quick-footed they were—those happy traffickers in the blessed merchandise of purest charity! And now they reached the gamekeeper's cottage, they hastened round it to the little yard behind; there rose the piled-up stack of wood which the friendly winds had strewed all ready for those youthful gleaners' hands—branches large and small, branches old and sere—piled up in a stack as high as Herbert from the ground. And there beside it stood the gamekeeper's two younger boys.

Jonathan and Benjamin; and there stood the mother with her infant in her arms, curious to see the young Squire's reception of so new and uncommon a gift; and there stood the tall game-keeper with one hand upon the stack he had stooped to help his children to rear, with a smile upon his pleasant face in which many a feeling mingled—the consciousness of effort for the needy, of labor whose only recompense was love, and not the least, perhaps, a sense, a welcome sense, of one work upon earth, and that the noblest, in which his own young boys stood side by side with their young master.

" Well, this is capital," said Herbert, " capital, I declare! you good little fellows! that was being of some use in the world." And the boys looked on in silence, with faces of delight—ad-mitted in that moment to a partnership of heartfelt interest for the poor and needy.

" It was a capital thought, Linton," said Herbert, now address-ing himself to the gamekeeper. " I was terribly done up how to get firewood for old Willy just now, and never thought of the dead branches about, and if I had, I should have been a month getting up such a stack as this; but now the question is, how to get it to the cottage?"

" Well, sir," said the gamekeeper, " that 's soon settled. I can put the horse in the light cart in a minute, and we can soon have it there."

" Well, I wish you would, Linton, the sooner the better. And Jonathan, you must run to the stables, and say I am not going to ride this morning." And then Herbert, and gamekeeper, and children, and the mother with her infant on one arm, all laid in and threw in the gathered branches, till not a useable twig re-mained behind.

" There Linton, thank you, that will do, we can manage the rest. Now, Richard and Jonathan, in with you, and let us have

little Benjamin, too—he can hold the horse;" so Benjamin was
lifted in, and then the gamekeeper ran to open the gate, and he
looked after the light cart from the gateway, and his wife from
the cottage door, the children hidden by the piled-up wood behind them, associated in one work with the young Squire—and
that the work of love and mercy.

Old Willy was sitting with his cottage door wide open, for the
day was bright, and, sheltered by his fireside, he liked to look
out on the pleasant face of nature, while the sun did gleam a
little after the long cold winter. Up drove the light cart. Herbert jumped out ; and, while the boys were getting out, he hastily
took down the movable stile, and running up the straight garden-
path, exclaimed, " Here is no end of wood coming for you, Willy ! Linton's boys have picked it up in the Park; we will put
it all in the shed." And then he ran back to the cart ; the boys
had already tilted it, shooting the wood into the road, where it
lay in large scattered heaps. Little Benjamin stood at the
horse's head, just high enough to stroke the creature's face,
which was stooped down in recognition to the child, proving
also a signal to the horse, that this was a time to stand still.
Backward and forward went the boys, laden with the old man's
wood—who could tire in such a labor !—while with a smile of
peace the old man watched them at their work.

" Come, Benjamin," at last said Herbert, " the horse under-
stands it well enough, you may help us carry." And little Benjamin came to the heap, and caught up a sear old branch
higher than himself, clasping it round with both arms, his little
pinafore dragged up by the first stooping act of embrace, running off with it to the shed—and the horse looked round after
his little watcher, but he saw evident proof that the business was
pressing, so he did his part and stood perfectly still.

When the light labor was over—labor in which the heart

eased the hand—Herbert, looking with complete satisfaction at the well-filled shed, said, " Now let us each carry a .og up for the fire." Little Benjamin, as was to be expected, chose out the biggest he could see—perhaps because most inviting to the yet unmeasuring thought of his infant spirit; he toiled with it after the bigger boys, the young Squire going first, and when at last, with desperate effort, he cast it on the hearth—his brothers laughing at its size—his still sturdy figure overbalanced, and, but for Herbert's instant spring, he would have fallen himself upon the burning wood in this his first ministry of love for the poor and feeble.

" There, Willy !" said Herbert, " now we will all shake hands with you, and be off again." So they had each a hearty shake of the hand ; but little Benjamin lifted his baby face to old Willy for a kiss—that being the only token of good-will he as yet understood ; and then they all ran down the narrow path, fixed in the stile, sprang over it—little Benjamin tumbling after them—then up into the light cart, and merrily home again : while old Willy, raising his eyes and hands, exclaimed, " Sure of such is the kingdom of heaven.!"

The gamekeeper, still on the watch, was at the open gate with his bow and smile of welcome ; never had he looked on his young master with such hope and reverence as now—when he drove in with the light cart by his children's side, from their labor of love. " Benjamin was a capital helper !" said Herbert, as the child's father lifted him down.

" Shall we get any more, sir ?" asked Richard.

" O, yes, when you like," replied Herbert. " It 's worth any thing to have a store in hand !"

And the boys made their bow in response to Herbert's " Good-by," and returned to their cottage quite decided that there was no pleasure now like gathering wood for old Willy and their young master ; and it was fully evident that old Willy was in no further danger of perishing for want of firewood.

CHAPTER IX

*" Better is the end of a thing than the beginning thereof; and the patient in spirit
is better than the proud in spirit."—ECCLES. vii. 8.*

FEBRUARY passed away, and the morning came of the first of
March. A whole month Herbert had found himself left
without the aid of money; and during that month he had discovered that true wealth consisteth not in gold and silver, and
houses and lands, but in the love of earth and heaven. In that
month Herbert had also learned how to become possessed of this
true wealth; he had cultivated prayer, and faith, and effort,
and they had all taken root within his heart—there they grew,
watered by the Divine Word, and love from above and from
around responded to them. Herbert had set himself to learn
the lesson that at first looked so hard to him; he turned to the
heavenly Counselor—to whom none ever turned with their
whole heart in vain—and he had found that the knowledge of
Wisdom was sweet to his soul, and that verily in keeping God's
commandments there is great reward.

Herbert remembered what day it was, when he woke, and
thoughts of the past, the present, and the future filled his mind;
but he knew where to take his thoughts now—even to a heavenly Father's feet; and when we take our thoughts and plant
them by prayer at our heavenly Father's feet, they are sure to
spring up and bear sweet fruit, in God's best time, to His glory
and our comfort—however bitter they might be when we took

them there. The light of the early spring morning was shining peacefully into Herbert's room; **he opened his** window and breathed the keen freshness of the **air ;** the first bright beams of day seemed lingering **in** the heavens—their **vailed** radiance gently dispersing the darkness of earth, before they rose above and poured their beams upon it. Leafless and still lay **the misty woods ; but** the wakeful **deer were already** feeding, side by side, on the young herbage ; for the creatures not made to labor in **the** sin-defiled service of man need but short slumber **to refresh them.** Herbert heard the sheep-bell tinkle in the **distance—the** sheep-bell of his father's flock, and the sound led **his** thoughts **to Jem, and on to old** Willy ; and then he looked **on the gamekeeper's cottage, just visible** from his window among the **tall fir-trees, and his kindly** feeling gathered round **his little helpers there; and his thought turned** homeward, **where** one short **month seemed to have made all doubly** dear **to** him—and **from that hallowed resting-place he looked up** into the rosy sky, and **remembered the dark wintry night and the** heavy gloomy clouds **on which he** had gazed only **a** month before, and he thought **again of his sister's** words, "There is **no** darkness upon earth that God can **not** lighten ;" and in **the** peace-giving assurance **of the** same **faith, he** shut his window ind turned in quiet feeling to his studies.

"What can this be ?" said Herbert to himself, as he took up a small white paper parcel lying beside **his desk ;** it was not there when **he went to rest, some** one must have **been into** his room after **he had fallen** asleep. It was directed in **his father's** hand-writing. **He opened it ; there was a note within.** .

"My dearest Boy,

"The pain of a month ago was **well** worth enduring for the thankfulness of heart that, I trust, we both feel to-day. I did not wish to make you poor, but only to lead you to discover what poverty really is—lest you should be deceived by the outward show of wealth, and have supposed that, having that, you were of necessity rich. But now, I trust, my highest wish may be realized, and you found rich even in poverty—if this world's poverty should ever be your lot—rich in the love, and grace, and the blessing of God, from which nothing can separate—rich in the will, the wisdom, and the power of effort. I therefore gladly renew your allowance of the useful coin, on which I trust you will not now place a false dependence and value. And **as your** interests in life are so happily enlarged, I enlarge your means of meeting them by doubling your monthly income. Only remember, that you will need the heavenly Counselor quite as much with your purse as without it ;—it was the wisest of men who said, ' He that hearkeneth unto counsel is wise !'

" Your affectionate father,

" H. CLIFFORD."

The golden treasure lay folded within. Herbert could scarcely believe himself possessed of so much money ; he put it safe in **his** desk, determined to keep it with **the** greatest care ; then he looked at his watch, for he longed to go to his father, but it was too early yet to hope for that, **so** he took his books ; but his thoughts wandered away **to his** new possession, and a ceaseless succession of things that might be done with it, presented themselves to his mind. A new world of living interest lay freshly discovered around him, and he had never yet tried the effect of money's aid on any object in it ; so that his fancy was busy with a thousand thoughts, and his lessons lay unlearned. But suddenly a voice spoke within Herbert's heart—a still small voice—and it whispered there, " Every good gift, and every perfect gift is from above, and cometh down from the Father of

lights, with whom is no variableness, neither shadow of turn
ing." The words were familiar to him; he had himself hid
them within his heart; he had read them, learned them; they
were part of the very first chapter he had turned to in his time
of trouble, and now in his hour of prosperity they rose up
within his soul and spoke to him, and taught him now as that
same chapter had taught him then—it had led him in his
trouble to pray—it led him now in his prosperity to give thanks.
Herbert remembered that while he had longed to run to meet
his earthly father, he had not hastened to give thanks to that
Heavenly Father—the Father of all his light and comfort, from
whom this good gift came to him. O, happy child, who binds
the word of God by memory's help upon his heart—" When he
goeth, it shall lead him; when he sleepeth, it shall keep him;
when he awaketh, it shall talk with **him.** For the commandment is a lamp, and the law is light; and reproofs **of** instruction
are the way of life." Herbert had been afraid to **go so** early to
his earthly father, but our Heavenly Father's presence is always
open to His children, His ear always ready to listen to their
voice; and when Herbert had hastened where the Divine Word
called him, then he found that he could return to his lessons
and learn them—strengthened against the imaginations that before had led his thoughts wandering away from his books; for
when we have been speaking to our Father in heaven, whatever
it may be that we have had to say to Him, we are sure to come
back to our next duty better able to fulfill it, than before we
went into the presence of God and talked with Him. Now
Herbert studied diligently; so quickly he learned that he was
able to lay by his books—his lessons all prepared—ten minutes
before the nine o'clock prayer-bell rang. He hastened down to
look for his father; he knocked at the study-door, and was admitted there. No one knew what Herbert said to his father, or

what his father said to him; but every one could see the gladness of Herbert's face as he came in to prayers by his father's
side. His mother and his sister were happy in his joy, and all
was brightness at the morning meal.

Herbert thought that when he had finished his lessons he
would go and call on old Willy : he did not mean to be in any
haste to lay out his money, he only thought he should like to
know how he should feel in old Willy's cottage, now that he had
money to spend ; so after his studies were over, he set out for
the cottage. Old Willy was walking about in his garden, where
every thing looked fresh after the rain that had fallen the whole
of the day before, and the early part of the night. Eighty years
old Willy had lived in that cottage ; it was there that he was
born, and he had never slept a night from under its roof; and
now he watched the dwelling's decay much as he watched the
failure of his own bodily powers ; sometimes with an anxious
fear that the old building after all should not cover his aged
head **to** the last, for it had been left so long without repair **that**
its decay had become very rapid. Many people wondered that
the old man would live in such a place, and still more, that he
went on paying the same rent for it as they did for their warm
abodes ; but Willy had a hard landlord ; he must pay his full
rent, or he must go ; and **the** thought of changing that old
place for any other would have seemed to him like leaving his
native land for a strange country. Herbert stood in the cottage-
garden beside old Willy ; but a black cloud overhead burst in a
pelting shower, and Herbert and old Willy took refuge within
by the low embers of the wood-fire. " I will make **that** fire up
when the storm is over," said Herbert, as **he drew** out the low
stool and sat down close in front of old Willy, to make him hear
the more easily when he spoke to him. And then he looked
round the room with the eyes of one who felt that he had money

at his disposal, but who also felt that he had learned the use of his own hands.

" Why, I declare," at last exclaimed Herbert, getting up, and going to the middle of the room, " if there is not a hole here a foot deep—what a frightful hole !   Why, it is a foot and a half deep !   I could fill up that in no time, and lay in a couple of bricks to match the rest of the floor, which is all about as bad as it can be !"

" No, thank you, master," replied old Willy, " it would be no charity to fill that hole up ; I could not live in the old place without it, and I am often trying after making it a bit bigger."

" What do you mean, Willy ?" said Herbert, still standing over the hole; " such a place as that can be of no use except to break one's leg in, just in the middle of the floor here !"   And Herbert put his own foot in, which went down up to his knee.

But old Willy made answer, " Ah, master, there are those who know the use of many a thing, that some above them would do away with, and never think of the trial they would leave behind !" Old Willy did not mean to make any allusion to his log when tumbled into the ditch ; but Herbert remembered it, and stood silent, looking down into the hole.   Then old Willy, rising slowly, said, " I will show you the use of it, master.   There is never a heavy rain but the old roof drips all over, and just above that hole the water pours down in a stream sometimes enough to drown the place ; you may see the light through, if you look up that way," said old Willy, pointing to a particular place in the roof with his stick ; " and so I scooped out this hole, and then, if the rain be not long, the water settles there, instead of flooding the old place ; but if it holds long there, I fall to ladling it out as it comes ; but it is dangerous, I know, for all that, and I always keep a slip of an old board over it ; but last night it rained piteous ; I was up half the night ladling it out as I best could, and I left it open to-day ;" and even as old Willy spoke the rain-drops began to drip from the roof, and a small stream to pour down into the ready-made hole.

"Is it always like this when it rains?" asked Herbert, indignantly.

"No, master, not when the rain is soon over ; but you see **the** old thatch was ringing wet before this shower came, and it is always bad when the rain holds any while. I was dragging about my old bedstead in the dead of last night, trying to get some place to lie down in where the rain would not drip on me, and I could not find so much as a dry corner to lay my head under. I was wholly worn out, and I thought it seemed so hard to pay the rent I did so regular, and then not to be able to find a place to lie down in ! And I sat down on my old bed and cried ; but then those words rose up in my heart, 'The Son of man hath not where to lay his **head !'** And O how ashamed I felt to be fretting there, just as it seemed because **I was like my** Lord ! and then I thought how all the world was His, and He had made it so beautiful for us sinful creatures to dwell in ! and yet he had not so much **as** a place He could call His own in it, but was forced to go up the mountains, when He was seeking after getting by Himself alone. And so I felt wholly **ashamed, and** lighted up my fire and my candle, and got looking into my Book, where it speaks about that place He is gone to prepare for the like of me, whom **the** Book says he came to save ! And then, when the rain gave over, I laid down, and, to my thinking, I had one of the best sleeps I ever had under the old **roof,** thanks be to Him **who** gave it."

"But," said Herbert, "I should just **like to** know who it is that pretends to let you such a **place** as this, and call it **a** house ?'

"It's a Master Sturgeon that owns the place, sir; this house and the bit of land round it was left to him by a relation; 'tis all that he has in the parish. He is well to do in the world, I have heard say; but to my thinking it's sometimes them that have most who see the most use in laying of it up, instead of laying of it out; for if I have asked him once, to be sure I have twenty times, when I carried in my rent, to. be so good as to lay out so much as a few shillings of it on the old place; but he never gave the least heed in the world, nor yet to lower the rent, though I never owed him a shilling; so I have given up asking, and now 'tis too bad for mending."

"Then let him put on a new roof!" replied Herbert.

"Well, to be sure, sir, that might mend it; but them that love money, why, 'tis hard for them to part with it when there is not a necessity."

"But there is a necessity! are you to lie all night long with water dripping over you, when we should not suffer a drop to rain through in our dog-kennel?"

"No, master, 'tis very true; but an old man like me, that's past being any use to any body, and only lies like a burden on the parish, why, 'tis not to be expected that any one should look after me! and no doubt Master Sturgeon thinks the old place will hold out the old man; and then may be he will do something different by it; but you see them that are after money, why, 'tis not their way to be after parting with it for them that are past being any use to any one, like as I am now."

Old Willy had seated himself again in his chair, and Herbert had drawn his stool close to it, his face raised to old Willy's; and now he laid his hand on old Willy's knee, and said, "Willy, dear old Willy! you are of use, you are of the greatest use to me; I have been a great deal happier, and get on a hundred times better since I first came to see after you!

I should not know what to do without you, now; and no one can or shall think you a burden!"

"The good Lord above bless you!" said the old man, as he laid his labor-worn hand on the little soft one that rested on his knee. Old Willy said no more, and Herbert sat lost in thought a few moments, then looking up again full of earnestness, he said, "I tell you what, Willy, you shall not lie without a dry roof over you, to be rained upon all night long; I say it, Willy, you shall not; and if your landlord has no thought for you, there is some one who has, and who has the power, too!"

"Yes, master, blessed be God, don't I know His own words —'I go to prepare a place for you!' and they come in to comfort me after every trouble, like the bow 'cross the dark cloud."

"Yes, Willy, but I don't mean our Saviour; I mean some one here who can help you, and who will. I mean that I can, and I shall; and it won't be like the coals, Willy, for I have the money now of my own!"

The aged Willy looked inquiringly on the bright young face, in which love for the old man, joy at the power, and earnest purpose to aid and comfort were all blended in full expression; but he did not say any thing, for he did not quite take in the idea that any one except the landlord, and still less the child at his knee, could think of new-roofing his cottage. But while he looked in inquiring silence, Herbert suddenly remembered the time, and wishing him then a hearty "good-by," not without another assurance that old Willy would soon see what would be done to the roof! he took his leave.

As Herbert pursued his homeward way he began to think, what would his father say to his new promise? He thought of his letter that morning received, and the only part that awoke a fear was the last sentence in it, "Remember, he that hearkeneth unto counsel is wise." "Perhaps, then," thought Herbert, "I ought to have consulted papa first; but who that had the money could help saying it should be done! I don't believe papa could, and I will tell him so if he objects; but he will not object now, because I have the money all my own, and he has never found fault with me for spending my own money as I liked, and he must be glad I should spend it in keeping old Willy dry; though his landlord ought to do it; yet if he won't, some one must, or old Willy must be left to perish!" So Herbert braced up his courage and went to dinner, but still he felt some difficulty in telling of an engagement that must consume his whole month's allowance, entered into on the day of receiving it; but what could he have done better with it? again he thought; so after being silent through dinner, he ventured when the dessert was on the table to begin, "Papa, I hope I have not cut my fingers again, but if I have, I really believe you would have done the same if you had been in my place!"

"Very likely," replied his father, "I have done so in your sense of the phrase, more than once or twice, and it is the experience I learned by such mistakes, that I would gladly use to guard you."

Again Herbert thought to himself, "Ah! papa means I should consult him ;—I wish I had, but it's too late now!"

"Well, papa, I may as well tell you at once; I have been to see old Willy, and, would you believe it? every rainy night his thatch drips with water from every part, and a stream pours down in the middle of his room, and he has dug a hole in the floor to catch the water; a deep hole in which he might break his leg any day, and his landlord won't do any thing to the roof to mend it!"

"And so my son Herbert is going to do the landlord's work for him, I suppose?" said Mr. Clifford.

" Not for the landlord, papa ; I would send him to prison if I could ! but for old Willy ; he can not do it for himself, and if no one will do it for him, why he must die from wet and damp. What else could I do, when I had money of my own, papa ?"

" You could not do otherwise if the love of God was in your heart, and the means in your hand, and no reason against it strong enough to prevent: but I am afraid there is a strong reason against your doing it, which, if you had consulted me first, I could have told you."

" What reason, papa ?" asked Herbert ; and again his heart sank within him, and the secret wish again was ready to rise, that in this case he had let charity alone.

" There is this reason against it—that there are men in this parish comparatively poor, owning a cottage or two, and keeping them in good repair, when I know they must often feel the want of all the money they can get: and there is this one wretched dwelling, owned by a man who could rebuild it and not miss the money so spent ; but, because he will not spare enough to put a dry roof over it, are those poor but honest men, who have made it their care to keep their tenants comfortable, to see the aid, never extended to them, bestowed on an unprincipled man who withholds the right of his tenant from him ?"

" But then, papa, should old Willy be left to perish because that miser of a man will not do what is right ?"

" Old Willy need not perish ; and though I have no doubt it would distress him to leave the house in which he was born, still we must not discourage good and honest men by aiding a bad one, to save old Willy this pain."

" But, papa, I have promised !"

" O, my boy, why so hasty ! Could you not have asked your father first ? But if we afterward find that any thing would make the fulfillment of a promise a wrong act toward others, we must acknowledge it, and endeavor to the utmost to obtain the same object in a right way."

"Well, papa, I am sure I don't know who could ever have stopped to think of the whole parish of landlords, when they saw that one poor suffering old man! What can I do to keep my promise in another way?"

"I think the best thing would be to go yourself to the landlord, and try to awaken a right feeling on the subject."

"It's no use to ask him, papa; old Willy asked till he gave up in despair."

"You have not tried him yourself yet," replied Mr. Clifford; "and you can not say that it would be of no use till the trial is made. The prophet Nehemiah, in his appeal to the heathen king, will teach us better—if we only set about our requests to others as he did, with prayer to the God of Heaven, we may be answered as he was. So do not be discouraged, my boy, but try it in prayer and faith, and you will most surely find, sooner or later, that you went not alone to the work."

"But, papa, I should hate to see the man; I should be sure to get into a passion with him."

"Then you had better not put yourself in his way, for if you have no rule over your own spirit, you certainly have no hope of success with another!"

"But how could I help it, papa?"

"Only by having more of the spirit of Him who commendeth His love toward us, in 'that while we were yet sinners, Christ died for us.' And in truth old Willy's rich landlord is more to be pitied than old Willy. Old Willy can suffer but a little time: a little moment—and his light affliction will be over for ever; for he is the heir of an eternal kingdom; but the other must have his portion with that rich man we read of in the

Bible, who lifted up his eyes in torment—and that for ever, if his heart is not changed."

" I am sure I wish it may be changed, papa, for old Willy's sake as well as his own ; but I don't seem to feel any hope."

Here the conversation was interrupted, and Herbert was soon at his sister's side. " Is it not dreadful, Mary, to have to talk **to** such a **man ?**"

" Yes, dear Herbert, **I** dare say you **feel** it so ; but **you** remember our Saviour was continually talking with those who were **always** sinning against His Heavenly Father ; and if we follow His example, we may do even the wicked good—with the help and blessing of God."

" Well," replied Herbert, "**I** am sure charity is the steepest hill I ever climbed ; I get a slip every step I try at; and how to get up again is more than I can tell !"

" But have you not found that there is One standing on that steep hill-side, to lift you up again when you fall ? Did not the Heavenly Counselor stoop to lift you up before ? **and** did He not show you a friend to help you ? It is better to fall **at His** feet, than to stand where He is not ! And if the hill be steep there is always sunshine on the top. Was there not sunshine **for** you when you stood on the last of old Willy's log, and saw it all ready for his use ?"

" Yes, that was pleasant enough."

" And so **it will** be when you stand in old Willy's garden, and look with him on the new roof of his cottage."

" O, Mary, do you think it really will be done, then ?"

" Yes, I have no doubt about it—when the right time comes— if we do not give up hope and effort."

" O dear," sighed Herbert, " how glad I shall be when to-morrow is over ! I think this is a worse job than the old log—but I will try at it for all that."

" You will not think it worse when the end comes, dear Herbert."

"But, Mary, you don't know the end; what is it makes you sure it will be good ?"

" Because I am quite sure whenever we try to help the poor, in a right spirit, and in a right way, that God is with us, and will not suffer our effort to fall to the ground."

" Well, Mary, now we shall see—I will try to do it as you and papa say I ought, because I know you understand all about charity, and then I will see what the end of it is !"

" Very well," said his sister, with a smile, "I agree; for I know none ever leaned upon and watched that unseen Hand in vain !"

Herbert then stood pledged to go forth the next day in the cause of the poor and needy—the young child of earth and Heaven was to stand, for the first time in his life, face to face " with the man of the earth," the poor man's oppressor; no wonder that he could think of little else ! He went early to his room, and, like the stripling David, preparing to encounter the champion of Gath—he made ready to meet the stronger giant of Oppression. I do not mean that Herbert ran to choose himself smooth stones from the brook for his sling—no, the weapons of his warfare were of another kind : Herbert went to the living stream of God's most holy Word, the pebbles he wanted lay there ; he went to the very part from which he had gathered often before, even the Epistle of St. James ; he chose the texts he thought would suit him best, and his heart was the sling in which he laid them ready for use ; he had learned all the epistle before, but now he looked upon it that he might choose what seemed best for his purpose, and, having chosen, he lay down to sleep.

The next morning Herbert did the best he could with his

lessons, but his heart was heavy, and he met his tutor ill-prepared; happily for him he had worked so well for the past month that his tutor readily listened to his assurance that he had done his best, and seeing that something lay heavy on his thoughts, allowed him to carry on the imperfect lessons to the next day, to be prepared with his fresh tasks—instead of detaining him after hours. So at the time for his afternoon ride his ponies were ordered round, and, having been in to his mother and sister, and asked them to think of him all the time, he set forth slowly on swift-footed Araby, and his groom, on young Ruby, followed slowly behind.

First he went to old Willy's to tell him the sorrowful tale of a disappointed purpose. He found him seated by his wood fire, with his Bible, that constant companion of his blessed old age, before him. Herbert had no doubt that old Willy's thoughts were full of the new roof, and he feared that the old man would never trust him again after such a disappointment as he had now to bring. But the truth was, that old Willy, not being quick of understanding, had never taken the idea of a new roof into his mind; he was looking again upon the precious words that told him of the mansions in Heaven that his Saviour was gone to prepare, and he had forgotten all about the last day's conversation. Herbert began, " Willy, I don't see any use in my making a promise to help any one, for I can never keep my word when I do !"

" Well, master, I have read in those good sayings that stand next to the Psalms in my Book, how that ' the desire of a man is his kindness !' I can show it you, for I always keep a bit of a mark tucked in at that, and it often comforts my old heart when I think upon others, and there's nothing but a prayer I can do for them. Here 't is, master ! I don't know the numbers—not to say where the words are, but you will if you look."

"Yes, Willy," said Herbert, heavily, "but it puts me quite out of heart that I must not make a new roof to keep you dry! Papa thinks it would go against those who keep their houses as they ought, if I did it for a rich man who could so easily do it for himself. So I am just going to tell your landlord how bad it is, and to see if he will not be persuaded to do it himself; but I declare I don't see much hope any way!"

Old Willy, perceiving that something troubled his young master, had strained his utmost powers of attention; but Herbert's tone was low, and the sentence long, and all that old Willy laid hold of were the last words—"I don't see much hope any way!" he did not understand what the hope related to, but his bright faith had always an answer to the tone of despondency, so he replied at once, "O, master, there's always a hope up above! and that's always a leading me on, and sure that's enough for them that have it!"

"Well, Willy, good-by," said Herbert, with a sorrowful look at the old man and the old place; and the ministering boy passed away in his sadness, and the old man looked with troubled face after him, troubled not for his unrepaired roof—for the thought of that he had not taken in—but troubled because he saw the shade upon the bright young face that of late had entered his dwelling like the first glad sunbeam of spring; and the old man breathed a silent prayer for the child, and then looked again on the Words of Life.

Herbert reached the town—the town where Mr. Mansfield lived and little Jane, the town where little Ruth and Patience dwelt—the town was reached, and then the street, and then the house; there was the name of Mr. Sturgeon in large letters on the brass-plate on the door. Mr. Sturgeon was at home, and Herbert went in. Herbert took the chair Mr. Sturgeon handed to him, and said, "I am come to ask you to repair the cottage of Willy Green; the roof is so bad that the rain drips through all night long, when the weather is very wet." Mr. Sturgeon's countenance fell, and he replied, "I make a point, sir, of knowing the state of all my property, and I am sorry that in this case I can not meet your request."

"Is there any reason why the roof should not be mended?" asked Herbert.

"Yes, the best of reasons," replied Mr. Sturgeon; "I long ago made up my mind not to lay out another shilling on the old place; my wish is to sell it, and I might have done so several times over before now, but I could not get my price; and when I have once named my price, I never take less, let the risk of loss to myself be what it may."

"Do you mean that you would sell the place over old Willy, and turn him out?"

"Well, I suppose whoever buys it will hardly wish to keep him in: the fact is, that three cottages might be built on that piece of land, and three times the money made of it. I do not wish to undertake the thing myself, but I mean to sell it as a piece capable of bringing in three times the money it has done."

"It would break old Willy's heart to turn him out!" said Herbert, earnestly; "and you would not like to take away all his comfort for a little more MONEY?"

"Indeed, sir, I am sorry for the old man; but if his affection is so strong for brick and mortar, I am afraid I can not engage to secure his comfort to him! I look upon money as a means of comfort to many; I am a general supporter of charitable institutions, but if I turned out of my way for the fancies of every old man or old woman, I must soon curtail my charities."

"But," said Herbert, "when our way is not God's way, it is best to turn out of it—is it not?"

"I beg your pardon, sir, I do not understand you," replied Mr. Sturgeon.

Then Herbert took the first of his treasured pebbles from the brook—even his first text from St. James, and he replied, "The Bible says, that 'the Lord is very pitiful and of tender mercy'—that is God's way."

"Indeed, I hope so," replied Mr. Sturgeon, "or, I am afraid the best of us will stand but a poor chance."

"But," added Herbert, taking another of his texts, "the Bible says also, that 'he shall have judgment without mercy that hath showed no mercy;' so won't you show mercy to old Willy?"

"You want me," replied Mr. Sturgeon, "for the sake of one old man, to curtail my means of bestowing charity on the many."

Herbert had tried hard to keep his indignation down, but now it rose, and he replied, "You have taken old Willy's rent for a place not fit for any one to live in, and you can never do charity with such money! God asks poor people in the Bible if rich men have oppressed them; and will you not be afraid when God asks old Willy?"

Mr. Sturgeon replied, "I must be allowed my own opinion of justice, as well as you; the old man would not stay, I suppose, if the place was not worth more to him than the money he pays; there is nothing but his own will to detain him."

"But there is not an empty cottage in the village," replied Herbert, "to which old Willy would go, if he wished ever so much!"

Mr. Sturgeon replied, "Every one knows there is a house large enough to receive him close by; and, for my part, I think the work-house the best place for such helpless old people."

"O, Mr. Sturgeon, you do not understand the thing, and so you do wrong, and think it right! Old Willy is not helpless, he can do every thing for himself, and read the Bible, too; and if he were forced to go into that heap of people in the workhouse, he would lose all his quiet. The Bible says, 'Thou shalt love thy neighbor as thyself!'" This was the last pebble Herbert had chosen for his sling—the last selected text from St. James, but the oppressor felt it not. Every rejected word of Holy Scripture, which seems to fall powerless at the hardened sinner's feet, will one day rise again, to **descend upon** him with a millstone weight, crushing his soul for ever. O, let the sinner then beware how he reasons away and **rejects** the awful Word of God!

Mr. Sturgeon only replied, " My principle, sir, is, ' Let every **one see** to his own interest ;' and, in a free country like ours, where the laws are good, and the observance of them strictly enforced, I do not know a principle likely to work better for all."

" Have you read the last chapter of the Epistle of St. James ?" asked Herbert.

" Certainly **I have, sir** ; I am fully acquainted with all **you** may wish to urge on such a foundation."

" Will you not, then, put a new roof over old Willy with the **money he** has **so long** paid you for rent ?"

" I have given you my answer, sir, and I must decline all interference between me and my tenant."

" Then I must wish **you good** day, Mr. Sturgeon ; and may old Willy's God forgive you !"

Herbert rode away. When free from the town, large tears came fast ; he felt overcome with his effort, but the sweet air kissed his burning cheeks **and** breathed over his temples ; he looked up into the clear blue sky, as only the child of the Holy Heaven—the child of the God of the poor and needy—can look. Yet his heart was heavy, and on his face the shades of sin and sorrow rested—how could it be otherwise ? He would not pass old Willy's **house ;** he felt as **if** he could not bear to see the old man on this his sad return, so he took the further road to his home, which led round by Mr. Smith's farm. Suddenly Jem appeared in sight—coming along the distant road ; he had just folded his sheep, and was returning home to his supper. A moment more, and Araby bore his young master to the side of honest Jem. Jem stood still, and Herbert threw himself from his saddle, intent on his subject of thought, and stood leaning on Araby's neck—the most effectual way of keeping his impatient steed quiet. There stood the eager boy—the child of fortune, looking up to that poor lad, as if his earthly treasury of hope and help were garnered in his breast : and there stood the shepherd youth with head uncovered, looking down with loving reverence on that young face upraised to his.

"O, Jem," said Herbert, "there is no one in the world I should have been so glad to meet as you ! I am in another trouble, and if you can not help me, there is no one can now. Old Willy's roof lets all the rain-drops through upon him ; I have been to his landlord, and he will not do any thing, but talks of selling the place over his head ! It will break old Willy's heart ! What can be done ?"

Jem passed his hand across his forehead, " Well, sir, excuse me ; but one thing at a time, as the saying is, and maybe we shall manage them all."

" What ! do you see any hope, Jem ?"

" Well, sir, 'tis a hard case when hope be clean gone ! But the roof—did you say that 's bad ?"

" Yes, terribly bad—holes all over !"

" Maybe I could stop them up," said Jem ; " master would not be against letting me have a little straw for that—that 's certain."

" No, Jem, old Willy says it 's past all mending ; and so I am sure it is ' why, it drips all over when the rain lasts any time !"

"That's a hard case," replied Jem, "**when** mending won't do it, and there's none to make! as the saying is. But I never found the trouble yet that I did n't see a light through when **I** had been after it a bit—and may be I shall in this."

"O, that's right, Jem! I don't mind any thing now I have met you. But what do you think of that wretched landlord saying he means to sell the old place, when he can get his price for it?"

"Well, sir, 'when' is a long day—sometimes longer than they think for that fix it! And there's more than ONE to be considered in this, I take it."

"What do you mean, Jem?"

"Why, sir, when my poor mother was left a widow and **I** was but a child, with nothing to look to but her, many's the time I have seen her cast down till her spirits were wholly gone, and then she would say, 'Well, child, "the king's heart is in the hands of the Lord," and so things may turn yet.' And, to be sure, **how** they did **turn**! Once, I remember, we **were as** near as any thing to being sent right away to our **own parish**, where we had not a creature to look to; mother **took on won-** derfully; she was **al**ways praying and fretting about it; and then, at the last, they turned the right **way** for us **to** stay. So I have never forgot that saying. I take **it to be** from the Bible, and that it's a certain thing, if **the Lord** holds him that has the biggest power, he holds **them** too that have the less; and so may be the landlord won't have his way with Willy after all!"

"That's right, Jem; I shall think so too. How glad I am I met you! Good night!" and Herbert gave him a hearty shake of the hand—to which gratitude, hope, and affection all lent their force, and springing again on swift-footed Araby, was soon at the door of his home. The shade had passed from his brow, the weight from his young spirit—the chill of the cold-hearted oppressor lost in the sense of Jem's voice of hope and hand of power—and the spirit of the rich boy leaned on the poor boy, as the honeysuckle depends on some stem of sturdier growth, which the God of nature has caused to spring up at its side.

Meanwhile, Jem went home to his supper; the frugal meal was waiting his return; a log blazing on the hearth, Mary sitting close beside it, knitting him a pair of stockings, the worsted bought with the money saved by the firewood, which set aside the expense of coal; his mother at work in her large old spectacles, that fastened by a spring on her nose. They soon sat down to supper: Jem was unusually silent. "What 's the matter of it, boy ?" at last asked his mother; " you are not thinking about your supper, I 'm sure."

" Well, no, mother, I suppose I was not," said Jem, going on no less thoughtfully with his meal. After supper, Jem took his hat and went out, saying he had not done yet for the night.

" He is a working at something !" said his mother; " may be he will tell us after a bit."

Jem walked thoughtfully along, his feet seemed to guide him, rather than he them, up to the farm. He looked at his folded sheep; but it was plain his thoughts were away—for he took no notice of the bleat of his favorite lamb, who had heard its shepherd's step, and pressed its white head against the pen that shut it in. Jem came round by the back of the farm; a storm was gathering in the evening sky; Jem looked at it, then anxiously around; he was standing then in the stack-yard, and on the further side of it his eye fell on a large old tarpauling. that had been used the evening before to cover over a stack only partly removed to the barn; the remainder had now been carried in, and the tarpauling not yet put away. " 'Tis the very thing !" exclaimed Jem, and as he spoke he hastened to the back-door of the farm.

" You are wanted, Master William, if you please," said Molly, at the open door of the keeping-room, and William went out to the door of the back-kitchen.

"Well, Jem, any thing wrong with the sheep?" asked William.

"No, sir; I wish all was as right with others as 'tis with them, and then I had not need be after disturbing you."

"Never mind that; what's the matter now?"

"Why, Master Green's roof lets all the wet through upon him, and there's a terrible storm now coming up, and I don't seem as if I could rest if he is to be rained upon all night long."

"Well, but what can be done?" asked William; "there's no time and no light to be mending it to-night."

"No, it's not mending will do it, it's past all that; the more shame to them that have suffered it."

"But what's to be done, then? You can't make a new roof, I suppose—and to-night into the bargain!"

"Why, that's just what I was thinking if I could, for as I came down by the barn, I saw the old tarpauling lying there; now the old roof is no bigness but what that would cover it, and I'll be bound not a drop would get through, if it rains ever so."

"Well, to be sure, that is a new roof after a fashion!" replied William; "and if the old tarpauling was mine, you should have it in a minute; I am only afraid it will go against father to .end! But you wait about, and I will hear what he says."

Away turned Jem to stand and look at things without seeing them, and back went William to the keeping-room. His father was resting in his chair by the fire, and his mother was busy at her needle; William stood a minute at the window looking out at the gathering cloud, then walking up to the fire, he said, "There's a terrible storm coming up to-night!"

"It's a good thing it held fine to clear in the stack," observed farmer Smith.

"Yes, it was a good thing for the wheat," replied William

" but it will not be a good thing for them that have not a dry roof over them to-night, by what I can see !"

" Who do you mean ?" asked farmer Smith, looking up.

" Why, old Willy Green," replied William ; " I find he might as well lie in our fields, and better under one of our hedges, for all the shelter he gets from that moldy roof of his !"

" There 's the more to answer for by them that suffer it !" observed farmer Smith.

" Well, father, that 's just what I was thinking ; I don't see how we can suffer him to lie so !"

" 'Tis his landlord, not us !" said farmer Smith ; " what can we do ?—Make a new roof for every hard-hearted man that won't keep his own tenants dry ?—that 's not my idea of charity !"

" No, father, but there 's that old tarpauling lying down in the stack-yard, if we were to draw that over the roof, he would lie as dry as we do."

" And I should like to know what we are to do without it ?"

" Why, you know, father, we have housed the last stack to-day ; we are sure not to want it before harvest : we have others, and better too, for the wagons."

" Well, I can't say I take to it," said farmer Smith ; " I am always ready to give a trifle, but if you once take up with lending, you never know what 's your own !"

Impatience had long been gathering in Mrs. Smith's face, and at these last words she broke silence, " Yes, Mr. Smith, that 's all the difference ! you are always for giving, giving, giving, till no one knows the end of it ! I say, let them earn an honest penny that may do them some good, instead of all your givings, or lend them a bit if they be hard pressed, and let them work it out ; but no, you will always be giving, and taking out the little spirit that is in them ; and now, when an old tarpauling lies down in the yard, you won't let the boy roof over the best

man in the parish, and the oldest too, because you will stand out
against lending ! it 's too much for me, Mr. Smith, I declare !"

" Well, I suppose you are right," replied farmer Smith, in a
grave low tone; " I won't stand against it, boy." William was
sorry for his mother's rough words, but he could not say any
thing, so he hastened off to Jem, who was watching for the
first sound of the latch of the back kitchen door, and off set
William and Jem, hastening off together with the tarpauling
between them ; they laid it down at old Willy's door till they
returned, each with a thatcher's ladder, and then by climbing
and scrambling, and stretching and pulling, the old roof was
covered over, the covering made fast by the strings at its cor-
ners—and now the storm might come, old Willy would sleep
dry beneath it.

Herbert was leaning back on a sofa in the drawing-room,
while his sister played upon her harp ; a book was in his hand,
but he was not reading, his thoughts were with old Willy ; a
servant entered and asked of Herbert, " Can you be spoken with
to-night, sir ?"

Herbert sprang up and went out ; Jem stood in the hall. " I
beg pardon, sir," said Jem, " I thought maybe you would like to
know we have roofed it in as dry as dust !"

" Has Mr. Sturgeon been there, then ?" said Herbert.

"No, sir, to my thinking he is best away ; there are some that
seem to have no good to bring with them when they do come !
but Master William has roofed it all over with an old tarpauling
from the farm. Daddy's as pleased as any thing; he says he shall
be lying awake to feel the comfort of it !"

" How came you to think of that ?" asked Herbert, in delighted
surprise at the work already done.

" Well, sir, I saw the old tarpauling lie, and then the thought
came to me, but Master William it was that gained it."

Herbert went back with his brightest smile, " O Mary, it 's done, it 's done !"

" What is done ?" asked Miss Clifford.

" Why, old Willy's roof all covered over as dry as possible ! Jem and young Smith have covered it over with an old tarpauling !" His sister smiled and said, " Then we have seen that the end is good !" And with Herbert still leaning at her side, she sang to her harp a psalm of thanksgiving.

" Papa," said Herbert, after a while, " I don't see that money is of much use in charity, at least I don't find it so !"

" Wait till the call for it comes, my boy, as sooner or later it is sure to come, and then give it freely. The mistake is, when we think money can do everything ! it has its distinct work like other creatures of God, and when we apply it amiss we do harm with it instead of good."

That night as farmer Smith read in his mother's Bible, the words met his eye, " Do good, and lend, hoping for nothing again ; and your reward shall be great, and ye shall be the children of the Highest : for He is kind to the unthankful and the evil." Luke vi. 35. And the peaceful sense of its being a Divine command he had obeyed, came down into farmer Smith's heart, and the oil and wine of the living Word poured into and healed the wound rough words had left. From that day, farmer Smith was as willing to lend as to give, when his judgment approved of the case.

Sweet was the slumber of the ministering boys that night—within the Hall, the farm-house, and the cottage ; and sweet the link between them ! And pleasant thoughts smoothed the old man's pillow ; as, dry and warm through the youthful love of earth, he turned to rest beneath the shadow of the Eternal, turned to the well-spring whence those bright and blessed rills of human sympathy had risen and flowed at his aged feet.

CHAPTER X.

"Let mine outcasts dwell with thee.—Be thou a covert to them from the face of the spoiler."—ISAIAH xvi. 4.

THE spring advanced with silent step and hand unseen, strewing the earth with beauty. Woods, pastures, lanes,—all flower-enameled, tempted the step to linger. The countless branches of the trees—through winter black and dreary—now wore their rosy hue, while the oily chestnut and the silver birch already put forth their buds beneath the clear blue sky. Often did Herbert tread the path between his own fair mansion and old Willy's lowly dwelling—the younger and the elder heart fast linked in pure affection's blessed bond. The old tarpauling covered the roof; and Herbert had, with unspeakable satisfaction, filled up, with **his own** hands, the **hole in the** floor—no longer needed now.

" I wonder," said Herbert one day to old Willy, as he looked over the page of the open Bible from the low stool on which he sat, " I wonder why you are so often reading those words about the mansions in heaven, when you know them all by heart? I should be for reading what I did not know."

" Well, master, you are right enough, I dare say, but it seems to do me good to get a look at the real words ; it helps an old man's faith ; for when I see them, I say, ' There they be !' and I can not doubt them. You see, master, the thought of a mansion **in** heaven for an old sinner like me, and my Lord gone to prepare it, and **coming back to** take me to it—why, it 's all so wonderful : **if** I could not get a look at the words sometimes, I'm afeard I should be just doubting again—though I pray that the good Lord would keep me from that ! But it's wonderful to come and see **them** all written there just when I want to be building up my poor faith ; for then I know it's not man's **word**, nor the thought of my old heart, but the Word of the **Lord that** endureth for ever !"

When the black thorn's thin chilly blossoms had given place to the redundant May, scenting the hedges, Miss Clifford **was al-** lowed to take her first drive. Herbert was in high spirits, and took his seat on the coach-box by old Jenks—whose silent joy at driving his young lady out again, had shown itself in his at- titude, as, holding reins and whip in his right hand, he had leaned down from the carriage-box to see her safely seated within ; then bowing in response to her smile, resumed his up- right position ; and once more, after many months, set forth with the whole of his master's family for a drive.

They had not gone far before the old coachman asked Her- bert if he had heard the news about Mr. Sturgeon and old Willy Green.

" No ; what news ?" asked Herbert, eagerly looking up, all impatience, into the old coachman's deliberate face.

" Why, I thought you must have heard it ; it's been all the talk of the village since yesterday ! They say that Mr. Sturgeon has bought that place of Squire Crawford's for his country- house, and they say that he and the builder, in whose hands it was, could n't come to terms, and Mr. Sturgeon would not go from his offer, nor the builder from his price, and so Mr. Stur- geon threw in that plot of old Willy's, and by that got the place some pounds less, instead of more than he first offered. The builder was over yesterday at old Willy's—no one knew a word about it till then !"

"It can not be true, Jenks! I do not believe it!"

"Ah, it's too true, for all that!" replied Jenks, shaking his head; "and it don't surprise me, for there's something belongs to money, that, when once you get the love of it, there's no saying what you will stop at! They tell me old Willy never spoke so much as a word; it seemed to turn him to stone to find he was sold out in that way."

"But do you think the builder will turn him out?"

"O yes; he has served him a notice to quit in a month, and they say it will all be pulled down in another month. Poor old fellow, it will be the finish of him here, and then he will be better off, and out of the way of them that can trouble him now; that's my belief!"

"Stop, Jenks, and let me get inside. I declare I will tell papa this moment!"

"No, sir, not for the world," replied Jenks, driving faster; "if my young mistress were to hear of it, it would do her more harm than a hundred drives could do good!"

"Then stop at the pond, Jenks, and I will run across to old Willy's."

"Ah, but then," replied Jenks, "I'll be bound she'll guess there's something amiss!"

"No, I will not say a word about it, but I must and will go; and if you do not stop at the pond, I shall get down without!"

Jenks knew his young master too well, not to think it better to pull up when the pond was reached. Herbert, faithful to his engagement, only looked into the carriage, saying cheerfully, "I want to run across to old Willy's." And then, without giving time for any inquiries, he leaped the stile, bounded over the meadow, and was soon out of sight. But a little further, and his step grew slower; for over his young spirit passed the awe of a first contact with overwhelming grief. "How will it be when

I get to him?" thought Herbert. " I can not comfort him!" A shudder passed over that bright young spirit, and the boy looked along another path that led to his home, and stood a moment in doubt which to take. Then a thought of that ministering angel he had seen in his dream watching over old Willy, came back to his mind, and he thought he would venture to go and see what the love of God could do for old Willy now.

The afternoon sunshine of the sweet spring-day was warm and bright, but the cottage-door was shut. Herbert knocked and waited—no answer came ; so, with a beating heart, he opened the door, and looked in. There, at the further side of the room, old Willy knelt—his hands clasped on the top of his stick ; he had not heard **the** knock, he did not **hear** the boy's gentle step, nor know that any one was there, till Herbert, having quietly shut to the door and laid his **hat on the** table, knelt down by old Willy's side, and said in his heart, " O God! comfort old Willy!" The old man turned his pale and tearless face and looked some moments in silent wonder on the boy, then slowly said, " Why, I had but then begun to ask the God above to send you to the sight of my eyes, before they be too dim to have the sight of you any more!"

" **Then**, Willy, you need not pray for that, because I am come. I am going to stay and sit with you, and God will comfort you, dear Willy ; I know he will!"

The old man made no answer; he seemed like one stunned with a sudden blow; he knelt on with an almost vacant expression a few moments, then said, " If you be come, why, then, I must thank the God above who sent you so soon!" Herbert waited while Willy gave thanks, and then the old man rose slowly and with difficulty, and made his way back to his arm-chair. Herbert took the low stool and sat down by his side, **but knew not what to say.**

After a short silence, old Willy looked round and said, " They are going to take the old place from me ; they say I must leave it ; but I don't seem to know one thing from another, nor what will be done, and my sight is turned dim, and I can't see the words of the Book, so now I can't seem to lay hold on any thing, only I have a hope that the good Lord above, who came down to save me, will keep hold of me still—is not that right ?"

" Yes, Willy, quite right. Once, do you know, Willy, it looked quite dark to me; I could not see a way out of my trouble any how, and then I prayed, and then I did see a way."

" Yes, sure enough," replied old Willy, " prayer will show the way any day ! don't I see the way—and is n't it just my Saviour ? Sure enough He says, 'I am the way,' and now it comes to me, how she I call my blessed angel came to me one day, and read me a rare beautiful story about the dove flying **back to the ark,** because there was no rest in all the world for the sole of his foot ! I have a bit of a mark tucked in against it, for I have looked on it times and often since then, but my eyes don't seem as if they could get **hold of the** words to-day."

" Shall I read it to you, **Willy ?"** asked Herbert.

" Ah, do, master, if you will be **so good,** it will come back to me then !"

Old Willy clasped his **hands** upon his stick, and listened while Herbert read the eighth chapter of the book of Genesis, where the mark was **tucked in.** He listened to the boy's clear voice breathing the living Word. Well might the old man feel like the desolate bird on the wide waste of **the** unstable waters ! But at the words that told of the dove's return and shelter in the ark, his stricken heart revived, **he raised** to Heaven his own bright smile, and when the chapter was ended, he said at once,

"Ah, I mind it all now; it all comes back to me, how she rea..
it just like that, and then she said to me, 'Willy, there's no
rest but in our Saviour; we must be like the dove and fly to
Him, and He will put out His hand and take us in!' I mind
it now how earnest she said it, and sure enough I have never
seen the ring-dove cross the sky at evening, but I have thought
of that, and prayed in my heart a prayer that I might get to
my Saviour, and that He would be pleased to reach out His
hand and take me in. And now I see it plain—how I am just
like the poor lost bird—there's no rest left on this side the grave
for the soles of my old feet; **so I** must only be looking after my
Saviour, and then, when it pleases Him, why, He will reach
forth His hand and take me in!"

Herbert left the old man in the light of the faith his aid
had helped to rekindle. But his heavy tidings spread sadness
in his home, and left a flush of deeper crimson on his sister's
cheek.

"Can you think of nothing, Mary, that can be done for old
Willy?" asked Herbert, as he wished her good night.

"**I** can think only of ONE, dearest Herbert; I know that
nothing is impossible **with God,** and **that He** loves old Willy
better than we do!"

While Herbert was in his room that evening, the thought
crossed his mind that he had **not told** old Willy of his sister's
drive; it must surely comfort him, he thought, to hear she had
been out, and might soon call on him. He treasured up this
piece of good tidings as the only earthly comfort he could
find, and making a desperate effort the next morning, he fixed
his attention on his lessons, with as few thoughts of old Willy
as possible; and having succeeded in accomplishing his tasks to
his tutor's satisfaction, he set off, as soon as he was free again,
for old Willy's cottage. He found the old man sitting calmly

in his chair, his Bible open on the table ; but he was not reading.

" O, Willy, only think, I did not tell you yesterday, my sister has been out for a drive, and she will soon come and see you !"

At these words the old man burst into tears.

" Why, Willy ! I thought that would make you glad ?"

But the old man only wept on ; the frozen fountain of his tears had melted at this touch, and the pent-up torrent flowed—he wept and sobbed till Herbert was terrified.

" Willy, why do you cry so ? Is it because they are going to turn you out of your home ?"

" O, master," said old Willy, at last, " 't is a great sin to fret against the will of God, but it came upon me so sudden ! 'T is the very thing I have been thinking upon so long and praying for day and night—to see her blessed feet come in, and hear her tongue again, and now 't is come—but not for me !"

" Yes, it will be for you, Willy !"

" No, master, no, they are going to take all my quiet from me, and an old man like me that 's lived so long a time alone—why, if other folk were by, I should not so much as know the words she said ; it 's no more use for me ! O, I wish I might go to my grave before they take my quiet from me ! I shall never know the words I read or hear when other folk come crowding by, and then, may be, I shall forget it all again. O, if I might but go, now while I have it in my heart, before I have clean lost it all !"

Herbert stood in a child's despair ; his cheek was pale and his heart faint ; he knew not what to say, but he thought perhaps **God's** Word might still have power to comfort. He looked down anxiously upon the open page ; it was the well-worn leaf that told of the mansions in Heaven. " That will do," thought Herbert, " if any thing will !" So, looking up, he said, " Willy, you listen to me, I am going to read !" Then with a slow, dis-

7

tinct utterance, he read, "Let not your heart be troubled ; ye believe in God, believe also in me. In my Father's house are many mansions ; if it were not so, I would have told you. I go to prepare a place for you. And if I go and prepare a place for you, I will come again and receive you unto myself ; that where I am, there ye may be also." And as the boy read—the joyful sound woke up the old man's smile again—twice over Herbert read the life-giving assurance, and then old Willy said, " 'T is all there, then ! just as I used to see it ! I have been trying all day, and could not get a sight of it, and I thought it was all going from me, but now I can find it 's all there for me still, and sure enough I must be getting ready for Him that 's preparing a home for me above, and not a fretting for this !" And the light and love of Heaven drank up the tears of earth, and Herbert saw the old man's smile still beaming on his face when he looked back at him from the cottage door, as he left for his home.

But the sense of the old man's sorrow had sunk into the heart of the child, and he walked slowly homeward. At last a thought sprang up in his mind, then a resolve, and with the re-solve his step grew quicker and more decided than childhood's is wont to be. On his return home he went at once to his father.

" Papa, I want to speak to you ; I can not be happy without doing something to keep old Willy's quiet for him. Papa, I think he will soon die if he is taken into a heap of people : he says he can not understand what he reads or hears when he is not alone, and all his comfort comes from his Bible—he says he shall lose it all, papa, when he loses his quiet ; and he wished he might die now while he had it still in his heart !"

" The poor old man's trouble is great," replied Mr. Clifford " and I don't wonder that he is overwhelmed at the thought of the change ; but the same Holy Spirit who puts good things into our hearts when we are alone, is able to do it no less in the midst of a crowd; and even if we did lose the recollection of the holy words we love more than any thing, our God and Saviour would not the less remember us."

"But old Willy wont know that, papa; if I tell him, he will forget it again, and then all his comfort will be **gone**! and, papa, shall I tell you what I have been thinking?"

"Well, **what, my** boy?"

"Why, there are **some verses in** the Gospel of St. John that **old** Willy is always thinking about, only he could not remember them to-day till I read them to him, about our Saviour being gone to prepare a place for him in Heaven, and coming back to take him to it: and I have been thinking, papa, that when our Saviour comes back for old Willy, if He finds we have let him be taken away where all his comfort will be gone, He will not be pleased with us?" Herbert's father remained silent. **Herbert** waited a minute, and then went on, "You see, papa, it says in the Epistle of St. James, that if poor people be destitute, and we speak well to them, but don't give them what is needful—it says, 'What doth it profit?'"

"How do you mean, that we could give **old** Willy what is needful to his comfort now?" asked Mr. Clifford.

"Because, papa, **it is** to lose all his quiet, **and** his reading, and his thoughts, that makes old Willy most unhappy; and you know, papa, what a great deal of land we have; why there is all this great park! And if I might have just one little corner **of** it—any where, or of some field—just any place, then I could build a little house **on it**; one room would do for **old** Willy; **and I** have two sovereigns and half-a-crown, **and** some shillings besides! Do you think you could let me have a little piece of land, papa?"

"How much do you suppose it would cost to build this little cottage you talk of?" asked Mr. Clifford.

"I don't know, papa, perhaps a great deal! I could help make it, I know I could; and I would sell Ruby to build it, and do without a groom—Jenks would see to Araby's being looked after. I would part with Araby sooner than have old Willy die in that way! Jenks could be sure to get him a good master"—and the tears of mingling feelings gathered in Herbert's eyes—"would not that do, papa?"

"Yes, indeed it would, my boy, less than that, I hope."

"O then, papa, do you think you will let me build it?"

"I will certainly think it over, and try to decide on what may seem best. I do not refuse your petition—God forbid I should; but I must take a little time to consider what can best be done."

And so the weight of despair was lifted at once from the child's young heart, and his buoyant spirits rose again with the chastened brightness only gathered by those who tread the path of sympathy and love. And now he went day by day with cheerful step to see old Willy; he had learned how to refresh the weary soul, and replenish the sorrowful soul—even from the weil of the Living Word; and now he would open the Book at some one of the many marks tucked in, and the attempt never failed to brighten the old man's eyes and lips with the smile of joy and peace in believing. Meanwhile old Willy, relieved by the tears he had shed at thoughts of his lady's visit, began to recover more use of his aged senses, and could manage to make out all the most familiar passages of Holy Scripture, and he bowed in meek submission to whatever might befall, while he tried to set his affections more entirely on things above, and not on things on the earth.

"Herbert, I want you," said Mr. Clifford, one morning not many days after the conversation about the cottage. Herbert ran from the lawn to his father's study.

"There, I have considered your request, and I now give you

the title deeds, by which I make you sole possessor of a piece of land suitable to your purpose; there is an old cottage upon it, and I think you will find it better worth while to repair than build; and perhaps with a little of your father's help, the ponies may not have to go!"

"O, papa! have you done it, then?" asked Herbert, taking the parchment, and looking eagerly upon it. "What does it mean, papa? I can not understand it: it says, ' **Roodes' Plot !'** I thought Roodes' Plot was where old Willy lives now?"

"So it **is**," replied Mr. Clifford, "will not that do as well as **any** other?"

"Have you bought old Willy's house for me, papa?"

"Yes, of the builder, for you, with all that belongs to it, except old Willy, who is not to be bought or sold—but he is to be kept, I suppose, if you wish to detain him, as your tenant!"

The cheek of the ministering boy turned pale with emotion, he threw his arms round his father's neck, he did not speak, he did not weep, the clinging clasp of those young arms alone expressed that moment's unutterable joy. **At length he said,** " Papa, did it cost you a great deal!"

"Not so much as I have spent, many times over, on my own pleasure; not so much as the quiet is worth to old Willy; and not so much as I would gladly consecrate in the service of that Saviour, who, I trust, is preparing a home for me and mine in Heaven, and who has said, ' Inasmuch as ye have done it unto one of **the** least of these my brethren, ye have done it unto me.' "

Herbert left his father's side, but O! how strong the bond of love and reverence with which his father's act had bound him ! **His** father had met him in his heart's first gushing sympathy with sorrow, met him and filled his hand with a gift, the priceless worth of which the child was prepared to estimate: the occasion had arisen, and he had seen his parent carry out to the full that parent's own expressed principle—money at length had been needed, and it had been freely poured forth. Such moments as those then passed through by the boy have almost a creative power to enlarge the soul and ennoble the character.

"O! mamma, O! Mary," exclaimed Herbert, running into the drawing-room, "old Willy's house is mine; papa has bought it for me, for my very own, and I shall be his landlord! I can't stop a minute till I have told him." And off bounded the boy —never foot bore tidings more swiftly; no pause was made till, breathless and panting, he stopped at old Willy's door. It was no time to delay for a knock of inquiry; he burst in at once. "O Willy! Willy! you will never have to leave your home; papa has bought it all for me, and I shall be your landlord, and make you so comfortable! Won't you be happy now?"

Old Willy was in the act of crossing the uneven floor of his room when Herbert burst in with the tidings of joy, and now he stood fixed to the spot, where Herbert first arrested his attention, and looking up with a bewildered expression, replied only, "SIR!"

"Can not you understand me, Willy?" asked Herbert, and then with slow utterance, he shouted, "Papa has bought your house and given it to me, and I shall never let you leave it all your life, but I shall be your landlord, and make you so comfortable! Can not you understand me now?"

"Ah, master, I be afeared it's but a dream after all, and I'll be a waking soon, and then it will be gone!"

"No Willy, you are not asleep, you know me? look here, it's I, Willy, I have run so hard to tell you! look, I will shake hands with you. Don't you see it's all true?"

"What, then, am I to stay in the old place after all?"

"Yes, Willy, and I am to be your landlord, and I shall make

you so comfortable, and you shall not pay me any rent, and then you can have plenty of food! Papa will not mind, I know —though he is always thinking of what will be just to others, but every body knows you have paid good rent for a bad house, and so you shall have it all back in a good house and no rent. Won't you be happy now, Willy? O! I hope you will live a very long time, that I may take care of you!"

"Praise the Lord!" exclaimed old Willy, as he lifted his hand and eyes to heaven. "Who could have thought of this?" And then, making his way to his chair, he added, "Sure, 'tis He that's preparing a place for me in heaven, has let down a drop of His love into His young child's heart, to keep me a place on earth. Who could have thought it?"

Herbert ran back to be in time for his tutor. And when old Willy had mused a little, and offered up his fervent thanksgiving, he took his stick and went round his garden, and looked again on every aged tree and young green plant—on which his eyes had never rested since the hour in which he heard that he must leave them.

How bright the summer work, how sweet the labor that opened on young Herbert now! How dear was every inch of this his landed possession!—Yet was old Willy always the first thought in all. And now workmen were summoned; bricklayers' men began with walls and floor. All had to be so managed, in the warm summer-time, so that old Willy should not have to sleep away a single night. The walls were of brick and still firm, white-washing and a little repair would do for them; but the floor was, as Herbert said, "about as bad as a floor could be." It was all laid fresh with the smoothest bricks, and Herbert, under the bricklayer's directions, must needs lay the four bricks himself under old Willy's feet beside the fire. Then came the thatching, and piles of the brightest and firmest straws were laid beside the cottage walls; and the thatchers came; and the villagers stopped as they passed, with a lingering look of surprise and pleasure, and bowed with a kindling smile to the young Squire; and the village-children gathered in a group outside—to see the old house done up at last! and Jem, when his sheep were folded, thought not of supper-time; but, kneeling beside the cottage, he laid the wet straws side by side, ready for the thatcher's hand; and Herbert must needs climb the ladder, and stuff in one handful, and smooth it down, and fix in the twig—to help at last to roof old Willy over warm! and when Jem was forced to be off the next summer day, and the work still in hand, young Smith took his place; while old **Willy sat** calmly within—one while lost in his Book, reading again of the dove, and thinking how even he had an ark found him on earth; then on to the mansions in heaven, where his heart had so long had its home; and then, falling gently asleep, he would rest and dream of the faces and tones of love that met his waking senses. And Herbert would call and say, "Only see how nice it looks, Willy!" And the old man would answer, " 'Tis wholly a wonder to see the old place, and I to stand in it after all!" And once he added, "To my thinking, 'tis making wholly fit for a king!" And Herbert remembered the words that tell how all such as old Willy are "kings unto God," and the thought blended its hallowing awe with the eagerness of a child's interest and feeling.

At last the house was finished, and Herbert stood beside old Willy, and watched the tarpauling out of sight—carried back by faithful Jem, with old Willy's duty, and Herbert's thanks, to Farmer Smith; its friendly shelter being no longer needed now, for it was vain for rain-drop or blast of **wind ever** to try again to penetrate the roof that covered old Willy. Then Snowflake stopped at the stile, and Herbert led his sister up the narrow path, and old Willy received them both. Who shall tell the joy within those cottage walls—the old man, on whose face the tear and smile were meeting; the youthful lady, in whose eyes the light of Heaven already beamed, by whom the old man had been led to seek and find a home above; and the bright boy, whose heart and life had lent their aid to preserve and enrich with comfort a home on earth, where the old man might enjoy rest and peace, with all his need supplied!

And now came the garden, every foot of which Herbert resolved should be turned to account; so he set to work diligently in the study of gardening books; and was often seen deep in discourse with Dix, one of the under-gardeners at the Hall, who took a particular interest in assisting the young Squire. Happily, Herbert's holidays began early in the summer, before the heat of the season, that he might with more freedom enjoy exercise; therefore, he had leisure now when he most needed it for the improvement of his little estate. The evening saw him planning with Dix, and the early morning plying his spade, inhaling the air's first freshness and the scent of the newly-turned earth.

"If you take my advice, sir," said Dix, "you will clear out every one of those old trees; they are all past bearing, and stand for nothing but to cumber up the ground."

"No, Dix, you do not understand; there is not a tree old Willy did not plant, or his father before him; I would not have one of them touched; why, they are all like friends to old Willy!"

"Well, sir, that's reason enough," replied Dix; "there are two things to be thought of sometimes, I believe, when one is apt to set to work upon one."

Herbert was hasting through the Park to his early labor, the second morning of his work in old Willy's garden, when at the gate he found the gamekeeper's children. "If you please,. sir," said the eldest, "father thought may be you could set us to work; we have got our spade and hoe, and Ben can pick stones." So on went Herbert with his willing helpers, and the birds sang forth their morning carol over the boys' young heads, bowed low in their service of love.

"I guess, by what I see," observed Farmer Smith to his son William, as they drove home one afternoon from market, "I guess, by what I see, that our young Squire will be likely to understand how to keep dry roofs over his tenants!"

"Ah, and warm hearts within them, too," replied William; "I will answer for that."

So passed old Willy's trouble, like a summer-evening storm, after which his setting sun shone out in clearer brightness than before.

CHAPTER XI.

The law of the Lord is perfect, converting the soul. The statutes of the Lord are right, rejoicing the heart. More to be desired are they than gold, yea than much fine gold. Sweeter also than honey and the honeycomb."—Psalm xix. 7, 8, 10.

THERE came a bright morning in June, when the farm was al'
astir with even more than usual life. The dewy mist "that
tarrieth not for man, nor waiteth for the sons of men," was lav-
ing every leaf and flower, and nourishing the ripening corn—
first of all creation in the day's work of blessing, it hung between earth and sky, preparing every herb and tree to meet
uninjured the sun's noontide ray, from which the vegetable
world **can seek no** shelter; soft and cool, it bathed all nature,
even as when it rose in Eden, obedient to its Maker's will, to
water the sinless Paradise that God had made for man. The
sun had not long risen, nor the birds long begun their morning
song to greet it; but Mrs. Smith was down; she had opened
the windows, flung back the doors, and seemed intent on raising
an early commotion, **in order to** the earlier attainment of after
order and repose. Ah! the child was expected from school
that day, and the mother would do more to welcome her in act
beforehand, than in word when she came. And the boys **were**
out early, kneeling on the dewy grass-plot beside **the** gosset-
lamb, tying a bit of blue ribbon round its **neck** that had been
treasured up for the occasion. And William came in to breakfast, with his hand full of the wood's wild-flowers, all wet with

pearly dew; and he stuck them up in a glass, all crowded and pressed together, their delicate beauty half hidden in confusion; but their witness none the less clear—their silent witness to a brother's thoughtful love. The day wore on, and Mrs. Smith had put on her afternoon gown, and all the house was in afternoon order, and Molly had put on the kettle, and Mrs. Smith made a plum-cake, the last time of baking, for tea that day and now she looked sometimes from window and sometimes from door, along the distant road by which William in the gig would bring the child home from her school.

"Just you listen," said Mrs. Smith, "I am sure I hear them!" and Mr. Smith stepped out at the front-door, and Molly went round to the back, and the yard-boy, who saw her watching, shaded his eyes and looked along the road. Yes, there they came! and the boys ran to meet them; and when the horse stopped at the garden-gate, Rose sprang from the gig into her father's arms, then ran on to her mother, and Molly stood smiling in full sight, and the yard-boy led off the horse to the stable, looking back as he went. And glad was that evening meal, for the sunbeam of the home had returned.

It was the hay-time of the year, and Rose was often in the meadows among the haymakers. One day a woman of the name of Giles said to another woman working at her side—

"My mother-in-law is very bad; I doubt if she will ever get about again."

Rose heard the words, and her ready sympathy was called forth

"Is your mother-in-law very ill?" inquired Rose.

"It seems mostly weakness," replied the woman; "but she can't do a thing for herself, and I don't believe she ever will again."

Rose said no more, but she thought of the poor old woman lying weak and helpless, and she wished she could take her

something to comfort her; she could think of a great many
things, but she dared not ask her mother, for Mrs. Smith had
not spoken to any of the old woman's family for many months.
The old woman's name was Giles; she lived by herself in a cottage under the shelter of a lonely wood, and her son, with his
wife and children, lived in a cottage that was under the same
roof as the old woman's. There were no other cottages near,
and the old woman's son had been convicted of poaching in
the wood behind his cottage. Farmer Smith had dismissed
the man from his employ; and, if Mrs. Smith had had her way,
the whole family would have been denied employment also;
but farmer Smith refused to send away the wife and children
for the man's fault, so they still worked on the farm when
work could be found them; but Mrs. Smith refused to take any
notice of any of the family. Therefore Rose knew it was hopeless to ask her mother for any comforts for widow Giles. But
Rose had in her possession a treasured shilling, given by her
father in one of his visits to her at school: she had thought of
a great many things that might be bought with this shilling
when she went to the town with her father—which she was
always allowed to do once every holiday-time; but she had not
yet decided on which of all these thought-of purchases would
be best; and now it occurred to her that she might, with her
shilling, buy a quarter of a pound of tea for poor widow Giles.
Rose no sooner thought of this, than she resolved it should be
her final choice. So she went off in search of William, to
consult him as to how this quarter of a pound of tea could be
obtained from the town. William told her that they **were**
going to send in the next morning; so Rose intrusted him
with her shilling; and by twelve o'clock the next day Rose
was in possession of the tea from Mr. Mansfield's shop, done up
in its double paper, of white inside, and blue outside. Rose

managed to get it into her pocket, and felt a great deal richer, now that her shilling was turned into so much comfort for the poor old woman. But now Rose wanted to take it herself, and she was afraid her mother would not let her go to the cottage; but she remembered what her minister at school had said— "Ask, and it shall be given you." And she thought it must be right to go and see the poor old woman ; and when she had asked in heaven, she got courage then to ask on earth. Those who go oftenest to heaven in prayer, are sure to · have most holy courage on earth. So after dinner little Rose said—

"Mother, widow Giles is very ill ; they don't think she will ever get about again."

Mrs. Smith only replied, " I don't know any thing about those Gileses, I am sure ; I only know if I had my way, they would never be at work on this farm again !"

"I thought, mother, I should like **to go and ask poor old** widow Giles how she is ?"

" And what would be the use of that ? she won't be any thing the better for your asking how she is ?"

"No, mother; only then she would know we did think about her."

" Think about her !" replied Mrs. Smith ; " that's a family that **don't** deserve thinking about, after all your father's done for them, and the man worked on this farm from a boy, and his father before him, and then he must turn against it all, and go a-poaching !"

" But if widow Giles should die, mother, and we did not speak a word to her, she would think you had not forgiven her."

" I don't know any thing about forgiveness, I am sure," replied Mrs. Smith, "till people show a little sorrow for their ingratitude."

" But, mother, our minister at school says, that it's when people are forgiven that they are often most sorry."

" Well, child, I never heard such preaching as you seem to

hear; I only know 'tis a fine thing to have good schooling to help you to understand what it is you do hear; for my part, I have been all my life to church, and I never understood our minister's preaching—not to go on by it in that way."

"I don't think it's schooling, mother, makes me understand. Our minister does not preach about what we learn at school; he preaches all out of the Bible, and so plain that any body must understand him."

"Well, child, it's a **fine thing** to understand, let it be as it will; that's all I have got to say."

"May I go then, mother?"

"O, please yourself; it makes no difference to me."

Little Rose set off, at first gravely and slowly, under the chilling shadow of her mother's darkened heart, but she soon felt again the sunshine of heavenly truth and love in which **her** own young spirit lived, and then with quicker step she climbed the stiles, passed through the hay-meadows, and along the lane, **where the sun** poured his sultry heat upon her, till she reached the shadow of the lonely wood. She stood at the widow's door and knocked—no answer came; so she knocked again, then a feeble, anxious voice said, "Who is there?"

"It's me—it's Rose!" said the little girl.

"O dear, I am so glad!" said the poor old woman; "but I'm locked in; they have got the key in the hay-meadows."

"I will run back and get it!" shouted little Rose; so back she turned, forgetful of the summer's sun, running fast along the high unsheltered lane, back over the stiles and through the meadows, to where the women turned the fresh-cut grass.

"I can't get in to widow Giles; and she says you have got the key," said Rose to the daughter-in-law.

"Yes, I always lock the door, for fear any thing should ter- rify her; she lies so helpless."

" Could not some one stay with her ?" asked Rose.

" No, there is no one to stay, except the children," replied the daughter-in-law, " and they are a deal more trouble than comfort when one's well ; and I am sure they would be ten times orse to bear in sickness."

" Could you not teach them to be kind ?" asked Rose.

" Well, as for that, I don't know that they are bad dispositioned ; but children will be children—at least, I have always found it so."

Then off set little Rose with the great key from the daughter-in-law's pocket, and soon stood again before the helpless old woman's door ; she put in the key, turned it round, opened the door, and went into the desolate room. No hand of affection had been there to leave the trace of its skill around—all looked comfortless and dreary. Rose went up to the bed, and said, " I come to ask you how you are ; I did n't know you were ill till yesterday."

The poor old woman wept.

" I am so sorry you are ill !" said little Rose.

" O, dear young creature, who would have thought of seeing **you** ! They say Mrs. Smith will never so much as look at one **of us** again ; perhaps she does not know you are come ; does **she,** dear ?"

" O yes ; I asked mother if I might," replied Rose, " and look here, I have brought you a whole quarter of a pound of tea !"

" Bless you, dear. O, if I could but think your family had forgiven us ! but they say it 's no use to look for it ; they say your mother never really forgives any body that has once got wrong. I am sure if man be so far from forgiveness, I don't know how it will be with us when we come before God, for sure He has most right to be angry. I lie here thinking of that, and it 's a dead weight on my heart,"—and the poor old woman wept on. The tide of anguish was much for a child to stem; but the infant of days who stands at the feet of Him whose word is Peace, may so receive of Him as by its feeble utterance to soothe the storm into a calm.

"I am sure God will forgive you if you ask Him," said little Rose; "our minister at school preached about the wicked people who crucified our Saviour being forgiven, and made so sorry for what they had done, and quite **different; so I know God will** forgive **you, if you ask** Him."

" Ah ! dear ; but how can I know it ?" asked the old woman.

" I will read it to you out of the Bible," said little Rose, " and **then you** will **know it ;** our minister preached it all out of the second chapter of Acts. Have you got a Bible for me to read it in ?"

" No, dear, I can't read ; my son has one, but it's locked up in his house."

" Then I will bring my own Bible next time I come ; father **has bought** me such a beautiful Bible, and I always take it **to** church ; so I know all where our minister at school preaches from."

" Ah ! dear, I wish enough you could read to me, for I lie here, and there's never a creature to tell **me** a word of advice or comfort. I know I am **going, and there's** no one to tell me what to do, or which way **to look.** O ! 'tis a dreadful feeling, dear !"

"**I** will come—I will **promise to** come !" said little Rose ; "and I can say you a whole chapter now, if you like, without the Bible. Mercy Jones tells me the chapters Miss Clifford chooses **for her to** learn, and then **I** learn them, as **many of them as I** can. I can say the whole of the fifty-fifth chapter of Isaiah !" Then Rose began : " Ho every one that thirsteth, come ye to the waters, and he that hath no money, come ye, buy and eat; yea, come buy wine and milk, without money and without price." The old woman's eye was fixed upon the child, as death drinking in the balm of life; and when she reached the words, " Let the wicked forsake his way, and the unrighteous man his thoughts, and let him return unto the Lord, and He will have mercy upon him; and to our God, for He will abundantly pardon," the old woman asked, " Does it say like that in the Bible?"

" Yes, it's all just as I say it; I know it quite perfect," replied little Rose.

" Then there's hope for me!" exclaimed the poor old woman; and, lying back with closed eyelids, she said no more, and the child went on.

" That's all," said little Rose, when she had ended the chapter, " but I will come to-morrow, if I can, and read you where our minister preached about the people who crucified our Saviour."

" O do, dear; words like them are life from the dead; why, it's like as if an angel had come to bring me comfort!"

" Have you any thing to take?" asked Rose.

" No, dear; I was ready to faint away before you came, only those words so revived me up again! but I must wait, for there is n't a bit of kindling; if there had been, I think I must have tried to heat a little water to make a drop of tea to sop this crust in; I could not eat it dry, nor touch the cheese, and they went off in such a hurry, that was all they had to leave me, and the day seems terrible long, when they only come home once in the noon-time."

Rose looked at the fireplace; there was a little coal by the side, and a match-box over the mantel-piece, but neither stick nor straw.

" I know what I can do!" exclaimed Rose; " there is sure to be dry wood enough under the trees to make a fire in no time." So, lifting up her frock, she hastened out, stooping under the shel-

tering trees heavy with their summer foliage, picking up the little branches, sere and dry with sultry heat : when her frock was well filled she returned ; then kneeling down, her little hands soon kindled up a fire. But now there was no water— a minute more and Rose stood on the lowest step cut out in the field-side, dipping a pitcher in the pond, then back again to the cottage ; she poured just enough water into the tea-kettle to make **one** tea-pot full of tea, then finding an old fork **in** the cupboard, she toasted the dry piece of bread while the water was heating ; then she found **a** small basin, into which she **broke up** the toast, and **sprinkled** some brown sugar from **the cupboard. By this** time the water boiled, and Rose, from **her** own quarter-of-a-pound, made a tea-pot of good tea ; then filling up the kettle, she hung it again over the fire, and pour-ing out the fragrant tea, she took it to the bed-side, while the old woman's look on her was blessing. When Rose **saw how** the dying woman, faint and parched with **thirst,** received and fed on what her hand prepared, could she fail **to learn** how blessed was the **power** to help and **comfort?** She **waited** till the repast was finished, then, when the water boiled again, she filled the tea-pot up, and, setting it with the basin on a chair close by the bed, where the old **woman** could reach it, she tied **on** her bonnet, and, locking **the door, ran** home—down the same open lane, over the **stiles, and** across the hay meadows, leaving the **key** with **the** daughter-in-law, and reached the farm just as preparations **for** the family tea were beginning— calm, and bright, and sweet was that summer evening **to the** ministering child.

Day after day, when Rose could be spared **from her** home, she crossed the meadows, and trod **the lane to the lonely** wood, with her precious Bible hanging **in its little** bag upon her arm, **she sat** by the **old woman's bed and** read to her the words which lead the heart to Jesus. O, happy England! where the youngest and the poorest may as freely as the oldest and the richest gather the healing leaves of that Tree of Life—the Word of God—where it grows within the reach of all, and children may turn from their play and bear its seed of eternal life to the dying, and they may receive it and live for **ever!** And happy those who are found obedient to the injunction, "Freely ye have received, freely give!"

"Don't you like strawberries, child?" said Mrs. Smith, as Rose was gathering peas one morning near the strawberry-bed with her mother.

"Yes, mother, may I gather some?"

"You may as well have them as the birds, I suppose!"

"May I have some every day, mother?"

"Yes, I have no objection."

"How many, mother? may I have my little basket full every day?"

"Yes, I tell you; why do you ask a dozen questions, when one would do?"

"Shall I gather you some, mother?"

"No, thank you; when I eat strawberries, I like to gather them for myself!"

"Shall I gather father **some** of a day?"

"**That's as he** pleases!" replied Mrs. Smith, and Rose went silently on with the gathering of peas.

That day before dinner, Rose ran down the straight garden path, and filling her own little basket she set it safe and cool under the lilac-tree; and **then** gathering a plateful, she brought them **in** and put them **away in the** pantry till after dinner **when** her father sat down in his arm-chair before going out to his business again, then Rose brought out the plate of strawberries and offered them to him.

" Thank you, my dear," said her father, " that 's the way to enjoy strawberries—to have you gather them for me, and be able to sit still and eat them ! I have no time to stop after them while I am out."

When Rose **was** free to **run** off for her walk, she hastened down the garden path to the lilac-tree, and covering some of its green leaves over the fruit, to keep it cool from the afternoon sun, she **set** off, with her Bible on her arm, and her basket in her hand, **to** the cottage of the poor **dying** woman.

When widow Giles saw the strawberries, she exclaimed, " Why, if **it is** n't the very thing I have longed for more than **meat or** drink ! I thought there seemed nothing so tempting **as a** strawberry ; but if one has a penny to spend on such comforts, there is no one going to the town this busy time to lay it out for one, so I had no thought to see any." Meanwhile, Rose had spread the green leaves on the old woman's sheet, and laid a bright red strawberry on each, and the cool fruit was drink, and meat, and reviving medicine to the dying woman.

" There," said Rose, " I will put all these in a plate where you can reach them, and the leaves over them, **and** you may eat them all up before I come **again, because then I shall** bring you some more !"

The scarlet berries were piled **up, day** after day, by the little maiden, with eyes **of** gladness and hands of careful love ; the daily transfer of her whole portion involved no self-denial to her—she had tasted the " MORE BLESSED TO GIVE," and having drunk at that mountain-rill of higher, purer pleasure, **it** was **no** effort to her not to return to the stagnant pool of **self.** In her young ministry of love, self was lost sight of, not by the attempt to subdue it, but by finding within her reach a far higher principle, whose exercise had power to change the touching aspect of want, and sorrow, and tears—into comfort, and joy, and smiles. A child naturally loves sunshine, and is impatient of the cloud; let them early learn their Heaven-intrusted power to brighten **earth's** gloom with the sunbeam of love, to span its dark sky with the rainbow of hope, and many a child would turn to its exercise who little dreams of it now. And is it not **well** to lead childhood onward and upward, unconscious of effort, wherever possible?—the call **for** resolute self-denial is sure to come soon and often enough, but every step gained unconsciously **is** vantage ground, leaving the points of effort higher, and involving further advance.

At last the day came for Rose to go to the town with her father: the long drive, and to walk about the town with him would be very pleasant, **but poor** widow Giles would want her strawberries! **So** Rose **was up and** among the straw-berries before breakfast-time; she **filled her** basket, covered it with leaves, and **set it** under the **lilac-tree:** then when William came in to breakfast, she took his hand and led him down the garden-path, and holding back the **lilac** branches showed him the little basket, and asked him if he would just take them to poor widow Giles, who would be looking for them?

"**Yes, I will** see to that," said **William.** So Rose ran to breakfast, and then off in high spirits with her father, and Wil-liam no **sooner saw** them started than **he** hastened back to the tree, and carried the little basket at once to widow Giles.

Rose came home as full of delight **as** she went out, having a great variety of things to tell, **which** her mother heard with pa-tience, and her brothers with sympathizing interest.

"Did you take my strawberries?" whispered Rose, the **first** opportunity, to William.

"**Yes,** that I did, and I was glad enough you sent me, for the poor old woman had fretted herself, thinking I was as hurt with them all as mother ! and I am sure I had not stayed away from ill-will, and if I had known she worried about it, I would have gone in to speak to her any day, but I never gave it a thought !"

" O dear !" said the old woman, clasping her hands, as Rose went in the next day, " I think I can die now ! I little thought what a day I was to have yesterday !"

" What happened ?" asked Rose.

" Why, dear, first in the morning part came Master William. It was fortunate enough my daughter-in-law was home next door washing, so I was not locked in ; he came in at the door just as he used ! O, dear, I never thought to see him again, and I loved him like one of my own, having had so much to do in the nursing of him ! He stayed some time, and I saw I was all right with him, and then I thought I could rest—for I seemed to think there could never be a hope with your mother. Well, I was lying here in the afternoon-time, thinking how he came in and spoke so pleasant—when who should I see come up but your mother herself !"

" My mother ?" exclaimed Rose.

" Yes, dear, what, didn't she tell you ? Yes, she came her-self ! I was altogether overcome by the sight of her, and burst out a crying, and, to my thinking, she spoke kinder than ever, and she brought me a bottle of her own wine. No medicine could have done me the good of her kind words ! I have felt a wonderful comfort ever since. It seems to me as if Him you read to me about, had sent me a pardon for this world and the next. I had been getting hold of a hope for the next ever since that first day you came, but I thought it was all over for this, but now I see He that can give the one can give the other too. And now that dread I had is wholly gone, and I don't seem to see a fear now—looking to Him you read of to me !"

After a few more peaceful days, widow Giles died. They laid her body in the village churchyard, and in the evening, when all the mourners and the people were gone, Rose went alone·and stood by the grave, and she looked up to the calm blue sky, and felt as if the blessing of that poor old widow fell down upon her from Heaven. So passed away her holidays, and Rose went **back to her** school.

But one little girl there was who had done with school, who had learned her last lesson, and was gone Home for ever— **Home,** not to a house made with hands, which trouble, and sorrow, and sickness, and death can enter ; but Home to a House not made with hands, **a mansion in** the Heavens, where darkness and **evil cannot** come, **where** there is no more crying, or sorrow, or pain, or death, but God wipes away all tears, and every one is happy for ever. It was not little Mercy who had done with school—no, she was never absent from her place there, she had many sweet lessons yet to learn, and some hard ones too. It was not little Jane—no, her school-days had not yet begun, she still learned at **her mother's** side, and dropped with patient love her weekly penny into **her** little box to clothe the orphan Mercy. **It was not** poor Patience—no, she had not learned the first and **best of all** Heavenly lessons yet, that GOD IS LOVE : she was to **learn this lesson,** but she had not learned **it yet, so** she must still **be kept in** this world at school to learn the lessons that can only be learned here. Who then was the happy child who had done with school for **ever, and was** sent for Home ? It was little Ruth. Heaven's shining gate often opens, and the holy angels come down to fetch little children **home to** their Heavenly Father **long** before those little children expected to be sent for. Then **let every** child **try** to please God in all things, as little Ruth did, because no one knows how soon the call may come. The spring had been and the summer followed, but they had brought no bloom of life to the cheeks of little Ruth. She was sitting in her comfortless home one Saturday afternoon with her Bible on her knee, learning her texts of Scripture, when her **father** came in : something had made him angry, **and** little Ruth **trembled** at the words he spoke. " Oh, father," she gently said, "we must not take God's holy name in vain !"

" And why not ?" said her father, turning sharply **to** the little girl, as she sat on her stool near the sleeping infant.

" Because, father, the Bible says so."

" And what 's the Bible to me, I should like to know ?" asked her father.

" O, it 's just every thing, if you did but know it, father; it 's just every thing to me !"

And little Ruth looked up, her eyes filled with tears, **and her** father-in-law was looking down on her, and the sight of her pale sweet face, the Bible open on her knee, and her trembling voice declaring it was every thing to her, was too much for the hardened man ; the thought broke in upon him, how **he** had left her no other comfort ; and he went out **of the** house unable to look at the child **again.** **He never rested till** he found work, and then he toiled **as if he felt he had a life to save ;** but it was too late for little Ruth ! she **seemed to** have done with earth **from** that Saturday evening **when she** bore her young witness to **the Word** of God, and when **the** next Saturday came she lay on her **pillow** unable **to speak or** move ; her father-in-law hurried **home** with his earnings, and stooping over her, said, " I have **brought** all my wages, you shall have every thing now !"

Yes, little Ruth would have every thing now—for in the home where blessed children dwell in Heaven, **no** want can ever come. There God our Father, and Jesus **our** Saviour and Shepherd,

8

and the Holy Spirit dwell: there the holy angels live; and all is love, and joy, and gladness for ever. Miss Wilson had been several times to see the little girl, and now she came again, but the dying child had done with earth, she did not know her friend, though her eyes were open, and she was looking upward.

"Sure she sees the angels coming for her!" said her weeping mother, "see how she smiles—O! what a heavenly smile!"

But no one knows the blessed sights that God's departing children see! and with that smile upon her lips, little Ruth passed away. Little Ruth, who loved the Saviour, and prayed to Him; who loved God's Holy Word, and tried to please Him; little Ruth, her mother's comfort, whom her little sister and infant brother loved so much; the favorite of her school-fellows; and one of the best children in the school: little Ruth, the friend and teacher of the poor dying child, passed away from earth! Little Ruth was never forgotten by any of her friends; nor by her father-in-law—she was gone far away out of his sight, but he could not forget; he took her Bible and tried to follow its words as she had done; and he took care of his two poor little children, and made their home and their mother's happy.

> —"Seated on the tomb, Faith's angel
> Says, 'Ye are not there,'
> Where then are ye? With the Saviour,
> Blest, for ever blest are ye;
> 'Mid the sinless little children
> Who have heard His 'COME TO ME!'
> 'Yond the shades of Death's dark valley,
> Now ye lean upon His breast—
> Where the wicked cease from troubling,
> And the weary are at rest."

CHAPTER XII.

"Let all your things be done with charity."—1 Cor. xvi. 14.

"PAPA" said Herbert one day at dinner, as the year was closing in, "I have long made up my mind to give Jem some valuable present this Christmas, and to-day I have hit on the right thing. It will cost £3, but I can manage it, because I have had the thought so long in my mind that I have been saving up my money for it; and now I am so delighted to have found the very thing! Can you guess, papa?"

"I am almost afraid to try," said Mr. Clifford, smiling; "for **sometimes your** right thing and mine do not recognize each other at first sight, and I may disappoint you."

"Do try, papa, this is not charity, you know; so there is not the same fear; and you must think it a capital thing, for Jem is not the easiest person to find out a right sort of a present for; is he, papa?"

"No, perhaps not," replied Mr. Clifford, "because his wants do not extend beyond life's necessaries, and his own honest hands provide those."

"Yes, papa, and my present is something to do with life's necessaries—something to do with Jem's work! Now, papa, **can you guess?**"

"Something to do with Jem's work, and to cost **£3**," said Mr Clifford, in a **tone** of reflection. "**I confess I** am puzzled; I did not think Jem made use of such costly assistance in his simple labor."

"No, papa; it's something quite new to Jem; such a thing as he never had, or thought of having. I am full of the suprise it will be to him!"

"Is it a watch?" asked Mr. Clifford, doubtfully.

"No, not a watch; I could not get any thing of a watch for £3; could I, papa? Besides which, Jem's watch is in the sky; he always keeps time by the sun, without any trouble of winding up!"

"Is it some implement of husbandry?" asked Mr. Clifford.

"No, papa, Jem is a shepherd! only Mr. Smith sometimes puts him to other work when he wants him."

"Is it a shepherd's dog of some superior excellence?"

"No, papa, Jem has hard work to keep his old mother and little niece, he could not keep a dog! though to be sure that is a good idea."

"Then I confess I must give it up," said Mr. Clifford.

"Are you sure you can not guess, papa?"

"Yes, I give up in despair."

"Well then, papa, I have seen the most perfect collection of all sorts of carpenter's tools in a box for £3; every thing you could possibly want! Won't it be just the present to give to one who does every thing for himself?"

"Is Jem a carpenter, then?"

"No, papa, he is a shepherd! but he does every thing for himself; so that there must often be carpenter's work wanted."

"I think you will certainly make him a little work, in keeping his tools bright; for I am afraid his use of them will not be likely to do it."

"Then you do not think that it would be a nice present for him, papa?"

"No, I can not say I do. I think when you give your friend a present, it is a pity to give him a trouble. I have no doubt you would find that Jem is quite as independent of carpenter's tools, as he is of carpenter's aid in his mending and making."

" Can you think of any thing then, papa ?" asked Herbert, in a tone whose gladness was gone.

" Why not give him a good winter great-coat ?   I should say that would be far better."

" No, papa, I don't want my first present to Jem to be clothes ! I don't **want it to be like** charity !   **I want him to see** I have thought about how best to please him."

" And do you think that charity **admits no** thought of how **best** to please **?**"

" No, papa, I don't think that ; only I don't want my present to Jem to look like charity."

" What then do you suppose charity to be ?   Let us have your explanation of the word."

" O papa, every body knows what charity is ? though **I am** pretty sure nobody knows what a mess they may make of **it** till they try at it, for it 's ten to one if they hit it right when they do try !"

" But what do you explain this same charity to mean **?**"

" Well, papa, one can not always explain what every body knows, but of course it 's doing for the poor !"

" Very true, my boy ; only remember, there is no one **on** earth so rich as not to need this heaven-born charity !"

" What do **you mean, papa ? you don't** want charity !"

" Yes, dear Herbert, I do ; ana so do you.   To be poor in money, is but one point **of poverty** ; just as to be rich in money, is but one point of riches."

" What then are you poor in, papa ?"

" I am so poor, that there is no one I have any intercourse with who may not make me richer."

" What do you **mean,** papa ?"

" I mean that my earthly comfort depends more upon that
spirit of love or charity, in those with whom I am associated,
than upon any thing else; and this is true of all. One of the
chief reasons of the happiness of heaven is, that there every
thought and feeling, every word and action, is governed by
CHARITY ! And the nearer you come to the practice of this
spirit of love on earth, the nearer you come to the spirit of
heaven."

" But then, papa, if I could think of any thing to please Jem
more than a coat, I might give it to him, and yet not go against
charity ?"

" Yes, certainly, whatever most proves your thoughtful interest in others, and care for them, is the best and brightest
exercise of charity."

Soon after this, Herbert was left alone with his mother and
sister, when he said sorrowfully, " I declare I feel ready to cry !
I never felt so sure before about having hit on the right thing ;
and now papa thinks it quite wrong ; and papa comes down so
grave upon one, that the thing never looks the same afterward
—I don't care about that box of tools the least now !"

" Did old Willy's cottage not look the same when papa had
made it yours ?" asked Miss Clifford.

" O, Mary, you know that was the best thing that ever
happened to me in all my life ! Of course I did not mean
that."

" Then perhaps you only mean that papa shows you your
mistakes ?"

" I don't know, I am sure," replied Herbert ; " but I often get
so full of a thing, and it looks as pleasant as possible, and then
I am off to talk to papa about it, and he makes it look as dull
as can be. I wonder how it is that I can so seldom think like
papa beforehand !"

"Shall I try and help you to understand how it is?" asked Mrs. Clifford.

"Yes, mamma, I wish you would."

"You have often been out early these last nine months; have you not observed how different objects looked to you in the misty light of the morning, how large some small things seemed, and how the dew-drops looked like diamonds in the bright sunbeams, and the grass you walked upon sparkled with countless points of brilliant light and color?"

"Yes, mamma, but what of that?"

"That is like your early morning of life, my child, when, for want of clearer knowledge, many objects appear to you different to what they really are. But, your father has reached life's afternoon, when the misty light deceives no longer, and the diamond dew-drops are gone from the earth, and therefore when he puts things in the clearer light of his fuller knowledge, they appear to you very different."

"Well, mamma, I wish things were always bright! I am sure it is much pleasanter when they are."

"They will be always bright in heaven, my dear boy; no light of fuller knowledge can ever change the forms and hues of heaven—except to increase their beauty. The day's loveliest dawn, and your life's glowing morning, are but to picture to you a little of heaven. But there the bloom and the fragrance, the glory and the freshness, never pass away. If we could always keep earth's brightness here, we might seek less earnestly for that inheritance which can not fade away."

"I know you must be right, mamma, but still it seems sad to have things that looked so pleasant changed."

"Many true things are sad on earth, dear Herbert. He who is Himself the Truth—your Heavenly Counselor was a Man of sorrows here on earth; but, in heaven, Truth wears only her beautiful garments,' and will be known by all who dwell there, only in her brightness for **ever**."

"**It was** Herbert's Christmas holidays, and the next morning, when he went into **his** sister's room after breakfast, to read to her, he was still feeling his disappointment about the box of tools.

"**It is** a pity about Jem, is it not, Mary ?   I did want to give him something that might always please him."

"But why need you give up the hope to do so still ?" asked his sister; "is **a** box **of** tools the end of all useful and pleasant things ?"

"No, but for Jem it is not easy to find any thing really pleas. ant to give; now I have given up the tools, I can not think of a single thing."

"Shall **I** tell you what I think would please him more than **any** other present ?"

"O yes, do tell me—you always bring back one's hope even when it 's quite gone—do tell **me** directly !"

"You **know** how fond Jem is of his dear old mother; did you not hear of his saving up a little money he **had** for her, to buy her a winter gown ?"

"No."

"He did so, and she was delighted with her son's present, as **you can** suppose; and I have often thought, if the dear old wo- man **could have one** of those bright red cloaks, it would keep her warm all her life; she would look **the very** picture of com- fort in it; and Jem would hardly know how **to** be happy enough. **And** you could send for **Jem** on Christmas eve, and let it be his Christmas morning present **to** his mother."

"That will **be** the **very thing !**" exclaimed Herbert, with de- light as fresh as ever. "I will **run and** tell papa !"

Mr. Clifford thought that nothing could be better, and Mrs, Clifford approved **it as** the best thing possible; so Herbert returned to his sister, and the rainbow-hues around the gift were bright again, as when his own heart first framed the thought—bright in truth's own radiance now. After Herbert had talked with his sister a while about the red cloak—where it was to be bought, and how it was all to be managed—he sat silent for a moment on the side of the sofa where she was lying, and then said, "**Did you hear** what mamma was saying yesterday about **my** seeing all things in the morning's misty light; and papa **seeing them as they** really were ?"

" Yes, dear, I heard it all."

" Well, then, I can not make it out! because you always bring **the brightness** back when it 's all gone, and if you think differently from me, yet you don't take the brightness away, you only put it on something else, and yet papa is sure to say you are quite right ?"

Herbert looked inquiringly at his sister; the **tear started to** her **eyes,** but **she** did not speak.

" Dear Mary ! what makes you sad ?" asked Herbert.

" Only the thought that perhaps if I answered **your** question, it **would make** you sad, **dear."**

" O, no ; do tell me if you can ; I want to know !"

" Well, then, in the morning, **as mamma** said, the dew lies thick upon the grass, and leaves, and flowers, and the soft mist half conceals many objects; but the dew and the mist are only of earth, **and** the sun's fuller rays absorb the dew and the mist, and they **are gone : and** then comes the clear day, when every thing appears **as it** is in itself : and then, dear Herbert, what **next ?"**

" The evening comes next," replied Herbert.

" Yes, the setting sun--and then the brightness is all from Heaven ! You see the golden sunbeams fall, and they light **up all they touch ; but they do not** make any thing appear

what it is not; you see all things truly, only you see them
gilded by light from Heaven—a softer, stiller brightness than
the morning's dazzling light, a brightness that lasts till the sun
has set; and that, dear Herbert, is the brightness in which I
see all things; and because it does not mislead, papa agrees
with it."

"What do you mean, Mary?"

"I mean that my sun is setting, and I can not help but see
the brightness it casts on all around me."

"But what do you mean by your sun setting, Mary?"

"I mean that I believe I am dying to earth, but rising to God
and Heaven."

"O, Mary, you can not mean *dying!* you know you were ill
last winter, and then you got well again—almost well; did you
not? And so you will this time, indeed you will! God would
not take away the happiness from every thing, and it would be
all gone if you were gone!"

"If we put our happiness in any thing more than in God, He
may take it away, dear Herbert, if He loves us, to teach us to
find it first in Himself."

"I will try to find my happiness still more in God, if you stay
with us, Mary."

"Perhaps God may teach you to do so, by taking me away!"

"O, no, I could not learn any thing then!"

"We do not know what we can learn, or how we can learn
best, till God teaches us, dear."

"I am sure papa and mamma can not have such a thought
bout you, Mary; they could never bear it!"

"Papa and mamma will try to bear God's will, whatever it
may be; and will not you try also, dear Herbert?"

"How do you know that papa and mamma have such a
thought?"

" Because we often talk about it."

" I never hear them !"

" No, they do not like to tell you, for fear of making you unhappy ; but I wanted you to know, that we might talk together of that blessed home to which I am going."

"Do you like to think of going, then ?"

" O yes, I love Heaven more than earth, and my God and Saviour more than all beside ! I used to be afraid that when I was gone, papa and mamma would have no companion to walk with them in the way to Heaven, and my poor people no earthly comforter ; but you took away these fears, dear Herbert ; or rather God took them away by you ; and now, instead of tears of sadness, you make me shed tears of joy sometimes."

" But, dear Mary, if you were to stay, I could help you do all this. I am sure the doctor can not think you so ill, because he has told me so many times that you were better ! If he says that he thinks you will get well, will you think so too ?"

Miss Clifford smiled, and asked : " If you could see the gate of our own home before you, could you easily believe any one who told you that a long journey still lay between you and it ?"

" What do you mean, Mary ?"

" I mean that I see the better world, and but a step between me and it !"

" But you may see it, Mary, if you will not go to it yet ! If the doctor says you will get well, will you believe it ?"

" He can not say that, dear."

" But if he says he thinks you will, will you try and get well?"

" Yes, I will promise you, whatever the doctor may say, that I will do any thing I can that might help my recovery."

" I will go off directly then and ask him !" exclaimed Herbert.

" No, stop, dear Herbert, do not go !" but the boy was gone.

" Papa, I want to go to the town, if you have no objection ; I shall soon be back."

" No, I have not any objection," Mr. Clifford replied ; and Herbert was soon on the road. He requested to speak with the medical man, who quickly appeared, asking, hastily, whether " Miss Clifford were worse ?"

" No, I hope she is better," replied Herbert, " but I want you to tell me whether you do not think she will get well when the spring time comes ?"

" It is not always easy to speak positively on such subjects," replied the doctor.

" But you do think my sister may get well again, as she did last summer, do you not ?"

" Yes, I do think that, with the greatest care, Miss Clifford may recover again as she did last summer."

" Thank you, sir, I could not rest without asking you." And Araby bore his young master swiftly home again.

" Dear Mary, I was right ! the doctor does think that with the greatest care you may recover again, as you did last summer ! Will you not think so too ?"

" Yes, I will think that, dear !"

" And then, when you have recovered, there is no reason why you should be ill again, more than any one else who has been ill and recovers !"

Miss Clifford only smiled, and Herbert did not read the meaning of that smile.

Herbert had put away all fear of losing his sister from his mind : but the momentary distress of the thought had made him cling closer to her than ever. He talked with her still oftener, and whatever gave rise to her words they continually ended in Heaven—till her young brother learned to feel the better world a familiar place to him, and a home in which, while still on earth, thought and affection, as well as hope, found their true resting-place. He talked with her—and the sweet links of hallowed sympathy that bound her to the poor, drew **him** also to them, in the tie of true feeling and warm interest. **He** read to her from the holy Scriptures—and the clear undoubting words of one who had learned almost her last lesson of God's unfolded truth, led him on in the understanding of that which was the Light of Life to her.

A few days before Christmas, **Herbert was** sitting talking with old Willy **on the stool** opposite the old man's chair, beside the blazing hearth, when suddenly his eye fell again on a large hole he had often observed in old Willy's coat.

" I wish, Willy, you had a new coat; you have worn this old thing ever since I knew you, and it is getting quite a rag."

" Ay, master, I can't count the years I've worn it, and for certain it's none the better for use. I have a Sunday coat that I bought the last harvest I made—and that's some years **agone** now—but if I take my Sunday dress for common days, I **shall** never look decent on the Sabbath then."

" What! have you not had a new coat **since you could go** harvesting, Willy ?"

" No, master, that was the last time **I earned a** bit of gold, and I'm never like to earn so much as silver now. No, I have stood king of the reapers many a year, and led them on with green bough and sickle, but that's all over now, and I am thinking **of** Him that **is** coming, as it says in my Book, ' to gather His wheat into the garner, and to burn up the chaff with unquenchable fire'—O that I may be found a true grain then !"

Herbert sat silent, pondering on how **it** might be possible to **get a new** coat for old Willy. The bright red cloak would take all his store, and was more important than even old Willy's coat. The old man too seemed musing upon something; at last he first broke silence, saying, "It's no time, I say, for me to be thinking of finery, when I can **never** get up money enough, for such **a** place as this **is about** me. I've tried hard these last quarters to make up **a** little above what I paid him that kept it so bad, but I could n't live **on** less, and so it's just about the same **as** I saved up before; but it don't seem the thing to have the old place done up like this, and yet pay no more for the comfort **of** it."

" Why, Willy, you are not to pay me any rent! **I told you** so at first; don't you remember ?"

"O, yes, master, I remember how you told me I was to stay in the old place; I can never forget the wonder of that !"

"And not to pay any rent, Willy !"

" Not pay any rent ?" repeated old Willy, in a tone of inquiring astonishment. **"Yes,** master, I hope I'll not turn like that against such goodness **as yours; I have saved it** all up as careful as I could !"

" Now, Willy," said Herbert, standing up **in despair,** "I don't mean to let you pay me any rent; so all the money you have saved up—is yours! Can you understand that ?"

" Yes, master, I can UNDERSTAND, **but I** can't see the thing to be right for all that !"

" Never mind, Willy, it must be right if I say it, because **it's** my **house;** and I want you to be happy in it, and to live a long while ! I will tell you what papa says—papa says that TO GIVE is the BIRTHRIGHT of every child of God! so it is quite right for me to give you back your rent. And now, Willy, you can buy a new coat with that money **you** have saved up ! Do you understand !"

" Yes, master, I understand, and thank **you too."**

Herbert could **not** help thinking what a picture of comfort old Willy would look at his fireside, in his pretty cottage, if he had but a nice coat; so in two days' time, he called in again to see if it was bought.

" Well, Willy, have you got a new coat ?"

" No, master, I can't say I have as yet."

" But you must make haste, Willy ;—you know you have money enough now."

" Yes, master, that 's true that I have, but there is a thought come in my mind that hinders me a bit."

" **What thought, Willy ?**"

" Why, my Jem, as I call him, was in here a few evenings ago, and he was telling me how he had been over to a meeting holden some where in these parts, where they told about places a longful way off, where they have not so much as a Bible ! and I have been thinking how I sit reading here all about those mansions in Heaven, and Him that 's the way to them ; and out there, in such places as those he heard speak of, they can't so much as get sight of the Book !"

" Well, Willy, that 's all true ; but what of that ?"

" Ah, master, you see I 'm just thinking it 's a deal of money to spend on a coat for an old man like me, that may never live to want it ; so I was thinking to get this patched up a bit, to .ook tidy like for me ; and then, maybe, if I could get to them just that money you give back to me, why they might get a Bible out there, to show them the true way to Heaven !"

" O, Willy, not all that you have saved for your rent ! you might send enough for one Bible, and have a coat too !"

" Well, master, it must be as you please, for sure enough it 's all yours, and not mine ; only I 'm thinking how I live like a prince, to what that poor beggar did I read of in my Book ; and yet the angels carried him into Heaven : but how those poor creatures are ever to get there, that never heard the words of the Book to show them Him that 's the way—it hurts me to think !"

"Dear Willy! I do believe you are right, and I won't mind about your coat! Papa can send the money for you if you like," said Herbert, rather sorrowfully. But, O! the joy that lighted up the old man's eye, as he poured out the saved up contents of his little leathern-bag, sixpences and shillings, and saw Herbert bear them off; and then sat down to his Book with thoughts of those who, like himself, would hear and read the glad tidings of great joy through the Book that would now be sent to show them the way!

Mr. Clifford heard the touching tale, and took the old man's offering from the boy; and Herbert went on to say, "Papa, I ought to think of those who have no Bibles, as well as old Willy, and I could do it without having to give up my coat for it! What could I give, papa?"

"You could give me whatever you like, monthly, or quarterly, or yearly," replied his father.

"I should like monthly best, I think, papa; when I receive my money." So Herbert, led by old Willy, began to stretch forth his hand to aid those, who, in countries far away, "sat in darkness and the shadow of death."

Then came the Christmas Eve. The cloak, the scarlet cloak had arrived, directed for Herbert, and his eyes kindled with joy when Mrs. Clifford put it on, wrapping it round her black satin dress, which showed all its warm beauty to perfection.

"Widow Jones's son is waiting to see you, sir," said a servant to Herbert, after tea.

"Show him into the dining-room," replied Herbert. "Now, mamma, you must come, and, Mary, you must come!"

"I think we had better not," said Mrs. Clifford. "J will nave quite enough to encounter in the red cloak without t you can tell us about it afterward."

"Perhaps that will be best," said Herbert, and he went out alone : he was gone a long time : at length he returned.

"Well, what of the cloak ?" asked Mrs. Clifford.

"O, mamma, I am glad you did not come ! I could not even tell you all. I am sure I love that good fellow, and I think he loves me. I could not get him to believe at first that it was to be for his mother, and a present from him ; he said he had never thought to see her look like that ! And when he found out that he was really to take it away, he said, 'I haven't got any words, sir, but 'tis a comfort we will never see the end of !' I don't believe, Mary, any one but you could have thought of it ; it was the very best thing in the world for me to give to Jem, and I am sure he thinks so too."

On Christmas day, Mr. and Mrs. Clifford always provided some presents for their children. These presents were always placed on the breakfast-table ; and a large brown paper parcel lay, this Christmas morning, beside Herbert's plate.

"O, papa, what a parcel !" said Herbert, as, impatient of all delay, he slipped off the string, and unfolded the paper. "O Willy ! O papa ! why, it's a coat for old Willy—what a beautiful coat ! why, it's the very thing I used to fancy him wearing —a blue coat, with brass buttons ; how delightful ! Now he will have a coat, after all !" and Herbert turned, with his kiss of grateful love to his parents. "I should not have cared for any thing so much as that, papa ; I shall take it myself this afternoon !"

As Herbert entered the church-yard, at his parent's side, who should he see coming down the snowy path from the other end but widow Jones, in her red cloak, with little Mercy at her side, and Jem at a short distance, in full view of his mother's bright appearance. The old woman saw her young benefactor, and she courtesied so low, that her red cloak rested on the pure white snow. Herbert bowed, with his heart-warming smile ;

and the rich and the poor entered the house of prayer, there to kneel before the God and Father of all, who is rich unto all who call upon Him.

When luncheon was over, Herbert set off to old Willy. The old man had had his Christmas dinner, of roast beef and plum-pudding, sent from the Hall; and was seated beside his fire in peace, with his "Book" to talk with him. Herbert was wise, and laying the parcel aside, he first made old Willy fully under-stand that all his money was gone for those who had no Bibles, and that it would buy for them, not one Bible alone, but many Bibles; and when the old man clearly understood, and had fully taken in the joy of this blessed thought, then Herbert told him that his father had bought a coat on purpose for him. The old man rose, and took it with a bow of grateful reverence to the elder Squire who had sent, and the younger who had brought such clothing for him! and then he wondered at its beauty, and thought it little fitting for such as him to wear, and promised never to put on his old coat again, but to wear his Sunday dress on common days, and his new coat on Sundays. And Herbert, quite satisfied, returned to his home.

Meanwhile, at the farm, William in the gig had brought Rose from her school. She had received there the tidings of the birth of another brother in her home, and her first eager visit was to the cradle of the sleeping infant. Rose became at once the infant's nurse, and full occupation and delight were found in this new interest. The day for the christening had been put off till her return, that she might be present on the occasion. Farmer Smith had decided on the infant's name, which was to be Timothy; "For by what I can make out," said farmer Smith, "it is him of whom we read in the Bible as hav-ing taken most to the Scriptures from a child!" so the infant boy was baptized by the name of Timothy, which, according to the custom of using short names at the farm, was contracted to Tim, and little Tim soon became an object of interest to all around him.

Mercy too kept a merry Christmas in her cottage home; her grandmother's red cloak was the delight of her eyes; she had also knitted a pair of new stockings for her grandmother, and a pair for her uncle Jem, the worsted bought with the money saved by her uncle Jem's hedging and ditching. And the young orphan herself was now freshly clad; she had run about with warm feet all the winter, through little Jane's first effort to darn stockings a year before; and now the last penny had been paid in, the club-day had come, and widow Jones, laden with the warm clothing, had once more stopped at Mrs. Mansfield's door. Mrs. Jones was had into the parlor, Jane was sent for down from the nursery, and Mr. Mansfield was called in from the shop; and blue print with the little white spots upon it, warm flannel, and white calico, were displayed by the tall old woman in her bright red cloak before the earnest eyes of little Jane. As Jane looked on in silent wonder, the full conscious-ness—because the full knowledge, was in her mind, that, but for her saved-up pennies, those warm garments would not have been bought for the orphan Mercy; it was a feeling to enlarge a child's young heart, and to give added strength to her char-acter—resulting from a continued effort with its realized attain-ment. And so the little orphan was clothed, warmly and well as when her careful parents watched over her infant years. And the passer-by through the village lanes might see her, with the rosy hue of health upon her cheek, braving the freezing air, which had no power to chill her now;—the passer-by might see the happy child, sometimes on her cottage door-step, scattering down the crumbs from the frugal meal, while the expectant robin, peeping from the thatched eaves, heard her sing—

"Little bird, with bosom red,
Welcome to my humble shed!
Doubt not, little though there be,
But I'll cast a crumb to thee!"

—and then without fear flew down to pick the crumbs at her feet. Or she might be seen hastening up the hill, just to light up dame Clarke's little fire, which the poor old woman was too feeble to manage ; or sitting beside it with her of an evening-time awhile, to read to her from the Holy Book—whose words the old woman could not read herself : or coming back on her grandmother's washing-day, from her early visit to the poor old woman, with the things she had found, that she and her grandmother could wash with their own. Thus was Mercy, to whom little Jane had ministered, a ministering child herself.

And now, before we leave that happy Christmas time, we will go back and pay one more visit in the town—not to poor little Patience ; no, we cannot climb the dark staircase to her cold empty home ; some one else must do that—and some one was coming who would, but not till that happy Christmas was past ; poor Patience must spend that, as she had spent all before it—in wretchedness and want ; no time brought her gladness as yet ; but the star was soon coming in the dark cloud for poor Patience, and she will have comfort enough by-and-by— though for all who dwell in this world, the cloud must still darken the bright stars sometimes ; but for such as little Ruth, who are gone to dwell in heaven, all darkness and trouble is passed away for ever !

Where then are we going if not to see poor Patience ? You are going to look into a shoemaker's home, and to see what was doing there. We must pass Mr. Mansfield's corner shop, go down the short street at the top of which it stands, turn to the right, and then again down a narrow street to the left, and there half-way down the street, you will see " Boot and Shoe maker" written up. The worthy shoemaker, who lived in this narrow street, was once in a much larger way of business, but his poor est days had been his best days, and what he had lost of this world's wealth he had gained a hundred fold in enduring riches — even the love of God, which made Heaven his home. He lived with his wife and children in one back room, with a small shop in front: but he was so sickly in health and so poor, that he could not have kept even that one room, if it had not been for his eldest son, who was gone abroad, and who was always **sending money** to his parents at home. The second son lived with his parents, and was serving his apprenticeship to a book-**binder.** Little Ephraim, the third son, went to a day-school; Manasseh was a baby in the cradle. Little Ephraim was troubled because the baby slept in the cradle instead of joining in family prayer; so when it was over one day he went to the cradle, and kneeling down by the side, he put the baby's hands together, saying, **as he held them,** "Lord, teach Manasseh to pray!" There was also a little girl named Agnes, who went to a **day-**school, and waited on her mother at home.

It was Christmas-eve in the shoemaker's home; for the blessed Christmas comes **to** all, to rich and **poor, to** young and old, telling year after year of the Saviour's love, to win them to seek him while yet he may be found—to call upon him while he is near. It was Christmas-eve in the shoemaker's home, the father was out, and the mother, with little Agnes to help, was making haste to get all in readiness for Christmas-day. There was no plum-pudding or roast beef preparing for the Christmas dinner; but the Missionary box! feel its weight, and do not think it is heavy with pence only, no, there are sixpences and shillings, not few in number—the thank-offerings to God of the shoemaker's family. **The children** will sit round the table;

each child will have a little farthing candle to burn, all at once, making a bright light, then the box will be opened, and they will count up the money that they have gathered for the poor heathen, to help in sending good ministers to them, to teach them to know that blessed Saviour, whose birth we celebrate on Christmas-day. The mother was busy, getting on with her cleaning up, when she heard a loud knock at the door. "Run, Agnes, and see who is there," said the mother. The door was at the end of a long passage; presently Agnes came back, and her book-binding brother with her, and a large brown paper parcel in his hand.

"Did you hear that loud knock, mother?" asked the boy.

"Yes, who was it?"

"Why, it was a friend of yours, only he did not wish his name mentioned; he brought a little Christmas present for you with his love."

"For me!" said the mother, "a friend of mine! Did you know him?"

"Yes, mother, and so would you if you had seen him; but I am not going to tell you as he did not wish it, so it's no use asking me; and as for Agnes, she saw no one but me, so she can't tell."

"What can it be?" said the mother, and wiping her hands and arms she came up to the round table in the middle of the room, where Agnes and Ephraim stood all expectation by their elder brother's side. The string was untied—for the shoe-maker's careful wife would be sorry to cut a knot and waste an inch of string, the paper was unfolded, and five small parcels tumbled out. "O mother!" said Agnes. "O dear! O dear!" said little Ephraim. The first parcel was a quarter of a pound of tea; the next, half a pound of coffee; the next, a pound of sugar; the next, a pound of currants; and the last, a pound of

plums. The mother looked hard at her book-binding boy—
" Now, Bob, if I don't believe that it's you, and no one else, has
been getting all these things for me ?"

" Well, mother, I could not stand your having no Christmas
pudding, and I managed to earn it all at over **hours !**"

So, to the children's delight, and the mother's **pleasure, a**
great Christmas pudding was prepared, and the whole family had
their Christmas feast of the provision made by the book-binding boy.

And so the Christmas came and went. And **some** young
hearts, and some that were no longer young in earthly youth,
loved still better than before, the " Holy Child Jesus," who **was**
born for their sakes, an infant in the stable of Bethlehem.

CHAPTER XIII.

Now the end of the commandment is CHARITY out of a pure heart, and a good conscience, and faith unfeigned."—1 TIM. i. 5.

CHRISTMAS had passed away, New Year's Day was over and gone, and the cold snowy month of January slowly drawing to a close. Rose had returned, for her last half year, to school. And poor little Patience had taken her place again in the second class, among her companions; the mistress said it was a disgrace for her to be still only in the second class, when many younger than she, had been months in the first; but no one else took notice of it, for the poor child was so small and thin, so silent and shrinking, that a stranger might have supposed her one of the youngest, as well as the lowest, which she generally was, in the second class of healthy happy children. It was at this same time that a traveling carriage arrived at the Hall. Mr. and Mrs. Clifford were at the door to receive their guests; a rather elderly gentleman stepped out of the carriage, and then handed from it a young slight girl, whom Mrs. Clifford received with a mother's welcome. The hall-door was shut, and the carriage drove round to the stables. This young visitor was the only child of Mrs. Clifford's earliest friend; that friend had died some years before in England, and the father had gone to reside with this his only child abroad, more from change of scene than from any necessity of health. A mother's sheltering tenderness had passed away from her,

just when she began to realize the power and blessing of it.
But that mother had led her from her earliest years to her God
and Saviour, whose love is more than a mother's love, **and whose**
presence can **never** be taken away; and the **motherless child**
knew where to turn in her heart's desolation; she **had been led**
so constantly to her Saviour's feet that **it was no** strange place
to her, she had learned to tell the wishes of **her** infant life to
Him, to carry to Him **her** childhood's **hopes and fears, and now**
when bereft on earth she **turned with her** aching **heart to**
heaven; and the love of God, **that** filled **the** blank **in life for**
her, filled also her life with sympathy for all. After her mother's
death she had little intercourse with any but her father, and **this**
older companionship, with her mother's loss, had made her
grave beyond her years; her face was full of thought; and when
she smiled it seemed rather the expression of her tenderness for
those she loved, or pleasure in others' mirth, than the bright
gleam **of** personal merriment. On the eager glee of others,
like herself in childhood, she seemed **to** look with distant **pleas-**
ure; but wherever sorrow rested she drew near—as **if she** felt
her call on earth lay there. Young as she **was, she had** drunk
deep of the cup of grief; death and separation **were** words, the
reality of which her hourly life still **learned; but she** had tasted
also the love that can sweeten **the bitterest trial,** and her sense
of joy was still deeper than **her feeling of** sadness. She, herself,
was comforted in all things—how **could** she then but long to
comfort others! **There was no** gloom in her sweet gravity, but
a depth of tenderness, **an** assurance of sympathy, that made **her**
very presence soothe. **Those** who shrank most from the thought
of intrusion in their grief would welcome **her, nor wish to** turn
from meeting her calm expressive **eye,** which **seemed** rather to
take in the object on which it looked, **than to** search into **that**
object with penetrating inquiry.

9

Miss Clifford had been like an elder sister to her; no place was like Miss Clifford's side to her, and no one else had so much power to waken the silent gladness of feeling, and the graceful play of thought—that had slept because there had been none to call them forth, or give responsive tones; but even when with her sister friend, her words were more often the earnest words that told of earnest thought. She looked upon the world around her, not as on a picture, as childhood for the most part beholds it —searching no deeper than its surface-hues of light and shadow, but as one who had already learned the deep realities that live beneath the pictured scene. When her eye rested on sorrow's aspect she instantly estimated the depth of suffering by her own sense of grief; and when she had tried to comfort or relieve, she still retained the feeling of the sorrow being like her own—not to be forgotten. Yet sometimes it was her's to sow the seeds of purest joy in the heart that grief had filled. Her friend, Miss Clifford, had known sorrow and want only as she had sought them out to relieve them; the feeling they called forth in her was, how best to aid and comfort; and when want was replenished, and sadness smiled on her, she passed away and felt only the joy of relieving. The one seemed to soothe by receiving the sorrows of others into her own deep sympathy; the other to brighten by shedding her own light of peace on the troubled. It was as one of earth's loveliest sights to see the two, so young in years, with all the world could offer of attraction spread around them, intent in converse how best to use the blessed power intrusted to them—to brighten the sorrowful, and guide them to the holy heaven to which their own youthful steps were bound. Such as these lead an angel's life on earth, and ministering angels love to watch and tend them unseen. And truly for such as these, the wilderness of many a sorrowful heart is made glad; and the desert of many a sinful soul rejoices and blossoms as the rose—planted and watered by their prayerful efforts, to which God vouchsafes the increase.

The young guest at the Hall was anxious to lose no time before taking a drive to the neighboring town to see her old nurse, from whom she had never been separated till she left England with her father, when her mother's faithful maid became her attendant. The first suitable day was chosen, and as Patience was creeping back over the snow from school, a few minutes after, four o'clock, Mr. Clifford's carriage drove up and stopped beside her at the door of the house where she lived, No. 9 Ivy-lane, from which the old nurse's last letters had been dated. " Does Mrs. Brame live here ?" asked the footman of the child. " Yes," said Patience, looking up. The man went in, and Patience slowly followed.

" How unhappy that little girl looked !" said Mrs. Clifford's young guest.

" Do you mean that neatly-dressed child now gone in ?" asked Mrs. Clifford.

" Yes, she looked as if she had never smiled !"

" You don't say so ! I was thinking how clean and comfortable she appeared."

Mrs. Brame lived at the top of the large old house ; and though aged now, and, for the most part, slow of movement, she descended the stairs almost as quickly as the footman had run up ; and tears, and smiles, and words of astonishment and gladness were the old woman's welcome to the child whose infancy had been cradled in her arms, whose opening life had been her one object of interest, and who through years of absence had still retained the entire possession of her nurse's heart, which had never glowed with affection towards any other object through life.

For one whole hour the devoted nurse was to be allowed the sole possession of the child so precious to her ! But as the time drew near its close, the youthful Lady Gertrude asked her nurse about the little girl whom she had seen enter the same house. Nurse Brame told her sad story, and her young listener sighing, said, " I thought she looked as if her heart were empty !"

" Ah ! it 's worse than that !" replied nurse Brame. " I doubt if she has a heart ! Why let happen what will, I have never seen her shed a tear ! and if I have given her once, I have twenty times, just because I could not bear to see such a miserable looking child—but I don't believe she cares a bit more about me than if I had never shown her a kindness !"

" I wish I could see her again !" said the young Lady Gertrude.

" It 's not the least use !" replied the old nurse. " I have tried it fifty times, there 's no getting any thing out of her !"

" I must see her again if she is here still !" said the Lady Gertrude, " I will go to her room and see her there."

The old nurse went reluctantly to inquire, in the hope of finding that Patience was not within. But she returned, saying, the child was alone · adding, in a tone of remonstrance, " If you won't be pacified without going, why then I must stand outside her door, for if I were to let you see that child's father, I should never forgive myself !"

The Lady Gertrude made no answer, but followed her nurse down the first flight of stairs to the room where poor Patience dwelt; there was not much evidence of any " pacifying" being needed in her noiseless step of youthful dignity, and her calm, earnest eye ; but her old nurse had always been wont to suppose the necessity of "pacifying," as a reason for yielding to her young lady's gentle yet decided will. The old nurse took her post to listen and watch at the top of the stairs, and the Lady Gertrude entered the room. One glance round the apartment was sufficient to show that no mother's care, no mother's presence was known there ; and a rush of almost sisterly feeling

passed through the heart of the motherless child of rank and fortune, as she looked on the motherless child of want and sorrow. Patience was standing with her usual expression of dull and hopeless wretchedness. The young Lady Gertrude went up to her, and said, in her low tone of tenderness, " Dear little girl, you are not happy !" She asked no question, she called for no reply, but she gave expression to her own sense of a fact, a simple fact, that none had seemed to notice before. Patience took up her little white linen apron, and hid her face in it, and wept. " Do not cry, dear," said the Lady Gertrude, " I want to make you happy. Are you not cold without a fire ?" and she laid her hand on the chilblained hands of the child. " Yes, you are very cold. If you have half-a-crown from my purse, then you could get some coal and some wood, and make a fire when I am gone, could you not ?" But Patience still only hid her face and wept. Warm tears they were, melting the child's young heart **so early** frozen, and leaving its surface to receive the first impression of human tenderness, which no after-time could efface or impair.

" Did you ever hear of Jesus ?"

" Yes," said the child.

" He wants you to love Him, and be His child, that He may make you happy. Will you love Him, **and try to** pray to Him ? if you do He will be sure to comfort you."

" Yes," said the still weeping child.

" I shall have to go away directly ; will you not look at me, that you may remember me ? Because I am your friend, and I love you, and shall often think about you !"

Patience looked up, but the time was gone ; the carriage **was** already within hearing. Then despairing to comfort the child, **and** feeling only, at that moment, the sorrow she could not bear away, the child of rank put her arm around the child of poverty, **pressed** a kiss of tenderness upon her forehead, and, putting the half-crown into her hand, turned away in answer to her nurse's knock on the half-shut door. "Do be kind to her!" said the Lady Gertrude, as she took leave of her nurse, and hastened down the stairs ; and in a minute more she was driving fast away.

Mrs. Clifford observed the shade of sadness on the face of her young charge, and naturally concluding that she felt leaving her old nurse, immediately planned in her own mind to obtain the consent of her young visitor's father, and then send for the old nurse to stay at the Hall. But far other were the thoughts of that gentle girl : her heart was lingering where she felt she had left an unsupplied want, an unsoothed sorrow— lingering with the motherless child in that bare and desolate room. She was thinking that she had done nothing, worse than nothing—had awakened the child's sorrow, and left her uncomforted. "Why," she thought, "**was** I so determined to speak to her! How much better if **I had** not attempted what I could not do!" Did she not know then how often the eye returns to look again upon the first, the only star, that has suddenly appeared to light up the gloom of a darkened, lowering **sky? Did she not know how,** when in all the lonely earth no music wakes, if suddenly the nightingale's rich melody fall upon the ear, the very heart is hushed to listen and recall the **strain?** Did **she** not know how dear, how unlike all that follow, **is the** first violet, gathered where the sunbeam has warmed the yet wintery bank, and called for ththe herald of spring? **Yes,** she knew that these things were so ; but she knew not that her visit **to the child** of want and suffering had been like them ; and so she passed away in sadness, and thought she had left no blessing—how many such misgiving fears will the light of eternity, when it falls on life past, dispel for ever !

Nurse Brame watched the carriage swiftly disappearing in **the** dimly-lighted lane, then turned within again, and taking up her candle, slowly reascended the staircase. The earnest tone in which the words, " Do be kind to her !" had been uttered, left them impressed on the old woman's heart, and the child seemed more associated with her young lady than any thing beside, and she turned into the room to speak to her.

Poor little Patience, when left alone, had ceased her tears for a minute in bewildered surprise ; then raised her hand to feel where that kiss **had been—to see** if her forehead still felt the same ; it felt the same, but she did not—she had ceased to feel alone in all the world ! She had met the first gleam of human tenderness, and to that her shrinking spirit turned. She did not reason, but she felt ; and feeling lies deeper than reason, and often in a child supplies reason's part—the lifeless chill was gone from her heart, its frozen surface thawed and left susceptible of passing impressions. Nurse Brame came in, and holding up her candle to see the child in the dark chamber, said, in a kind voice, " Here, come along with me out of this cold place, and we will have some tea together !" Patience followed, and was soon seated on a stool by the little fire-place ; nurse Brame stirred up the dull coals into a blaze, and telling the child to make haste and get warm, she set out the little round table with her tea-board and bread and butter ; and lifting the kettle on the fire, sat down in the twilight and watched till the water boiled. The substantial slice of bread and butter, and the steaming cup of sugared tea, brought a little color to the cheek of the child ; and nurse Brame cut the square white loaf with no sparing hand, and put more water on uncurled tea-leaves, that the poor child might be " satisfied for once !" and all the while the old nurse felt as if she **was** just doing her young lady's will.

" There, now you are neither cold nor hungry at last !" said nurse Brame, " and you had better go down and go to bed, and there's no doubt you will sleep sound enough!" Patience returned to her cold dark room, and crept to the side of the heap of rags that made her bed; but she too remembered the lady's words, and her gentle inquiry, "Will you try and pray?" led the child, as by the silken bond of constraining love, to make her first faint effort. Then taking from her pocket the treasured half-crown, she clasped it tight in her hand, and, lying down, was soon asleep.

Nurse Brame was sitting over her decaying fire that night, her candle was out, and it was her usual early hour of rest; but she was sitting as if watching the fading embers, and thinking on the past events of the day—her unexpected and joyful surprise in her Lady Gertrude's visit, and then the child —but the child, the poor child, came like a shadow across the sunbeam's track. Nurse Brame had never learned the pure and simple joy of doing good: she had showed many a little kindness to the desolate child, but it was, as she herself expressed it, because she could not bear to see so miserable a thing—not because she could not bear that silent suffering should be, if unseen! she thought that such things must be, and that it was only her call to relieve when forced upon her notice. "Out of sight" was "out of mind" with old nurse Brame, therefore a gift from her was nothing more to the receiver, than the same gift picked up on the highway side— it came as no living witness, therefore it left no living glow: the receiver's feeling was as shallow and transient as the feeling of the giver. But now the link between the old nurse and the child had changed—it was no longer the transient sight of want, but the feeling of her young lady's interest. Nurse Brame was sitting in the dim firelight, thinking upon how much it would be necessary for her to do for this unhappy and, to her, uninteresting child—uninteresting not to her alone, but to all save the one who had reached the child's buried heart! the old nurse felt she must be kind to her; she would not neglect a wish of her young lady's for the world, but she wanted to come to a conclusion in her own mind as to what amount of kindness would be sufficient. She knew not CHARITY's indwelling influence, which, far from consisting in this or that act, is the very atmosphere in which the spirit that possesses it, lives and moves and has its being! While so pondering, nurse Brame heard a hasty knock on her door, and looking round a little startled, the woman who rented the house, letting out its rooms to lodgers, and living herself on the ground floor, opened the door and came in. " I want you to tell me," said the woman, " what I am to do! I have just heard—that pest of a man is off to escape the constables; I have not had a farthing of rent for five weeks, and what is left in the room won't pay me a quarter of that; but such as there is, I shall make the most I can of it, and glad enough to get rid of him. But what to do with the child? I can see nothing for her but the work-house!" Now nurse Brame thought the work-house next in disgrace to the prison itself; and the question instantly arose in her mind, what would her young Lady Gertrude say when she saw her again and asked for the child, if she found that the next day she had been carried off to the work-house! Nurse Brame did not consider where the disgrace of the work-house lay—whether with those who could do nothing to support themselves, or whether, not rather with those who suffered the young and helpless, or the old and feeble, to be carried off and nourished by the forced contributions of others. Nurse Brame considered the work-house, in some way or other, to be a disgrace; and according to the readiest and most general custom, she associated that disgrace with the result, and not the cause of that result, and exclaimed, " Is there nothing but the work-

HOUSE!" "I can think of nothing else," replied the woman. Then suddenly within the mind of old nurse Brame rose the vision of the child, as she had been seated that evening on the stool by the fireside; the stool was still there, but the child was gone. Why might not that warm comfortable room become the child's **home?** Nurse Brame might feed the worse than orphan and yet have enough for herself—and she knew this; the child was clothed in the school, and rent of room, firing and candle, would have cost no more. All this passed before the mind of old nurse Brame; but the motive that influenced her thoughts was one of earthly limitation, not of Heaven's boundless charity; therefore it came short of such an attainment, and she only replied, "Well, I would not be the one to send a child off to the WORKHOUSE!" The woman stood a moment considering, then said, "I have a relation in the town who wants a girl, and perhaps if I spoke, she would **take the child**; though I doubt if she would think her strong enough for the place." Now "a place" to old nurse Brame had a respectable sound; she considered it no business of hers to find out what the place was— it was "a place"—a place of service; a way, in her estimation, of earning an honest penny—little considering how often the "honest penny" of the poor is paid by dishonest hands, who have wrung three times the penny's worth from the strength that has no redress on earth. But the day will come when the God of the poor "will plead their cause, and spoil the soul of those that spoiled them." And so because the name of "a place" was better than the name of "a workhouse," nurse Brame made no inquiry as to what the real thing might be, but gave her **judgment in favor of the** place, saying, "Well, I am sure I would try for the place, rather than send the poor thing off to the workhouse." Meanwhile little Patience, whose fate seemed pending above, was quietly sleeping below. No rest-breaking

father returned to disturb her slumber, and she did not wake
till the slowly dawning light shone into her dreary room; then,
hastily rising, she looked for her father—he was not there—she
saw at once he had not been there; so looking again at her
half-crown, and once more feeling her forehead that the lady's
lips had kissed, she rose and dressed. There was no fire, no
food; but the thought of spending the half-crown was not even
entertained—it was the lady's gift! the sign that made the past
still real and present to the child; so she put it at the bottom
of her pocket, and was thinking about what time it could be,
when the woman of the house came in and said, "I am sorry
for you, but your father is off, no one knows where, and he has
paid me no rent for these five weeks, so I must just take what
he has left, and hope for a better lodger; but I don't want to
be hard upon you, and if you think you would like to try service better than the workhouse, why I will go with you at once
and see after a place that I know of?". Poor little Patience!
the avalanche of frozen words fell upon her heart, still warmed
with yesterday's glow of feeling, making the chilling shock the
greater. Again she **hid** her face and wept! **"Poor thing!"**
said the woman in a softened tone, **"I** am sure none can treat
you **worse** than your own father **has done!** I dare say you
have not tasted food; come along **with me and I** will give you
some breakfast, and then we will see what can be done." So
taking the unresisting child by the arm, she led her down stairs,
and gave her some bread and butter and cold tea; and then
after awhile repeated her question, as to whether she would like
best to go to service or to the workhouse? Poor Patience did
not know—both names were alike to her—and beginning again
to cry instead of answer, she only wished in her heart that the
lady would but come again! She felt as if there was one who
would not let her be left alone in her misery! The woman

seeing that words were hopeless, tied on her bonnet, and, fetching the child's bonnet and cloak, put them on her, saying, "Well, come and see what you think of a place," and again taking her by the arm, she led her through the **town to** a distant narrow street, stopping at the door of a high house. Patience was left **in the** passage while the woman went in and talked with the mistress, and then calling Patience in, the mistress of the house asked her whether she thought she could run about **and do the work for her board and a shilling a week?** A shilling a **week** sounded like exhaustless wealth to the poor child, who **knew** nothing of the expense of necessary clothes, and she answered, "Yes." So the woman left the child, promising to send all that **she found belonging to her, and returned** well satisfied, to inform nurse Brame of the success of her attempt.

The next morning nurse Brame received a letter by the **post ;** it was from her loved young lady—the old woman put on her spectacles, and read, with astonishment and delight, that in the course of that afternoon, Mr. Clifford's carriage would take her back to the Hall, to stay there during the time of her young lady's visit. **The** old woman looked twice at the letter, to be **quite** sure, then **putting on** her shawl and bonnet she hurried **out** to buy such additions to her wardrobe as she thought **necessary for so great an** occasion, and then hurrying home **again, began** to make preparations. **The** sun had set when the carriage drove up to the door ; the footman ran up to summon **Mrs. Brame, and the** old woman stepped down, dressed in her neatest and best, and the footman carried her bandbox behind her. Her young lady was in the carriage alone, and when the old woman **was in and the** footman waiting for **orders,** the Lady Gertrude asked her nurse whether **that poor child was at home ?** "Ah, no, poor thing! she went off yesterday to a place," replied Mrs. Brame.

" That little girl to be a servant !" asked the young Lady Gertrude in a tone of surprise.

" Ah, yes, she is older than she has the look of, by a good bit."

" Home," said the Lady Gertrude, and the carriage drove on ; then turning, she talked with her old nurse, till, as they were about to leave the town, she suddenly, as if a thought for the first time crossed her mind, inquired, " Do you know where that little girl has gone to live ?"

" **Not the least in the world,**" replied nurse Brame ; " but she **is gone to** a place—and that's respectable ! they would have **sent her** off to the workhouse, but I set my face against having the poor thing treated like that, and now she is once in service she must work her way as I and others have done."

" But if she should not be happy, who will know it ?" asked the young Lady Gertrude.

" You need not distress yourself about that," replied nurse Brame, " she has led such a wretched life, that let service be what it will, it must be better than that !"

The Lady Gertrude said no more, she felt that the child had no place in the heart of her old nurse, and from that **time** she never mentioned her again ; and her nurse believed her satisfied, and the child **a** forgotten thing. **In a** fortnight more the young visitor and her father **left the** Hall ; and in the spring of the same year, they quitted England again for a residence abroad.

When Miss Wilson **next** visited the school, she missed Patience, and when she inquired of the mistress, she heard that the child had been **forsaken** by her father, and was gone to service. And then the mistress told her what she had now found out about the life of misery the poor forsaken child had led in her home. Miss Wilson felt very sorry, but it was too late now to hope to do much ; yet she could still go and see poor Patience in her place of service; and knowing that Patience had not

earned a Bible, she directly determined to go and take her one,
so she learnt from the mistress where Patience was living, then
going to a shop, she bought a Bible, and went on to find poor
Patience in her new place of service.

It was a narrow street, and when Miss Wilson knocked at
the door, a cross-looking woman opened it. Miss Wilson
asked for her little scholar. The woman did not invite her in,
but shouted to Patience to come down, and then went herself,
and left Miss Wilson standing at the door. Patience came;
just the same look over her face as when at school—as if she
expected something to be said to persuade her to try and do
more than she had done before. But Miss Wilson knew the
truth now, and gladly would she have comforted the poor
desolate child—but she could only speak to her at the door of
the house; she gave Patience the Bible she had brought for
her; Patience took it and courtesied, but she did not speak, and
Miss Wilson could never forget the look of illness in the poor
child's face. She went away feeling very sad about the child:
she had always been kind to Patience, she had never spoken
hastily or severely to her, but she had loved her less than she
loved the other children, and poor Patience had wanted more
love than others—not less.

Miss Wilson waited some weeks, and then she went again to see
Patience in her place. The same cross-looking woman opened the
door, and Miss Wilson asked if she could speak to Patience.

" O, she is not here," replied the woman; " she fell ill of brain-
fever, and we had her carried off to the workhouse !"

Poor Patience ! she had no strength for work; half-starved as
she had been and miserable, her feeble limbs could stand no
labor; she had toiled on till all power was gone, and now at
last she was in the workhouse ! We will not leave her yet,
but will go and see her there. She was laid on a little bed in

the sick ward of the workhouse, and nursed till the fever left her, and she was able to sit up. When she was well enough to sit up and walk about a little, she was not sent to another place of service; no, she was taken two miles away from the town to a house in the country, where the workhouse children **were** kept. **It** was the beginning of May ; the trees were all in bud, and the hedges growing green, and the lark was singing in the clear blue sky. Patience had never been so far in the country before, she wished the drive would last very long, for she liked it very much, and she did not know what she might find at the end. It was not long, however, before they stopped at a large house that stood alone. A strong, kind-looking woman came out, and took Patience in, saying, " Never mind, my dear, you will soon get better here !" Patience heard the words, and she looked up at the strong kind woman with something like inquiry and wonder.. But it was all true, it was the strong kind woman's heart that spoke in those first words **to** the timid stranger child, and Patience was to live with her. And now the cold nipping winter of the poor child's life was gone, and its bright spring-time began. Yes, its bright spring-time began in the workhouse, under the care of that strong kind woman ! Patience began the **next** day to do a little work, but the woman saw directly the tired look came over her face, and made her leave off. Breakfast, dinner, and tea all came, with strengthening **food for** Patience ; and now that she was no longer faint and hungry, she began to think of all that she had heard long before. And first she got her little Bible, and read to herself, and she felt happy, reading all alone, and trying to remember what Miss Wilson said at **the** school. After a little while, Patience thought that what made her happy would make the other children **happy ;** so in their play-time she often persuaded them to come and sit round her ; and she read out of her Bible, and taught them texts and hymns, and read to them from her other little books, and the children liked to listen. So it was that poor Patience, who seemed at school as if she could not learn, and would never remember any thing, was the first perhaps of all the children there, except little Ruth, to become a ministering child to others.

Poor Patience had never known a parent's tenderness; but she soon learned to love the strong kind woman who took care of all the workhouse children ; the woman moved about quickly, and spoke fast and loud, but her heart was kind, and Patience loved her, and tried to please her. When the months of May and June had passed away, and Patience was well again, there came a day of holiday in the workhouse ; and the matron told Patience that she might go to the town and see her friends. Patience had no friends except Miss Wilson, and that lady far away! but she thought she should like to go and see Miss Wilson. Though Patience looked very small, she was older than she looked, and quite old enough to go to the town alone. She knew where Miss Wilson lived, and easily found the house. Miss Wilson was much surprised at seeing Patience, but very glad to find how happy she was in the workhouse. And now Patience not only answered every question put to her, but she told how she employed her time, and how the workhouse children came round and listened while she read to them, and told them what she had been taught at school. Miss Wilson gave Patience some new books for her own, to carry back with her : and not being able to walk so far herself, she asked her father to go, and one day he went, and found Patience happy herself, and trying to make others happy. And there for the present we must leave her—a ministering child in the workhouse.

CHAPTER XIV.

"The words that I speak unto you, they are spirit, and they are life."—JOHN vi. 63.

WHILE Patience in the workhouse was gathering other children round her, and teaching them the blessed words that had so long lain silently on her own heart; little Jane led by her mother's thoughtful care, had a mission of love to the aged. In the town where Mr. Mansfield lived, there stood, in a narrow street, a row of old almshouses; the walls were of white plaster: the one single shutter to each lower lattice-window and the doors, were black; and the old chimneys rose thick above the red tiled roof. In the spring of the year, an old man and woman passed under the almshouse door-way, and up the white deal stairs, to end their days in one of the almshouse rooms, which the friendly compassion of some people in the town had obtained for them. They had come from a large farm-house, where much had been under their care; but the old man had failed, and now all was gone—except one four-post bedstead with its white dimity hangings, their two arm-chairs, a chest of drawers, a small round table before the fire, and a square one in the window, and such few other articles as were necessary to the furniture of one room. The old woman spread a white cover on the little table in the window, and hung at both small lattices muslin blinds, and, to a stranger's eye, the room looked a picture of neatness and comfort, and the old people were thankful for such a refuge, but still they felt the change; the old woman most of the two—and her stirring active manner changed to a look of silent dejection. They knew not that HOPE that can shed its brightness no less on poverty than on wealth, and is the only abiding light of either.

Mrs. Mansfield had known something of them in their better days, and now she hastened to visit them in their affliction; she **saw the** silent dejection of both, and the thought occurred to her mind, that very probably it was as much owing to the loss of all active interest in life as it was to any sense of present poverty; and that to provide the old woman a little employment might prove a great help in cheering their spirits. She knew also that Mrs. Blake was a good knitter; so after sitting with them in sympathy a short time, she said, "I have a little plan to propose to you, Mrs. Blake: I know you are a superior knitter, and I want my eldest little girl to learn the art, and if you would not object to take a little pupil, I would send her to you three times a week for an hour, and then send for her again. I should thankfully pay a shilling a week for her instruction till she can manage it well enough to go on by herself."

"I am sure I should be thankful," replied Mrs. Blake, "it would seem a little company, and cheer us up every way!" So **the** next day was fixed for a beginning.

"Jane," said Mrs. Mansfield, that afternoon, "I am going to send you to-morrow to take your first lessons in knitting; you are **going** to a kind old woman who is willing to teach you. I am sure you will be very attentive, and try to give her no trouble."

"Is she very old, mamma?"

"I dare say you would think her very old, so you must be careful not to tire her by making her tell you the same thing over a great many times. You know you have often wished **you** could knit like me, and now you will learn."

Jane took the first opportunity of getting off to the nursery, being always anxious to **tell all** that concerned herself to her nurse.

" Nurse, **I am** going to learn to **knit** like mamma ; there is a very old woman who is going to teach me ; mamma says I shall think her a very old woman ! Do you think, nurse, I can do any thing for her ?"

" Yes, to be sure ; I never saw the old woman yet that a child could not be a comfort to if there was the mind to try !"

" What do you think I can do, nurse ?"

" How should I know ? that 's for you to find out when you are there."   .

Little Jane had no love for suspense, and she thought it would be much pleasanter to know at once just what she could do for this very old woman, and though it was her nurse who had taught her to reverence old age, still **her** mother was always her final appeal, so she did not stay long in the nursery, but made her way back again to her mother's side.

" Mamma, nurse says I can do something for the old woman. What can I do ?"

" I hope you will be her little comforter, Jane, and that will be doing the best thing for her, for she is very sorrowful."

" How can I be her comforter, mamma ?"

" Only by loving her, and **trying to make her** happy, as you try to make me when I am sad."

" I read to you out of the Bible to comfort you, mamma, will that comfort the old woman ?"

" Yes, I hope **it will**. You will find an old man also ; the old woman's husband ; and when you have knitted three quarters of an hour. you can tell the old woman that you read to me to make me happy, and that if she **will** let you, you will read to her."

"How shall I know when it is three quarters of an hour, mamma?"

"Mr. Blake, the old man has a watch, and he will tell you if you ask him."

Now, little Jane was perfectly satisfied, and with a path before her clear and bright as the shining light, she waited for her next day's lesson.

Her nurse led her to the almshouse, up the white deal staircase, knocked at the black door where the No. 3 was painted in large white letters, and left Jane seated on a stool by Mrs. Blake's side. Jane was a timid child, and she felt a little strange, and the color came to her cheek when left alone with the old people; but she remembered that she was to try and be a comfort to them, and any sense of power soon dispels the slavery of fear. Jane tried to do her best, but the knitting-pins were strangers to her little fingers, and she longed to get to the pages of the Bible to which those same little fingers had so long been used.

"Is it three-quarters of an hour yet, do you think?" asked Jane of Mrs. Blake.

"No, my dear, not more than one as yet, I should say."

Jane knitted on in patience, but the time seemed very long, while she grasped as tight as possible pins, which as yet she knew not the skill of holding with easier pressure. "Do you think it is nearly three-quarters now?" At length she asked again. Then the old man's pity awoke, and taking out his watch, he laid it on the table by the child, and said, "There, dear, now you can see for yourself!"

"I don't know what's o'clock when I look," said little Jane.

"Come, wife," said Mr. Blake, "you have had time enough for your teachings; I will give mine now. Come here, dear, and I will show you all about it!" So Jane stood at the old man's

knee, and he taught her how to find out what it was o'clock, and spun out his lesson till the three quarters were fairly over.

" Is it quite three quarters ?" asked Jane.

".Yes, dear ; do you want to be going ?"

" No, I don't want to go, but mamma said, would you like me to read in the Bible to you when it was three quarters of an hour ?"

" Yes, to be sure !" said the old man. " Wife, where's our Bible ?"

" It's here where it always is," said Mrs. Blake, going to the chest of drawers, " but it's too big for a child !"

" I can stand at the table," said little Jane ; " I can find the place where I read to mamma this morning—I can find places in the Bible now all by myself !—shall I read what I read to mamma about the sheep and the goats ?"

" Yes, dear, that's just what I should like !" said the old farmer.

So the child stood up between the two old people, and her young voice bore on its feeble breath the seed of eternal life— herself unconscious of the enduring influence of the words that " are spirit and life," thinking only of its present power to comfort.

When Jane had done, the old man said, " Ah, thank you, dear, those are cutting words !" but Mrs. Blake only praised little Jane's reading. Jane looked at her, surprised and disappointed—as having expected a far higher result than any thought of her reading, and said, gravely, " It makes mamma happy when I read her the Bible !"

" Ah, dear, that's as it should be !" said the old man.

" Does it make you happy ?" asked little Jane, turning to him.

" God grant it may ! God grant it may !" he replied, and

little Jane satisfied with his words, shut up the great Bible.
Mrs. Blake saw that she had answered wrong, and that the child
had expected what was read to have some effect on her; she
said no more **then**, but she determined next time to listen, that
she might see whether she could find any thing in the words
themselves.   Then rising up, Mrs. Blake went to her closet and
brought out her wheaten loaf **and** slice, of **butter**, and cutting
some bread and butter for Jane, she offered it to her.   She had
been used to bring **out** her home-made cake **and** wine to her
guests; and now, though bread and butter was all her store, she
would still offer that.   Little Jane received the offer of the poor
old woman as she would have received the same kind care from
the rich; and then, her nurse arriving, she returned to her home,
to give to her mother her simple account of all that had passed.
And on through the summer weeks little Jane knitted her three
quarters of an hour, then told the time from the old man's
watch, and read her **chapter out of the great** Bible—and thus
the child became a ministering guide to Heaven!

Before we leave the town we will pay a farewell visit to the
shoemaker's family. We saw them before, on the Christmas-
eve; and it was still the winter-time, when, if you could have
looked in **of an evening after the** day's **work was** done, and
when the mother's candle **was** lighted, and she was sitting
by the round table at work, you would have seen on the
table a pile of loose pages, and Agnes and Ephraim seated
side by side, sorting and arranging them : they were pages
of the New Testament, which Miss Wilson had found in
one of the school closets—a heap of old and torn copies of
the Holy Testament; so she sent them to the shoemaker's book-
binding son, for him to see what he could do with them. The
book-binding boy set his little **brother and** sister **to** work, and
every evening after, they sorted the sacred pages, till they had

some Testaments complete, and some separate Gospels complete, and some Epistles complete; then the shoemaker's book-binding son carried them off, and in his spare time, with the pieces his master allowed him to use, he put them all into neat dark covers, and then he **gave** them to Miss Wilson, saying, " **I have** not money, but I have a little time to give, and I want **it to be** my offering to those that have need." He brought eight volumes—Testaments and parts of Testaments, refusing any payment, leaving **the** words that **are " spirit and** life," again ready for the use of the poor and **needy.** So **it** was that the shoemaker's children ministered **to others,** " according to their ability."

While little Patience gathered health and strength in the warm summer-time beneath the workhouse matron's care, the life of the young sweet lady of the Hall was passing from the earth. Every one around her watched her gently fading from their sight; her parents knew that she was dying, and looked upon her day by day as if each look might be their last **upon** her living form; the servants watched her whenever in **their** sight, and thought of all that devoted service could do—as **if** they felt each act might be the last that loving reverence might offer **her; the** villagers looked **from their** labor when the carriage passed—and if she was in **it,** they turned and watched it out of sight; the cottage women looked from door or window, **then** sighing turned again **to** their **work** within; the very children **of the village knew that** their lady was departing, and looked **into her face** with **silent** questioning, which there was none to answer—for their young hearts spoke by looks alone; all knew that she had well-nigh reached Heaven's gate, all but her own young brother—he looked on her, but her smile, unchanged, still threw its veil of beauty over weakness and pain; he looked no deeper than that smile, **and** thought that however her strength might change, that smile would be always beside him; and lest he should find that others thought differently, he never asked of any what they thought, and so he knew it not, but still believed that, with the greatest care, she might recover again, as she had **done** before.   It was now some weeks **since** he had **been to old** Willy's, for the last time he **went, and** expressed **his hope that** his sister would soon be well again, **old** Willy had shaken **his** head ; Herbert saw **and felt** that shake **of** the old man's head ; he said nothing, but **he kept away from the** cottage after that, afraid **to** venture again.

It was the close of June, the air breathed the fragrance of **the** new-mown grass **over** the hills, the **song** of the birds was hushed at mid-day, **and** the heavy foliage hung its soft shade between the earth **and** sky.   Miss Clifford came down in her shawl and bonnet, and Herbert, ever on the watch, soon had her leaning on his arm, crossing the unsheltered lawn.   " You will not go this way, Mary, you will **want the** shade of the trees," he said—without arresting by a pause the frail steps he supported.

" No, I want to go this way to-day," she replied ; " and as I can not talk while walking, we will sit down on this seat, and I will tell you why."

Herbert sat down **beside** his sister, and she said, " There is a **poor old** woman who lives not far from the Lime-avenue Lodge ; **she is** very ill ; I fear they think her dying, **and** I want to go to-**day and** visit her."

" Indeed, Mary, you must not go! you **know** mamma never lets you go and sit in sick rooms ; and now, when you can not take a little walk without being tired, I am **sure** you must not go !"

" Yes, dear Herbert, mamma does **not** mind to-day ; she knows I am going, **and** you will **go** with me. I fear the poor woman is dying without a hope beyond the grave, and there is no one to tell her of ' the precious blood that cleanseth from all sin.' "

Herbert was silent; he thought, could he go and tell **the** dying woman of the precious blood of Jesus, that could cleanse **her** from her sins? No, he thought he could not; he feared he should not know what to say to her; he had never seen sickness and death, and he was afraid to venture; so he let his sister take his arm, and he led her gently **on**; they were silent till they reached the cottage. The dying woman was lying on a bed put up for her **in** the lower room; **she** looked toward Miss Clifford, but did **not speak.** Herbert stayed by the open casement, **and** Miss Clifford went **to the** bedside. "I am sorry to **see** you **so ill,"** said Miss Clifford.

"O, dear, yes, and I am as **bad** in mind as I am in body!" the dying woman replied.

"What is it that troubles you?" Miss Clifford asked.

"What is it! why it's every thing, even to the look of peace on my husband's face—for to my belief the peace he has is as much above my reach as the Heaven itself!"

"It is the peace of God your husband has; the peace of one who has found the Saviour; none ever reached that peace of themselves; but God who gave it to him, **can give it** also to you."

"Yes, our minister has been here, and he told **me I** must repent; he said, that there was no mercy without that, and I told him it was no use, for I could **not** repent; I don't feel it, and I told him so."

"You can not get repentance any more than peace of yourself; they are both the gift of God; but it is written in the Bible, 'Ask, and it shall be given you!'"

"Yes, I dare say it's all to be had by those who have not set themselves against it all their life-long **as I** have done, but there's none can tell how I have turned against it—therefore there's none can say that it's for me!"

10

"Shall I tell you what God, who knows all things, says in His Word?"

"Yes, I don't mind hearing now!"

"He says, 'O Israel, thou **hast** destroyed thyself, but in **Me** is thy help found!'"

The dying woman looked up; those words, "Thou hast destroyed thyself," reached the depth of her sense of misery; they included it all, and made her feel that if over those "destroyed" there was hope, then might there be a hope for her. Clasping her hands together, and fixing her dying eyes upon the young speaker, **she exclaimed,** "O, how you comfort me!" then, closing her eyes, she listened while again the same words which **had proved so** instantly "spirit **and** life" to her were repeated. **After** telling her of Jesus—the One mighty to save, on whom help for the sinful **has** been laid, whose precious blood can cleanse from all sin, the young lady took her leave, and left her to the hope she had set before **her** in the Gospel—that one declaration of divine truth, which, admitting all her sin and misery, turned her eye not on herself for repentance, but on Jesus for help, and touched her heart; the seed of hope was **planted, and** in the **last** great **day** it may **be** seen to have brought forth fruit to life eternal.

Herbert led his sister gently home, he laid her on her couch to rest—wearied with her effort she did not speak, but laid her **hand** upon his head and smiled upon him—one long sweet smile that met his earnest and inquiring look: then Herbert turned away thoughtfully to his room; he had a purpose in going there—it was to take his Bible in his hand; to hold again, himself, in his own hand, the wondrous Book, whose words from his sister's lips he had but just seen change the face of dull despair to the eager gaze of sudden hope. He held his **Bible, he** looked **upon** its pages, he saw the words so thickly

traced, and thought again upon the living, the creative power
he had but now seen them possessed of, and he resolved that
the highest object of his life should be to make them his own
by hiding them within his heart—that he might both live himself by their help, and use them in aid of others. He held the
sacred volume as the young soldier grasps his sword—for personal and relative defense: but Herbert's was "the sword of the
Spirit, the Word of God"—which wounds but to heal; which
destroys—not man, but sin, man's enemy; a sword given to
be used—not to defend one human being against another, but
to defend all against the powers of evil, to rescue all from Satan's
dreadful dominion. Happy the child who goes forth early in
this blessed warfare—who, taking the Word of God, first proves
its power in his own heart and life, then tries to use it for
others' good; "he shall stand in the evil day, and having done
all, shall stand," and those beside him whom God will have
given him to be his glory and joy in the day of Christ's appear-
ing!

CHAPTER XV.

"O, I stand trembling
  Where foot of mortal ne'er hath been ;
  Wrapt in the radiance of that sinless land
  Which eye hath never seen.

"Bright visions come and go,
  Shapes of resplendent beauty round me throng,
  From angel lips I seem to hear the flow
  Of soft and holy song."

IT was the summer night. The heavens, so softly blue, were gleaming with their host of countless stars : the village slept in the calm hush of midnight's hour, it slept and knew not that its best and dearest treasure was passing from its sight forever. Horses' hoofs trod swiftly through the village street, but they roused not the laborer whose healthful sleep is sweet to him after the long day's toil ; then all was silent, till after an hour's space, carriage wheels rolled rapidly by, it sounded like the doctor's carriage, and affection's wakeful ear and heart were roused—many a villager listened, and some looked anxiously out, but the distant sound had died away, and all was silent again. With the dawn, the village rose, " Man goeth forth to his work and to his labor till the evening." Far over the bright pastures the grass had withered—the flower faded beneath the mower's scythe ; and one, the sweetest flower that ever grew within the village bound, one that every village hand would have been raised to shield and to retain, had fallen too beneath the scythe of death—the young sweet lady of the Hall

lay dead ; that night her spirit had departed, and the place that
had known her, knew her no more. The villagers soon learned
the tidings, and one told another, till every cottage knew and
mourned its loss. Yet they said not, " She is DEAD ;" but only,
" She is GONE !" They thought not of death, but of Heaven
as her portion ; so they said one to another, " She is gone !" and
the laborer raised his arm, from turning the new-made hay, and
wiped away the tear that dimmed his eye ; and the widow wept
alone within her cottage door ; and the village mother, silent
and sad, prepared the morning meal, and the children cried beside their untasted food—the village mourned, for the friend, the
loved of all, was gone !

The windows of the Hall were curtained—the stately home
of her birth closed in ; guarding the still repose of that lovely
form in death which it had sheltered through life. The grief of
the home was calmed by the near approach to Heaven's gate
with the bright spirit who had, manifestly to all, entered in ; and
for a time the glory that received her, struggled with the sadness
her departure had left behind—even as the sun's parting rays
cast their light back on the gray shades of advancing twilight.
Poor Herbert alone had been surprised as by a sudden shock,
he knew not that she was going, till, lo ! she was gone ! Grief
held him in its heavy fetters, he could think of and feel nothing
but the first overpowering sense of death and desolation ; he
knew too little yet of what it is to rise in heart and live in Heav-
en, to be able to feel communion of spirit still with her whom
he had lost on Earth.

The day of the funeral came, and the whole village gathered
to the grave—there came the old and feeble, whom her hands
had clothed and fed, her lips had taught and comforted : there
came the dark transgressor, whose chains of sin had melted
under her fervent utterance of Heavenly truth and love ; there

came the strong-built laborer, whose dull mind had gathered
light under her gentle teaching, whose hand of iron-strength
had followed her frail finger, tracing out the sacred lessons of
holy writ; there came the village children, the lambs of the
Chief Shepherd's fold, whom she had fed with the living Word
of the Lord of Life—all came to see the form they had loved
laid to its rest, till the resurrection of the just.   Respect brought
some, but it was love unfeigned that led the many there : they
filled the churchyard, lined the wooded lane that led down the
hill-side, reached to the park-gate and stood beneath the trees
that grew beside it.   Old Willy had climbed the hill, and lean
ing on his staff, stood beneath the churchyard Yew.   Then the
long procession came in sight, the servants of her home would
suffer no hired hand to bear her honored form and lay it to
its rest ; slowly they came, the snow-white border of the sable
pall gleaming between the old trees of the park ; telling of
purity and light that encompasseth the blessed, hidden from
earthly sight by the dark shade of death.   Herbert was led by
his father, and the long train of mourners followed.   There
stood the mourning village, and the mourners from many a
village round.   The great men of the Earth have a name
through its generations, and then, if their greatness has been
of Earth only, their very name must pass away and be lost for-
ever : but the childlike spirit, who lives to minister to others'
good, to ease the burden of the weary-hearted, to sweeten and
bless life's bitter cup, to win the lost to the Saviour's feet—
luring on, by **words** of truth and bright example of Heavenly
love, from Earth to Heaven, from darkness into light, from
death to life—has a record written on human hearts whose
records are eternal.   A suppressed sob heaved the breasts of
the villagers as she—who had ever come among them in life to
bless—was borne into the midst of them sleeping in death.   The

village children had filled their pinafores with the summer flowers, they had been wont to gather them to win her smile, and now they cast them down before the feet of those who bore her to her rest ; she who most endeared the flowers to them had passed away from earth forever.

The clergyman of the village, an old man, had served that village-church for thirty years, but not a single voice had blessed him, for he knew not the power of that love by which the minister of Christ unlocks the sinner's heart. He had now stepped from his garden to the vestry on the other side of the church, and it was not till called to meet the departed that he saw the assembled village. As the sight from the church porch first broke upon him, he stood for a moment overcome—such a company of mourning people—children whose sobs answered to the silent tears of strong-built men and helpless age, was grief too real not to raise the instant question within him, " What woke this burst of love ?" and he stood silent and awe-struck at the church's porch. Meanwhile the bearers waited, they had reached the churchyard gate, and would not enter without the words of holiest greeting for the earthly form they bore ; then, in that moment's solemn pause, old Willy, standing beneath the Yew raised his voice, and calmly and distinctly exclaimed, " Welcome the holy dead !" At the sound of those firm tones of age, the Minister recovered speech ; he came forward with the words of Life, and the bearers followed him into the church. The service went calmly on ; but when the white coffin was borne within the tomb, overcome by the hopelessness with which they hid his sister from his sight forever upon Earth, Herbert fainted and fell. The servants came forward, but meanwhile Jem had darted through them, and kneeling on one knee at Herbert's side, looked up at the father's face for permission to raise the boy : the servants would have put him aside, but the father

moved his hand to them to retire, and lifting Herbert from the
ground, placed him in the arms of the faithful Jem, sending a
servant hastily forward to prevent needless alarm to Mrs. Clifford. The throng separated for Jem to pass, bearing his precious burden—the child of fortune—the only hope of his
father's house, trusted to one of themselves, borne by the village lad to his home. Jem made his way down the hill side,
then stopped a moment to raise the boy's arm, which had fallen·
from its posture of rest, and as he laid the small, soft hand on
the breast of the boy, he thought of the day when he had
taught it first to use the tools so large and heavy for its strength,
in labor for the poor and needy! and the tear of past and
present feeling gathered in the eyes of the faithful Jem. Jem
was met on his way to the Hall, and accompanied by some of
the maid-servants to the house. Mrs. Clifford waited anxiously
at the door.

" It 's only a fainting, ma'am," said Jem ; " it was all over too
much for my young master, but he will come to quick enough
now !"

Mrs. Clifford bent a moment over the fainting boy, almost as
pale herself—her vision almost as dim. " Bring him in here
and lay him down," she said ; and she opened the nearest door,
while the maids gathered to the Hall, bearing various remedies
and helps. Mrs. Clifford preceded Jem into the dining-room
—the very room where Jem had stood before alone with the
young Squire to receive his mother's scarlet cloak.

" Come in and lay him here," said Mrs. Clifford, and she placed
the damask cushion for the boy's unconscious head. Jem had
felt no hesitation in raising the heir of that stately dwelling in
his arms, to bear him to his home ; but now that by daylight
he saw the rich carpet that lay before his feet, he held back
with his precious burden, hesitating in his rough shoes to tread

upon a thing so costly—even so it is that the poorest can r'se in a moment to feel and act up to the universal tie of nature's one brotherhood, but they pause at the threshold of wealth's display ; and own, as if by instinct, that the separating line lies there !

" Bring him in," repeated the housekeeper ; and friends within the house were gathering, and maid-servants were waiting round, and so Jem bore the child of the mansion across the soft-carpeted floor, laid him gently´down with his pale cheek on the crimson cushion, and then, as he stepped back, while Herbert's mother knelt beside the couch, and friends drew nearer and servants waited—Jem, bowing, asked, " Will you please that I should fetch the doctor ?" but the housekeeper shook her head and whispered " No ;" then Jem, with another bow of lowliest reverence, and a look of anxious love toward the fainting boy, withdrew. He saw the long train of mourners descending the hill, and made his way straight to the farm, there to solace himself among his sheep.

The evening shadows fell and closed that summer **day ; the** folded flowers, the folded flocks, the birds with folded wing— all sought repose ; while softly calm the moon rose over all in the blue heavens. Old Willy had vainly tried to comfort his troubled heart—his eyes were dim, he could not see the words of the Book ; he sat awhile within doors, then stepped into his garden, then back again within the cottage in wearied restlessness, wanting some human voice to fall on his aching heart with tones of comfort ; but all that summer day were mourners, and no earthly comforter drew near. When the hush of evening shed its soothing silence round, and sleep seemed far away trom old Willy's tear-dimmed eyes, he took his staff and set forth to climb once more that day the steep hill-side, and look **upon the** tomb where they had **laid his** blessed guide to Heaven.

All were gone from the hill-side; and the Hall, with its far-stretching slopes, lay silently and beautifully in the summer evening twilight. Old Willy looked round once from the hill-top on his lady's home on earth, then turned to the church-yard gate, and leaning upon it, rested there a little while before he ventured further, for the place where they had laid her seemed to the old man holy ground—too sacred almost for his feet to enter. So he leaned upon the gate, looking on into the distant azure of the sky, looking almost without sight or thought, his senses lost in one deep feeling—they had laid his sweet young lady in the grave, they had left her there alone, the night was darkening over her, and he alone kept watch above the form so loved of all! How long he stood he did not know, but suddenly he saw in those blue heavens before his eyes a shining star, full on his sight its radiance beamed, the only star in heaven, risen there in view, and looking down to comfort him, it seemed! "Ah! sure I see it," the old man said, in a low tone, "sure I see it 's no use looking down in the dark grave for her that 's up above the stars in glory there! I see it!" again he murmured low, as with a lingering gaze on that bright star he turned to depart; but then again he looked toward the tomb, and thought he would stand beside it once before the night came on, and so he climbed the stile beside the now locked gate, and reached the silent grave; then stopping short gazed in surprise, for at its foot a child lay sleeping, her head reclined against the lady's tomb, her lap full of fresh-gathered flowers. "Poor dear," said the old man, "she has fallen off asleep; why, 'tis little Mercy Jones! Mercy, child! I say, wake up there!" And the child sprang up from sleep like a startled fawn, and her flowers dropped from her pinafore; but when she saw it was old Willy, she stood still, looking down on the fallen flowers.

" Why, Mercy, child, you must not stay sleeping here, it's no place for you !"

" Yes, but it is," said the child, without looking up ; " it 's the best place in all the world—to be near to my lady ! I nave not been so near to her since that last day she came and stood among us all in school, only I can't see her **now** Oh, if I could but see **her** !" **And the** child sat down agair. at the tomb's foot beside her fallen flowers and hid her face and wept.

The tears again dimmed old Willy's eyes, but still he saw that beauteous star shining so brightly down from the blue Heaven—looking full upon both him and the young child, as **they watched there beside** the tomb within the churchyard dreary ! and he answered quickly, " Why, child, your blessed lady is not here, look there, she 's shining bright in Heaven !" The child looked up with sudden start, as if expecting **that** angel face to beam upon her from above, or to get some distant glimpse of her lady's white-robed form in glory ; she looked where the old man pointed, and her eye too rested on **the** star —on those calm blue Heavens above her, and that beaming star so full of softened glory—she looked, **then said,** " I only see a star !"

" Well, child, what more would you **see ?** Is not that star enough ? is n't it just come shining down from Heaven upon you to tell you that the blessed lady is up above it far away in glory ? **For** what did God send **it in** the sky there, if not to put you in mind that there 's a world of glory up above, all shining bright like that same star, and that He took the blessed lady straight up to it to dwell with Him forever ?"

" Yes, I know it," said little Mercy, " and **I** wish I was with her there !"

" Then, child, you must be walking the path she went."

" What path was that ?" asked Mercy, looking up to the old man's face.

" Why, the blessed path of love, child ! love to God and man ; her mind was always on her Saviour, and trying to bring others to the love of Him.   Oh, child ! it 's written in the Book that ' God is Love,' and there 's none but a path of love that can lead up to Him."

Little Mercy was silent ; she had tried to tread the path of **love, in** which her lady had taught her to walk, she had tried to please God her Heavenly Father, and Jesus her Saviour, and to be a ministering child to others ; and now she knew not what more to do ; all looked dreary and dull around her, and she was silent.

" Come now, child," then old Willy said, " it 's best to begin at once !   You know right well your poor grandmother is fretting at home for that blessed lady that 's gone, now, do you go back, and be cheerful, and comfort her up."

" Yes," said little Mercy, " I came here because I could not bear it.—Granny cried, and said, ' the summer time seemed gone from the earth !' and though I had set the supper all ready, Uncle Jem turned away and never eat a bit ! so I went **and** gathered those flowers and came here."

" Well, child, you know you have seen that star, there it is, **look** at it, see how it shines right down upon us here—a bit of glory as it is !   Now, you go and be like that, you go and try.   He who sent that star to light us up with comfort here, sent you to your good grandmother to be a bit of light to her in this lonesome world—you mind that, and go and try, till the day comes when you will go, as the blessed lady 's gone, to Heaven."

So little Mercy rose, and took her bonnet from the ground, **and** the old man laid his hand upon her head, and blessed her, and she left her fallen flowers at the foot of the tomb, and back she went with many a look upon the star in the blue **sky;** from whatever point she turned to look, the star still beamed upon her,—seemed to watch her still, so she went back with light in her eyes and fresh life in her young heart, gathered from the old man's words and the bright star in Heaven. Old Willy, too, went home, **and** from his cottage door beheld the same bright star, then laid him down to rest— to sleep and dream of glory.

CHAPTER XVI.

"The memory of the just is blessed."—Proverbs x. 7.
"Being dead, yet speaketh."—Hebrews xi. 4.

THE old clergyman could not forget the scene he had witnessed, but the love and the sorrow were both incomprehen-
sible to him; he felt their reality, but could not understand
their cause. At length it occurred to him, how often, in driving out, he had seen Miss Clifford's ponies at the cottage doors;
he instantly concluded that it must be the notice she had
taken of the poor that had endeared her to them; and thinking it would be pleasant to win the same feeling for himself,
pleasant to have the love of all his people in life, and their
tears above his grave, he determined to visit, himself, from
house to house with this object. He thought also that it would
be pleasant to be kind to those who showed so much feeling,
such warm return of gratitude: so he set forth. He went
through the village street, calling at every house, leaving his
gifts of money, and saying a few words to all, but he returned
dissatisfied: he had met no smile of welcome, seen no tear-
dimmed eye grown bright; heard no blessing. What made
the difference? Why had he no power, and she—the departed
so young in years! why had she so much? He could not tell:
he did not know that a difference, as real as that of Earth and
Heaven, lay between his visits and the visits of her the village
mourned. He had gone in his own name, his words were of
Earth, his gifts the dole of the richer to the poorer; his object

was to please, and to win affection and gratitude to himself;
but she they mourned, had gone to none but in the Name of
JESUS; her words breathed to all the love and truth of Heaven:
her gifts were ever the expression of her thoughtful sympathy
—warm with compassion's tenderness, and bright with the
glad power of administering aid; such was her way of giving
that her gift ever elevated, instead of seeming to degrade or
lower the receiver; her highest object was not to win feeling
toward herself, but to win the whole heart and life of those
she visited to her Saviour and their Saviour, that they might
be happy in Him, and He glorified in them: therefore an over-
flowing recompense was poured out for her—for "with what
measure ye mete, it shall be measured to you again." But the
aged clergyman knew not that the difference between his
Earthly kindness and her Heavenly love, was wide as the east
is from the west. He was disappointed, and resolved to give
up the vain attempt, and go on as before. But then a recollection of that old man who had stood within the churchyard
gate, and uttered those words of blessing on the departed,
crossed his mind, and he resolved to go and call on him, and
see what he would say.

Old Willy saw his minister coming up his cottage garden,
and stood at his door with his hat in his hand to receive him:
old Willy had learned to behave himself lowly and reverently
to those whom God had placed above him in station, and cour-
teously to all. There is no such teacher of true courtesy as pure
Religion—if we would only learn of her!

"Sit down, my good friend, sit down," said the clergyman.
"What a nice house you have here! I think I remember this
quite a tumble-down building?"

"Very like you may, sir; for that was the fashion of it many
a long day!"

"I think I saw you at Miss Clifford's funeral the other day!" observed the clergyman.

Old Willy sobbed out, "Yes, sir!" overcome at the sudden mention of the subject.

"Never mind my good friend, I am sorry to distress you. I suppose Miss Clifford was very good to the poor?"

"Ah yes, sir! if I might have given my old life for her's, there's hundreds would have blessed me!"

"Miss Clifford came to see you, I suppose?"

"Yes, sir, sure enough she did, but it was Him she brought with her, that made her wholly a blessing."

"Who was that?" asked the minister.

"Why our Saviour, sir! she never went any where to my belief without Him, and you never saw her but you seemed to get a fresh sight of Him."

The clergyman was silent; at length he said, "Well, my good friend, you come very regular to church, I wish I could see a few more of your neighbors there."

"Yes, sir, but then you see we want teaching! and there's some of them that can walk after that."

"To be sure they want teaching, and have not I preached two sermons every Sunday for thirty years? Why don't they come to hear them?"

"That's true enough, sir, there's none can say to the contrary of that; no doubt there's teaching enough in your sermons to do any body good; only poor dark creatures as we are, can't get hold of it, because the Light isn't set up in the midst of it."

"What Light do you mean?"

"Why, sir, I mean him that is the Light of the world, without whom 'tis groping in the dark. I mean our Saviour, sir! why when one gets a sight of Him, then one can see and get a hold of **all the good** that lies round; but when there's no getting a sight of Him, why it seems all the same as leading a poor creature out when the sun is not in the sky—there's no getting a right understanding of any thing."

The aged minister was silent again; old Willy waited, but when the silence lasted, he laid his hand upon the Bible at **his** side, saying, "I never look in here for teaching, but I see Him before me! He is just the very light of my old heart, that was as dark as death before. I first got a sight of Him, out of this Book, and now I never so much as look into it but I see Him, and I find that it holds but dark where there's no setting up of **Him.**"

"**Well,** my good friend, I will think of your words," said the **old** clergyman, **and with** that withdrew.

The summer sun had three times risen and set since Herbert sank beside his sister's grave; he was lying on his mother's couch: his cheek almost as pale as then; his Bible lay beside him, but he had ceased to read, and was lying with a look of sad and earnest thought: his mother watched him anxiously, but feared to question him, lest she should but wake her **own** deep grief and his into expression.

"Mamma," at last he said, "you **see it is** harder for me than for any one."

"What is harder?" asked Mrs. Clifford.

"To lose Mary, mamma."

"Why is it harder for you, dear Herbert?"

"Because you and papa are so good! but I was always getting wrong, **and** never should have got right again if it had not been for Mary's smile."

Mrs. Clifford was silent, she could not question more on such a subject. Herbert soon went on to say,

"You see, mamma, when I got into trouble, you and papa of course were displeased, and you looked so grave, and then I lost all hope in a moment, and it was so dreadful to feel as if one could never be right again!. And I never felt as if I could or seemed to know how; but when I went to Mary, she always smiled at me still, and said she knew I was sorry, and wanted to do right again—and so I am sure I did, though I did not always know it till she told me; and then she used to say it would soon be all bright again; and when I looked at her, and heard her say so, I believed it, and then I tried, and she used to tell me what to do, and help me; and then I was sure to get right again; only you and papa did not know how. But now I don't see any hope for me, I don't know what will become of me."

"Do you know who gave you your sweet sister to help **you** on your way?"

"Yes, mamma, of course it was God."

"And has God, your Heavenly Father, given you no better gift—one that still remains, one that death can never take away?"

"Yes, mamma, I know that God has given us Jesus Christ, and that He helps me when I pray to Him, I know that, mamma; but then I can not see Him, or hear him speak to me, as I could **Mary.**"

"You have not seen Him yet perhaps, dear Herbert, but you may see Him. He can and he does show Himself as clearly to the eye of the spirits of His children sometimes, as earthly objects are seen by the eye of the body; and he speaks as distinctly to their hearts as earthly voices to the ear."

"But would Jesus smile on me, mamma, when I get wrong, and am in trouble for it, as Mary used to do?"

"O yes, he would! Whatever may have been your fault, if you only turn to Him you will find His tenderness the same: if you only look up to Him—the moment you see His face you will see the smile of forgiveness and love upon it. His love, **my** child, is more than a mother's; and what His tenderness leads you to hope, His power can enable you to accomplish—He can work in you both to will and to do according to His own good pleasure."

Herbert lay silent, thinking on his mother's words, and she had gathered strength from speaking of Him who is the Life, to speak of her whom death had taken, and went on to say to her listening child, " It was so with Mary, she lived always in the presence of God her Saviour, always able to look up to Him and see His face at any moment, she lived in the sense of His love, it was her greatest joy to try in all she did to please Him, by doing His holy will—this made her life so happy, and so blessed !"

Then Herbert said, " I will try mamma, and do as Mary did Shall I read you a chapter from the Bible now ?"

" Yes, dear Herbert, that will help us both to do that of which we have been speaking—even to walk in the light of God's countenance." So Herbert read to his mother, and the words of Heavenly Truth and Love lightened the sadness of their hearts—as the rising sun illumines the mist **that hides the Heavens from** our earthly view.

Days passed away, and Herbert returned to his studies ; but the paleness did not pass from his cheek, nor the sadness from **his brow :** he had not mounted Araby, **nor taken a** single walk by himself since the day that **saw** him bereft of his sister. He was sitting one morning in the window of his father's study with a lesson-book before him, but his eyes were far away on the park's green slopes, where the deer were feeding. His father came in, and, going up to him, laid his hand upon the boy's dark clustering curls, but silently, as if he feared to wake into expression the saddened thought so plainly written on his face. Herbert looked up, then, after a minute's silence, said, " Papa, shall I tell you what I was thinking ?"

" Yes, my boy, what was it ?"

" I was thinking that I wished Snowflake might be unshod and turned into the park, to live always there, and no one ever ride her again ; she would look so beautiful under the green trees ! I am sure she has done good enough to rest all her life now, and I could not bear to see her led up for any one else to mount."

" No, perhaps none of us could bear that ; but how would it be if I had a new pony-carriage for your mamma, and you drove Snowflake and the groom's pony in it ? and then we could keep David on, and have a seat behind the carriage for him, to save your mother's fears ?"

" O yes, papa, I should like that ! I had not been into the stables till to-day, and David took the cloth off Snowflake, she looked as beautiful as possible, and turned her bright eye round on me, only she looked so sad ! I am sure she knows, papa— any one who saw her would think so too ! David said that at first he felt as if he could not bear the place, but now he feels as if he could do any thing to stay. May I tell him what you mean to do, papa ? I know he will be so glad !"

" Yes, if your mother does not object. Jenks can try Snow-flake alone in the pony-chair, I know he broke her in first to that !"

" Yes, papa, and then I can drive mamma out first with Snowflake alone, till the new carriage comes." And Herbert rose up with more of purpose and energy than he had felt since the day that the stroke of bereavement had first fallen on him. Mrs. Clifford made no objection, any personal fear being over-come by the sense of the new interest for her child. David met the proposal still to stay as groom very gratefully ; and Jenks said, " You could not put the creature to the thing she would not do if she had the power !" So it was finally settled, that

after one or two days' trial by Jenks, Herbert should drive his
mother with Snowflake in the pony-chair, till the new carriage
could be bought.

The day arrived when Herbert was, for the first time, to
drive his mother out. . Old Jenks led up the pony-chair with
Snowflake harnessed in it ; she did not stand with arching neck
and pawing step, but sorrowfully with head hung down, as if
she knew the hand and voice she loved, would not be now
awaiting her. Herbert felt all the responsibility of his new
privilege ; and some unexpressed anxiety that all should be
prosperous in **this his first** attempt to drive his mother, helped
to check **his** feeling at sight of Snowflake. Mrs. Clifford also
was not free from nervous apprehension, never really considering
herself safe except when old Jenks was her charioteer—she had
only yielded to the proposal for the sake of the interest to Herbert ; and now her feeling also at sight of the snow-white creature
was lessened by a sense of personal apprehension : she took her
seat, and Herbert his, by her side, and Snowflake gently trotted
from the door. There were only three roads by which to leave
the Hall for a drive ; one was the direct way **to the** town, and
led past old Willy's cottage ; Herbert had not yet summoned
courage to see old Willy, though the old man had been many
times up to the Hall to inquire **for** him since the day he had
seen " the blessed child," as he called him, fall beside the grave ;
therefore Herbert would not go that way, because of passing his
cottage. Another road led up the steep hill-side to the church,
past the churchyard gate, and then round by farmer Smith's, a
longer way to the town ; that could not be ventured on ; **so Her-**
bert drove out by the gamekeeper's lodge, and took a long
winding shady lane that led round by the back **of** the park.
Snowflake trotted swiftly and smoothly along ; but gentle as
the creature was known to be, Mrs. Clifford was still on the

watch for fear of some mischance. On they went beneath the sheltering trees, when, drawing near a lonely cottage, Snowflake suddenly quickened her **pace and drew** up at the door.

" What is the matter ?" exclaimed Mrs. Clifford. While she spoke, Herbert touched Snowflake with the whip; but all the advance that was gained was a few steps to a little window of one pane, rather high up in the wall—a window that opened with a push from within or from without, directly underneath which Snowflake took a determined stand. Herbert gave her a harder stroke; she shook her silver mane at the unwonted indignity, but did not move a step. Herbert's color mounted to his cheek, and Mrs. Clifford exclaimed, " Take care, Herbert, something will certainly happen !" But at that instant the door opened, and out came a neatly-dressed woman, courtesying, as if to expected guests.

" Do go to the creature's head while we get out !" said Mrs. Clifford. The woman obeyed, and Herbert sprang down and handed out his mother.

" Something is wrong," said Mrs. Clifford, as she stood on the door-step ; " the creature will not move !"

" O dear me, no, ma'am, the pretty dear is always used to stop here ; I don't know I have ever seen it pass by without !"

" What for ?" asked **Mrs.** Clifford.

" Why, you see, ma'am, my poor old mother is blind and bed-ridden, and that sweet lady that 's gone was the very light of her life, and I never saw her so much as pass by once ! She used to get off at this door-step, and the pretty creature knew it as well, and would never have wanted the telling ; and if she was all in a hurry for time, as she would be sometimes, why then she just rode up to that little window—it goes open with a shove, and it's just above my old mother's bed, and there she would speak a cheery word to her, and then be off again ; and, dear me, how that word would lift up my poor mother's spirits ! She used to say, the very sound of her voice was like Heaven's music to her, sent to comfort her up in her darkness ! So that is all the meaning of the pretty creature's holding to it so !"

The sudden alarm Mrs. Clifford had taken, and now the sudden disclosure of the cause, were too much for her ; she stepped into the cottage, and, sitting down, leaned her face upon her hand, and wept. Herbert threw his arms round Snowflake, partly to hide **his** tears, and partly to atone for the stroke of the whip he had made her feel. The poor woman waited beside Mrs. Clifford in distress to know what to do, then hastened and **brought her** water in a glass.

Mrs. Clifford soon recovered self-possession, and turning to the poor woman, said, " I will see your mother." The woman hastened into the inner room, and smoothing the bed-clothes, whispered, " Here's Madam herself from the Hall ! the pretty creature would not stir a step, and Madam is wholly overcome !" Then, hastening back again, she took Mrs. Clifford in. **Mrs.** Clifford went to the bed, took the old woman's hand in hers, **and** sat down, but vain were all attempts to **speak.** The poor old woman felt her silent grief, but while the big tears from her sightless eyes rolled down her **cheek, she** said, " Oh ! my lady ! this world is the place for weeping, but the blessed dear is gone to Him who wipes all tears away ! Don't I see her with my sightless eyes, shining as bright as the morning's ray up above in the holy **Heaven** ? and don't it lighten me up, as the sound of her tongue **did** here ! I never thought to hear her horse's feet ring down the lane again ; and now that you should come ! 'tis a wonderful condescension and lifts me up—that it **does."**

" I will come and see you often !" replied Mrs. Clifford, and she rose, strengthened by the old woman's vision of faith, but unable to say more, pressed her hand, and left the cottage.

It was the first visit Mrs. Clifford had ever paid to the poor and needy. The deep feeling and touching expression, and unassuming attention, the bright faith beholding what her own faith had not realized—all these surprised her with their charm · that brief visit had planted in her heart the seed of a personal interest in the poor ; she felt too the peace of having shed comfort on another, and she stepped from the cottage door, unwilling so soon to leave the spot, yet feeling unable then to stay. The fear too of safety with Snowflake seemed lost in the deeper impressions now awakened, and a creature who could so follow the track of its departed mistress's steps of love, was surely worthy of confidence, so Mrs. Clifford took her seat by Herbert's side, and ceased to look out for occasions of mischance.

On through the summer lanes they drove, and the sweet air relieved the oppression of feeling. The drive was a lonely one, farm-houses and cottages stood right and left among the fields, but none by the road-side, till at the foot of a hill, sideways from the winding lane, they saw a cottage : a little boy stood beside the wicket-gate, clad in a coarse round pinafore, his little cap, crushed up in his hand, left his fair curls uncovered, and his smiling eyes of blue looked down the winding lane as if with listening expectation.

The boy was Rose's little friend, Johnnie Lambert, the widow Lambert's only child. Quick as thought, the listening boy at sight of Snowflake darted into the cottage, calling, " Mother ! mother ! the lady's coming !" then back he ran to the wicket-gate, while the mother looked from the door.

" Stop and let us speak to that child," said Mrs. Clifford, for she saw the white pony was well known to the boy.

The child made his deliberate and never-forgotten bow, and then raised his bright face as if to meet the look of some loved familiar friend, but instantly the blank of disappointed hope chased his glad smile away, and running to the pony's head, **he** sheltered himself there.

Seeing the pony stopping at the gate, the mother **stepped out** and courtesied low.

" **Your** little boy knows the **pony ?**" said Mrs. Clifford.

" Yes, ma'am,—Johnnie, **come** here and make your **bow to** the lady !" but Johnnie **was giving his tears** to Snowflake. " **He** takes on, ma'am, **so about the dear young lady** that's better off, he is always watching **for her, and I can't** make him sensible that she **is** gone ! he **ran in just now, for he** thought it was her **when he got** sight **of the pony.**"

" **Was she** often **here ?**" asked Mrs. Clifford.

" O yes, that she was ! All the time my poor husband kept about, she used to come and read to him—for he could not read a word, and I never saw a man so changed ! he suffered a wonderful deal, for his complaint lay in the head, and **nothing** could ease it, and he lost all his spirits, and was **always** fretting to live and **get** well ; **but when** she had showed **him the** way to Heaven—all plain for him to walk in, and showed **him how his** Saviour called him to come unto Him **! he seemed to** think **of** nothing else, it was wholly **a** pleasure **instead of a** misery to see him !"

" Has he been long **dead ?" asked Mrs. Clifford.**

" Over two **years,** ma'am ; **but** to me it seems all as fresh as yesterday ! **He lay** six **weeks in** his bed, and all that time he never **saw the dear** young lady, only she used to send and in- quire **for him, but** he seemed past the want of her then, **though** before **when he was** about he would sit all **day long and** watch **for her** coming by, but when he took to his **bed, and** she could **not** come, he seemed to be hanging **only on** his Saviour. I have heard him say when I sat by his bed, " Oh ! I see Him ! I see Him !" and then he would let me leave him and get my night's rest—though he could not sleep a wink for pain, but it seemed as if Heaven had opened above him. Oh, it was a wonderful change! he said the **dear** young lady's words had been life from the dead to him!"

Herbert had slipped out **of** the carriage unperceived by his mother, and now standing **with** the reins in his hand, **was** trying to comfort the child, but he could not get him to speak, only **to** take a shy look at him now and then.

"Poor dear!" said the mother, looking round, "**it** puts me so in mind of his father to see how he listens for the creature's feet, the dear young lady took wonderful notice of him! he can **say many a thing she** taught him, only he's shy. When I ask him where **his** poor father is, he will point up to the sky, and say, 'With God!' but I can't make him sensible that the dear young lady **won't** come down **the lane again!**"

"Tell him **that we will come** again!" said Mrs. Clifford—with an effort **to** retain composure : **and** Herbert, hearing this assurance, **took** his seat, and they drove on—watched out of sight by the widow and her orphan boy.

But now it was necessary to decide which way to return—either back through the lanes, and so to risk another halt at the blind widow's door ; **or past the** churchyard gate ; or by old **Willy's cottage.** Herbert preferred the last—as best of the three, and before they reached the **old man's** dwelling, they saw **him** in the distance, advancing slowly **on** the road toward them.

"There is old Willy himself!" said Herbert.

"Do not pass him by," replied Mrs. Clifford, "stop **and speak** to him."

The old **man stood some minutes** beside the little carriage, **his** white head uncovered—the **very** picture of beautiful old **age!** Mrs. Clifford talked **to him,** and with true feeling the **old man** made **no** reference **to** the **one** of whom **each** heart was full, his feeling only struggled through in silent tears ; he had changed away his **week-day** garment for an old **coat of** black, and in this, and a band of crape about his hat, wore the signs of mourning for her who had been more than child to him. At parting, Mrs. Clifford said, " **I shall** come and **see** you with my son."

" A thousand thanks," replied old Willy, as he bowed **low to** the lady, but his look of love turned full **and** rested on Herbert.

" Yes, I shall soon come, Willy, **very** soon, and mamma too !" added Herbert greatly relieved at the thought of the first sight of his aged friend being over.

And so they returned to the Hall ; both had passed through much to try them in that morning ride, but not less to soothe and elevate. The mother and son felt as if they had that day entered on their sweet Mary's path of love and service, and they longed to follow her steps in all. Herbert now often drove his mother out, all fear of Snowflake was gone, **the creature was** allowed to stop at pleasure ; and when a visit could not **be** made, some kindly word was spoken, till in **every** dwelling where her child had shed the light of hope, and the peace of comfort, or the aid of knowledge, Mrs. Clifford followed her, gathering the blessed recompense that **even** the most aching heart must find in keeping God's commandments—watered herself with Heavenly consolation in watering others. While in Herbert's young heart—so trained and disciplined, earth daily gathered more of Heaven ; and a depth of feeling and **a power** of thought and action beyond his years, enriched his **life with** personal and relative happiness.

CHAPTER XVII.

"Bear ye one another's burdens, and so fulfill the law of Christ."—GALATIANS vl. 2

THE summer months left Patience in the workhouse restored to health. And now another place of service must be found for her; the workhouse made the choice, and we shall find what it was. Patience took leave of her workhouse home with a sorrowful heart; and a heavy dread came over her as she drew near the place to which she was now engaged. It was a small house, a short distance out of the town; and when Patience went in, she saw so many children crowded together in one small kitchen, that she supposed it to be an infant school! But no, it was a family of ten children, the youngest a baby of some few weeks, the next just able to step alone, the third a helpless little cripple, the fourth a rosy-faced girl of about five years of age, then twin-boys of seven, who, with the four elder boys and girls, went to a day-school. The mother was busy at the washing tub, and the children were all sitting and standing about, the elder ones home from their afternoon school; but when Patience came in, they all with one consent looked round on her.

This was now to be the place of service Patience was to fill—maid-of-all-work in the family of the foreman in Mr. Mansfield's shop—there were ten children, and all the washing done at home! It sounds like heavy work, but we must not, like old nurse Brame, be led by sound alone; and we may always

remember that work proving hard or pleasant depends far more
upon the minds of those who rule, and those who serve, than
upon the amount of labor to be done. Robert, the eldest boy,
had opened the door, and then run back to his mother to say
the new girl was there. " Bring her in then," said the mother ;
so in came Patience, still pale and timid, with her small bundle
in her hand. " Come in, come in and see us all at once !" said
the mother and mistress, without so much as making a moment's stop in her washing. Then, looking hard at Patience
in the firelight, she added, " What 's that all the show you have
to make of strength ! Well, if you are killed with hard work
that will lie at your master's door, for it was he hired you, not
I, remember that ! Here 's plenty of work—and plenty of play
too, so don't be frightened ! There, Betsy, you go and show
the girl where to put her bonnet and shawl and her bundle, and
then don't lose a minute, but come and be after tea." Betsy did
as she was desired, and quickly returned with Patience to the
kitchen. The early autumn evening was damp and cold, and
when Patience returned to the family party, preparations for tea
were beginning. The little parlor opened into the small kitchen, and Robert, the eldest boy, was kneeling down before the
parlor-stove, blowing up the flame he had just lighted. Polly,
the second girl, was setting out the tea-things ; and the moment
Betsy returned, she began to take her part in fetching out the
bread and butter and cheese, together with a large round cake,
whose only claim to the designation consisted in a few scattered
currants—more thought of because so far apart that each one
became a definite object, and this so-called plum-cake, with its
scanty sweetening of sugar, was much more approved by the
little group of children than slices of bread and butter. Patience
had not been five minutes in the house, but on no account was
she to stand idle. " What 's your name, child ?" inquired the

mother, still wringing out the wet clothes, and depositing them, one by one, in a large white basket. "Patience!" replied the new little servant.

"Patience?   **Well,** I have heard worse names than that! You may be sure you will have plenty need of patience here, though there is no hardship for all that! I hope you have an apron?"

"Yes, in my bundle," replied Patience.

"Have it on then, as fast as you can!" And up stairs Patience ran with a light quick step, there was something so animating in the universal stir below stairs, that she longed to be one among them all again, and in two minutes' time she stood aproned before her mistress.

"Now take that wide shovel and gather up all those cinders by the grate here, and put them every one on the parlor fire." So Patience gathered **up** the cinders, and laid them on the top of the knobs of coal, among which the cheerful blaze began to ascend. "Now take the kettle and fill it at the tap there, and set it on this fire to boil," said her mistress. Meanwhile, Robert had been out and shut the shutter; Betsy had drawn the chintz curtain within; Polly had lighted one solitary candle and set it in the middle of the tea-table; the mother had wrung out the **last** little garment—and the whole collection lay piled in the **large white basket;** the water was poured from the washing-tub, the tub set up, the stool on which it stood put aside, the whole kitchen then looked in perfect order, the mother drew down her sleeves, changed her coarse blue apron for a white one, and in they all went to tea. The baby sleeping in its cradle had waked up some minutes before; but Betsy had lifted it out and rocked it in her arms, till the mother, seated in the low black chair beside the parlor-fire, received it. The chil-**dren** dragged out their stools and chairs, little Esther, the child of five years—not having yet learned the division of labor, pulled hard at a parlor chair for herself with one hand, and **at** the poor little cripple's high chair with the other. Patience caught sight, amid the active group, of little Esther's attempt, and, running up to her, reached over her head, and laying hold of both chairs pulled gently also, when, to the child's perfect satisfaction, both chairs moved slowly and steadily to the **table.** Esther would by no means leave her **hold till the** chairs were drawn quite close, so Patience slipped **behind** them and pushed, till the little **Esther, stooping half under** the table, peeped up with a grave look, and **suffered** Patience **to** lift her into the parlor chair, **gravely** observing, " **I did pull two** chair !" And **through the heart** of Patience passed a warm feeling for the child ; and a sense of active life, with its native charm of cheerful energy, rose still more freshly within her at this first successful aid rendered to the child.   And now Betsy placed the little cripple in his chair, and Esther looked **up at Betsy, repeating,** " I did pull two chair !" and Betsy said, " **Good Esther !"** ard hastened away to fix up the next baby of **eighteen months old.** Now there was one small blue plate **set down** between Esther and the little cripple ; Esther put her hand **upon** it by way of claim, but did not take it nearer, **then the little** cripple reached out his hand and said, " **Me ! Me !" Esther** shook her head, for it was hard **to give up the plate that was the** earnest to her of food, but Patience, whose attention was all alive, caught sight of the difficulty, and put another blue plate close before Esther, who then pushed the other gently to her little brother, **and** looking up at Patience, said, " I did give it him !"

All the little ones being seated, Betsy cut the bread **and butter,** Robert a piece of cake for each, Polly filled the mugs half full of water, and poured water into the tea-pot for the tea, while all the little ones looked on. This divided labor was quickly

accomplished, after which the mother stood up with her babe
in her arms, the elder children stood also, and Robert asked the
blessing—for at meals, when the father was away, this was
always Robert's office.   Patience had a corner at the table, and
made as hearty **a** meal as any of them : the good mother seeing
her hesitate at first, took care to say, " Come, Patience, girl,
make haste, you have earned your tea, though you may not
think it !"   There was no riot at the meal—the children, trained
to good order, found no pleasure in confusion ; and having had
no food since their early frugal dinner, their best amusement
was to eat.   All the play had come before tea, and now the
moment it was over, and Robert had given thanks, while every
little one was silent with clasped hands, Betsy and Polly took
off the baby of eighteen months and **the** little cripple each in
their arms to **bed,** and the mother **bid** Patience follow with
Esther, who looked very **grave, but quite** willing to go with her
helper of the tea-table.   Patience found that Esther was to share
her little bed, in a room just large enough to hold the bed and
one chair.   The little cripple and the baby of eighteen months
were soon laid to their sleep, and Betsy went down with Polly
to bring up the twin boys of seven.   When Patience returned
to the parlor, the tea-table **was** cleared of all that had been
used, and what remained was set in order for the father's return ;
*.*he boys, **having so** arranged the table, were already at their
tasks for school the next day, and the mother putting the infant
to rest.   Patience was set to wash up the tea-things in the
back-kitchen ; while Betsy and Polly sat down to their lessons.

The baby slept in the cradle ; and when Patience had finished
washing up the tea-things, and had been shown where to
put them away, her good mistress said, " Now for your thimble,
as quick as possible !"   And Patience had a seat at the table,
and one of the children's socks given her to darn.   But Patience

was no darner, she had never been taught, for there are but few
schools in which any pains is taken to teach children to mend,
though to the children of the poor the skill to mend well is
hardly less needful than to make. Poor Patience felt her
spirits sink; she could not do the work, and now she thought
her troubles would begin, and the timid child, only so lately
warmed with the glow of kindness, dreaded a sharp word more
than any thing! But sharp words were not given in this her
new abode without a needs be. The good mistress saw the
color rise to the pale face of Patience **over** the sock; so calling
her to her, she **said, " I can see you are** no match for your task,
well, never mind, bring your stool here, and sit down and learn,
there will be no time lost in the end by good learning in the
beginning!" So Patience took her seat by her mistress, and
learned to darn, as little Jane had learned by her mother's **side,**
only that Patience, being much older, learned to darn **a great**
deal quicker, and did not want so much attention **as Jane had**
done. While Patience darned, the four children **who were sit-**
ting round the table repeated their lessons **to their mother.**
They had had tea at five o'clock, and all **their** lessons were learned
and repeated **by** eight, except those of the youngest boy. The
moment the clock struck eight the **books** were all put away,
and the boy whose lessons **were not** learned, with a sorrowful
face wished **his mother " Good** night," and went up to bed in
the dark. This was done without a word being said, for it was
the constant rule **of** the house; if the school lessons were not
learned from six to eight, no more time was given, as the lessons were not hard or long, and learned in less **time whenever**
the children were diligent; and the mother's principle was, neither in work nor lessons to allow time to be wasted. Then the
girls sat down to their work of mending or making, and Robert
to knitting—the **boys** being never idle when the girls were

busy. Presently home came the father to their glad welcome; he sat down to his tea and supper both in one, while the mother and the children worked and talked, and Patience darned her sock.

As soon as the father's supper was over, Patience cleared all the things **into the** back-kitchen, as directed; the great Bible was put on the table, the children brought theirs, Patience was sent **to fetch** her's—her own little Bible that Miss Wilson had taken her in her first place of service; and then father and mother and children all read a chapter verse by verse, and Patience had to read with them: then the father questioned the children, **and** he questioned Patience also, and looked pleased with her answers; and then they all knelt down, and the father offered up the evening prayer. After this, Robert and the girls went to bed. Patience washed up and put away the things from her master's supper; and then to her surprise she found her work was done; in fact every body's work was done, for all the house was in order, and Patience went up to her closet of a room where little Esther lay sleeping. With what a thankful heart did the orphan child offer up her evening thanksgiving and prayer! and then taking her treasured half-crown—which she had kept through all her troubles and changes, she looked at it, and wished that beautiful lady could but see how happy she was now! And she lay down to sleep—as if suddenly brought **in the midst of** a home's bright circle of her own.

The next morning her mistress called her **at six** o'clock, and to her mistress's surprise Patience came out from her closet ready dressed. She had heard her mistress rising, and had risen herself.

" What, up and dressed!" **said** her mistress; " well, you mind my word, I never knew a bad servant an early riser! Now then, we shall be at work before the girls to-day!" And the **pleasant stir** soon began below Patience had, as quick as time itself, to light up the back-kitchen fire; then to brighten up and lay the parlor fire, while Betsy followed to sweep the room and dust the chairs; and while the chairs were dusting, Polly set the breakfast. Robert was out in the little garden fixing the linen poles; and Thomas the second boy, chopping wood and filling the coal-scuttle, while the good mother fried bacon for the father's breakfast, and made the coffee. All as busy as possible, and all done by seven o'clock when the father came down; he had been reading his Bible in the midst of his six sleeping children, and now he came down to breakfast with his four eldest. Patience also was called to the table, and so they sat down to the morning meal. Each child repeated a text from the Holy Bible, and the father asked Patience if she could remember one, and Patience repeated the words—" I love them that love Me; and those that seek Me early shall find Me." After breakfast the father read a Psalm, then offered up the morning prayer, and hastened away to be at the shop by eight o'clock. Then Patience went up stairs with Betsy and Polly to dress the children—the mother prepared their breakfast; Robert worked in the little garden, which had its Autumn as well as its Spring and Summer flowers; but Thomas had to sit within and get his lessons perfect. At a quarter to nine, boys and girls were off to school; the twin boys were taken to an infant school by their elder brothers on their way to their own school; the poor little cripple played hour after hour on his sofa-bed with a doll: Esther talked to Patience and stepped about at her side, while the baby of eighteen months old sometimes played on the floor and sometimes slept. At twelve o'clock the children all came home, when, to the surprise of Patience, the baby of eighteen months and the little cripple were put into a light wooden carriage, and all the children went out for a walk together—Robert and Betsy taking charge. Then

Patience and her mistress ironed away till one o'clock, when **they** all returned. Betsy and Polly **made ready** the little ones; Robert and Thomas **set** the dinner-table, and all were seated with hungry appetite to **eat** the food provided for them.

Day after day passed on, till Patience felt more like an **elder** child **and** sister than a servant in the house. Betsy **and** Polly confided to her their secret hopes: Betsy's desire was to **learn** mantua-making, and be a lady's maid—as her mother had been before her; and to this end her mother trained her. Polly meant to be kitchen maid first, and then cook, with the hope **of** being one day a housekeeper, and taking charge of stores— **which** seemed to her the most interesting of work; accordingly every **jar and** bottle in the house was **put** under Polly's keeping; **she gave out the** daily supply, **wrote the** labels, tied down the jars, made some preserves in the summer-time, and took every opportunity of doing **the** cooking. **Robert had a** hope of being taken in Mr. Mansfield's shop, where his **father was** foreman; while Thomas had as yet no definite desire or prospect **in** life. Months passed away in this happy family, till all the paleness was gone from the cheek of Patience, and her figure, becoming stout and strong, seemed made for untiring work. She had taught Esther her own short morning and evening prayers— **learned by** her when **at** school, and **the** little girl now **never** lay down at night or rose up in the morning without offering **them up.** She had become a monthly subscriber to the Church Missionary Society—her master with **his ten** children **was a** subscriber; the children **would often earn or save** some offering for it also; and when Patience **received her** monthly wages, she always paid sixpence **for the same** blessed object. A year passed away, and Patience **went to** call on Miss Wilson, but **Miss** Wilson did not know her—could not believe the change, **till on** talking **with** her **she** found this **rosy,** strong, active-looking girl, full of life and cheerful spirits, was the pale, thin, silent child, she had known so long at school. Patience told Miss Wilson of her happy life in her mistress's house—with ten children, and she, maid-of-all-work, with all the washing done at home ; and how the little one who slept with her, had learned her prayer and said it night and morning, and how her master subscribed to the Church Missionary Society—and she subscribed also. And there, in the midst of life and cheerfulness, we leave Patience for the present.

Rose had done with **school,** happy at the thought of living always at home. **It was not** long, however, before her happiness met her first **sorrow in the loss** of Miss Clifford—she had stood between her father **and** William at the funeral, and in the long summer days she and little Mercy had cried together. The yellow harvest came ; and when the reapers' work was done and the last sheaf carried, and William had stood aloft on the point of the high round stack with the last sheaf in his hand, before he laid it under his feet ; and the men in a circle round had sung the " Harvest Home ;" and the fields were left **bare ;** and the thresher's flails sounded from the **barn :** then another sorrow came for little Rose—a sorrow for **her** home and for the **farm.** William had a good situation **offered** to him in a London shop. Farmer Smith's brother was a London linen-draper ; William had always **been a favorite with** his uncle, and now his uncle's **son had left the** shop to follow a business he liked better, and the place of trust which he had held was offered **to** William, and a high salary was offered with it—for his uncle wished much to have him, and knowing William's love **for the** farm-work, he was afraid unless he made the offer very tempting, **that** it would be declined. **But** it was **not money** that would have tempted William away from his father's farm, if it had not been **for his** father's and his young brother's sakes. It was some years since farmer Smith had been able to lay by any profits : in one bad farming year he had been obliged to borrow money on some cottages built by his mother, and left to him by her ; he had been unable to pay the money or the interest upon it, and now the cottages were no longer his—they had become the property of the man who lent him the money— they had cleared him from debt, but he had nothing now beyond the yearly produce of his farm ; and one bad farming year might **put** him in difficulty again. William worked like a laborer on the farm, and was worth two other men, because his mind and his heart were in all he did ; but there were four younger boys, and farmer Smith knew not how he should pro- vide for them.   If William went to London, it was not unlikely that he might find situations for some of his brothers there. So farmer Smith decided that William should go—with a heavy heart he decided that William should **go.**   William felt as if all the outward joy of life would be darkened for him—away from his home and his father's farm, shut up all day where fields were out of reach ; but he chose the higher pleasure of doing that which would be most likely to relieve his father and aid his younger brothers.   The boys thought it was **a** fine thing for William to go to London !   Rose tried to be as cheerful as she could, but Mrs. Smith never gave so much as one pleasant look, **from** the time that it was decided for William to go.

Mr. Clifford was sitting alone in his study, when an impatient **knock at** his door roused him from his **book.**   " Come in !" he said, in a tone that seemed to guess the intruder.   Herbert en- tered, out of breath with haste.

" Papa, what do you think I have just heard in the village ?— Young Smith is going off directly to a situation in London, to a shop, only think, papa !   I would not lose such a fellow as he **is from** the place for any thing, and I am sure he would not go

if he could help it! don't you think something could be done
to prevent it, papa?"

" We must first know whether his friends and himself would
wish any thing to be done to hinder his going; perhaps they
may feel it to be to his future advantage to go, however sorry
they may all be at present to lose him."

" Well then, papa, suppose I **just go down to the farm and**
hear?"

"I think it would be wise to **go and learn a** little more what
the facts of the case are, before you and I decide here what is
to be done **to prevent it!**"

" Well then, papa, so I will, and I will come and tell you."

So the father suffered the boy to go in his warm impulse to
the farm; seated in the great farm-kitchen he gave full expression to his thoughts and feelings on the subject; Mrs. Smith, for
the first time, heard opposition to the plan, equal to her own; she
brought the young Squire her home-made wine and cake, but
he was too intent on his subject to partake of such hospitality;
farmer Smith talked the subject long over with him, and child
as he was, told him the hopes he had built on his eldest son's departure, as if he had been a long-trusted friend—a due recompense for the boy's **warm** feeling! Herbert returned to his father
more than ever interested for the Smiths, and for William in particular—but convinced that it would not be the thing to attempt
to hinder **the London plan.** Deep in William's heart sank the
memory of the young Squire's unwillingness to lose him from
the place—the warm feeling that had been expressed soothed **the**
pain he felt at going; it cheered his father's heart to think how
his son was valued by those above him; and even Mrs. Smith
seemed softened into more gentleness on the subject, now she
knew that her favorite William was not likely to be forgotten in
his native village. Such the large results that oftentimes might

follow—lasting on enduringly, from the spontaneous feeling and unchecked expression of childhood's true appreciation ! When the autumn winds strewed the sere leaves upon the garden paths at the farm, there was no neat and careful William to sweep them away—the great and busy city had received him.

Herbert's tutor did not find in his pupil the love of books that he naturally desired in one whom he had undertaken to prepare for study at college, and he communicated to Mr. Clifford his anxiety and regret, that Herbert engaged by so many objects of interest, did not make the progress he could wish in his books.

Mr. Clifford replied, " It is very natural, and very right, that you should feel anxious on such a subject ; but we shall gain nothing by straining a point, no compulsion will implant the love of books ; and we have need to remember that books are but the scaffolding for erecting the mental structure. A mere man of books is rather a ready-made collection of material, than a living influence. It is my belief that a circle of human life, gathered by sympathy's natural tie around a child, exercising every good and self-denying feeling the young spirit has, is likely to rear and leave a far nobler character, far more excelling in power and influence, than the mere student of books. But I would not have you discouraged even as to Herbert's book-learning—I find him an increasingly intelligent companion, awake **to** every subject I bring before him, his mind free and unburdened by the weight of mere acquirement. He is following on in the right order—things Heavenly before things earthly, the heart before the head ; and though I may not **live** to see it, I am not without the hope that he, who as a child has learned to minister with such self-devotion to age and poverty may yet bring down his country's blessing on his head."

The tutor pressed his patron's hand and withdrew.

CHAPTER XVIII.

"SON, REMEMBER!"—LUKE xvi. 25.

WHEN the next summer-time **had** come, filling the land with beauty, **and fragrance, and** plenty—telling of His rich bounty who **" is kind to** the unthankful and to the evil," " and **sendeth rain on the** just and the unjust," a messenger arrived at the Hall, asking to speak with Mr. Herbert Clifford.

" I am come from Mr. Sturgeon, sir," said the man ; " he is very ill—thought to be dying, and he begs you to pay him a visit as soon as possible."

Herbert went **to** his father. When Mr. Clifford heard **the** request, he said, " Go, by all means." Herbert sent word by the **messenger that he** would follow immediately, and was soon on **his** way to Mr. Sturgeon's residence. Solemn thoughts filled **his** mind, he was sent for by a dying man—what could it be that Mr. Sturgeon wanted to see him for ? Perhaps he wished before he died to do something for old Willy ?—but old Willy had all he wanted **now** !

Herbert arrived **at** the house, and one of Mr. Sturgeon's **sons** took him up at once to his father's room. The dying **man** looked at him, and said, " I thank you, sir, for coming so soon. You are the only person in all the world I wished to see, for you, dear young sir, are the only one who ever came to me with the words of faithful warning. I **don't** mean to blame my fel-low-men, I have heard the best of preachers and the best of discourses, but from all this **I could—I did** shield myself. Oh, why did none come to me with the pointed arrow of truth, and say to me personally—'You are casting away eternal life!—you are putting Earth before Heaven?' You did **come to me**, you did **warn** me, and I wish to thank **you for what** might have been of eternal use to me if I had listened to your **counsel.**"

Then Herbert took, not as before the smooth **stone for his** sling, but the balm of healing and life, from the Epistle of St. James—all of which he had learned by heart. "It is written in the Bible," said Herbert, "'The prayer of faith shall save the sick, and the Lord shall raise him up; and if he have committed sins they shall be forgiven him!'"

Mr. Sturgeon seemed not to hear, or not to heed the words of peace. "Oh, it is not **the** future, but the past," he went **on** to say, "that presses on my soul with its iron yoke—wherever I turn I seem to hear a voice, and it says to me, "SON, REMEMBER;"—it says no more, but in those words there seems destruction. I do nothing but REMEMBER, and in remembrance there seems despair!"

"But," said Herbert, "our Saviour said we were to remember HIM—and that must be HOPE!"

"**Yes, I** know it—He said we were to remember HIM! and if I had remembered Him then, now I might have hope; but **I have** lived to forget Him—I have forgotten Him in the very church, where I professed to worship Him—I have forgotten Him in secret, where I might have found Him and made Him my own forever—I have forgotten Him in business, where I have taken the opinions of man, and not the heart-searching law of Christ for my rule—I have forgotten Him in the world, where I have been more careful to honor myself than to show forth His praise—I have forgotten Him in my so-called charities,

for I still dared to give in my own name that which but for the gain of oppression, might never have been mine—Yes, I have forgotten Him, and now He knows me not!"

The dying man made no mention of old Willy; he could take a just estimate of sin now, and the sin of forgetting God, of thinking more of himself than of Him—the Lord of Glory —who died to open Heaven's gate to sinners, swallowed up the sense of all beside. He had sinned against old Willy, sinned against man, it was true; but the thought of this for a time was lost in the overpowering sense that he had sinned against Heaven, and before God. The dying man gave Herbert his **hand, and** said, "Dear young sir! I can say no more; I wished **to** give you my thanks, and to tell you freely that you was right and I was wrong, and that 'the way of transgressors is hard!' May you reap the fruit of that truth which you tried in vain to plant in my heart!" Herbert rode slowly **and** mournfully away.

The road home lay past old Willy's cottage; and there **in** that warm summer afternoon, sat the old man **on** the bench beside his door, his hands resting on his staff, his broad-brimmed hat shading his eyes, and his head bowed in slumber; beside him bloomed the rose and honeysuckle—while over him hung the large leaves of the vine; Herbert's hand had planted them —meet emblems of the Earthly **and** the Heavenly love by which the old man's life **was blessed!** Herbert left his horse with the groom, and walked up the straight path to the **cottage.** Swiftly had he run up that same path at the head of **the** game-keeper's boys, to rear up a blazing fire **on old Willy's** hearth; he had rushed up the same narrow **path to shout the** glad tidings to old Willy that the home of all his life was to **be** his dwelling still; he had hastened with light foot, bearing the old man's coat, his father's Christmas gift: but now his step was slower, for it bore to old Willy's side a heart oppressed with thought and feeling. Herbert felt as if he wanted to see the old **man, to** hear him speak, to hear him tell of Heaven and his own bright hope, to dispel the gloom that had gathered round his spirit. Herbert went to old Willy, not now to give, but to receive. He stopped a little distance from the bench, unwilling to awake his aged friend ; he stopped and looked at him—his feeble, wasted frame, his white locks on his shoulders, his labor-worn hands ; and that green life and fragrant blossoming of nature round him—its bright freshness in strong contrast with his withered form. Herbert felt how he loved that lone and frail old man ; and as he felt how he loved him, he looked on **the** cottage his love had prepared—there rose the firm white walls, its close-fitting window and door, its warm and sheltering roof ; there lay the little garden before it, where plant, and herb, and tree seemed to grow rejoicingly out of the ground—pleasant to the eye, and good for the food of that old man : and then in the hush of that summer afternoon, a still small voice spoke within Herbert's heart, and said, " Inasmuch as ye have done it unto one of the least of these my brethren, ye have done it unto Me !" Herbert looked up to the cloudless sky above his head, as if he thought to see Him whose words then spoke within him ; **he** looked up, and he felt that old Willy's God and Saviour and his God and Saviour looked down in love on him, and the gloom and the weight were gone from his heart, and the light and the love of Heaven were there. Old Willy had slept in his young master's moment of need, but the God of all such as old Willy never slumbereth or sleepeth, and He hath said, " If thou draw out thy soul to the hungry, and satisfy the afflicted soul, then shall thy light rise in obscurity, and thy darkness as the noon-day !"

Now Herbert felt as if he no longer needed to stay and

speak to old Willy, for Heavenly peace had come without; and though he still felt solemnized and sad—for the sorrow **he had** witnessed of one who had lightly esteemed the Rock of our salvation, yet the chill and the gloom were gone, and his need supplied. But as he turned to go, old Willy raised his head, and seeing the young Squire turning away, he rose as quickly as he could, and taking off his hat, said, " I beg your pardon, sir !"

" What for ?" asked Herbert, as he turned again, and sitting down on the bench laid **his** hand on old Willy's arm, making him sit down by his side.

" Do you know, Willy, that Mr. Sturgeon is dying ?"

" **No, sir** ; sure ! not dying !"

" Yes, they think him dying ! and he sent for me, to tell me that I was right when I pleaded for you : but, O Willy, it was dreadful, for he has no hope, and I could not comfort him !"

" Well, master, 'tis better so, than if he had a false hope !"

" But nothing can be worse than NO HOPE, Willy, and he has NO HOPE !"

" Yes, master, 'tis better to feel it. If the true **Hope** be not there, 'tis better to have lost hold of every other ; **for then** maybe they will feel after the true Hope **and find it :** maybe they will look up to their Saviour from the very gate of death itself as the dying thief did. Oh what a look he cast upon the Lord !— And that look found salvation **in** the Saviour for him, and he **went into Paradise** with the Son of God !"

" Then, Willy, you think Mr. Sturgeon may find **hope in our Saviour even** now ?"

" I pray God he may !" replied old Willy fervently.

" Oh, I wish he might !" exclaimed Herbert. And then giving a smile to old Willy, in which love and hope struggled with his lingering sadness of expression he departed.

The dying man passed away from Earth, and never could the
boy, through life, forget the death-bed where the Saviour was
not.

The traces of bereavement and sorrow were marked most
visibly in Mr. Clifford. The mother and the boy had felt their
loss no less, but a light had sprung up for them on every side,
in the general service of love to which they had turned ; they
had taken their departed Mary's bright ministry, and the hearts
that mourned for her now looked to them for comfort. To
Mrs. Clifford the personal work was new, and its results
charmed with the sweet surprise of a power to bless, comparatively untried before. And then she was not companionless in
the work ; her boy, her precious boy, once so wild and willful,
was her ardent companion, and shared the new interest to the
full ! But the father had lost the one, who, from life's earliest
childhood, had walked and rode by beside him, visited, studied,
read with him ; he found but one thing able to soothe the
aching void her absence left—that one thing the Word of God,
that was his solace now, it took his lost one's place. It soon
became evident how high the fountain of eternal Truth rises
above its purest streams, how deep the well-spring of eternal
Love, compared with the most purified of earthly vessels.
Continual converse with the Divine Word irradiated all his life
with Heavenly Light—the " conversation in Heaven," the constant thought for others, the tone of deeper feeling, the calmer
firmness even of censure, all bore witness of a drawing nearer
to the Home of perfect Love and Truth, a rising now in spirit
to breathe more of its pure atmosphere while still on Earth.
But failing health denied him all active effort ; and his bowed
form and feebler step told of Earth's decay. Change of scene
and climate were urged as the only hope of imparting new
vigor. Mr. Clifford at first refused, but at last yielded to Mrs.

Clifford's anxiety a reluctant consent, and arrangements were made without delay for going that autumn to Italy.

When Mr. Clifford had consented to leave his home for a foreign land, he sent for the aged Minister of the place, and receiving him alone in his study, addressed him, saying, "I have sent for you, dear sir, to say to you as a dying man, which I believe myself to be, what I ought long ago to have said to you in health. You were appointed to hold the Lantern of the Word of Life to this people, but you show them not its Light: you preach its moral precepts, but He in whose light alone any can see the light of Life you shew them not, and therefore all your teaching is dark and dead—unable to quicken one soul unto eternal Life, unable to guide one wanderer into the narrow way. I beseech you to consider what I say, for your own sake, and the sake of your people. And let me entreat you to pray earnestly that the Spirit of Christ—by whom alone He can be revealed, may yet be given you to enlighten the eyes of your understanding, that you may yet know the sinner's only true ground of confidence—Christ in you the hope of glory. Forgive me for speaking plainly; alas! I ought years ago to have warned you in faithfulness, as I do now! I have also a request to make, I make it as the request of your dying patron—that you will allow me before I go to provide a curate to aid you in your ministry here. I will furnish you with his yearly salary. I will promise that he shall be one who will walk in all lowliness toward you and toward all men, one whom you may make a stay and comfort in your declining years; but one also who will teach and preach Christ Jesus—that Saviour who bore my dying child through the valley of the shadow of death, causing the dark valley for her to glow with the glory of His presence— that Saviour, to whom I look in humble hope of His infinite mercy to bear and carry me—that Saviour, dear sir, whom you

will need; without whom there is **no** salvation—and it will be
my earnest prayer **that in hearing Him** preached, you may be
enabled to lay hold **on the Hope set** before **you** in the gospel."

The aged Minister **did not refuse his** Patron's **wish, did** not
refuse to hearken **unto counsel**: it sounded to him **as a** thrice-
repeated **warning—first** heard **in the** sobs **of** his **people** who
wept **at** their **young** teacher's grave, **then in** old **Willy's simple**
words, and **now from** the lips of **one who had always** treated
him **with kindness and** consideration.

Before Mr. Clifford left, he assembled **all** his tenants and **dependants to a dinner** provided **in** his park. After the repast, the
different groups were gathered **in one,** and Mr. Clifford came
among **them,** his **hand** upon the shoulder **of** his boy, on whom
he leaned: **then uncovering his head,** he said, **in** a voice distinctly heard, **"My friends, I am going a** long journey, and I
wished to take my **leave of you. I am** not going by **my own**
desire, for I would **myself have** chosen **to abide the will of God**
here, whatever that **may be;** but our own **feelings must** sometimes yield to the judgment of others. **I** wished, before I left, **to**
thank you for the **affection** you have manifested toward **me and**
mine. **In** the earlier **days of** my residence among **you some pain**
might have been **spared to** you and **to me, if you had better**
understood my aims and wishes, and if **I perhaps had had** more
skill and patience in making **them known to you. But we** have
now, I believe, **lived long** enough **in** connection to gain mutual
confidence. **If there be any** among you who have any grievance
past **or** present to **complain of, I** ask them, with all friendliness
of feeling toward **them, to come and** state **it to** me before **I** go,
that, God permitting, **I may leave no thorn** behind in any heart
without the prayerful effort **to remove it** thence. For all in
which I have been wanting toward you, I ask your forgiveness
in the sight of Heaven: and most of all, that I have not done

more to teach you the good and the right way. I have desired
you should know it, but I have made too little effort to accom
plish that desire; I pray you seek it for yourselves more
earnestly than I have sought it for you, for the promise that
they shall find the Lord and Giver of Life is given to none but
those who seek with all their heart. One blessed child I had
who lived and died among you, and I may safely say to you,
'Be ye followers **of her, as** she was of Christ.' I commend
my son to your prayers, that he may have **grace** from above to
commend himself **to** your affections. And now, my friends, ' I
commend **you to** God, and **to** the Word of His grace, which is
able to build you up, and to give you an inheritance among all
them **which** are sanctified—through faith which is in Christ
Jesus.' "

Thus it was the Squire took his leave. One thing more he
did, and that was to see a white marble slab raised on the wall
within the village church, where all the poor could see it, **and**
on it was written his daughter's name, and age, and **place** of
residence, and this text, " Remember ye not, that **when** I was
with you, I told you these things ?"

Herbert took leave of old Willy. " Never mind, dear Willy !"
said the boy with choking utterance, " **I** shall come back again
to take care of you; I **shall never forget** you, and you will live
here in quiet, and every body **will be** kind to you when they
know I am gone !" **And** the old man blessed him, weeping !
The family drove from the Hall—the road side lined with those
who mourned their loss : they left their home for a foreign **land.**
There, with the same devotion with which he **had watched his**
dying sister, Herbert tended his dying parent ; and the natural
impetuosity of his character deepened into quiet strength. Mr.
Clifford lived six months abroad, **and then** he died. He said,
" I have not the same radiant **sunbeam of** faith that lighted my

12

Mary's steps through the valley of the shadow of death; but I have the peace of an assured hope that my Saviour hath loved me, and washed me from my sins in His own blood; and that because He lives, I shall live also."

Mrs. Clifford felt unable to return to her home after this bereavement; she decided to remain abroad until the time when it would be necessary for Herbert to return for his studies at college. Herbert worked diligently with his tutor; but the Book he loved the best was his father's Greek Testament—his father's constant companion in the last years of his life, and his parting gift to Herbert. With this he would wander forth before his mother's time of rising, while the early morning glowed in rose and purple on the snowy mountain heights and the overhanging clouds, winding alone through the steep mountain-path; or, when evening fell, seated in the Swiss peasant's lowly chalet, reading of the " Lamb of God who taketh away the sin of the world." Then again in some boat of transport on lake or river, while his mother yielded herself to the calm influence of Earth and Sky, as they glided on between the blue water below and bluer Heaven above, Herbert with the same Book of Life —the same small Book his hand could cover, but whose span was infinite, and date eternal—with that wondrous Book, Herbert would talk to the benighted sailors, or the traveling peasants, or not seldom to some company of Romish priests— winning the hearts of even those whose spiritual fetters he could not break, till sometimes the young priest would take his leave with his arms encircling the neck of his gentle, but dauntless opponent. Thus passed away Herbert's early youth—while he gazed intently on the volume of Nature's beauty; the volume of man's recorded thoughts; and the volume of Divine Inspiration.

CHAPTER XIX.

Pure religion and undefiled before God and the Father is this, To visit the fatherless and widows in their affliction, and to keep himself unspotted from the world."
—James i. 27.

" Why should we fear, youth's draught of joy,
    If pure, would sparkle less ?
Why should the cup the sooner cloy,
    Which God hath deigned to bless ?"

THE arrival of the curate in the village was a subject of great
interest, and tended more than any other event probably
could, to alleviate the sorrow felt on the departure of the Squire's
family. Many there were who went to church on the first Sunday, in expectation and hope, and among these was little Rose ;
her face gathered brightness when the prayers were read with
fervent distinctness, but as the new minister preached, it became
beaming with joy ; and no sooner had they passed the Church's
door, than Rose exclaimed, " Oh, father ! that is just like our
Minister at school, that is exactly how he preached, Oh, I am so
glad ! Did you not like that father ?"

" Yes, dear, I could sit all day to hear such words as those.
I thank God he is come in my time !"

Mrs. Smith had hastened on before with a still quicker step
than usual, and when Rose reached home with her father, her
mother was already preparing the dinner. If Rose had looked
at her mother's face she would have seen no pleased expression
there, but she was too full of delight to question the possibility
of any one feeling different ; so she ran into the family kitchen,

and exclaimed at once, "Oh, mother! was not that beautiful preaching? That was just like our minister at school!"

"I am sure I don't know," replied Mrs. Smith; "it may be beautiful enough for some, but certainly not for me!"

"What! did you not like it, mother?"

"Like it, child! I don't know who would like to be told that when they had done their best, and lived respected as I have done, and always kept their church, that for all that they must turn and seek the same way to Heaven as the worst of sinners!"

"O, mother! that is because Jesus our Saviour is the way, as the minister said in his text—'No man cometh unto the Father but by Me.'"

"Well, child, I don't know as to what the way may be, I only know I have lived a very different life from many, and I don't choose to be mixed up with them, as if I were the same as they!"

"But, mother, it's because Jesus our Saviour is the only way to Heaven, and every one must come to Him who wants to go to Heaven; and He can take all their sins away! Miss Clifford said she wanted to come to Jesus our Saviour!"

"Well, child, that might be, for Miss Clifford never did seem to consider herself above the lowest; but for my part, I can't come to that, but I don't mean to talk about it, there is no need for you to change your mind, nor I mine!" Rose said no more, her sudden joy was dashed as suddenly with disappointment. From this time Mrs. Smith made a point of never going to church when she knew the curate was to preach; her temper became more trying to all around her, and if it had not been for the comfort of the Sunday's sermons, Rose and her father would have found it hard to keep up their spirits through the week.

What was pain to Mrs. Smith was not only comfort to Rose and her father, it was also joy to old Willy. Twice on the Sabbath-day the old man climbed the hill, supported by his staff, and the glad sound was always new life to him. The weekly visits also of the curate were his delight; but he always questioned him as to whether any tidings had been heard of his young master; and he said it was a heart-affecting thing that he, an old man as he was, should live to see the young and good pass clear away like that—one taken **up** above, and the other into foreign parts! But when **at last a letter** came to the curate, and a message in it **to old** Willy, written with Herbert's own hand all those miles away, joy lighted **up** the old man's **eye,** and he exclaimed. " Who can tell, but I shall see him again before I die !" The faithful Jem seemed to consider old Willy now as his peculiar charge, scarcely a day passed that he **did** not look in at the cottage. The little plot of garden-ground **he** took under his entire care—there, early and late, **was heard** his busy spade; it was Jem who dug up and stowed **under** ground the bright red potatoes, to protect them from **the snow ;** Jem, who managed to buy the old **man's coals at less cost** in the town, and brought them back in **a** return waggon of farmer Smith's ; Jem, who, when **the snow had** melted, planted in the early vegetables ; tended the flowers **as** spring came on ; cut the garden hedge ; and trained the **vine above the** lattice-window ; in short, Jem, **the** old man said, tended him like a **prince !** Little Mercy, too, would often step up to the cottage and **find** out work **the old man** wanted done ; when his sight was dim **she** would read to him; and sometimes she would take her knitting up and sit and sing to him. Thus was old Willy tended still and comforted.

A year and six months had passed away since William left his home, and he **had** not been down once to visit it. His father had written in the autumn, and written again at Christmas, to ask him to come; but William returned for answer that he could see no prospect yet of doing any thing for his brothers, nor therefore of returning himself to live at home; **and that** till he did, he could not trust himself to come, for fear he **should lose** his resolution, and not return to his work in London any more.   But he sent his love to his mother, and he still hoped to sow and reap again with his **father for** her; his love to Joe and Samson, and he still hoped to make great men of them; his love to Ted, and the first good berth he could find on board ship should be his—if he would learn well at **school first;** his love to little Tim, and he would come home some day **and teach** him to plough, and till then Tim was to be sure and **take care of Black** Beauty; **and** finally his love to Rose, and she **must come up and see him in London;** and so, wishing a happy Christmas to them **all, ended** William's second Christmas letter.

When the Spring-time came, tidings arrived **in the** village of the death of the Squire, and **the** continued residence of his lady and her son abroad.   The loss was much felt, for the Squire was greatly beloved; and it was all the more felt because his affairs were left in such perfect order, that no tenant's sense of the loss of a friend was turned into anxiety as to personal concerns; all **felt a friend** and counselor was gone, and felt it still the more, **from the tokens of care for** their interest and comfort which the **communications received** made evident.   Old Willy mourned the **loss, and doubted now that** he should ever live to see his young master any more!

The hay-time was scarcely over **when an invitation came to** Rose from her uncle in London **to** pay **him** a visit.   Rose was much pleased **with** the thought **of** going **to** London; but her chief joy was the prospect of seeing William.   Mr. Smith's brother in London, Mr. Samson Smith, lived in a country-house, some few miles out of the great city. William met Rose at the inn where the coach stopped, and took her down to her uncle's house. There seemed to Rose no end of streets or people, but she had few thoughts for them; her joy at sight of her brother swallowed up all besides. Her uncle's house was very different from her home; there was a carpet all over the floor, paintings round the room, a pier-glass over the mantle-piece, and more than one sofa! Her aunt and cousins were very kind to her as well as her uncle; but Rose felt strange, and when William went away in the evening she could hardly keep from crying. But in a few days she was more at home; and her aunt took Rose into London with her cousins, and showed her some of the sights that make the great city so famous—Rose saw the wild beasts; she saw also the Tower, where, in days gone by, so many a noble prisoner heard the key turn that separated between him and all he loved on earth forever. Rose saw the river with its forest of masts; she saw the street again, and wondered how they could be all so full of people at once; but she saw nothing like her own sweet woods and fields, no rippling stream, no shading trees, no free bird warbling praise; and she began to think about the time when she would go home again She saw but little of William; he could seldom get down, except on Sundays, and then she could not talk much to him, before her aunt and cousins.

Had the ministering child then nothing to do for others away from her home? O yes! we have always something to do for others, and something to learn, wherever we may be. Rose tried to be useful to her aunt and cousins, but they were all very happy, and did not seem really to want her; her uncle was very kind to her, but he never seemed to want her; the servants, too, were attentive to her, but they looked well and satisfied. William could seldom come; and Rose thought of her own village far away—she knew that there were many who wanted **her** there ; **some** of the poor old people wanted her, she knew ; and her father she knew must miss her sadly, and little Tim, and her mother also—and Rose felt she would rather be where she was really WANTED, than seeing all the fine sights in the world. Was there no one, then, who wanted Rose where she was gone to stay ? You will hear.

One day, in her aunt's house, Rose heard a tale of sorrow. **A** poor man, a workman in a brewery near, had fallen into one **of the** great beer-vats, and been killed. He had left a wife and three little children, to live on Earth without him, and the poor woman's heart was almost broken with her sorrow. A kind lady went **round to collect a** little money, that a mangle or something might be bought for the poor widow to earn her bread, and Rose's aunt gave some money to help. The next day Rose heard the servants talking about this same poor woman, so she asked the housemaid about her, and the housemaid said, " While they are collecting this money the poor thing is almost dying of distress and want !" " But don't they go and see her, and take her some of it ?" asked Rose. " No, they are keeping **it** all to do something to get her a living with ; and she is so distracted with grief no one likes to go and see her !" Rose said **no more** that day, but she thought in her heart that the love of **Jesus** could **comfort any** sorrow, and that if no one else would **go,** she ought to try and comfort the poor widow. So she **asked** the housemaid where the poor woman lived ; and the next time she was out alone, she had to pass the end of the little path that led up to her cottage. **Rose** thought it might be terrible to see such grief, but **it** must be worse to bear **it** and have no comforter, so she turned up **the** narrow pathway that led to the house ; she thought if she could not comfort her she could give her some money she had, that would buy her food

for a little while ; so she went. She knocked at the door, and some one said " Come in !" Rose lifted the latch, and went in. There stood the poor widow looking very pale, as if she had cried for days and nights.

" I am so sorry for you," said Rose, " I came to see you !" The poor woman sat down, and wiped away her tears with her apron ; and Rose sat by her and talked to her of Jesus, and the poor woman listened to all Rose had to say, and took what Rose had brought for her, and was as gentle as the ministering child herself. Then Rose went away, and she saw there was no need to be afraid of sorrow when we go to it in the name of JESUS. It was the poor widow, with none to visit her, who wanted Rose.

William had to go some distance on business for his uncle ; he was away several days, and when he returned, the time had come for Rose to go back to her home. William came down quite early in the morning to take her into London to the coach ; and as soon as he was alone with Rose in the fly he said, " Rose, I have a secret I will tell you, if you promise not to tell father, or mother, or any one, till I write about it ?" Rose promised not to tell, and William talked low and earnestly to her, and Rose listened, all anxiety, till the fly stopped at the inn. Then William put Rose into the coach, and as he leaned on the door he said, " Oh ! I would give all I have earned, to be going back with you, if it was only myself I had to think of !" And then charging Rose once more to keep the secret, the coach drove off, and Rose soon lost sight of William at the turning of the street, while full of joy she looked forward to her home. It was a long day's journey ; but when the coach stopped at the little village inn nearest to her home, to change horses, there stood her father, and the horse in the gig, waiting for her. Very joyful was the meeting between Rose and her father. " And what of poor Will ?" said her father, when Rose was seated by his side in the gig, and they had started for home—"what of poor Will ?"

"Oh ! he wished so he could come with me !" replied Rose, "I could not bear to leave him !"

" Poor boy !" said farmer Smith, " I doubt we must have him home after all ; he will never settle, so far from the place."

" No, father, he would not live in London always, for any money ! but he would not leave it now, I know, for he says he shall stay till he has worked out a way for the young ones— all except Tim, he says he never could part with Tim, and he knows that if he can only get back in time enough to teach Tim farming, that he will take to it better than any thing else, and I am sure Tim is more like William than any of them !"

" Well, I don't know, I am sure," said farmer Smith, " but these are not times to settle boys out in a day, and I am sure I would not be the father to keep a son like him pining away from his home, seeking after what may never be found."

" O father, Will does not pine up there ! Why, he is grown into such a man as you would never believe—and as busy as any thing. I wish you could see him ; and I know a secret, father, only I am not to tell you or any one, so you won't say any thing, will you, father ?"

Farmer Smith looked down anxiously on his child's bright face, but she did not perceive the anxiety of the look ; she thought if the subject-matter of a secret was not revealed, the fact of its existence could only be an allowable communication of satisfying interest ; so she went on to say, " It 's only good, father ; and if it comes to be, then you, and mother, and all will know it ; but I promised Will not to tell !" And Rose thought she was only giving hope and pleasure by her intima-tion of the existence of a secret—for how should her inexperienced childhood understand a parent's anxious questioning!

Chestnut in the gig trotted swiftly along, and Rose soon gave a shout at sight of her home—with its white vine-covered walls, its sheltering barns and stacks; and then the yard-boy driving Fillpail, and Cowslip, and Rosebud, and all their companions back from the milking to their pasture in the valley. And then her brothers caught sight of the gig, and ran out with their welcome, and little Tim came trotting after them; and at the door stood her mother, in her afternoon gown of red-patterned print, and Rose thought how nice she looked; and how fresh and sweet and clean all seemed, after the London suburbs and the dingy city she had left.

When Rose was seated down after tea, her eager brother Joe and the little sprightly Ted, began their questioning, and Rose with no less animation replied. At last Joe said, " Well, I suppose William begins to find out that there is something better to be done, than walking backward and forward over a field after a plough all the days of one's life !"

" O, no !" exclaimed Rose, indignantly, " he says there is nothing he counts on more than the day when he shall lace on his plough-boots again on father's farm !"

" Poor boy ! poor boy !" said farmer Smith. " I am sure there is nothing I count on like having him back again for good !"

" Why then did you ever let him go?" asked Mrs. Smith. " You know it was all your doing. If I had had my way, he never should have set his foot in London; by what I hear they have people enough, and too many up there as it is, and why we should be sending our best off to them—I never did, and I never shall see the reason of !"

" Well, wife," said Mr. Smith sorrowfully " it seemed as if it might be for the best in the end ; but I am sure I don't know, and if we have not One above to order for us, I don't know who is to tell what is for the best !   It 's certain I thought I should get over the loss of him better than I have."

" I don't suppose you thought about how you would get over it at all," replied Mrs. Smith, " it never was your way; when you took a thing up you were for doing it—and then let the feeling come after as it might.   I could have told you that you never would get over the loss of him, only you would not have minded it if I had !"

Mr. Smith made no further remark during tea, and as soon as it was over he took his hat and went out into his farm, to **relieve** his burdened spirit with the freshness of the evening **air.**   And while the boys made haste to help their mother clear the tea-table, Rose slipped away after her **father, and** with her hand in his soon dispersed the gloom that had gathered on his face.

" I wish enough," said Joe that evening to Rose, " that I had not said any thing about William at tea, mother always takes it up so, and then it vexes father !   I only know, I wish I could go to London too, for it is as dull as dullness always to be walking over the same fields, and see no one but the same ten heavy men all the days of one's life.   I am sure I can't think **how** father can stand it, only I suppose he likes it.   Did Wil- **liam say any** thing about me ?"

Rose hesitated a little ; Joe's quick eye turned instantly at her silence, and fixed upon her.   " He said," replied Rose, " that he was sure you would not like uncle's shop any better than farming."

" No, so I told him," replied Joe.   " I don't see any more spirit in laying up and taking down bales of goods, and cutting yards of stuffs, than in putting in turnips and then taking them out again, and cutting them up for the sheep—all over and over year after year! what I should like, would be a merchant's office, where some day I might travel, and not have nothing but what grows at one's door to do with all the days of one's life ! Did Will say any thing about that ?"

" He said," replied Rose, " that he would never give up trying after it, for he did not believe that, so much as you had read and thought about it, you would ever settle to any thing else."

" What a good fellow he is !" said Joe, " he always did seem to care as much about what one felt as one did one's self—let it **be the least** thing in the world even ! If ever he makes a merchant of me he shall see what a memory I have for things **I have heard** him say, and **what I** will get hold of and do to **please him! I wish** I was off, for there 's no getting **on** here, all one tries to do seems to go for nothing, as to making any real difference. Just think what it would be to work one's way up there and buy this farm for father, instead of every now and then hearing it is likely to be sold over his head ; **or** pay the rent for him ; or any thing to keep off that harass that 's always upon him ; but somehow there seems no getting on, and no spirit in any thing here !"

" O, Joe, the spirit is not in THINGS, the spirit is in US ! I have heard William say that you may PUT spirit into any thing ! And he thinks there 's nothing like farming for the pleasure of it."

" Well, I am sure father says I do work well, but William said it was hard to settle to work you can not get a liking for."

" So I dare say it is," replied Rose ; " but only you try and be **a** comfort to father, and see if William does not **soon** find you something up in London !"

Joe took the assurance of sympathy and comfort, and went the next morning, with fresh spirit to his work.

Rose was often seen looking out from door or window about the hour of ten, at which time the postman generally arrived, and when she saw him climbing the green ascent to her home, she would run out to meet him and receive his store, but she still always **returned with** slower step—no letter from William was there! At length one baking morning, when Rose was busy in the back-kitchen making the harvest-cakes, farmer Smith called Mrs. Smith and Rose into the parlor, where he stood with an open letter in his hand! The heart of Rose beat quick for she guessed that the secret had come at last! Farmer Smith shut the parlor door, saying, "Here is a letter from Will, and no time to be lost in attending to it!" so saying, he read as follows·

"DEAR FATHER,—

"I hope I have gathered my first sheaf, after pretty near a two years' waiting for it; but I have **often** and often thought how you used to say, when I wanted to be hasty in housing the crops, 'Waiting time is often the time that pays best in the end!' Well, father, I told Rose a bit of a secret, but she promised **to keep** it, so **I** may as well tell you and mother from the beginning. You know how Joe has always been bent on **a** merchant's office? I was so certain nothing else would content him that I always kept that in my eye, but I never got so much as **the least** prospect, **or** chance of **trying for him.** Well, **a** week before Rose went home, I had to go a journey **on business** for my uncle; there was an elderly gentleman seated by me outside the coach, and we had not gone far when a terrible thunder-shower came **on.** I had an umbrella, for I **had** seen a threatening of it; the old gentleman had none, and he was seated at the end just where the storm beat, so I said, 'If you will please to change places, sir, I could shelter you better in the middle here.' At that he looked up and said, 'I am sure you are very good to say so, but I have no right to expect, shelter from you, and an old man ought to be better provided against a storm than a young one, don't you consider so?' 'Well, sir,' I said, 'I don't know but what the young have quite as much reason to look out as the old!' By this the old gentleman had changed his place, but he soon began to **call** out that I was getting his share of **the storm!** 'I am no way afraid of that, sir,' said I, 'I have been **used to** stand a shower all my days.' 'How is that?' **he asked.** 'Well, sir, I was brought up **to the farming, and you can't be** a farmer and afraid of **a shower! but a** soaking is dangerous sometimes, **when you are** not used to it.' Then the old gentleman put no end of questions to me, and I found he knew pretty well about farming himself; he told me he was born and brought up on a farm, and certainly he pleased me better than any one **I had** met all the time I have been in London—near enough **now up**-on two years. In all that time uncle Sampson has **never asked** me half so many questions about you, and the farm, and the boys, as that old gentleman did that day, and all **as** if he cared to know! **it did** me more good than **any talk I had** had since I left home. The old gentleman gave me his card at the end of the journey, and told **me to call on** him as soon as I re-turned to London, for he was going to return the next day. I found **by** his card that **he lived** not very far from my uncle's, and when I showed it to him, he told me that he knew **him** well by name, and that he was a man of excellent standing, **a** merchant in London. O, how I thought **of Joe—and what if** after all this should be the making of him! **I went** down the very first evening to see him; he seemed **to be** living alone by what I could make out, in a beautiful house, and certainly he was one of the pleasantest persons **I ever** spoke to; he remem-

bered every word I had told him, and there I sat, talking to
him, just as if I had been at home. Well, it so happened that
Joe being so much on my mind, I had told all about him outside the coach before ever I knew what the old gentleman was,
and how glad I was to think I had, for I should not have liked
to speak about it then, I could not have done it half so well.
The old gentleman never said a word of what I was so full of
hope about, and when I went away I thought all was over, for
he only said he should hope to see me again some day. Well,
two days ago what should come but a note from him to invite
me to dine with him. And then he told me that he had called
on my uncle, and satisfied himself as far as he could, that
he was not venturing too much, and that he now offered me a
situation in his office for my younger brother, provided he
proved capable on trial. 'But,' he said, 'my premium is
a hundred pounds; I require two hundred with the sons of
gentlemen, and I have never taken any with less; do you
think your father can provide that sum?' Well, I knew,
let it be where it would in a merchant's office, there must be a
premium, and I would not for any thing have put a hinderance
in the way, so I said, I hoped that might not be found to stand
in the way of so excellent an offer. Then the old gentleman
seemed satisfied; and I should have been sorry not to give Joe
as good a start as we could, and pay him regularly in; and as
I dare say the old gentleman knows my uncle is rich, it might
have looked encroaching on the kindness of his offer, if I had
made any difficulty. So now at last the thing is settled. But
for the money—take my advice, father, and do not worry
to think it over yourself, for I have thought it all over and over
again, and there is but one way—and that way will soon do it.
First, then, I have thirty pounds all ready at once, saved out
of these two years: then, to meet the rest there is but one

thing to be done, Black Beauty must be sold; don't keep vexing about it; but let it be done, and you will never repent it.
I say the more because I know you will think most about me
in selling him, but I have made up my mind, and it would
hurt me a great deal more, to have any difficulty in Joe's way
with such an offer as this. Tell mother not to vex about the
horse, I can rear her another such, some day, when I am your
farming-man again; he ought to fetch seventy pounds to say
the least, but if **you can not get that at hands** likely to do well
by him, then you can make up the rest without much difficulty,
by selling **off what remains** of last year's wheat. Let me
decide for you, father, as I think I best can in this case, because
I know the value of the offer. You must have Joe and the
money ready in a fortnight; and then tell mother when I have
seen Joe settled, I will come home for a holiday. My love to
all, and good wishes to Joe.

" Your affectionate son,

" WILLIAM SMITH.

"P. S.—At first I thought I would make an effort and ask my
uncle to lend me the seventy pounds, but then I remembered
what you have so often said to me—' Bear any thing rather
than borrow, Will!' So I did **not ask** my uncle, and I dare
say he supposes **we can** easily raise the money, for he never
inquires much as to how farming stands."

" **O,** father," exclaimed Rose, " that's the secret! May I run
and tell Joe?"

" And what **do you** mean to do?" asked Mrs. Smith of her
husband.

" Well, I suppose we can't do better than take William's advice; these are no times to bring up five boys on one small
farm, and Joe has no mind to the work."

" I," said Mrs. Smith, " always found I must put my mind in my work, and then my **work came** to my mind, and I have trained Rose to the same; but, as **I** always said, you must rule the boys; only don't let me see the horse led away—that is all I have to say !" and Mrs. Smith returned **to** the back-kitchen. Rose stayed by her father's side; what would he have done but for his little comforter ! " Never mind, father, never mind," she said. " **It's sure** to be right if Will **says so; you** know it **always is !"**

" Then you think it had better be as William says ?" asked **the father** of his little daughter.

" O yes, father; Joe is bent on London, and William must **know better up** there—among **so** many people, than we do **down here; only** mother never likes things different, but she **will be glad some day !** May I go and tell Joe now ?"

" Yes, if you like. Your mother's taking things contrary, makes them **a heavy burden. I am sure I am** sorry enough for the poor beast; **but it's better than** borrowing !" and farmer Smith took his hat; and Rose ran to look for Joe. She found him busy in the fields among the men; so calling him on **one** side, she told him all, except about the **horse, by which it was** to be obtained. Joe rushed to the house, wild with joy. **The first person** he found was his mother.

" O mother ! I am to be a merchant, **after** all ! William has **found me a** place in London !"

" **Well, I** can't help it," said Mrs. Smith.

" **No,** mother, I **don't want it helped; it's** the thing of all others I have most wished for !"

" And **what is the use of never being** satisfied in one place, till you are in another, I should like to know ?" asked Mrs. Smith. " There's William always sighing after his home, and **I dare say you will** like London no better !"

" Why, mother, Will never did like it ; he always said it was only for us he went away ; but it's the very thing I have always longed for, so I am sure to like it !"

" Well, I only hope it may be so !" replied Mrs. Smith ; **and** Joe went off to look for warmer sympathy in his father. He did not look in vain ; but after some conversation, farmer Smith said, " I am sorry for the horse ; but it can not be helped !"

" What horse, father ?"

" Did not Rose tell **you ? We must sell** Black Beauty, to pay the premium."

" Sell Black Beauty, **father ! no,** that you must not ; William **would** never bear the sight of me, if his horse had been sold to get me up **there :** I would sooner not go !" And the lad's voice faltered with struggling feelings.

" Yes, but it is William himself who says so," replied his father.

" Does William say so ?" asked Joe. " Well, I never thought he could have given up so much for me !"

Now it happened that the old clergyman had **long taken a great fancy** to Black Beauty, as a fine horse **for his** hooded carriage ; and he had more than once asked farmer Smith to let him know if ever he thought of parting **with it ; so,** acting on his son William's advice, farmer Smith lost no time in calling on the Rector. The **old** clergyman seemed pleased with a prospect of possessing the horse, but said that he had fixed the price that he would give, namely fifty pounds, beyond which he would not go. **Farmer** Smith stated that the horse was worth more ; that he felt no **doubt a** dealer would give him **more ;** that **it** was only **a** sudden necessity he could not meet, compelled him to sell the horse, but that he greatly desired **to** secure a good master for him. Now the old clergyman was rich, and had no children, but he made no inquiry as to why the horse had to be sold ; he only said, " I have stated the price I will give, you must take it or not, as seems best to you." Farmer Smith sat a few minutes in harassed thought; he wished his little Rose had been at his side, to say one way or the other; at last, feeling for the creature outweighed the hope of a larger price, and he replied, " Well, **sir,** I would sooner let him go for less to a good master, than strain a point and get a bad one. The horse is worth full seventy pounds, but as I am driven to it by necessity, **I will take** the fifty for him, if you please, sir."

" Very well," said the old clergyman ; I gave fifty pounds for the best horse I ever had, and I never mean to give more, or I may probably get a worse." So farmer Smith took the offer, and the horse was to be fetched away the next day !

It was late in the afternoon when the Rector's coachman came **for the horse. Ted saw** him coming and gave the alarm, then **ran off to** the stable to give Black Beauty his last supper.

Joe followed slowly, and Rose with him, trying to cheer him ; but he took his stand, pale and silent, within the stable, half concealed from view. Samson stood with great composure at the farm-yard gate, watching the approach of the man ; while little Tim, hearing from Molly what was about to happen, came running and crying as he ran, and lisping out his sobs, " No, no, naughty man, Black Booty not go ; Will said, 'Tim, take care of Black Booty !' " Ted had filled a measure to the brim, and the high and gentle creature stooped his head to feed ; but when little Tim came sobbing in, the creature turned from its food, looked hard at the child, and then stooped down its face to him, as if to caress and soothe.

Then farmer Smith and the coachman entered. Farmer Smith looked on the group one moment in silent feeling almost as strong as his children's, then stroking down his favorite's silky mane, he said, " There 's the horse ; I give him to you in good condition, and a better horse you can not find."

"I am sorry for you sir," said the coachman; and farmer Smith left the stable, unable to stay and witness the scene.

"You will let him get his supper first?" said Ted, looking up, and holding the measure afresh to Black Beauty's head.

"Go, naughty man, go quite away," said little Tim, "Will shall be very angry with you!" And the horse turned from its food again to the child.

"Come now, Tim," said Ted, "you won't let him have a bit of supper!" And Tim suffered Rose to compose and comfort him while Black Beauty eat his food, but the moment it was done and the halter was in the coachman's hand, his grief broke forth again, while Ted, and Rose, and Joe, at that sight, no longer kept from tears. The man tried to make short work of it, and led the horse at once away, but the creature threw up his head, his eyes that had looked so mildly on the child grew fierce and snorting, he seemed to bid the stranger defiance in his attempt to secure and lead him away. Then Joe looked up in blank distress, and said, "It's of no use, he won't go for you, a stranger never led him, give him to me, it's fit I should have to lead him away, for it's all for me he has to go!" So Joe took the halter, the creature hung down his head and followed, and the children followed also—little Tim stamping with impotent distress. The heavy laden wagon coming in at the stack-yard gate stood still, and the men looked round to watch; and the laborers, winding up the hill with their rakes upon their shoulders, turned to see the faithful creature go, and Molly and the yard-boy stood in view, and Mrs. Smith within the house kept up a more than usual stir, and Mr. Smith—no one knew where he was! Rose soon stopped with little Tim; but Ted ran on by the side of Joe, who led the horse to his new stable, then the boys hung their arms round his neck and left

him to his new abode : and long Black Beauty neighed in vain
for the children's hands to feed him !

" Never mind, my boy," said farmer Smith, as Joe turned away
from his **supper**, " you won't trifle with a situation **that has cost**
us all so **much !**"

" What in the world is this ?" asked Mrs. Smith, as she packed
her son Joe's box for London.

" O, never mind, mother, just tuck it in any where !"

" But what in the world is it for ?" asked Mrs. Smith.

" Well, mother, it's only just the old bit of rope with which **I**
led Black Beauty away; he would **not** let the Rector's man
halter him or lead him out of the stable."

" **And what can be** the use of taking that ?" asked **Mrs.**
Smith.

" O, never mind, mother, only for fear that I should ever forget that day !"

" Well, I am sure," **said Mrs. Smith**, " it's an odd fancy—to
hold feeling by a bit of old rope ! but **so it must be** if you
will."

Perhaps Mrs. Smith was really more **capable** of understanding Joe's feelings than she showed signs of **being ;** but so **it**
passed off, and Black Beauty's old piece of rope was tucked **in**
the corner of his box.   And Joe went to London, and the merchant was pleased with the **lad, and the** money was paid, and
William took Joe **to lodge with him, and when** he had seen him
comfortably settled, William went down to spend **a** fortnight in
his home—to the comfort of all, and **not least of** little **Tim.**
And Black Beauty drew the minister's carriage.

CHAPTER XX.

" Warm'd underneath the Comforter's safe wing,
    They spread th' endearing warmth around."

" Putting on the breastplate of faith and love."—1 THESS. v. 8.

WHILE these events had been passing in the village, little Jane had followed on her childhood's path within the town : and the energy of growing thought, and the courage of deepening feeling, strengthened within her heart. Her sympathy for the poor grew with her growth—a sympathy inherited by birth from her parents, and constantly nourished by the atmosphere of her home ; a respectful sympathy, a loving feeling of relationship a sense of some invisible tie existing between her and the poor which did not exist between her and the rich—even that most blessed bond, the power to aid and comfort !

There was a road which led out of the town, on the side nearest to Mr. Mansfield's house, the road led up a long hill, and then crossed a wide heath ; this was a favorite walk with Jane and her little brothers, and here they used to run, and play with the snow, in the winter time, to which we have now come ; —while William and Joe were together in London, little Mercy and her uncle Jem tending old Willy, Herbert away in a foreign land, Rose busy in her home, and Black Beauty drawing the minister's carriage. Thus on the fresh-blowing heath, Jane and her little brothers grew rosy with their play. There were scattered cottages and huts upon this open heath, and Jane often stopped in her play and looked at them, or passed them by with slower step—she felt that the **poor were there!** But there was **one** hut that stood separated from **any other, a mean abode** it was, and with no look of comfort round it; there **was a pile of** turf to lengthen out the smoldering fire, but no little stack of wood, no black and shining coal, no cheerful blaze within. No **Herbert** came and went that **way; no** faithful Jem lived near; **but** little Jane's eye of thoughtful love—so early trained to watch where any want might rest—her eye of thoughtful love had marked the mean abode, and again and again she had looked, wondering who might live there. At last one wintery day, **just as** Jane passed by, the door opened, and an aged woman came out with a ragged cloth in her hand which she hung on a snowy bramble that grew beside the door; the aged woman wore an old print gown, with a small black shawl pinned over her shoulders, and an old black bonnet on her head, her head shook with the palsy of age, and it was evident at first sight that she was old and poor—very old, and very poor.

"Look nurse," said Jane, "that poor old woman lives there!"

"Yes, I see," said nurse.

"Do you think mamma knows that old woman?" asked Jane.

"How can I tell!" replied nurse; "you don't suppose your mamma knows every old woman for miles round the town?"

Nurse was walking at a quick pace with the little boys, and she called to Jane, who was lingering with her eyes still on the open cottage-door, to come on; so Jane hastened on. As they returned, the aged woman stood outside her door again, putting out a few more ragged things to dry on the bushes in the wintery wind. Jane watched her as she passed, but said no more to nurse. As soon as she was alone with her mother that day, she said, "Mamma, what do you think! I saw such a very old woman in such a very old cottage, she looked so cold, and her head shook, and she was hanging out some ragged things to dry, and I saw no fire inside! Do you know her, mamma?"

" Where did you see her?" asked Mrs. Mansfield.

" Out on the heath, mamma, such a very old cottage—alone by itself! I am sure she is very poor, and she must be very cold."

" I don't think I know any thing of her," replied Mrs. Mansfield; " but if you think she is so very old and poor, you shall take me to see her, and then we shall both know her."

" O, mamma, will you let me ? shall we go this afternoon?"

" No, you could not walk so far twice in one day."

" O, yes, I could indeed, mamma, I am not at all tired !"

" No, we will wait till to-morrow, and then if the day is very fine, I will promise, if possible, to go with you."

" Shall you do any thing to make her warm, mamma ?"

" Yes, if you like we will take her a coal-ticket, and then she will be able to have some coals."

" O, mamma, I am so glad ! I wish I could do something for her as well !"

" We will observe when we go, what she seems most to want, and then perhaps you can make it, and take it to her some day in your walk with nurse."

" Do you mean I may take it in, all alone by myself, mamma?"

" Yes, if she seems a kind old woman, who would be pleased to have a little visitor."

" Are not all poor people kind, then, mamma ?"

" No, dear Jane, not all; an evil heart within them makes some poor people unkind and wicked, as it does some rich people. And then the poor often suffer a great deal; and when they have not the fear and love of God to comfort them, suffer-

13

ing often makes them speak, and feel, and act as they would not if they knew the love **of God.**"

"Can not they be **taught to know it** then, mamma?"

"Yes, Jane, we must try to help every one to know the love of God through Jesus Christ; God's love can change the hardest and most wicked heart, and make it gentle and patient—even in suffering. So when we find any one unkind to us, whether poor or rich, we must try and show them what the love of God **can teach and** enable us to bear and to do; and if we can we **must tell** them of His love, that they may seek it also."

"**Then if** the old woman is unkind, what will you do, mamma?"

"**I do** not think she will be; but if she should, we must speak the more gently and kindly to her, and perhaps she will soon find **that we want to be a** help and comfort to her, and then she will be glad to see us; **and our love may** lead her, perhaps, to seek the love of God—and **that will make her happy** in her poor **cottage** here, and then it will take her to Heaven."

Jane was satisfied, and asked no more; she had learned an **added** lesson of truth; no suspicion **had been** taught her; her mother had only reminded her of the fact—that from sin's evil **root** we must not be surprised to find its bitter fruit; and **she had** bound **upon** her child "the breastplate of faith and **love,**" to shield her from the painful effects of a surprise. The **youngest soldier of the cross** needs **to be** so prepared and guarded, when venturing on ground untried by others for his steps; and **care is needed—is** greatly needed—lest the older mind should teach by infusing suspicion and doubt, instead of giving the simple knowledge of the universal fact of man's evil heart, and carefully binding on the child's young spirit that breastplate of FAITH and LOVE which can alone guard it for its **safe** conflict **with** the world.

The next day Jane set off with her mother for the cottage on the heath. It was true she walked with more silent question ings in her heart—as to what they might meet in the old woman's cottage—but it was the questioning that belongs to Earth's uncertainty ; and whatever might be found, she was pre- pared to meet it now, without being driven back by a surprise. The cottage door was shut ; on Mrs. Mansfield's knocking, the old woman opened it, and Mrs. Mansfield said, " We have walked up from the town to call on you ; may we come in ?"

" It 's no place to come into," said the aged woman, " but you can if you like."

So Mrs. Mansfield went in, and sat down on a broken chair ; Jane found a seat on the bottom of the bedstead, and the aged woman sat down again by her small table, where she was taking her twelve o'clock dinner of a little tea and a crust of bread.

" You must feel the cold on this open heath," said Mrs. Mans- field.

" Yes, it 's enough to perish an old woman like me ; but I could never make up the high rent down in the town, so I am forced to bear it as I can."

" We thought that you might like a coal-ticket ; they are giv- ing some in the town ; do you know about them !"

" Oh yes ! I know about them."

" Would you like to have one ?"

" Well, I can have it if you like, but I don't suppose I can ever get the coals out here ; I am sure I can't carry them."

" No, you could not carry them yourself ; but I see some other cottages near ; perhaps you have a neighbor who could ?"

" No, there 's no one who neighbors with me ; I have no one to look to but myself ; what I can do for myself I do, and what I can't I have to go without."

" Could you not manage if you had a shilling with it ?   Then you could pay the sixpence that is necessary with the ticket, and give something to a boy to carry them for you."

"Yes, I suppose I could do that."

"Shall I write your name on the ticket, then? I have a pen and ink in my basket."

"You can if you please."

So Mrs. Mansfield wrote; then turning to the aged woman, she said, "You feel as if you had no one to look to; but there is a Friend who is able and willing to help and comfort you, if you ask it of Him."

"I suppose you mean there is a God above," said the old woman; "I know that!"

"I mean that the God above sent His beloved Son to die for you, that you might find pardon, and help, and hope in Him—even in Jesus the Son of God."

"Well, I dare say it may be; but those who have no learning, like me, can not come at the understanding of it."

"Oh yes you can, by God's help. It is to the poor, above all others, that the good news is sent. It is all written in the Bible for you, and if you only get its words into your heart, they are sure to lead you to Heaven."

"I can't do that, then, for I can't read them; and I am not fit to go to a place of worship."

"Oh yes, you are quite fit for that; there are many who have worshiped God in worse clothing than yours: but if you like, my little girl shall come and read to you sometimes, when she walks this way?"

"Well, I am for the most part busy."

"Never mind; if you are busy she can run on with her brothers; but if you are not busy, she can come and read the words of the Bible to you—those blessed words that are written for the poor!"

"I am sure you are very good!" said the old woman, softened at last. And Mrs. Mansfield and Jane took their leave.

"She was not really unkind, was she mamma?" asked Jane, anxious to clear as much as possible any censure from her old woman.

"No, dear, she was not at all unkind, only very poor and very miserable; and when people are very miserable, they often don't feel able to speak pleasantly."

"No, mamma; do you think she **will** like me to read to her?"

"Yes, I feel sure she will, after a little **time**. I think she will **soon begin to love** you, Jane; **and then** perhaps you may teach her to know the love of God her Saviour, and then she will soon feel very different, and look very different."

"Shall I go to-morrow, mamma?"

"No, I dare say she will go for her coals to-morrow; **you** had better wait a day or two, and perhaps by that time she will begin to look out for your promised visit."

"I saw something she wanted, mamma—did **you**?"

"Yes, poor old woman! I thought she wanted almost every hing!"

"But I mean her tea-pot, mamma; **did you** see it was tied together with a string?"

"No, I did not see that.

"It was, indeed, mamma! How much would a tea-pot cost?"

"You could get a small black tea-pot for tenpence."

"Ten weeks, then, mamma, it would take me before I could **buy one!**"

"Yes, it would; but you need not wait for that, because I think I have a tea-pot at home I could spare; it is a pewter tea-pot, a good deal bent, but it has no holes in it."

"May **I take it, then,** mamma, when I go?"

" Yes, and if you like, you shall make her a warm garment, and take her that as a present from me."   So Jane, with delight, gave her play-time to work, till in three days the garment was ready ; then, with the tea-pot packed in a basket, and a little tea and sugar from her father beside it, and with her mother's warm present tied up in a parcel, the happy child set forth with her brothers and her nurse.   O, how she longed to reach the cottage ! And when at last it came in sight, she said, " Nurse, may I run on now ?" and then swiftly she crossed the wintery heath, and knocked at the old woman's door.

" O, it 's you !" said the old woman ; " I have looked out for you !"

" Mamma has sent you this !" said Jane, unfolding her mother's present; " will it not keep you warm ?   I made it for you all myself, except the fixing !"

" Why, I never had the like of this before !" said the old woman, with evident surprise.

" And mamma said I might bring you this tea-pot," said Jane ; " and there is some tea and sugar from our shop !"

" I am sure you are very good to me !" said the old woman, with feeling in her tone.

" Are you busy to-day ?" asked Jane.

" No, I am not busy, I have nothing to be busy about."

" Shall I stay a little while ?"

" Yes, dear, if you can content yourself."

" O yes, I like to stay with you, you must be so dull here all alone !   Do you like me to read to you ?   I have brought my own Bible."

" As you please," replied the old woman.

" I can read to you about Heaven in the Revelation," said Jane ; and she read from the seventh chapter of Revelation, the ninth verse to the end of the chapter.

"It's very fine, I dare say," said the old woman, "for those who can get hold of it, but I have no understanding."

"Can not you understand it?" asked Jane, with disappointment.

"No, I never had any learning."

Jane looked down on the sacred words, and pondered what to say.

"I wish you could understand!" at last said Jane, looking up earnestly at the old woman's face; "if you could it would make you happy. Shall I read them once over again?"

"As you please," replied the old woman, "but I have no understanding."

Jane read a few verses again, then stopped, saying, "Do you know who the Lamb means?"

"No," answered the old woman.

"It means Jesus, God's Son, because he died for us!" said Jane. Then Jane read on about the white robes, and stopped again, and said, "Every body in Heaven wears a white robe, because Jesus has washed them all white in His blood! I can teach you a prayer about that—it is a very short prayer out of the Bible—"Wash me, and I shall be whiter than snow." Do say it after me, and then you will know it!"

The old woman tried; at last she seemed able to remember it a little:—and when Jane was gone, she still sat on her broken chair, saying over to herself, "Wash me whiter than snow! Wash me whiter than snow!"

It was simple teaching, and simple learning; but we must estimate the full meaning of the few words left in the aged woman's heart, before we can estimate the value of the lesson given and received. "Wash me!" there lay the assertion of her need of cleansing—a need only to be truly learned from the entrance of that Word that enlighteneth the eyes. "Whiter than snow?"—there lay the assurance that there was a power that could make clean, make without spot the heart and life, that needed washing, unable to cleanse itself. When the Word of God, that gives at once the knowledge of sin and the only remedy, is thus fixed within the heart, the nail is fastened in a sure place—though the Master of assemblies deign to work by the infant of days in fixing it there.

Jane's pence were now saved up by her eager, joyful hand of love, for her own old woman. First two lilac print aprons were bought and made, with a white one for Sundays. Mrs. Mansfield added a large handkerchief to pin outside the gown over the shoulders, which Jane hemmed; and when these were about to be taken, Mrs. Mansfield said, "Suppose, if I can find a piece of black silk, I make her a little black bonnet?"

Of course the thought of this was delightful, and Jane kept back her gifts till the bonnet was ready. The neatest old woman's bonnet was made, the silk put plain on a small close shape, and then Mrs. Mansfield made a plain net cap, with a net border, while Jane watched her mother's needle with eager interest. The bonnet and cap were put in a little blue bandbox; and then Mrs. Mansfield found a shawl of her own for the old woman; and so, richly laden and over- flowing with gladness, Jane set out, with her nurse and her brother to help, and the little ones to share the interest, on the way to her old woman's cottage. Tears started to the eyes of the poor old woman—tears of love and grateful feeling; and Jane saw the old woman at church—in her white apron, and neck-handkerchief and shawl, and her little black bonnet and white net cap. The hand of love had clothed her, the voice of love had warmed and cheered her; there were tones that make the heart's music now on earth for her; and, led by these, she

went to hear of the love that these bore witness to—the **love that passeth** knowledge !

Before the cold of winter had passed away, Jane discovered that her own old woman had stiff limbs from rheumatism ; she told this, as she told every thing, to her mother ; and on **Mrs.** Mansfield's learning from Jane that the old woman's floor was often damp, and she without any covering for it, Mrs. Mansfield found up a variety **of pieces of** carpet, **some** old and some new, and showed Jane how to join them. With an old **pair** of gloves on her hands, fine twine, and **a short carpet-needle, Jane sat on a low** stool **on the nursery floor and** made her patchwork rugs. **It was kept a great** secret, the old woman was to know nothing about **it till it** was done **; and never** could work have afforded a child more pleasure. She was to take the many-colored rug, when finished, and lay it down herself ; it would fill up all the space between the bed and the fire, just where the old woman sat, and light up with its variety of patterns and colors **the old** woman's dreary dwelling ; the little window had long been cleaned by the old woman's own thought, to let in more light for Jane to read, **and** Jane had secret **thoughts of** asking her mother if she might not make a new curtain **for it ;** but the carpet-work fully engaged her spare time **for the** present ; and sometimes her mother, and sometimes **her nurse,** gave her advice as to how best to arrange her various-shaped pieces. One day, while Jane was intent on her work in the middle of the nursery floor, the daughter of a neighbor and friend of her mother's knocked at the nursery-door, and on nurse saying, " Come in," she opened the door, saying, by way of excuse for her appearance there, " I found your mamma was out, and I got the servant just to let me run up, because I have no time to stay, and I want you to come to drink **tea with us** on Friday. I am to have a party. **Mamma has bought me** a new best frock of green silk, and I shall wear it then! What is your best frock?"

"I have no best frock," said Jane, "only one old stuff and one new stuff, and I wear white on Sundays in summer, and when I go out with mamma, if you mean that?"

"No, I wear white sometimes in summer; but how very odd you should not have a best frock! Shall you come in your stuff frock, then?"

"I don't think mamma will let me come at all," said Jane, "I never go out to tea without mamma, unless it is with nurse into the country in the summer-time."

"Well, but you will ask, will you not?"

"Yes, I will ask mamma," said Jane.

"What are you doing here, then?" said Jane's young visitor, looking down on the patchwork carpet; "sowing bits of carpet, I declare! what terrible hard work! I never have such work to do."

"It is not hard," said Jane, "I like it very much; it's for a poor old woman who has nothing to lay on her floor, and her floor is damp!"

"O, well, I don't know any old women, but if I did, I think I should get my mamma to buy her a bit of carpet!"

"Mamma says," replied Jane, "that it is much better to give what we have made; and I know my old woman will like it a great deal the more for my having made it. And mamma says it will be much stronger and warmer than a new piece, because of all the joins I have made!"

"O yes, I dare say it will; but if you come and see me on Friday, I will show you my work; I am working a little boy and girl in worsted, sitting on a stool, and they have such rosy faces! I think I shall give it to mamma when I have finished it, but I don't know, because mamma says she is tired of the sight of it; but if I don't give it to mamma, I shall find some one to give **it to."**

When her young visitor was gone, Jane said to her nurse, " Do you think mamma would like it if I were to work some children sitting on a stool for her?"

" Nonsense!" said nurse, "your mamma sees enough of children sitting on stools, without your wasting your time in showing her. I have no patience **with such** folly; you had much better make carpets all your life for those who have none!"

" I never made any thing for mamma," said **Jane.**

" Well, you may **be sure your mamma is best** pleased when **you are working for the poor;** but if you want to make something **for her, I can tell you what** would be a great deal better than children sitting on stools!"

" What, nurse?"

" Why, net her a purse! she uses one of those wove things, that look old before ever they look new; you might make her one that would look and wear well, and there would be some sense in that."

" But I can not do netting, nurse."

" O, I can soon teach you that; if you **save up your** pence for three weeks, you can buy **a skein and begin.** I have got a needle and pin."

" But will mamma know?"

"There is **no** need she **should:** if you like to be up these light mornings you may work an hour before breakfast, by three weeks' time **it may be a** great deal warmer than now; but then you must save up all your money, because there will be the rings and the tassels as well as the silk."

The agreement was joyfully made. Now came the finishing of the patch-work carpet, and Jane, with her nurse's help, carried it **up to** the old woman, and laid it down before her wondering eyes, and then looked round with delighted feeling at the change in the cottage, **and** the change in the dear old woman since the day when first she entered it.

The purse could not be begun till the first three-pence **was** saved up.

"You don't know why I save up my money now, mamma!" said Jane to her mother.

"No, indeed, I can not tell; do you want a few of my pence **to** help yours a little, that I may know the sooner?"

"O, no, mamma, that would not do at all, it must be all my own money!" but while the child answered so, she felt the confidence that would have helped her secret purpose without even **asking to know it.**

Jane could not quite forget her young visitor's remarks, so one day she **said to her nurse,** "Mamma never buys me a best frock!"

"No, nor does not need," **replied nurse,** "it's only those who don't look always as they should, and who want to look sometimes as they should not, who think about best dresses! Your mamma always keeps you neat, and fit to be seen according to your station, and so you have no more need to think about wanting a best frock than any lady in the land."

There was something so decided and satisfactory to Jane in **her nurse's** reply, that she thought no more upon the subject, quite convinced that to be always neat was the only point of importance. But she could not so readily forget the worsted-work, and though she was intent **on her** secret purse, she still thought it would be very pleasant to do some work with colored wools; she did **not go** to her young visitor's party, so she had not seen the work of which she had heard so much. "Mamma," said Jane, one day, "should you think that children sitting on a stool would look pretty done in worsted-work?"

"I do not know, unless I saw them," replied her mother, "**but I do not generally** admire such pieces **of work;** they take a **great deal** of time and attention, more, I think, than they are **worth.** Did you wish to try some worsted-work?"

"**Yes, mamma,** I should like very much, only nurse said it was nonsense to do children sitting on a stool, and I don't know what else could be done."

"A great many things can be done! I think the best would be to work your father a pair of worsted slippers, to put on when he comes in from the shop; nurse would **not** think that nonsense."

"O, yes, I should like that a great deal the best! May I do that, mamma?"

"Yes, you shall go to the shop with me and choose them for yourself."

And so the child found full employment now, in her early work for her mother, and her later work for her father—all through the spring's bright weeks; and then the joy of presenting her gifts, **and** seeing the lasting pleasure with which they were used—the smile of remembrance that fell on her glad eyes **when the purse was** drawn out sometimes, or the slippers put on. **And thus,** within and without her home, every pure and hallowed **sympathy was** strengthened in her **young** life **by** natural and **easy exercise.**

CHAPTER XXI.

"The world's a room of sickness, where each heart
Knows its own anguish and unrest;
The truest wisdom there, and noblest art,
Is his, who skills of comfort best."

IN the following spring an invitation came for Rose, from her mother's only brother, a farmer on a large grass-farm in Derbyshire : it was a long journey for Rose to take, and her father was very unwilling to **lose his** little comforter from his home : Rose also did not like the thought of another visit to unknown relations, but her mother was resolved—Mrs. Smith said that her brother would have good reason to be offended as Rose had been allowed to visit her other uncle, if his invitation was now refused ; so the engagement was made, and Rose was to meet **her** uncle in London, to which place he expected to travel **up in about three weeks' time ; and as in those days it** was not **thought worth while for children to take a long** journey for a **short period, it was settled that Rose was to** spend three **months beneath her Derbyshire uncle's roof.**

When Molly, the maid at the farm, found that Rose was to leave for **another long visit,** her patient **endurance gave way to** despair, and **after nine** years' faithful **service she told her mis-** tress that she **must leave her place—unable to bear the** prospect of her mistress's trying temper without Rose to soften it. Things **were not improved in the** house by **Molly's giving** warning ; Mrs. Smith **really** valued her and **was very sorry to lose** her ;

302

but the pride of heart which made Mrs. Smith's temper so trying to all, would not now suffer her to express any regret—she only showed resentment at what she called Molly's ingratitude; and Rose left her home with a sorrowful heart.

When the time for Molly's departure arrived, she came to take leave of her mistress in tears—little Tim had run off crying, to hide himself in the stable—and Molly gathered courage and said, "I am sure, ma'am, I never would have left your place for another, if I might have but reckoned on a pleasant word sometimes; but I don't think, since master Joe and the horse went away, you have given me so much as one smile—and I'm sure that their going was none of my doing; and I can't stand it, ma'am, and I don't see who is to stand it!" There still were moments when Mrs. Smith's pride had almost more than enough to do in keeping down and hiding up the buried feeling of her heart; and now when her faithful, her really valued servant stood before her and confessed that her mistress could have bound her to her service by a smile, when that servant was really departing, Mrs. Smith found the only disguise for her feeling would be silence—she did not therefore speak a word—she held out Molly's wages without looking at her, and then turned another way; while poor Molly, quite overcome by what seemed to her the unkindest act of all, left the farm for her mother's distant village, with a feeling of unreturned affection and heart-broken distress.

There was one person—and only one—with whom Mrs. Smith had to do, to whom she had never spoken a harsh word: it was not Rose, it was not little Tim, it was not her favorite William; no, it was the orphan child, Mercy Jones. It was true the orphan's grandmother, Widow Jones, had always stood as high as possible in Mrs. Smith's regard; Jem also, Mercy's uncle, Mrs. Smith considered worth all the other men and boys on the farm

put together, because she said, "If you make him understand
what is to be done, you may give up the worry yourself!"   But
it was not her grandmother's and her uncle's good qualities that
procured such favor for Mercy, Mrs. Smith was a strict examiner
of each individual with whom she had to do, and nothing but
personal integrity could ever win her regard.   Mercy was a tall,
delicate-looking, gentle child, with a thoughtful heart, a willing
mind, and a ready skill, that far more than compensated for her
lack of strength; and now that for the first time in nine years
the farm was left without a maid, widow Jones and Mercy both
came in to help.   It might have been supposed that these two
helpers would prove equal to Molly's former service, and so they
might have been but for Mrs. Smith's apprehensions on Mercy's
behalf: "Here, give that to me, girl," she would continually say,
taking the work from **Mercy's** hands, and finishing it up with
equal energy and sevenfold power; then, kindly adding, "It's
not, as I say, because you have not the notion, but because you
have not the strength!"   While to her husband Mrs. Smith was
constantly declaring, "Slave as I may, I am sure that girl will
be overdone! she's too willing, and the work's beyond her, and
an orphan too as she is—I wish enough I could meet with some
one I should not always be afraid to put upon!"   Many girls
came and offered themselves, but Mrs. Smith declared that there
was not so much as one among them who had any right to the
name of a servant; **she could tell** that without any need of a
trial!   **All** this time, while vexing over Mercy's toil, over-work-
ing her own strength, and objecting to every girl who came
before her, Mrs. Smith never named the absent Molly: in all the
vexatious trouble **she** daily made **for** herself, she cast no fresh
censure on Molly; and could Molly have seen her mistress's real
feeling, the probability would have been her instant return to
offer her services again; but pride lay between Mrs. Smith's

heart and her lips, and kept her continually back from the confessions that would have led to peace in her family, instead of strife and debate.

All through the years of which we have been speaking, Patience had lived on in her place of service with the family of Mr. Mansfield's foreman; but her master and mistress had for some time felt that the increasing expenses of their growing family were putting a servant beyond their means; and a still stronger reason for doing without one lay in the good sense of these excellent parents, who both felt that the best way of teaching their children diligence and method in accomplishing work, would be to bring them up to get well through all that their own home required. But how to send Patience away was the **painful** part, and month after month, then week after week, her dismissal was delayed, till at last the foreman's wife said, " Well, I can not help it, she has worked like a child for me, and you must tell her, for I can't; you hired her, she knows, **and** so it will come natural to her!" It was very seldom that the good woman's resolution failed her, but now it did; and her husband's mild firmness came in to the rescue of their home principles. He told Patience quietly and decidedly that he felt the time had come when his girls must do all the work of their house; that both he and his wife valued her faithful services, but still more the example she had set their children ; he said she had earned what was better than any wages—the lasting regard of those she had served ! and he told her to come to his house, as a home always open to her, while she maintained the same character she had earned in his family. The color left the cheek of Patience, but she could not speak; her master added, kindly, that they should not think of parting with her till she met with a comfortable place, and that, therefore, she need feel no anxiety on that subject, and then left her. When Patience returned to her mistress and the children, her tears broke forth, her good mistress cried also, and the children cried, but her mistress making an effort, said, cheerfully, " Come, child, it 's not for you to fret ; you have done your duty here, and your reward will follow ; you are only going to make more friends, and not to lose those you leave behind ! So cheer up, and be as busy as you can—that 's the **best** cure for low spirits of most kinds." So Patience tried, but the spring of her work was gone. She worked as well as before, but it was the work of habit and principle, not the energy of life ; and often through her heart a faintness passed, as she felt the home was her's no longer ! she must wander out again into the world her childhood found so rough ; and thoughts of her **early life** and of her first place of service came back with a sinking weight on her spirit.

Having spoken to Patience, her master now named the subject to his employer, Mr. Mansfield, and Mr. Mansfield promised to name it to some of his best customers. Among the first of these on the next day, being market-day, was farmer Smith.

" It's no **use** to ask you, Mr. Smith, whether you want a servant girl, for your's knows the value of her place, it seems, too well to leave it !"

" Ah, she is gone at last !" replied farmer Smith, gravely. " **Yes,** her's was nine years of honest service. She earned her wages fairly enough ; but she is gone **at** last !"

" Well, then, I can find you just such another. My foreman, here, like a wise man, is giving up servant-keeping, and he wants a place, he says, for one of the best girls who ever called herself a servant."

At this the foreman came forward and talked with farmer Smith, and Mr. Mansfield waited on his other customers.

Now, Mrs. Smith had often said that she would rather by far teach **a** girl farm-work and farm-ways from the beginning, than have one who thought herself clever at every thing! So farmer Smith went home, thinking he had met with the very girl most likely to satisfy his wife; but Mrs. Smith was not in a mood to be satisfied with any thing, or any body, and only replied to farmer Smith's pleasant description: "And what's the use of a girl who never stirred from the town, and knows only town ways, out here in the country?"

"Why, a good servant is a good servant," replied Mr. Smith; "and as for our ways, why, she can learn the country ways, I suppose, as well as she **learned the town** ways—if she has a mind to them!"

"But it is not the least likely she would have a mind to them; girls **who have been** used to the town never settle in country places like this; she had a thousand times better stay where she is," said Mrs. Smith.

Mr. Smith found it was hopeless to urge the point; so he dropped the subject. On the next market-day he made one more attempt, asking Mrs. Smith if she would not like **to go** in and just see the girl? But Mrs. Smith replied, that she could judge about it quite as well, without **having to** go seven miles to come to an opinion! **So Mr. Smith** took his drive to the town alone. He called at Mr. Mansfield's shop, and requested the foreman **to wait one week** longer for his answer, which he readily consented **to do, as** he thought the place must be a good one, where the last servant had remained nine years; farmer Smith's character also stood very high, and Patience was quite willing to go. "Moreover," the foreman added, "my opinion is, that the girl will settle all the better a little distance from my wife and children, of whom she is wonderfully fond!" **So** farmer Smith, very anxious to secure a good girl for his wife and home, waited for the forlorn hope of Mrs. Smith's change of feeling by another market-day.

The week passed by; every girl that applied for the place was pronounced by Mrs. Smith to be as unfit as could be, and the last person she would think of engaging with! while she was stil. vexed at having no servant to do the work, and protested that Mercy would be ill with overdoing—but Mr. Smith heard all in perfect silence. The next market-day arrived, but Mr. Smith asked no questions; he prepared as usual for market; when, just as with hat and whip he was leaving the house, Mrs. Smith followed him and said, "There is not the least use in the world in my going all that way after a girl that is not likely to come, or to stay if she did come; but if she has a mind to come after the place herself, why, that's another thing!"

"When would you like her to come then?" inquired Mr. Smith, "supposing she is willing?"

"Why, the sooner the better! I am sure I am in a fidget about that child Mercy, every day of my life; it's a wonder that she is not overset already, and I also, with the work of such a place as this is!"

Mr. Smith stepped quietly into his gig, and drove off. In the evening he returned with Patience seated beside him.

"What have you been after now?" exclaimed Mrs. Smith, in dismay, calling farmer Smith aside privately. "That's just the way with you, never giving one time to turn round; you think a thing is no sooner said than it can be done! I never meant the girl to come for good till I had seen her!"

"Well, wife," replied Farmer Smith calmly, "there is no harm done; the girl could not make her way out here alone. If you don't fancy her, Jem can drive her back in the light-cart after tea, or you can keep her a week on trial; both her mistress and the girl were willing either way."

Hearing this, Mrs. Smith was somewhat pacified, and she went out to receive Patience, who stood waiting at the door,

There stood Patience, a stout, strongly-built young woman, with a fresh color and pleasant face, her dress neatness itself. When she saw her expected mistress, Patience made a low courtesy, such as she had always been used to in her school days in the town, and she stood silently before Mrs. Smith. Now Mrs. Smith was not naturally without kindness of heart; it was pride and selfishness which she had suffered to grow within her unrestrained, that blinded her to the feelings of others; but when she saw a stranger girl before her, one of whom she heard so good a character, her natural kindness rose unimpeded, she received her with a welcome, and made her take a comfortable tea; and said that as she was come so far, and had brought her things with her, she had at all events better stay the week.

Patience rose the next morning, almost at break of day. She opened her little window, and wondered at the fragrance of the air; she looked over the land, and while she sighed for the sleeping children far away, and the cheerful call of her mistress's kind quick tone, that could not reach her now—while she sighed for these, she felt **that** she could love those pleasant fields better far than the town, and that if she could but bring her master's family to her, she should never wish for the town again; but then the feeling of a stranger in a strange place came over her, and she could only turn from the window to commit herself in prayer to Him who is the stranger's God. As soon as Patience heard her mistress moving, she left her room, and, greatly to the surprise of Mrs. Smith, her new maid stood before her at five o'clock in the morning, in her neat gown of dark blue, with short sleeves, **and** a stout apron—as fit for farm-house work as for any other. There was about Patience a quietness of look and manner that made a strange contrast with her active figure and step, quick without haste, and quiet without dullness—it might be that the exterior of her early sorrow had never been quite effaced, but left its gentlest shade upon her life's after vigor and brightness. There was also a propriety of manner about Patience that could not fail to produce a pleasing impression, and a readiness of attention and willingness of movement that made it no effort to tell her to **do** any thing; while her thoughtful care more frequently prevented the need of her being told. Mrs. Smith's quick eye soon read these qualifications, and the consequence was, she instantly made up her mind that Patience would consider herself too good for the place, and would be certain not to stay; but still, as she felt her deserving of attention, she put her **in** the way of farm-house work, giving her daily instruction in milking and other peculiarities of the dairy. Patience was very **grave,** for her heart was still in her last place, she was always finding herself back again in thought with those she had left, and Mrs. Smith failed not to set this down to discontent. "But, surely," said Mr. Smith, "the girl does every thing in as pleasant a way as can be, and what would you have more?"

"O! that's only by way of keeping up her character," replied Mrs. Smith. "You will see she will never stay a day beyond her week; I am sure she will never come down to the place, her manners are above it!"

Mrs. Smith did not know she had one beneath her roof who had been humbled in sorrow's bitter school; one who sought not pride but love; whose heart no money could win to her place, but which affection's power or feeling's claim could bind to any service; and so she made up her mind that Patience would consider herself above the place and go; and she said it was very hard to have nothing before her but teaching the same things over and over again to perhaps a dozen girls one after another, for she was sure the place would never suit this girl, and it was not likely she would find a girl in a hurry that would **suit** her! Mr. Smith heard in silence.

The end of the week came. Patience said nothing; so Mrs. Smith felt it incumbent upon her to speak.

"Well, girl," said Mrs. Smith, "you have done full as well as any one might expect; but of course the place is not one to suit you, any one can see that, so I can only wish you a better. We will make out a way to get you back to your friends."

Patience looked up in surprise, and the color deepened in her cheeks. "I have no wish to leave the place, ma'am," she replied, "if I could suit you; I am not likely to find a better."

Mrs. Smith was now more surprised than Patience had been, and not altogether pleased at finding herself mistaken; for Mrs. Smith always felt a secret satisfaction in seeing her predictions fulfilled, even though she considered the events to be evil. Happily Patience had said that she did not think herself likely to find a better place, and this single expression of feeling from a heart in which pride had no indulgence, went far to relieve the involuntary annoyance Mrs. Smith felt at finding her own impression a wrong one. So Patience stayed.

But from the day on which Mrs. Smith looked upon Patience as really her servant, she began her usual tone of harsh authority. Patience was neither slow to learn nor frequent in forgetting; but the dread of her mistress's voice made her painfully anxious about every possible thing that could be expected of her. The heavy, anxious look of her childhood began again to steal over and shadow the pleasant expression of her face. She would stand sometimes and watch little Tim in the farm-yard, by the side of his father, or talking with Jem, and she would think that child seemed the only one that she could love; but he was seldom within, always running away as soon as possible from his mother's harsh voice. He was a favorite with all the laborers, and they would do any thing to please him. But Jem was his chief friend. From the time that William had left, he had taken to Jem, as if he considered him to be most like his lost brother, and no one could so easily wake the clear tones of his merry laugh as honest Jem. He would ride on his shoulder, wander down to find him with the sheep, share his homely food; and now that Rose was away, he would get to him whenever he could. Poor Patience used to watch the child, and wish that he would turn to her as he did to Jem; but Molly was still fresh in the memory of little Tim, and he scarcely looked at Patience. So Patience felt more and more desolate, while closer round her heart pressed the warm memories of the home she had left.

While things were in this state, Jem, who had been sent on an errand to the town, came into the back-kitchen to have some provision on his return. It was evening, and Patience was sitting there alone. Jem had often observed her disconsolate look, and it hurt his kind and honest heart to see so little comfort for her; and now as he sat on the back-kitchen bench, cutting his bread and meat with his great pocket-knife, he ventured a remark: "Living out here in the country, I take it, does n't suit you like down there in the town?"

"No, it's very different," replied Patience; and there was silence again.

"You seem hard done up in your thoughts," again observed Jem; "I hope you have n't happened with any misfortune."

"No, not that exactly," Patience slowly replied; and then, encouraged by Jem's friendly tone, and not less by the expression of his honest face, which she had seen most days since she had been at the farm, she went on to say—"I was thinking how little wages I could do with! I think I could do with less than my last mistress would have liked to offer me; only then I remembered there's the food, and one must eat if one's to live!"

Jem had no skill in arithmetic, and could not render **much** aid in such a calculation; but he had a far quicker estimate, perhaps, than many an arithmetician of the heart's joys and sorrows, and he came in with his friendly aid at the root of the matter. " Are you after a change, then ?" he asked.

" Well," replied Patience, " I was thinking if I could get back anyhow where I came from, I would rather live there on dry bread, among those that were one with **me,** than here, where no one has a care for one, on any wages !"

" But," answered Jem, " they said you could not hold the place, because the family **gave up** servant-keeping ?"

" So they did," said Patience, " **and I'm** afraid they would not **take me** back **if I could** go without **wages; only** I can't help thinking about it !"

" Well, now," said Jem, " take my advice. You will never do yourself or others a straw's worth of good thinking on what can not be, and don't be down-hearted here. Mistress is hasty, I know ; but I have served her from a child, and if once **you get** right with her, you will never have a trouble from **her again.** She is always for thinking every one will go wrong till **she** finds they go no way but right. Once let her get **persuaded** of that, and she would not believe the whole world **if they** stood out against you. I know it's hard in the **coming, and** she has been put out of late more than common one **way** or another, and the last maid could not put up with it, nor wait for things to work round again, **so she** left; **but** only you keep right on as you have begun, and you will **be sure** to find things mend in good **time."**

This conversation was the first encouragement poor Patience **had had;** it eased her spirit also to have been able to speak on the subject, and for a time she went more cheerfully on. But the same harsh tone, the same cold short manner, met her every effort, and after a while she lost heart again, and began to think

she **must** give up, and **try to** find **some** other place. But where
could she turn? She **had no** opportunity, so far from the town,
of making inquiry, **and she** was ashamed to write **to** her mistress,
and say she could **not stay** in the place she had been **so** glad to
secure for her. She was sitting at her needle on the **low chair
in the** back-kitchen, and as she thought on these things her tears
fell on her work. Little Tim had come, unperceived by her, to
the back-door, and as he stood there looking in, he saw Patience
crying. The sight touched his heart, for little Tim **was** no
stranger to tears, especially since Rose had been away; so he
went up to Patience, and said in his kindest little voice, " What
for you kie?"

" **Because** no one **loves me** here," said Patience.

" I will **love you,**" said little Tim, putting his hand upon her
cheek, and then, when Patience still cried, slipping his arm
round her neck, he **said** again, " **I will** love you very much;
don't kie any more."

Patience clasped her arms round the child, and laid her head
one moment on his little shoulder, as he stood beside her, and
sobbed; then looking up, she made an effort, and wiped away
her **tears,** and said, " If you love me, then I will not cry!" From
that time little Tim seemed to feel that it depended upon him to
keep Patience from crying. He would often come and look at
her from the back-kitchen door, and when she was alone would
stay **beside** her **and** talk to her; and the heart of poor Patience
grew content in her place, because **of** the love and care of that
one little ministering child.

Rose had now been more than **two** months away, and they
had proved happy months for her. Her uncle met her in London—a grave and silent person, of whom Rose felt afraid; but
her aunt's kind face, and her cousins' warm greeting, soon made
her at home among them. She found every one of them full

p. 314.

of occupation; but each one seemed ready **for** her, and always able to find her a help and comfort. She helped her cousins tend their poultry, and make the summer preserves—learning many things unknown in her home. She helped them in their garden, where she learned from them **to** bud roses, prune trees, and as the summer advanced, to distill **rose-leaves** and herbs. She helped them in their work—she **learned to cut out** and make by herself garments for the **poor; and often while** she worked with them one **read aloud, and Rose learned** more of general knowledge in that **visit than in all her young** life before. Here she heard histories **of missions, all new to her;** and read of other **countries, also** new and strange **to** her. She sat **by** her cousins while they taught the village children in the **school,** till at last they made her take a little class of her own; this gave new interest and delight to Rose, and she thought it would be **as** hard to leave the little children of her class as it would to **leave** any thing. She wondered how she could have lived so long **without** knowing and loving relations **so** dear **to** her **now!** but **the** distance had been great between them. Still Rose **often** thought of her home, and longed to see it again, though she did not like to think of leaving her aunt and **cousins so far away.** But when the harvest-time came, and Rose **was** expecting **to** return, a letter arrived to say **that** little **Tim was** ill with a dangerous fever, and the letter asked that **Rose** might still remain at her uncle's house, for fear **of** taking the fever if she returned. This was unexpected **sorrow for** Rose—little Tim, whom she loved so much, dangerously ill, and she could not nurse, or comfort, **or** see him! Poor Rose was overwhelmed with grief, but **she had** those around her now who knew how to comfort; they **loved** her more tenderly in her sorrow than they had done before, and they reminded her to whom to look—even **to the** Saviour who can comfort any heart that turns to Him.

Little Tim lay in his cot at home, and the doctor said that his life was in danger. Now a real trial was come to Mrs. Smith at last; she had long been making troubles for herself and others, but trouble was come now, and she felt it was; and all that before she had made so much of was forgotten. Day and night she watched by the cot of little Tim; he did not like to lie in her arms when restless—he seemed uneasy there, and cried for Rose when his mother took him; so, weeping, she would lay him back upon his pillow, and sit long hours and watch beside him. As she sat there a sense of the past came over her—a sense of years of harshness and ill-temper, of peace destroyed by her, and sorrow made for others; she thought too of how the child had always seemed glad to slip away from her, as if uneasy in her presence, and she looked down on his burning cheek, and felt as if it would kill her to see him die. Patience, too, would watch beside the cot while widow Jones did her work below—and it seemed to ease the heavy grief of Mrs. Smith to have her there. The men were constantly inquiring for the child, and Jem was always waiting about the house when possible, helping his mother to do the work, and asking of all who came from the room how the child seemed now?

Mrs. Smith was leaning over the cot, and Patience kneeling beside it, when little Tim called "Rose! Rose! do come to Tim, come now?" "What do you want, my darling?" said Mrs. Smith, "I will do it for you." "I want to pray," said little Tim, "and Rose can teach me, I forget it now!" Mrs. Smith was silent.

"Mother, can you pray?" asked little Tim. Mrs. Smith hid her face and wept, she felt she could not pray, she had never taught her child, and she could not teach him now, she could think of nothing!

"Can you pray, Patens?" asked little Tim, in his anxiety.

'Yes, dear, I do pray for you."

"Oh, then you can teach it to me! I forget it all now !" said little Tim, and he joined his hands together in act of prayer.

Patience repeated the prayer she had taught to little Ruth in her last place, and Tim, quite satisfied, repeated it after her.

"Can you say my texes, too ?" asked little Tim.

Patience made a guess, and said, "Suffer the little children to come unto Me, and forbid them not, for of such is the kingdom of Heaven ;" it proved quite right, and little Tim added, " I can say my other, ' Speak, Lord, for thy servant heareth.' "

"Now I can say my hymn," said little Tim, "that Rose did teach me ;" and looking up with folded hands, he repeated, in his broken utterance—

> "Lord, look upon a little child,
>   By nature sinful, rude, and wild;
>   O put Thy gracious hands on me,
>   And make me all I ought to be.

> "Make me Thy child—a child of God,
>   Washed in my Saviour's precious blood;
>   And my whole heart from sin set free,
>   A little vessel full of Thee.

> "A star of early dawn, and bright,
>   Shining within Thy sacred light;
>   A beam of grace to all around;
>   A little spot of hallowed ground.

> "Lord Jesus, take me to Thy breast,
>   And bless me that I may be blest;
>   Both when I wake, and when I sleep,
>   Thy little lamb in safety keep."

And then, satisfied, he said, "Mother, don't kie any more—

Patens can teach it me all!" and turning his cheek on his pillow, he fell peacefully asleep.

Day and night Mrs. Smith repeated to herself, and tried to keep in her memory continually, the prayer that Patience had said for little Tim, in the hope that he would ask her again to teach him—but he never appealed to his mother any more: when he woke from sleep, if he had his senses, his first look was for Patience, and with folded hands he waited for her to teach him "how to pray."

"Does it hurt you very much, dear?" asked Patience, as she helped Mrs. Smith to dress a blister on the child's head. "No, nothing hurts me now!" said little Tim. And he fell asleep, and woke no more on earth.

It was grief for all: but the mother's heart was broken up; she took to her bed, the fever that had taken little Tim from earth came upon her, and her mind wandered in sorrowful delirium. Patience was her devoted nurse; while widow Jones sometimes gave Patience a little rest from the sick-room, or helped her in it, and at other times did what she could of the work below, with Jem to aid.

"I see it now," said Mrs. Smith, when for a short time her senses returned, "I see it all now, it is right I should be left to die! I turned from our young minister who would have taught me how to live; and now death is come, and I see plain enough that I am not ready to meet it!"

"Don't you think the minister would come, if he was asked?" said Patience to widow Jones.

"What's the use of it?" asked widow Jones, "she is scarcely a moment reasonable, and she has been so set against him, it might be too much for her now."

Widow Jones had seen their aged minister sent for many times to the dying; but he had never unlocked the exhaustless treasury of the love of God in Jesus Christ for his own heart—— therefore he knew not how to dispense its balm of Life, its soothing peace to others: widow Jones had never seen the servant of the most High God, the faithful minister of the truth as it is in Jesus, draw near in his Master's name to the dying bed **where** hope was not—this she had never seen, and so knowing **only** what she had seen, she only replied, " What's the use ?"

But Patience was not to be so easily satisfied. She waited awhile, and then she went to her master : " My poor mistress keeps lamenting so," she said, **" to** think how she turned from the minister ! Don't **you think he would come to see her** if you asked him, **sir ?"**

Farmer **Smith** stood silent. " It 's a hard case !" he replied ; " I am sure I don't know ; I have been ashamed to meet him for ever so long now ; and it 's more than a year since he has been into the house, your poor mistress was so set against him ; and now such a fever as it is, and her senses gone, I don't know that I dare to ask it !"

" May I go sir, and just tell him the state my **poor mistress is** in, and hear if he would please to come ?"

" But," said farmer Smith, " it **might overset** her, so bad **as** she is, and then if she were **worse for it,** I **should** have to answer for it. I dare not engage with it !"

So Patience returned to **the sick** chamber. The sun was setting in the autumnal evening, **she** sat down by the window and looked into the glowing sky, and thought of little Tim. The thought was sad, yet full of peace. Lost in the feeling, she watched the sun's decline behind the purple clouds ; then looking down below again, she saw a distant figure crossing the pasture in the valley. It was the curate ! **Could** he indeed be coming to the farm ? or would he take the road that led **to the** cottages **by the wood ?** Patience watched, breathless between hope and fear! He crossed the farm-stile, he turned to the bridge over the brook, and then began to ascend the green slope —he was coming indeed! Patience ran down. Farmer Smith was still within. He hastened out to meet his visitor, and Patience to see that all was in readiness above.

"I am grieved to hear of your heavy trials," said the curate, as he entered the house with farmer Smith. "I was absent at the death of your child, and only now heard on my return of the illness of your wife. I thought she might be willing to see me, but if not, I hope I may be permitted to speak a word of comfort to you."

"I am sure, sir, it is more than I could have expected!" said farmer Smith, hardly able to speak from overburdened feeling.

"It is a dark and cloudy day for you!" said the curate. "Indeed a storm has burst upon you; but you remember how after the storm the bow is set in the cloud for all who will look above to the Hand that smites them. The storm has come, and now we must look up and wait and watch, in prayer and faith, for the rainbow of promise and comfort. Will your wife be able and willing to see me?"

Mr. Smith went to the sick room, and returned, saying, "She is not sensible, sir, and I am afraid it is but putting you into danger."

"Oh, I am not afraid of that," replied the curate, "if you are willing I should go. We may pray for her, and more may be known by her than you think."

"Well, then, sir, if you please," said farmer Smith. And the feet of the publisher of peace, the bringer of good tidings, entered the chamber of sickness and sorrow. He stood a moment by the bed, and looked upon the poor unconscious sufferer, then said, "Let us pray," and kneeled down beside the bed, while farmer Smith and Patience knelt also.

"O God of the spirits of all flesh, thou who art a just God, and yet a Saviour, hear us, we beseech thee, in the prayer which we offer up, through thy son Jesus Christ, for the body and soul of this sick woman. In thy most merciful hands are the issues of life and death. O suffer not the king of terrors to destroy, but raise her up, we beseech thee, that she may live in thy sight. O spare her, most merciful Lord, now that thou hast dug with thy chastening hand to her roots. **O spare** her, we pray thee, yet another year, to see if she may not now bear fruit to thy honor and praise and glory! Open thou her ear, good Lord, to hear thy still small voice in this hour of tribulation; open thou **her eyes to** behold the Lamb of God who taketh away all sin; open thou her heart to receive Him whom thou hast sent to seek and to save that which was lost. As thou hast plowed up her soul with affliction, O cast in the precious seed of thy word, and so water it with thy grace, and nourish it with thy blessing, that it may bring forth fruit unto life eternal. And cause, we beseech thee, the doctrine of thy grace and the word of thy lips to distill as the dew, at this time, upon the parched spirit of this poor sufferer, that she may know the power of its heavenly refreshment. We ask all for His sake whose precious blood cleanseth from all sin, and whose spirit quickeneth the dead, even Jesus Christ our Lord. Amen."

Then, sitting down beside the bed, the minister repeated softly and slowly, "Come unto me all ye that labor and are heavy laden, and I will give you rest." "Come now and let us reason together, saith the Lord; though your sins be as scarlet, they **shall** be as white as snow; though they be red like crimson, they shall be as wool." "The blood of Jesus Christ cleanseth from all sin." "Look unto Me and be ye saved, all the ends of the earth; for I am God, and there is none else." "Ask, and it **shall** be given you; seek, and ye shall find; knock, and it shall be opened unto you; for every one that asketh receiveth, and he that seeketh findeth, and to him that knocketh it shall be opened." The words, the tone of peace, seemed to soothe the sufferer—she lay still and composed. Standing up, the minister said, fervently, "The Lord bless thee and keep thee; the Lord make his face to shine upon thee, and be gracious unto thee; the Lord lift up the light of his countenance upon thee, and give thee peace!" And then he left the room.

The curate talked long with farmer Smith below, and farmer Smith found, to his surprise, that there was no resentment at the conduct poor Mrs. Smith had shown toward him. He only spoke the words and breathed the spirit of sympathy, and counsel, and comfort. Oh, what a weight was lifted that evening from the heart of farmer Smith! The opposition expressed and shown in his home to the curate, had kept farmer Smith back from venturing to speak to him; but now he had been seated with him in his own parlor without fear, and there had been able to utter the long pent-up and hidden feelings of his heart. Oh, how the father thought of his little Rose as he returned with thankfulness and peace to his kitchen!

"Patience, child, is it you?" asked Mrs. Smith that evening, when the light of day had faded, and the candle was lit. "Patience, child, is it you? I hardly seem to know where I am, and yet I think I am better, I have had such a heavenly dream—I thought I was carried, all so bad as I am, in my bed to the church, and there I saw the new minister again! O how it seemed to give me hope, for I thought I had turned away from him, and now I should never be suffered to see him any more! I thought he stood up, but he seemed to speak only to me, and to look down at none but me, and he preached about "rest," and it seemed as if he came with the message for me, straight from the God above! and then I thought I looked round for little Tim to hear the sweet words too, but he was not there, and then I remembered he was gone! but still **it** did not seem to strike me down as the thought of him did before, for I seemed to know he was gone to that "rest" that the minister was preaching about. O how it did ease me to hear our new minister again! Patience, child, do you think I shall ever be able to get to the church any more before I am carried to my grave?"

"O yes, dear mistress, I do think you will live, by God's mercy; and that was not all a dream you had, **it was part true,** for the minister has been here to see you!"

"What! our rector?"

"No, the curate himself! and O, I feel sure since he came and prayed for your life, and your pardon, and peace, that God will give it!"

"What! our curate been here to see me!"

"Yes, and he stood up here by the bed, and he said those words, 'Come unto me all ye that labor and are heavy laden, and I will give you rest.' "

"Why, those are the very words I thought I heard him preach upon. Who could have thought it! Do you think he will come again?"

"Yes, I am sure he will," replied Patience, "and he will find you better when he does!"

The next day the curate called again. Mrs. Smith had been saved all anxiety of expectation—not thinking he would come again so soon: she was much overcome at seeing him, saying to him, "O sir, I thought I should never have seen you again!"

"My Master has sent me to comfort all who mourn," said the minister, "and I hope by His grace to be able to comfort you."

"O, sir, I don't know, but I fear not, I fear my comfort is dead, and I dying myself!"

"The Lord my God," said the minister, "is one who quickeneth the dead. He can not only restore you, but comfort you also "

" Ah, sir, I fear you don't know how bad I have been! I was set against your preaching from the first, because you said there was but one way for all, and you invited the worst sinners to come and try that way, and it hurt my pride—I thought they were not fit to be put so along with me! but now I have seen that I am not fit to be put with them—for I am the worst of all!"

" I have then a message for you," said the minister, " you have often heard it before, but now that God is chastening and teaching you, you will be able to understand its meaning, and I trust to receive its comfort. 'If we say that we have no sin, we deceive ourselves, and the truth is not in us. If we confess our sins, God is faithful and just to forgive us our sins, and to cleanse us from all unrighteousness.' You see, then, there is forgiveness for you—pardon and peace with God through Jesus Christ our Lord, if, confessing your sins unto God, you look to the Saviour, whom God has set forth to be a propitiation for sin."

Mrs. Smith listened to the words, and that truth which before had been so bitter, was now sweet to her hungry soul. The visits of the minister were her greatest comfort. Till at last from that sick-bed, the tones of hope, and peace, and praise were heard: and the always pleasant but now softened smile of Mrs. Smith would fall on those who watched beside her; and on Patience it fell with something of a mother's feeling.

The evening hearth shone bright when Mrs. Smith first came down to tea. Samson and Ted had done their best to make all things cheerful and full of comfort. Widow Jones had put away into the parlor the chair of little Tim—but the mother's eye fell on its vacant place. It was a long sad lesson that mother's heart had still to learn; but, sweetened by Heavenly mercy, and soothed by Heavenly peace, the longest lesson will only the more establish the heart, and root it the deeper in faith, hope, and **love.**

The autumn passed away, but fear of infection still made the anxious mother keep Rose from home. At last all danger was considered over, and the day was fixed. Rose was to return, and her two brothers also, William and Joe, were to join her in London, and return with her. O, what a day of expectation that was! Jem drove the horse in the gig to the next village **inn,** where the coach always stopped; then leaving it there he walked back, and the two brothers, with Rose in the gig between them, drove home together. Far over the now empty fields gleamed the **light from the farm-window,** of the blazing logs heaped up by **Ted upon the** fire—the mother, in her gown of black, **sat** in her chair beside it; the tea was prepared, and the pile of buttered toast, which Samson made in Rose's absence. Patience had had an extra baking, with widow Jones to help, and all her skill could do to welcome was added to the prepared reception. Patience had never seen Rose as yet, and even **her** heart **trembled** at thought of the one for whom the dying child had **called,** returning to the home where he was not. But in they came, Rose first, "Mother! oh, mother!" said the child, and the mother held her long pressed in that close embrace—as if she feared that she too might pass away from her sight like little Tim! Then in came William and Joe, with their tender and gentle greeting; and with softened feeling on every face, and deeper love in every heart, the circle, from which one had **been** taken, drew round to **their evening repast.**

CHAPTER XXII.

" Enthroned upon a hill of light,
A heavenly minstrel sings;
And sounds unutterably bright
Spring from the golden strings.
Who would have thought so fair a form
Once bent beneath an earthly storm!"

THE winter passed peacefully away at the farm. There was a hush about the place—a shadow evidently hung above it, the former active bustle of the **house went on** more quietly; but it was a stillness that told **of greater depth, a shadow** beneath which the best feelings of **the hearts there, strengthened** and grew. The look of anxiety which used **so** often **to cross** the young and blooming face of Rose, as she feared in **time** past her mother's hasty feeling at every fresh proposal or event, changed now **to an** expression of peace—yet with a quietness about it that told the sense of something gone, which steadied the light **spirits** of her happy youth, steadied **but** did not sadden—for she shared the happiness of little Tim ; and she often sung aloud the first verse of one of Mercy's hymns—

" There is beyond the sky
A heaven of joy and love:
And holy children, when they die,
Go to that world above !"

And though her mother never noticed it in words, yet did she often listen to the low tones as Rose sang on to herself, listened **in fear lest the sweet words** should cease; but happily Rose ac

quired the habit, till she would begin and keep on almost uncon
sciously to herself. Sunday was now a day of rest indeed, a day
made holy and a delight by the glad sounds of the good tidings
of great joy, preached every Sabbath in the village church
Patience had again found a home, and the heart of her mistress
cherished for her a deeper feeling than any that Patience had
known in service before. With Rose **it was** always pleasant to
work, or to speak—and when Patience discovered the mutual
friendship existing between Rose and a variety of the living
creatures upon the farm, Patience took pattern, **and trained her**
cows to an intelligence that seemed to give promise of rivalling,
in time, tl e very horses themselves !

In the following summer, to the delight of Rose, her Derby·
shire uncle and aunt and two of her cousins came down, at Mrs.
Smith's earnest request, to make a visit at the farm. Mrs. Smith's
brother soon returned to his home, on account of his business ;
but he left his wife and daughters, who made a stay **of** six weeks
—to the comfort and profit of Mrs. Smith, the satisfaction and
pleasure of farmer Smith, and the ceaseless enjoyment **of Rose.**
This intercourse tended to raise and enlarge Mrs. Smith's already
softened and rightly directed feelings. And six weeks **of** so
much peaceful enjoyment had **never been** known before within
the farm.

William and Joe obtained an early holiday this year, and to
their father's comfort **and** the pleasure of all, they came down
for the last fortnight **of** the harvest-time. How merrily did
Rose prepare the harvest-cakes the last baking before their **re-**
turn, obtaining from her mother's pleased and willing hand a
large supply of plums—because Will and Joe would be among
those to be fed with the harvest-cakes? And though it was
four years since William had held a sickle, the reapers declared
that Master William might stand king of them, for all he had

been up in London so long! But it was only a fortnight—and
the time drew to its close. The father had felt again the comfort
of his eldest son at his side in the anxiety and joy of harvest, and
his spirits sank at the approaching separation.

"Do you see any prospect for returning for good?" asked the
father, a few evenings before the last, as they sat together, after
supper—the young boys having retired to rest.

"Well, father," said William, "I should wish to do what I can
for my brothers. Joe stands on his own feet now: as for Ted I
think I may leave him to Joe; if you and mother consent to his
going to sea—on which he seems so bent—Joe is much more in
the way than **I am** of hearing of an opening in that line. But
then there's Samson; I don't know what you would wish about
him. I am afraid he has not spirit enough for a farmer!"

"No," said the father; "but I would sooner risk it, than have
you stay away for him, till no one knows when!"

"Well, I need not do that, father; for if you thought he
would do better in business, my uncle made me an offer before I
came down, to take him on trial; and he might, I think, with
his steady head, make a good man of business. If you liked him
to come up to me this Christmas, I would see the boy fairly into
his work, and then in another year I think I might hope to be a
farmer again."

It was agreed to give Samson leave to decide for himself the
next day. William said he could never consent to bind down
his brother to what he had felt so much, unless he was inclined
for it himself; and Mrs. Smith said she should be satisfied if the
boy made his own choice. So the next morning, before separating after breakfast, the proposal was made to Samson. He waited
a minute in grave consideration, then said with a deliberate tone—

"I should wish to come and see the place sometimes; but for
the rest—I would as soon be up there as down here!"

Mrs. Smith looked out of the window, and tears started to her eyes.

"Never mind, mother," said William in a low voice, "there's many a heart wakes up away from its home, that lay fast asleep in it!" But Mrs. Smith made no reply : she felt again the refluent wave of bitter memory, reminding her how little she had done to call forth and bind the hearts of her children to their home—their mother's dwelling-place! Yet William seemed as if he could love no other—but it might be only his father and the place he cared for! it was always for his father Joe talked of earning money! little Tim had seemed uneasy with her! and now Samson cared not whether he went or stayed! Oh, how bitterly around the heart flows sin's returning tide! But then back to the mother's memory came the first utterance of Rose on her return—the first words half smothered by her feeling, "Mother! oh, mother!" and looking round, as if to see whether the child who breathed them still were her's, she met the earnest eyes of Rose—bent in their full and tenderest expression upon her, as if only one thought were in her heart, and that one how her mother would bear the decision for Samson to go! It was enough, the mother felt one child to be at least a gift from Heaven to her—a gift most undeserved ; and her strengthened heart was ready to endure in patience and in hope ; to wait the influence of better feelings—now breathed and lived by her—on all around. So it was decided for Samson to go.

Ted had stood in breathless attention, while the fate of his brother was deciding : but the moment it was fixed for Samson to go, and farmer Smith had taken his hat and hastened out to his men, Ted exclaimed, "And what's going to be done with me? I mean to go to sea! Joe said he would find me a ship, and if he does not, I shall just run away and find one for myself!"

"Heyday!" answered William, "I shall look after Rover's old :nain! How do you think you are to climb a mast?"

"I will just show you!" said Ted, springing into his tall brother's arms, then on his shoulder, his merry face looking down at his brother's, as he asked, "Is not that something like it?"

"Well done!" answered William, "but there are no friendly **arms** on ship-board, I warn you!"

"Just you come off, then," said Ted, "and see me climb the barn-roof—I can do it all over! And if you and father don't find me a ship, I will find one for myself!"

"I tell you what, my little man," said William, stopping suddenly short, as Ted was leading him to the barn, "I shall not go a step further, nor see you climb, till you have listened to me." So sitting down on a cart-shaft that rested on the ground, he made a prisoner of the impatient boy, and began his discourse.

"Now, Ted, I tell you what, if you talk so I shall expect to hear that you fall down from the barn-roof and kill yourself, before ever you see your ship!"

"Well, but I want to go to sea,—and father said I should,— and father never said Samson was to go to London,—yet he is to go, and I am not!"

"I would not have Samson in London if I could not trust him," replied William; "and if you were only a runaway—who would trust you? You must try to earn a ship, and then I have not the least doubt but we shall find you one, and then you will go on board to serve like a man, and not like a runaway slave!"

"But why may I not go now? I can never earn it, so it is not any use to try; and I can climb well enough, and that's all a sailor wants to know."

"Yes, but you can earn it, and you will not be happy in it if you do not earn it," said William.

"How can I earn it?"

"By trying to do your duty now—being a comfort while you are at home; and learning all you possibly can to make you worth taking on board ship."

"But I tell you I can climb—and that is all a sailor wants to know."

"If you think so, you are very much mistaken; and it is a very happy thing for you that the ship is not yet lying in the harbor waiting for you."

"Why, what do I want to know more than climbing?"

"What? why, a sailor ought to know as many things as any one! The very first voyage you go you may be wrecked on **some uninhabited** island, and what use would you be then to **yourself or** to any one?—Nothing better than a poor helpless child! You must set to and learn the use of your hands for something more than climbing—a monkey can do that better than you already! but you hope to be a man, and I hope so too, and you must begin to act like one, and then **I shall begin to** think we may look out for your ship."

"But, Will, what must I learn?"

"Why, go off to Lewis, the basket-maker in the next village, and get him to teach you how to twist the willow withes, and don't you give over till you can make mother a basket strong enough to send her eggs to market in. And then get old master Newsom to teach you carpentering; and help him make hi wheels, and his barrows, and his carts. And then you must take to thatching, and learn how to bind a roof in dry—before you reckon yourself all ready for a life that may cast and leave **you** any where! And I advise you these next **winter** evenings, to get Rose to teach you how to work with a needle."

"So I will! and then, William, I can go to old Dawson, I know there's plenty of room for me at his stall, and I will be a cobbler, and mend and make shoes, what fun! I will make haste and learn every thing!"

"Yes, to be sure," replied William, "and then think of what use you might be! Why, you would be the last man to be parted with, if you were of use for every thing—what a busy, happy life you might lead! And then, Ted, do you think I have told you all you would want to know?"

"I don't know," replied Ted, looking up, at William's earnest tone.

"What if there came a storm at sea, and the ship went down, and you went down to the bottom with it? do you think your spirit would rise, like a little diver, and know its way to the Holy Heaven—where Tim has gone to dwell?"

"Did Tim know the way?" asked Ted.

"Yes, don't you remember how he loved to pray, and to learn and repeat the texts and hymns Rose taught him, which told of Jesus who is the way to Heaven?"

"Yes, I know that," answered Ted.

"Then don't you think you will want to know as much as little Tim knew, before you go on those great deep waters? And suppose you should find poor sailor boys, or men, who don't know the way to Heaven—you could teach them; and that knowledge would be the best of all, both for yourself and others."

"Yes, I dare say it might," replied Ted, "but I don't see that I can learn that."

"Not of yourself alone, but if you really try to learn, God will teach you both to know and to love it. Little Tim learned from Rose; would you like to go and see our Curate with me, and for me to ask him to take you into his class of boys, that you may learn that knowledge?"

"Yes, I should not mind that."

" Very well, then, we will go; and I think by when we have
bound the ship you will be ready for it—with knowledge to
make you happy yourself, and a comfort and blessing, I trust, to
others."

William returned with Joe to London, leaving Ted full of
spirit for his trades; and received under the Curate's care to
learn that which hath the promise, not only of the life that now
is, but of that which is to come. Ted inherited his mother's
energy, and being a general favorite, he found little difficulty
in persuading the village tradespeople to teach him something
of their skill—some idea how their work was done, and their
tools handled; besides, a refusal was not very easily given to one
who had no idea of taking it. The Curate, in his walk through
the village, would see his little scholar busy at the wheelwright's
side; or look down upon his merry face in the cobbler's stall—
intent with earnest gravity on mending some worn-out boot
Samson went to London at Christmas: and so passed away the
village winter.

Old Willy's health had long been visibly declining; there
were those who thought the old man would not see another
spring, and not without reason—for in the frost of February he
took to his bed, from which he never rose again. Widow Jones
was his nurse, Mercy his comfort, and Jem his earthly stay and
dependence. Rose was often sent by her mother with something warm from the farm; and Mrs. Smith herself was not
seldom seen making her way to the old man's cottage. Ted, to
his own perfect satisfaction, had soled a pair of old Willy's boots,
for which Dawson, the cobbler, said nothing was to be paid,
because the work was none of his; so Ted carried them home
and set them down close by old Willy's bed—ready for him as
soon as he might be able to get up; and from time to time the
ministering boy looked in to see whether the old man had yet

made tria. of the first completed effort of his skill. But old
Willy had trod the rough path of the world to its end; he had
put off his shoes from his feet, and he needed to be shod no more,
save with the preparation of the Gospel of peace—which time
and use, so far from impairing, can only serve to strengthen on
the heavenward pilgrim's feet.

At the approach of spring, notice arrived at the Hall, of the
return of Mrs. Clifford and the young Squire, and immediate
preparations were made. A request was sent that there should
be no demonstration of joy on their return; it was to be as quiet
and private as possible. The servants were to be arrayed in the
garb of mourning; and every circumstance to mark the event,
not as a family return, but as that of the widow and her fatherless son. The day was not made known, in order more effectually to prevent an assembling of the people. Jem now watched
with anxious impatience and fear, lest the fast-waning life of
old Willy should depart before his long-cherished wish had been
granted—to see his young master again! Widow Jones and
Mercy had for some time kept watch by day, and Jem slept in
old Willy's room by night. And still the feeble lamp of life
burned dimly on with that old man—as if no outward circumstance now affected its slow and gentle expiring. Widow Jones
and Mercy were in the cottage, when at the sound of carriage-
wheels Mercy ran to the door; it was a traveling carriage, and
there could be little doubt that it was on its way to the Hall, but
no one was visible within, no one looked out as it swiftly passed
by old Willy's door. Could it be the young Squire and the
Lady of the Hall? Yes, Jem, when he came in the evening,
brought word that it was said in the village they had arrived.
Widow Jones had sat up through the previous night, and Jem
was to keep watch through the first hours of this—till his mother
should come, after necessary rest, to relieve him. The evening

closed in, Jem drew the little window-curtain, lighted the candle, and opening the old man's Bible sat down to read. But he found it difficult to stay his thoughts on the sacred page, his mind was full of the young Squire's return—would he be altogether changed? Jem feared it must be likely he would—away so long, and in foreign parts, he could hardly return the same! Yet Jem believed the good were not given **to** change, he had heard his mother say so when **he was** a child; and surely the young Squire was good if ever any were! so it might be he would prove still the same. Then rose the question, would old Willy know him if he came to see him? Was there consciousness enough still left for the old man to know his hope fulfilled? **And Jem looked round on old** Willy in anxious inquiry. While thought was thus busy within, he heard a knock at the door; then a hand, to whom its latch seemed familiar, opened it; and and a stranger gentleman looked in; Jem started up, but in a moment he knew the face, he knew the friendly smile, he knew the form, yes, he knew the very hand that was raised to silence his exclamation and then extended to him! Jem bowed **his lowest** bow, then took the offered hand, and grasped it in both of his, while such a light of sudden joy suffused his countenance that words were little needed. Laying his hat on the table, the young Squire turned to the bed where the old man lay with his eyes closed as if in slumber. **He** stood and looked on him in silence. Oh then what a wave from memory's sea overflowed his heart! the past, the long past became present again—he thought of his dream, and as vividly as then in his sleep did he now seem **to** see the bright angel who watched over the old man—the heir of glory. He thought of that time when his work of love was not even begun, he remembered how hard that work had seemed at first—then how pleasant; how the difficulty again grew worse than before—then brightened into joy. And with that remembrance came the thought of his father--how he had met him in his childhood's feelings and made him possessor of the home where old Willy dwelt—the recollection of all passed before him, till he wiped away his starting tears, and turned round to Jem, saying softly, "He sleeps!"

"No, sir," Jem replied, "I doubt if he does; he lies mostly in that quiet way—as if his doings with Earth were all over, and we don't disturb him except for his food. But I will just speak to him now, if you please, sir, for he has longed sore to see you, and maybe he will still have the knowledge to understand that."

Jem went to the pillow, and stooping above it, said gently, "Daddy, look up! I say, daddy, look up and see who has come to you here!"

The old man looked up, the voice had aroused him and called up his half-slumbering senses. Herbert knelt down before him; and the eye of the old man fell on him, and he gazed with that long earnest look that the departing spirit seems to cast back from a still lengthening distance—its last glance through those eyes that have been its earthly portals of vision. The old man gazed on Herbert, but he did not speak. It might be he thought himself lost in some dream of a hope yet unfulfilled; however it might be, the old man gave no sign of recognition—save that fixed, earnest look on the face that now, after long years, was before him. Herbert in that sacred moment felt afraid by the name so familiar to appeal to the old man—who seemed so calmly departing; afraid to bring back before him the dim visions of Earth, when he was just landing in Heaven. So he thought of the words that old Willy most loved, and said in his clear, softened tone, "Let not your heart be troubled; ye believe in God, believe also in me. In my Father's house are many mansions: if it were not so, I would have told you. I go to prepare a place for you. And if I go and prepare a place for you, I will come again and receive you unto myself; that where I am, there ye may be also." The old man's dying ear caught the joyful sound; he listened with clasped hands and eyes upraised, while Herbert thus performed for him the last sacred ministry his spirit needed on Earth. There was silence again, and the old man seemed to muse on the words he had heard. Then, as if waking afresh, he looked up to Jem, who still stood beside him, and called, in his feeble **tone** and words **of** endearment, "Jem, my poor boy!" Jem stooped to his pillow again, **and the old** man said, "I have seen him! he is grown up to a heavenly man! and he spoke those same words from my Book that he had read me often and often before. I knew him, for the voice was his own!" There Herbert still knelt—by the side of the bed, but the old man had ceased to discern him, his dim eyes now failed him. Then Herbert rose up, and taking his seat on the bed he leaned over old Willy, and laid his hand softly on the old man's, and said, "Willy, dear old Willy, your young master's here! I am he! don't you know me?"

Then the old man wept, and raising his hand, **as had been his** custom when feeling overpowered **him, he** said, **"It is** granted then! my young master's come!" **And** looking through his tears to where Herbert sat before **him, he** said with calmer utterance, "I have waited **for you!** I knew you would come! and now I have seen you, **I am** ready to go. I heard those sweet words you spoke from my Book, and they have lifted me up to those mansions **above.** I am now at the door, I shall soon be gone in, and you will come to me there! You have sheltered me here, I have not known a want! but the good **Lord** above **has** sent for me home. His angels are come, but He would let me stay till I had my last wish—to **see you** once more. Will you care for my Jem? and please let him have my Book to show him the way; and the coat that you brought me—it will serve

15

him for years. And when I am gone, let them lay me to rest
at the feet of my lady; I have stood at the foot of her tomb in
winter and summer, I went there most days to look where she
lay, and 'tis there I would lie—where I always have stood to keep
watch over her. I know that the angels keep sight of her grave,
and they 'll watch over me—whom she taught the way to Heaven
where they dwell. She is sure to see me when I enter in—with
robes all washed white in the blood of the Lamb! She will
know then how fast in my heart I have kept the Name of my
Saviour; long nights as I lie here, I still say to myself, 'Jesus,
my Saviour, Lord Jesus, my God!' and it keeps me so close by
the Heavenly gate that I have only been waiting for you! I
leave you my blessing, dear young master, God grant you may
know what the blessing of the poor man can be; 't is the God up
above who makes the poor's blessing rich, and with my dying
prayer I commend you to him."

Herbert had already bowed his head on the old man's hand,
which his own hand still held; and, at his parting blessing, the
old man raised again his other hand in act of prayer, then spent
with **the** effort, it fell by his side, and he seemed **to** repose.
Herbert at length rose, and spoke softly with Jem, and would
have sent further assistance to watch through the night, but Jem
said his mother had had already some hours of rest, and would
be there by midnight, and he would rather be alone till then.
So Herbert returned to the Hall; but a servant soon arrived at
the cottage bringing warm cordials; Jem again roused the old
man, to take some, and he well understood who had sent the
warm cordials for him! then turning again to rest on his pillow,
he slept. Jem watched **by** him there, while his breathing became stiller, till it **ceased; and** Jem—watching beside him—
knew not when he died.

Herbert called at the cottage again the next day, and looked

on the smile that still lingered on the lips of the departed. Jem
was away at the farm, but **Widow** Jones and Mercy were there.
Widow Jones **took** from a **drawer a** small bag of money, saying
to Herbert, " I made my **promise to the** old man, sir, that I **would**
give that for his burying ; he said he considered it was right **that**
he should make a provision for that."

" Keep it then for yourself," replied **Herbert ; "I** shall lay him
to his rest."

" Thank you, **sir,** I am sure," replied Widow Jones, **"but if you
won't be** offended, sir, I could not be satisfied to take **it, because**
he had laid **it all by, and I promised him to** give it for that."

" Then let **me have it,"** said Herbert, " and I will send it for
Bibles **to be** given in Heathen lands—that was what lay nearest
his heart, and so in that way his own money shall embalm him !"

The winter's rain was over and gone, the flowers had appeared
on the Earth, the time of the singing of birds was come, and **the**
voice of the turtle was heard in the land—then **it was they bore**
the **old** man's **body to its** rest. Herbert walked on **one side of
the coffin, and Jem** on **the** other, **and the** village mourners followed. **They had dug** the old man's **grave, at the** young Squire's
direction, across the foot of the lady's **tomb, and** there, with the
words of blessing and the tears **of affection,** they laid him to his
rest. Herbert lingered the last—Jem waiting near, at his desire ;
Herbert spoke not **of** the past, **but it** rose in fresh remembrance
before him ; **till at last,** turning slowly away from the hallowed
spot, he **descended the hill in** heavenly converse with Jem. **The
cottage was shut** up, the young Squire kept the key, and the
dwelling mourned for three months, in desolation, the life it **had**
sheltered **from birth, and** now lost **from its** shelter for ever.

CHAPTER XXIII.

" Ready to give thanks and live
On the least that Heaven may give."

"Godliness with contentment is great gain."—1 Tim. vi. 6.

WE must return for our last visit to the town, and **take a** final leave of the childhood of little Jane. She had **grown** what her father called "a great girl;" she went daily, alone, to a good school in the town; and was often useful to her mother in **the** errands she could do for **her.** She still looked **upon** Widow **Jones** and her granddaughter Mercy, the **old** people **in the** almshouse, and the lone old woman on the heath, **as** her particular friends; and now a whole family were to be added to **the** number. Jane heard of a poor old man in the town, **a** cobbler by trade, but scarcely able to earn bread for his family. He had been a shepherd on the very heath where Jane's **old woman** lived; but he was obliged to give up keeping sheep, and now he earned his food by mending shoes. Jane heard that he was as happy as he was poor: and she thought how delightful it would be to help him. So she told her mother all she had heard; and asked if she might not go herself, and take her own boots **to** be mended by him.

Mrs. Mansfield replied, " Yes, you may **take** them if **you** like, and tell the poor man to mend them up **for** giving away; he **will** be able then to do them in a stronger way and for less money, **or I should not think them worth doing at all.** But are you sure you know **exactly** the place where he lives?"

"O yes, mamma, I know it exactly! I have been and looked down at it; only I would not go without your leave." So Jane set forth with her boots in a little basket, and in her pocket a purse that had for some days held a piece of silver. Eager, rich, and happy went the ministering child, gliding through the busy streets of the town! Her's was the joyous sense of power—how easily taught, how easily learned, and yet how often unthought of, unknown! She had love in her heart, work in her hand, and money in her purse—what could she not do! One thing was certain—she could help and comfort; and strong, and bright, and fearless in this undoubting faith she hastened on. She reached at last the narrow door at the top of the steep flight of steps that led to the little court where the cobbler dwelt. Jane stopped a moment, looked down into the strange place, then carefully descended the steep steps, made of red uneven bricks, and edged with rotting wood, till she arrived in safety at the bottom. The cobbler's dwelling was No. 2, and at the second cottage before her Jane noticed the clean-washed bricks before the door—it looked like the entrance to a good man's dwelling. Jane gathered fresh pleasure at the sight, but now the shyness of a stranger came over her, and she knocked with some trembling at the door. A tall woman in a brown calico gown opened it, with a snow-white handkerchief under her partly-opened gown, a cap of thick muslin as white, and her sick-looking face, almost as white also.

"Does Mr. May live here?" asked Jane.

"Yes, miss," said the woman, with a curt'sy; "will you please to walk in?" And Jane entered as neat a little dwelling as ever met a visitor's eye. A very small fire a few inches wide and deep, burned in the grate; over the fire was a high black mantle-piece; on one side of the fireplace was a black closet-door, and on the other another black door leading up stairs; the walls were whitewashed, and one little book-shelf suspended upon

them, with a small store of books in neatest order. There was a
long hutch opposite the fire, and on it a store of large new-baked
loaves; the floor was neatly sanded, and before the large lattice-
window stood the cobbler's low stall—not even a straggling
leather or tool had escaped from it, to litter the brick floor; and
before it sat the small old man on a low round stool of homely
manufacture, with his apron tied round him, busy at work. Two
daughters rose up at Jane's entrance, and the old cobbler took
his spectacles from his nose and looked round. Jane turned at
once to him, and said, "I have brought a pair of boots, which
mamma thought you might like to mend, and I was to tell you
that they were to be done for giving away."

"Thank you, miss, I am sure," said the cobbler; "it's well to
know that, because you see then a patch outside, here and there,
does not signify, and that's a deal less trouble to do, and lasts all
the longer—because it don't wear out the old leather, like so many
stitches as you must set into it for that fine particular mending
that must be done for gentlefolks." The old cobbler had risen up,
and did not begin his response to the message till Jane was seated, so that Jane listened with a settled feeling to his long reply,
which gave her complete satisfaction, as she had not quite liked
to say they were to be mended for giving away! But she thought
now how wise her mother was—who must have known all that
when she gave her the message! Though only a child had entered, the mother and daughters still stood, and Jane, uncomfort-
able at that, said, "I may stay a little while, if you are not busy,
and can sit down?" upon which they were all seated. The old
cobbler had fastened his spectacles again on his nose, and was
busy at his work; but he seemed to feel the responsibility of en-
tertaining their guest rested with him, so he lost no time in going
on to say, "It's a comfort, that many can little think, to see
work come in at the door; for to sit here and earn the food one

eats makes it seem to be doubly sweet.· and I believe too that it does do you more good, for I believe that s the order God has written upon this world—that the bread of idleress shall do none the same good ! And I am sure," said the cobbler, looking round, as he did for a moment at frequent intervals of his discourse, " I am sure, miss, we are thankful to you for the bringing it."

" I liked to come," answered Jane, " I heard that your wife was ill."

" Well, miss," replied the cobbler, looking round kindly at his wife for a moment, " she is never well. I do what I can, but one pair of hands can hardly keep four in food and clothing and house-rent, by shoe-mending. **And** she has been sickly now **a** long time. But, as I say, we do what we can, and there's the comfort of knowing that the trial is the will of the Lord. My poor girls there," the cobbler went on to say, " would be thankful to do what they could, but the Lord has not blessed them with the sense he has given to some; but still I say, if He be graciously pleased to keep them from evil, **and teach them the** knowledge of Himself, why that's mercy enough to **keep from** fretting about the other. My poor boy is much the same, but he has got a place, and I hope he may keep it, for it brings in a little." Jane looked at the daughters, clean and neat as their mother, and almost as pale ; they sat upright on chairs by the wall, and the unexpressive stare of their large round eyes gave evidence of some want of sense within. The father's face was very like his children's, except that in his eyes and on his lips was a smile as bright as a sunbeam ; and the whole expression of his face when speaking, was of one in earthly want already irradiated with heavenly faith.

" Can your daughters do needle-work ?" asked Jane.

" Yes, miss, they can sew very neatly, when they can get it tc do ; and the eldest has been in a place, but she had not the strength to keep it. I hope, however, she may get the better of it again, and look for another situation before long, for it's trying to sit at home when there is not work or food; but, thank God, we have managed as yet, and we would do any thing we could to keep the house and home together."

"You have bread now!" said Jane, in a tone half expressive of her pleasure at the sight of the large loaves on the hutch, and half inquiringly as to the reality of the fact.

"O yes, miss, and I don't know that we have ever been a day altogether without. That bread that you see will all wait for a fortnight. We always bake one fortnight under another; that's a rule we never break when we can possibly buy the flour, for no one would believe the difference it makes—how far a little bread will go to satisfy your hunger, when once it begins to turn moldy. My wife can show you our bread now; we are now beginning the last fortnight's, and that must hold out, or we should never be able to manage at all." All this was said in the earnest cheerful tone of one who had discovered a fortunate secret of sufficiency, while the wife and daughters removed the hot loaves, lifted up the hutch, and showed the hard-looking bread now coming into use. Jane was distressed, it was a study in poverty new to her, and the thought of this constant denial of pleasant food fell more heavily on her heart than would the knowledge of the occasional want of bread—a want, the experience of which she never knew, and therefore the suffering of which she would not fully have realized. The cobbler through his spectacles read the look of distress on the face of Jane, and in a moment turning his quick bright glance from his low stool again upon her, he said, in a tone of cheerful comfort, "There's no riches promised us here, if we be the Lord's; only the riches of faith and the riches of His blessing—and thanks be to Him, we have that; so we can say, He is faithful that promised! And 't is my belief there 's nothing makes the true riches increase so fast as trial does : so we must beware how we fret at the one, lest we lose our best gain of the other along with it !" Jane looked at the beaming face of the cobbler, with its kind and lingering expression of inquiry on her, as if to see whether he had removed the cloud he had cast over her, and she thought she had never seen any one look so happy as that poor man; and her heart grew warm again in the sunshine of his faith—for the sudden shock of what she heard about the bread had chilled her with distress.

"Are you never unhappy because you have not better food?" asked Jane.

"Well, miss, trouble is always ready enough to spring up ; it's got its root in my heart, and so it will have as long as there's any sin there for it to grow in, but, blessed be God, I know what to do with it. I never let it hold up its head long. I take it right away to our Saviour in prayer, and I leave it with Him, for I believe he knows better than I do how to manage with it; and so sure as I persevere in doing that, it comes right in the end, or I come right out of it."

Jane listened, and she loved to listen, for that old man's faith was truly making sunshine in the cloud of his deep poverty. But now she began to think that perhaps she ought not to stay any longer; so, rising up to go, she slipped her piece of silver, which she had managed to get unseen from her purse, into the cobbler's hand, saying softly, "Will you take that little present from me?" and then, in a minute more, she was climbing the steep stairs that led out of the court.

Jane waited in hope of some more shoes needing repair, and it was not long before her mother, who never forgot a case of want when once made acquainted with it, called her, and packed into a basket some of her children's shoes, which she told Jane she might take to her cobbler. So Jane set out on the pleasant errand.   As she descended the high steps she heard some one singing; it was a bright spring day, and the cobbler's lattice window was open; Jane felt sure the voice came from there; as she passed the window it stopped.   Jane delivered the work she had brought into the hands of the cobbler, and then sat down on the chair he had set for her near his stall, quite disposed to linger in the tempting-looking cottage, now lighted up by the spring's sweet sunshine.

" Do you sing at your work ?" asked Jane.

" Well, miss, I do amuse myself a little that way sometimes," said the old man, going on as fast as possible with his work, " I find it keeps troublesome thoughts out, and cheers my spirits up. I was singing a verse, as you came, that 's seldom long from my thoughts;" and the cobbler took off his spectacles, and looked up with his face of unchanging sunshine and said—

" Though **vilely** clad, and meanly fed,
    And, like **my** Saviour, poor,
    I would not change my Gospel bread
    For all the worldling's store."

Now Jane was surprised at the cobbler's happiness, and could not quite understand why he should seem to be the happiest of all the good people she knew, so she said, " Every one who loves God is not so happy as you are ?"

" Well, miss," replied the cobbler, " perhaps it is not given to all alike—we see a deal of those differences in the Bible.   It pleases God, I believe, **to try his people** some one way, and some another.   I am very poor, but maybe there's another who is not —then he must have his trial some other way : let it be as it will, each must have a trial !" said the cobbler, looking up over the top of his spectacles earnestly at Jane, as if anxious to impress that truth on her mind.   " All must have a trial some way—because it is written, 'Ye must through much tribulation enter into the kingdom of Heaven!'"

"But," asked Jane, "is it not very difficult to be always happy?"

"Well, miss," answered the cobbler, without pausing in his busy labor, "I should soon be dull enough if I were left to myself; but I will tell you what I find the best help, I always try to keep a flame of praise lit up in my heart, and that burns up the dross of unbelief and discontent in a wonderful way! That's one reason why I so often take to singing a hymn—when I find that flame of praise is getting low, and I can only work on, and so little coming in often for my work when it is done, then I get singing some hymn of praise to that Saviour, who worked out my salvation at such a cost as His own blessed life, and gives it to me without money and without price; and then when praise to Him kindles up in my heart, it burns up the discontent in no time. And then, dear me, what mercies come in! It was only last night I lay awake thinking entirely of our Mary; you see, miss, she is the youngest, and I have had many an anxiety about her, not but what she is a good girl to us, but she is very silent, and I was afraid whether the love of her Saviour was in her heart. Well, as I lay awake last night, I kept praying that the Lord would give her grace to choose the better part, like Mary we read of in the Scriptures, but I did not say any thing to her, well, this morning she said to me, 'Father, there was a text in my mind last night that I could not seem to forget, "Mary had chosen the better part, that shall never be taken from her"—I hope I shall do that! father.' Now what a mercy that was: who could but know that must be the Lord's doing!"

It was no wonder that Jane loved to visit the cobbler's bright cottage. There she saw faith, not so much contending with difficulties as triumphing over them, and its victory could not but

appear beautiful, even to the eyes of a child. One day, as Jane
was looking at a hymn-book, she suddenly caught sight of the
very same verse that the old cobbler had repeated to her as the
one he had been singing.   Jane showed it to her mother, with
the greatest feeling of interest; and her mother, always quick to
meet and strengthen every pure and hallowed feeling, found an
embossed card she had somewhere laid by, and in her plainest
writing copied the favorite verse, in the center of the card; then
finding four little brass nails, and showing Jane how to cut up a
piece of scarlet cloth in small rounds to fix the nails into, she
gave all into Jane's possession, who went the next day, after her
morning school, by the mother's leave, to carry the treasure. She
stood up in a chair, and nailed it herself with the cobbler's little
hammer over the mantle-piece, while all the family stood ad-
miring; and there the cobbler, whenever he looked up, was reminded of his hymn of praise.   Jane gave so warm an account of
the feeling called forth by the card upon the wall, that her
mother said, "If you save up your pence for a month, I will show
you what more you can do to adorn the cottage."   Jane could
not imagine what fourpence could do to adorn her old cobbler's walls; she tried to find out, but she could not guess,
and her mother still kept back the secret. At last the fourth
Saturday came, and Jane was possessor of fourpence. "Now,
mamma, what can it be? do tell me!" "You shall go out
with me, and then you will see," said her mother. So Jane
went out with her mother, and when Mrs. Mansfield had accomplished her business, she took Jane to a stationer's shop,
and asked for some pasteboard; she chose three penny sheets,
dark purple on the wrong side, and white on the right; then
Mrs. Mansfield asked for some tissue-paper, and chose a penny
sheet of lilac color. "Now, Jane," said Mrs. Mansfield, "you
have spent your fourpence, and this afternoon you shall see

what you can do!" On their return, Mrs. Mansfield looked
out with Jane some of the most interesting **pictures on** the
Church Missionary papers; then making some paste, she bade
Jane put on her pinafore, and laying the nursery ironing-board on
the nursery table, Mrs. Mansfield showed Jane how to divide the
large sheets of pasteboard in half, then to cut the tissue paper in
broad strips, and paste it round the margin of the pasteboard,
laying the Missionary picture in the middle; then pressing them
under something heavy, and large enough to cover them, they
looked, when dry, like pictures mounted on colored cardboard,
and the broad lilac margin made the effect very pretty—but it
required care to lay the thin tissue-paper smoothly on, when wet
with the paste. Jane was delighted with her work, and the
next week, when the pictures were quite dry, her mother provided the scarlet cloth to be cut into very small rounds for each
nail, and four nails for each picture, there being six pictures, and
Jane carried a hammer at the bottom of her little basket, for
fear the old cobbler's small wooden hammer should not prove
sufficient; and attended by the cobbler's wife and daughters,
while the old cobbler looked up from his work continually, Jane
put up the pictures to the pleasure and admiration of all. Then
the old cobbler stood up and looked round with delight, not
alone on the brightened aspect of his walls, but on scenes that
told of the triumphs of his own pure and Heavenly faith over
the dark and cruel superstition of idolatry. From that time it
was a favorite amusement with Jane, to save up her weekly
pence and make pictures to adorn the walls of all her poor friends.

And now we must say farewell to Jane in **her** childhood.
We leave her gathering around her the hearts of the poor.
And He who guides the sparrow's fall, guided her steps, so that
never breath of evil, or sight of sin, fell on her childhood's ear
or eye, among the poor.

CHAPTER XXIV.

"It grew up together with him, and with his children; and was unto him as a daughter."—2 Samuel xii. 3.

WHEN three months had passed away, the young Squire went alone to old Willy's cottage; he stayed some time in the house, then walked in the garden, and seemed engaged in a general consideration of the place. The next day workmen arrived, and the young Squire went down to meet them. Then began pulling down and building up; the front of the cottage remained as it was, the room in which old Willy sat by day and slept by night was untouched, but other rooms were added behind, till the dwelling rose with its three chambers above, its back kitchen and little dairy, and out-houses, complete. Some said the young Squire was going to turn the place into a farm; but no, it was a simple cottage still, too large for one person, but with every comfort for a family. The young Squire often walked down to the spot, looking with interest on all, and giving his directions to the workmen.

Meanwhile the summer months were gliding by. Snowflake and Jet again drew the pony-carriage, and Herbert again drove his mother out; and still sometimes Mrs. Clifford would call at a cottage, but more generally she only stopped in passing, to make kind inquiry; it was evident that any general intercourse with others, was, as yet, an effort to her. But one day she stopped at widow Jones's door, and finding her at home, went in. Mrs. Clifford had never forgotten Mercy—the child in whom

Miss Clifford had always seemed, perhaps, to take more interest than in any other; and Mrs. Clifford, knowing her to be of an age for service, and remembering her delicate look, was afraid lest any place of common work should prove beyond her strength, so she called on the widow Jones to ask whether she had any wish about her granddaughter that she could be aided in. Widow Jones replied that she had long been on the look-out for a situation for Mercy; the field-work was too much for her, she had not the strength for it—and that was her fear about service, but she believed she must make inquiry for a place in the town before another winter came on. Hearing this, Mrs. Clifford offered to take Mercy, and have her trained under her own maid, adding, "I should have her a good deal with me, she would have to read to me, and to carry out many little plans I may not feel able to undertake now myself, in the village. I believe her to be capable of this, and if it meets your wish, I shall be quite willing to try her." This proposal was received with over-flowing gratitude by widow Jones; and when Mercy heard of it, with delight by her. To live still in her own village near her grandmother, to live in her young lady's own home, and wait on madam—all this was more than hope could have believed, or imagination pictured! So Mercy went to service at the Hall, to wait on Mrs. Clifford, and be trained under her **maid.**

When September hung its ripe fruit upon the trees in old Willy's garden, the cottage stood complete; the bricklayers, and carpenters, and thatchers, and glaziers, and painters were gone. The door was again locked, and the place stood silent and peaceful. Then early one autumn evening, just as Jem returned home from his work at the farm, the young Squire called at his cottage, saying, "I came to ask you and your mother to come and see the dear old man's dwelling. I have had it enlarged; and you always took so much interest in it, that I wish to show it to you myself."

Widow Jones put on her bonnet, and walked up the lane with her son Jem and the young Squire. The sun was setting, and his parting beams fell upon the cottage-roof, and gilded the garden trees. The young Squire crossed the garden-stile— the very same that used to be—then turning round, he said with a grave smile to Jem, " Do you remember the dark morning when you and I first crossed that stile together ?" " It was a good morning, sir, for him that dwelt within !" said Jem ; and on they passed.

The young Squire unlocked the door, and they went in. There was the same look about the open fire-place ; the very chair old Willy always sat in, with its crimson cushion, was there ; there stood the little table, and the very stool on which the young squire used to sit. The bed was gone, and in its place stood a bureau, and a larger table, and chairs round the room—while flowers in pots bloomed in the window. " What do you think of it ?" asked the young Squire, as Jem and his mother looked round with wondering eyes, " 'Tis made wholly beautiful, I am sure !" said Jem.   " There is not the cottage like to it in the place !" said widow Jones.

" Then, Jem, what do you say to being my tenant, and bringing your old mother to live here in comfort ?"

" Well, sir, I am afraid I should fail more in the doing than the saying, so far as that is concerned—my best wages could never clear the rent of such a place as this !"

" And I suppose," said the young Squire, " you would be as hard as my dear old Willy himself, to be persuaded that a house could be honestly tenanted without the payment of money ! But you need not fear robbing me when I say you shall pay me no rent, for I hold this dwelling a sacred place, for many reasons, and so long as I can find a faithful heart to inhabit it, I mean never to let it for money ! I make it your home now, and your mother's, till such time as you may receive notice to quit it—which will not be with my desire, so long as life is granted you, if you are enabled to maintain the same character as that which wins my regard for you now. You will find the upper rooms furnished as well as this. The furniture is all your own : I purchased it for you ; the house and land you hold as my tenant—in proof of which you may always send up to the Hall the first dish of rosy apples you gather from the trees I planted ! There is a small field, that was part of the little place when bought ; I let it to the farmer who had hired it before—old Willy having no use for it—but I have now attached it to the cottage, and had a gate made into it from the garden : you can let it or use it, as you like, only seeing that it is kept in grass, and not dug up without my consent. And may old Willy's God grant you to live as blessed and peaceful an old age as he enjoyed beneath this roof!" Widow Jones and her son were filled with surprise and gratitude. The Squire let them speak their broken words of thankfulness, that they might not afterward feel distressed at having said nothing. And then talking a few minutes more with them, and telling widow Jones that he should request his mother to let her granddaughter be sent to them the next day to help them move in, he left them with the key in their possession.

The move was soon effected—where every thing was prepared beforehand for use and comfort. Widow Jones sold off most of her old furniture, saying there was scarce a piece of it that was fit so much as to see inside of such a place as the Squire had prepared for her Jem ! and there, with Mercy's help, they slept in peace the following night ; widow Jones only expressed her fear, as to how she could ever bring her

mind to the care of such things as stood on every side there
—look which way you would! When the young Squire went
to college in October, he left Jem quietly settled in his new
abode. The whole village rejoiced in the good fortune of Jem
—honest Jem; for Jem was, as may be supposed, a general
favorite. Was he not always ready to lend a helping hand,
to tender some kindly office in sickness or trouble, and at all
times to speak a pleasant word? None but the bad could
have failed to look kindly on honest Jem. But among the
general pleasure felt, none was more warmly expressed than
Mrs. Smith's; her regard for both mother and son seemed to
make her pleasure in the event double : and never could honest
laborer, and faithful servant, and dutiful son, have entered a
new abode with more pleasant feelings to himself and others
—than honest Jem, when he called the home of old Willy his
own!

William's return had been anxiously looked for this year at
the farm; but when the time drew near, he wrote word to his
father, that though very sorry to be absent longer, he did feel
a wish to stay one year more. His uncle, he said, would be
glad to detain him, and offered to raise his salary again—but
he did not feel bound on that account; still there were reasons
that would make him glad of another year, and though he felt
the disappointed hope more, he was sure, than any one else
could, yet, if his father was willing, he certainly should wish to
stay till the following July, when he hoped to be down in time
to put the first sickle to the corn. Samson was getting on well
in his uncle's business and favor; Joe was as happy as possible, and plainly giving satisfaction in the merchant's office—
and by next year Joe hoped to have found a ship for Ted.
So the hope of the parents was still deferred; and a short visit
from their three sons, all they could that year enjoy. William

said nothing as to his reason for wishing to remain longer in London; but every thing seemed going on well with the three brothers; and it was not difficult for farmer Smith to believe that to have William to watch over the other two was a great security for them.

In the following winter the old Clergyman died. Much anxiety was felt in the village as to whether the Curate would remain; the anxiety of Mrs. Smith equaled that felt by farmer Smith and Rose, and great was the universal joy when it was known that Mrs. Clifford had presented the living to the Curate, and that now the villagers might hope he would live and die among them. The late Clergyman's widow remained some months in the rectory, and every thing went on as before; till one day farmer Smith returned from market with an unusually clouded brow.

" I never saw you look more like bad news," said Mrs. Smith, " what has happened ?"

Farmer Smith was silent.

" Come now," said Mrs. Smith, " bad will be none the better for waiting ! I may as well know to-day as to-morrow."

" Well, it 's only the horse," said farmer Smith, " I saw a paper in the town, and there 's to be a sale at the rectory, and Black Beauty is in the list."

" Well," replied Mrs. Smith, " he is none of yours now ! and you can't take up with vexing over the sale of other people's creatures. Not but what I am sorry enough myself, but I have seen the good of his going since, and you must think of that. If Will laid the first stone of Joe's good fortune, it was the horse helped you set him on it, you could not have done it without him. I am sure I made sin enough of it before, so I have reason to bear with it now. I am only thankful the child does not know of his going—he used to count so of seeing the crea ure pass by! but he is better off; and we, why we must take the rough with the smooth as it comes, and be thankful there's One who can make them both 'work together for good,' as the Minister tells us."

Farmer Smith felt relieved, for he had dreaded the telling his wife, or her knowing that the favorite horse was to be put up to the highest bidder. The young Squire was absent at college; and many a time farmer Smith thought, had he but been at the Hall, there was little doubt that he would have bought the favorite, and then the creature would but have exchanged one good stable for another, still in sight of his first possessors. But the young Squire was away, so there was no prospect but that of soon looking his last on Black Beauty.

No further mention was made of the subject, till a day or two after, Ted rushed in exclaiming, "Mother, where's father? there's to be a sale at the rectory, and Black Beauty's down in the list! the bill is up on the blacksmith's shop—I saw it myself!"

"Well, child, the rector's lady has as much right to sell the horse as your father had—it was his then, and it's hers now."

"What, don't you mind about it then, mother?"

"Mind! child, what's the use of minding? I have vexed too much already for the poor beast! Don't you say a word to your father about it; I shall mind that if you do; let him forget it if he can."

"But, mother, father can't forget! How can he forget, when he must hear and know all about it?"

"Well, don't you say a word to make him think the more; you try and make the best of it, not the worst—that's what you have to do."

"I know what I shall do," replied Ted, "I shall just write off and tell William!"

"No, that I do forbid;" said Mrs. Smith, "for why in the world should you want to worry him with it? do you think he has not felt enough about it already?"

"Yes, mother, but then I know William has some money, I am quite sure of that, and a great deal too, for when I asked him if he **had** not last time he was down, he said, 'What you would call a great deal perhaps!' so I know he has, and then he could just send and buy Black Beauty away from them all!"

"That does not signify," replied Mrs. Smith. "If William has money he has earned it hardly enough, and I would not for the world have it taken from him to buy back a horse."

"Well, mother, William does not care for money, I am sure, **for** he said when I asked him if he had not got a great deal, that he would have given all up over and over again to be only yard-boy on father's farm—if there had been none but himself he had to think of! so I am sure he can't care **for** money; **and** every body knows how he cared for that horse!"

"Never mind, child, it's plain enough he did not wish to be after buying him back, or he could have said as easy as not, 'If there's a sale, you might let me **know!'** but he never said a word about it in any letter, and if **we** write him word, why it will put him up to do it just to please us, and I would not have that on any account. I will not have a word written to any one of them till the sale is over; you remember I have said it!"

"Well, mother, if **I** must not speak to father nor William, I declare I will go off to the sale and see after **the horse** myself! **and I** will speak a word to whoever buys him—let it be who it **will,** and if it's no more than to tell them what our Minister told us in our class—it may stick by them, and fright them a little, if they don't use him as they should! I would not have him bought, and led off, and no one to speak a word for him for any thing !"

"Very well," replied Mrs. Smith, "so long as you keep to what our Minister says, you are safe enough." And Ted, satisfied at having at last fixed upon something he might do, grew more composed on the subject, and when alone with his father, he said, "Never you mind, father, about Black Beauty's being sold off again, I have just got a word to say to whoever buys him that may be of good use to the horse: I mean to be up at the sale, and see all about it, and then I can tell you, father!" And the thought of this seasonable address that was to be made to the buyer of Black Beauty, with the care necessary in composing and recomposing it to make it as brief and forcible as possible, changed the prospect of the approaching sale into an event of effort and interest, rather than of distress to Ted.

The morning of the sale arrived. "Mother," said Ted, "I must be off now, and I want my best jacket; no one will care for me if I don't look something respectable." So Mrs. Smith brought Ted his best jacket, which was of dark blue, having been his particular request as most suitable for one who was soon to be a sailor; arrayed in this, with his round straw hat on the side of his head, and his little cane in his hand, he set off to the sale. "Never you mind, father!" said Ted, as he stopped to speak to his parent on the green slope from the house, "I am off to the sale, just to do what can be done, and then I will come home and tell you. And there's sure to be good come of it, father, though we may never know it, for the Minister says, when the right thing is done, if people don't think of it at first, they will sooner or later; and I know just what he said about those who have to do with dumb creatures ! so never you mind, father, I am now off for the sale. Tell mother not to think about dinner for me, there's no saying when I shall be back." "Take care what you are after ?" said the father.   But off ran the ministering boy to watch over Black Beauty, and speak the word of warning he had heard from the Minister's lips, to whoever might purchase the horse.

It was a heavy day to farmer Smith—this second sale of the favorite horse, close by his own door, and he not able to purchase it back, nor **now** to have any control over the hands into which it passed, troubled him not a little.   The creature had been born and reared on his farm, had played with his children, fed from their hands, he had himself broken it in for use, and it would leave its food or its pasture at any time at the first sound **of** his voice—the after-tie may be strong between master and steed, **but it is** on the farm where the creature is born, and reared, and trained, that the feeling becomes all but a family bond !

Mrs. Smith took the event more quietly ; her heart had been broken up by the bitter anguish of remorse—remorse for years of pride of heart and self-will; and though the balm of Heavenly love may bind up such broken hearts, **yet must the** surface-changes of life have but comparatively little power to distress —where sorrow so far deeper still lies within.   Yet Mrs. Smith did feel it; and the point in which it touched her most, was her sense of what the sorrow of little Tim would have been to have had his favorite **sold away a** second time, where he could never see **him pass.** But Mrs. Smith spoke not of this ; she had learned to endure in silence, conscious of the past—when **her** personal annoyances were always made a subject of distress for others ; so she now made an effort to hide **her own** feeling, and comfort those around **her.   Rose saw** her father's grave expression of face, and stepping **out** beside him, after dinner, said, "Never mind, father, **I think it**'s better the horse **should be taken quite away before Will** comes home, or he

would always be seeing him, and then you know, father, perhaps
he could not help wishing for him, and that would be wrong
now he is sold away; and it would be vexing to William, and to
Joe—if he knew that William could not help wishing him back:
so I think it's best, father!"

"So it is, Rose, I dare say, if I could but be sure of his being
well off."

"But, father, God made the creatures; and when we **can't**
take care of them any longer we must leave them to Him. I
am sure, father, you did the best you could, and then if we don't
feel satisfied, that looks as if we could not trust God Almighty;
and you know it says in the Bible, the sparrow does not fall to
the ground without our Heavenly Father!"

"So **it** does, Rose; I will think of that. Oh, if my mother
could **but** hear how you comfort **me**! But I have a hope now
that I shall show you to her some day in Heaven, and tell her
how her prayers were all answered, though she never knew it."
So farmer Smith passed on with livelier step to his men, and
Rose went back to iron at her mother's side.

Ted had not returned to dinner; and now his mother, each
time she paused in her work and set the iron down upon the
stand, gave a glance from the window.

"I can't think what the child is stopping after, all this time!"
at length said Mrs. Smith.

"I dare say Black Beauty came near the end of the sale," replied Rose, "and he said he should not stir from the place till he
saw what became of him."

Mrs. Smith said no more; only looking from time to time
along the distant road. Four o'clock—five o'clock passed, and
Rose prepared the tea; the ironing was finished and all cleared
away, and the table was set, the toast made, Mr. Smith came in,
but no Ted appeared.

"I can not think what the boy is after!" said Mrs. Smith. "I wish you would just step and see; and tell him he must come home. I would not have him stay after dark among a set of horse-dealers for any thing!"

Mr. Smith took his hat and went; and Mrs. Smith watched at the window—watched till she saw him returning alone. "Where's the child?" asked Mrs. Smith, "I wish enough you had brought him!"

"I don't think he will take any harm," replied farmer Smith. "I saw Beetlebright, the horse-dealer, there, and I asked him to have an eye on the boy—who was in the very thick of it among them all, looking on as earnestly as possible; I could not catch a sight from his eye; and Beetlebright told me the horse was coming on directly, so I came off, for I could not stand to see him led up. But I was not sorry I went, for I heard some good news."

"Did you?" asked Mrs. Smith; and her tone betrayed how far she was from indifference on the subject.

"Yes, Beetlebright told me he knew who had given orders to have the horse purchased, and I might be sure he would have a good master, if ever he had!"

"Well, that's a comfort," said Mrs. Smith, "I am sure I am thankful enough! Did he say who?"

"No, he turned off at that; and I thought no doubt he would not be free of speaking beforehand, and I heard them call for the horse, so I came off."

Upon this, Mrs. Smith, and Rose and her father sat down to tea, but with more feeling of mind than hunger of body.

"Just you look here, Miss Rose!" said Patience, stepping quickly up to the door of the family kitchen, which always stood open.

All ran to the window, being ready for any alarm. There

16

came the boy, in blue jacket and straw hat, mounted on Black Beauty—as large as life, and as steady as Time, stepping down the old familiar hill—the home road to the farm, which he had never trod since the day that Joe led him away. All hurried out from the door; Rose flew down the sloping green to the valley at the foot of the hill, where Black Beauty stopped of his own accord, and arched his neck, and put his nose into her hand.

"Now, Rose, that will do; do n't you see I want to be off to father?" said Ted. And off Black Beauty started on the accustomed canter along the path up the greensward that led to the wicket-gate of the garden.

"Do go and see," said Mrs. Smith, " what the boy is after!"

But farmer Smith stood still with Mrs. Smith beside the garden-gate, at which, in a minute more Black Beauty made a stand.

"What in the world have you been after, boy? What are you doing with the horse?" asked Mrs. Smith; while Rose came breathless from her run, and stood beside. But now Black Beauty's turn was come to give expression to his feeling: he stood again upon home ground, close to his master, who had never spoken to him since the parting day; he rested his head upon his master's shoulder, stepped from side to side, reached down his nose and courted the caress first of one and then the other—while all seemed to fail in its power to express the noble creature's joy. The men were turning home from the farm, laden with the implements and baskets, and they gathered wondering round. Jem and the yard-boy and Patience too, were there all looking—intent on the mystery; while Mrs. Smith hastily repeated her inquiry.

"What in the world are you after, boy? Make haste, I say and speak it out!"

"**Now, mother,**" said Ted, seated like a chieftain on his charger, " lon't look as if you thought it must be wrong because I have done it !"

" Done what ?" said Mrs. Smith, " what have you done ?

" Why brought the horse home, mother !"

" But how came you by him ? that 's what I want to know !"

" Well, mother, I did not steal him—though you look as if you were afraid I had ; nor beg him, nor borrow him, he was given me right away for father as I stood there !"

" Who by ?" asked farmer Smith, anxiously and earnestly.

" Why, I don't know, father, only it was the man who bought him, so I suppose he had a right to give him if he liked."

" I am afraid there 's some mistake in it," said farmer Smith, seriously—looking along the road to see if explanation, clearer than his boy's, might be coming there—but no cne was in sight.

" Well—now, father, you listen, and I will just tell you," said Ted, still seated on the creature—yet restless with its joy. " As soon as ever they led up the horse there was a man came and stood near where I was. He seemed, I thought, to be thinking of buying, and I wished he might; for I liked the look of him. Well, they kept bidding, and I got in such a way, for the man seemed ever so many times as if he would let him go, and he kept so quietly at it, that at last I did not know who had the horse; but I found he was gone down to some one, so I kept asking, 'Who has him? who has him?' and they pointed to this man. So I watched my opportunity when he was pretty well alone, and then I went up and just said what I had to say to him! Well, he listened, and when I had done, he said, 'You come along with me, and see what you think of my usage ?' so I went with him, and he never said a word more, but unpacked this saddle and **bridle—only you see,** father, what a saddle it is!" said Ted, tumbling himself off and lifting up the lappets, more thoroughly to display **the** saddle's excellence.

" Well, child, what then ?" asked his mother.

" **Why, when** he had done putting them on, and seeing they were all **right,** he said, 'Now, little master, have you a mind to **ride ?' and** before I knew what to say, he had lifted me up. O **how the** good creature did paw the ground when I was once **upon** him! he knew me as well as any thing! and thought he was coming off here, I know he did !"

" Well, child, but go on !" said Mrs. **Smith.**

" Dear me, mother, **I** don't know any more! only when the **man** had lifted **me on, he** said, ' You **go** and preach your sermon to your father, for **he is the** owner **of this** horse now ; and you tell him **that if he does not know how** to take care of him, he has a son that can **teach him!** And I will **be down after** you presently, when **I** have settled some **other** business.' "

" Was it Beetlebright, the horse-dealer ?" asked farmer Smith.

" I don't know, father, but I think I have seen him before in the town."   .

" But **did** not he say a word of who sent him ?"

" **Why,** he sent him, father ! he bought him, **and** sent him !"

" **Nonsense,** child ; a horse-dealer would never make me such a present !"

" Here 's some **one now** coming down the road, sir," said one of **the men.** They all watched ; and farmer Smith soon descried the substantial figure of Beetlebright the horse-dealer, who made his way to the assembled group.

" **I** am afraid," said farmer Smith, stepping forward, " we are under some **little** mistake in stopping the horse at our gate !"

" **Not a** bit **of** it," replied the horse-dealer, " if you can trust **that hand-writing,** and I think it 's as good and honest a hand as

I have seen for many a day." So saying, the hor.. dealer gave a sealed letter to farmer Smith, who opened it, and read :

" DEAR FATHER,

"It was my sorrow to cost you your favorite h rse; you did not spare him, neither did William, and now it is my joy to have earned him back again. I have been so a rid I should not get money enough before—for some reason or other—he might be sold off I I have never spent so much as a sixpence, no, nor a penny, I think, that I could do without; and now I have twenty pounds in hand, over and above what you had for him, so I am sure of it now ! I hope I am thankful, I am sure I think I am. Don't let a word be said to William, but when he comes home let the horse be taken to meet him—be sure you con't let him know till then ! My love to mother, and Rose. and Ted. Your affectionate and dutiful son,

" JOSEPH SMITH."

Farmer Smith put the letter into his wife's hand, and turned to the horse to hide his feeling.

" Well, I suppose it 's all right ?" said the horse-dealer. " Here 's my commission too, with the order for the new saddle and bridle ;" and he put an open letter into farmer Smith's hand. " As to what he says upon paying my charge on the commission, that 's all paid already in the pleasure of the job—I can say I never had a pleasanter ; and if such a lad does not turn out well, I don't know who will."

" Who 's done it, father ?" asked Rose.

" Why Joe himself !" said her father ; " he says he has never spent a sixpence he could help, for fear he might not have the money ready when an opportunity of buying the creature might come !"

" Well done, Joe !" said **Ted.** "**I** 'll be up to you, when **I** '**m
a** sailor, though !"

" Why, it 's master **Joe** ! it 's master Joe has done it himself'"
was repeated among the men ; and casting a pleased expressive
look **at the father** of such a son, they began to disperse **to their**
homes, to tell them how master Joe had never rested till he
brought back the black horse to his father's stable ! Mrs. Smith
gave the letter to her husband, and turned within doors, glad at
that moment to escape observation.

" Well, you will be thinking, I suppose, of leading him off **to**
his stable ?" said the horse-dealer. " I wish you joy of him, and
twenty times more of such a son ! And then I will just step in
with you, for I am altogether done up with my day's work."
Ted led the horse, **and** farmer Smith followed, and Jem to un-
saddle him, and **Rose followed also.** Ted made all haste to give
the **horse** a feed, **but the creature, while he** stooped to receive it,
looked round, as if **something were missing.** "**Come,** Black
Beauty, **eat !**" said Ted, impatient to give the first food **;** but the
horse, while he stooped his head in obedience, still **lifted** his
large eye, and looked to the **door.**

" Look, father, what 's the matter ?" **said Ted,** " Black Beauty
won't eat !"

" Never mind," said Rose, " do n't say a word, **he is** watching
for little Tim ! Here, put his food in the manger, he will eat
when we are gone ; **and come** in to tea, do, Ted ; you have had
nothing since breakfast !"

So Ted spread out **the food in the** manger, and followed his
father and the horse-dealer, with Rose, in to tea.

" What 's the matter, mother ?" **asked Ted, as his** mother
stooped to tuck him **up** in his **little bed** that night.

" Nothing, dear," **answered his** mother ; " **only I** was thinking
how good Joe had **been !**"

' Well, mother, I would wait till Joe was bad, before I cried about him!" said Ted.

" Ah, Ted," replied his mother, " perhaps you may know some day what it is to shed a tear for goodness you don't deserve; for the Lord's goodness, if not for man's!"

" But was that all you were thinking of, mother?" asked Ted, concerned at the sight of his mother's tears.

" Well, I was thinking of little Tim, and how delighted he would have been to see the horse come back."

" Well, mother, you need **not** cry about him; we read in our class to the Minister how they ride on white **horses** in Heaven! and he is better off there, mother."

" **So** he is, dear!" replied Mrs. Smith; and kissing her boy, she left him to sleep on his pillow, and turned away to think of her children on Earth, and her youngest in glory in Heaven.

Then came the warm bright harvest month, July; and before the sickle was put to the corn, William was to return. **And** Joe got leave of a few days' absence **also, having** obtained a berth for Ted on board a merchant-ship. **The two** brothers traveled outside the coach. Oh, **what a day was** that for William! all his best hopes **fulfilled, and** he returning, after so many years of **absence, to live at** home again and farm his father's land! **Chestnut was** put in the gig; and Ted was to ride Black Beauty for William, with the new saddle and bridle. What care had been taken to rub down the glossy coat of Black Beauty, to comb his mane, and show him to best effect! **All** day the farm had been in commotion; Patience scrubbing and cleaning the always clean house; Mrs. Smith baking her largest variety of best approved viands; Rose hanging the new little curtains she had made at the window of what was now to be William's **room**; men and boys getting all things in their best order—in preparation for Master William's return! while Ted devoted himself exclusively and entirely to the grooming of Black Beauty. Then came the starting-time, when farmer Smith drove off in the gig, and Ted—in blue jacket and straw hat—on Black Beauty, who ambled and capered along as if he knew it to be a festive occasion.

"Ah! you good old fellow," said Ted, "you little think who you will have to bring home again with you!"

Mrs. Smith watched from the door till the gig and the horse were out of sight, then turned within to hasten preparations with Rose. The coach was still miles away, when the gig and Black Beauty made their halt at the next village inn; but after long waiting, a cloud of dust came in sight—then the four gray horses, and men's hats on the top of the coach. Now Ted had made Black Beauty stand full in view across the road, while he concealed himself behind the gig.

"There's father!" said William, and standing up he seemed ready to spring from the top of the coach, before ever it stopped at the inn. And then, in a minute more, he added, " Why, Joe, I declare, if there is n't Black Beauty waiting for some one! how unfortunate, just when father's come there!"

" O, father's got over all that now," said Joe, "and does not mind the sight of him the least."

William looked at Joe as if he doubted not only the fact, but also that Joe could suppose forgetfulness possible; but he said nothing, and the coach stopped, and William was the first to set foot on the ground, and he wrung his father's hand with a grasp that said more than words; and then—quite unable to resist the temptation, turned to speak to Black Beauty. The faithful creature knew his young master, and had chafed and stamped after William's descent from the coach till he turned and laid his hand upon his neck.

" Why Ted, my boy, what are you doing here ?" said William, suddenly perceiving his young brother.

" Holding your horse for you, sir !"

" O Ted, Ted !" said William, half reproachfully , " do you know who the horse is waiting for ?"

" For you, sir !"

" Come, come !" said William, "no joking about that ! Now, father, if Joe has the luggage, we 'll be off."

Joe had been engaged in securing what William had seemed to have forgotten, and then stepping to Black Beauty's side, Joe took the bridle from Ted, and putting it in William's hand, said, " Your merchant-brother, William, has bought him back—the first-fruits of his earnings !"

" You don't mean it !" said William.

" Yes, Will, but I do ; and none can say he is the worse for being twice bought and sold for the sake of a brother !" William looked at Joe—and that look was enough, but still **he** said in a low tone, " O Joe, I little thought of this, when you were so bent on saving !" And he sprang on Black Beauty, who knew his rider, and gently rearing, darted forward on—by the well-known lanes, past the old familiar fields where every tree and hedge-row seemed **to** greet his return ; on—out of sight **and sound** of the tardier steed behind him, swiftly on, his horse bore him, to the home of his heart and toil ! There, in that sweet summer evening, his mother stood and watched with Rose, not on the door-step, but beside the garden-gate ; while Rover, at the first cadence of Black Beauty's measured trot, bounded down the sloping greensward, and hearing his master's greeting whistle, tried once and again to leap upon his horse, and welcome him there. But on Black Beauty bore his rider—till he sprang from the saddle to meet his mother's kiss and tear of welcome, and fold his sister to his heart ; while Black Beauty stood unheld beside him, looking on **as** if with sympathizing feelings.

It was finally decided by force of William's and Joe's persuasions, that as **there** was yet a fortnight at least before harvest, farmer and Mrs. Smith should accompany Joe and Ted on their return **to** London, to have the satisfaction of seeing Ted's captain **and** ship, and for their own refreshment and interest; while William and Rose kept the farm and house at home. So they went up accordingly, Ted in high spirits at the prospect before him, with William's full approval of the attainments he had made; and neither father nor mother harassed by any home anxieties to lessen the pleasure of their visit. The novelty of the complete change was very beneficial to both farmer and Mrs. Smith. They were most kindly entertained by their children's friends; **the** old merchant receiving them at his country-house to dinner, and promising **Mrs.** Smith the first opportunity that offered, to come down and spend a day or **two** at the farm, adding that he should take care to bring her son Joseph with him, for he was quite sure he was a son that never went down to his home without a welcome for himself and all he took **with** him! Mrs. Smith confessed that London was not so bad **as** she expected, and might do very well for people not used to the country! Joe insisted on paying all the expenses of the visit, which he said was a pleasure his labor had earned—and that having bought back Black Beauty, had his parents in London, and obtained a place **on** shipboard for Ted—he should begin life again with fresh spirit, **but** with, he still hoped, the same principles. Ted was left with Joe and Samson, ready to take his place on board ship as soon as necessary; and farmer and Mrs. Smith returned, greatly refreshed and benefited by the inspiriting change.

On the evening of the day after their return, William asked

both his father and mother to take a walk across the farm with him **and** Rose, **to** which they agreed and started; but Rose **seemed** to find it difficult to keep his meditative pace; while William, with gravest composure, walked and talked at their side. Rose was always before them, leading the way, till at last they came in sight of the two white little cottages with gardens stretching at either end, built by farmer Smith's mother, and lost by him through means of the only loan he ever borrowed. Rose still led the way, till her parents **had** nearly reached them, then turning round, she looked all expectation at William.

" O you secret-keeper !**" said** he, " you would tell it twenty times **over!** I shall know how **to trust you** again !**"**

" Why, Will, I never said a word !" replied Rose, coming to his side.

" No, nor much need you should !" he answered, smiling. And then turning to his father he said, " There, father, it **was grand-**mother's cottages kept me this last year **in London !"**

" Your grandmother's cottages ! What do you mean **?"**

" Because, father, when I went away **from home, I** came the last thing and looked **at them, and I** resolved I never would leave business in London—if **I** could help it, till I had bought them back for you ! **I got put from it** twice, with getting Joe up and Samson, but I kept on at my aim. Joe and I shared one room as we did at home, and no one would have believed, perhaps, for how little we managed ; but I found last year the man had no mind to part with them, and I was forced to **offer** a higher sum than I had by me, so the purchase was fixed for this year—and I stayed on to earn .t. **And** now, mother, if farming quite fails, there's a cottage rent-free for you and father and Rose, and another beside it for me—and my hands will be able, I should hope, with God's blessing, to earn bread for us all !

They are bought in father's name, and are as much his as they ever were. I know that was the best sheaf I could reap and bring home for him and for you !"

This was true—no earthly gift could perhaps have so met and gratified farmer Smith. His mother's cottages, left to him by will, lost by debt, and now restored by his son—effacing the memory of the loss to him so painful, were a treasured possession indeed !

"There's a refuge then, at least, now, mother!" said William, as his mother turned silently to take his arm home.

" Yes, Will, my son's refuge for me on Earth : and, I trust, my Saviour's in Heaven !"

So William, returned to his home, and began life as a farmer again.

CHAPTER XXV.

" God setteth the solitary in families."—PSALM lxviii. 6.

" For with the same measure that ye mete withal, it shall be measured to you again "
—LUKE vi. 38.

THE sun rose bright one summer morning, over the misty village, over the Hall with its long verdant slopes and spreading
woods, over the farm with its barns and stacks and sleeping cattle, over the lonely cottage of Jem—where fruitfulness and
luxuriance in trees, and vegetables, and flowers, bore witness to
" the hand of the diligent which maketh rich." The village was
still asleep, but Jem was in his garden, " tighting it up" as he
called it, though all looked tight enough, and neither leaf nor
petal, tree nor flower, seemed there, on that bright morning, to
show one trace of Earth's decay. Jem was not watching the
sun to tell the time at which to start off to tend his sheep, this
was no day of pastoral work for Jem, but a day of rest, and
gladness, and blessing—it was the wedding-day of honest faithful Jem. Nearly two years he had held his new abode; his
mother grew more feeble with advancing age, and Jem thought
to add comfort to her life, as well as his own, by the event of
that day. So thought Jem's aged mother also; and when the
sun sent forth his first golden beam through her lattice-window
on that bright morning, she had left her pillow, and was preparing to put all things "straight" within doors: and all the while
she stirred about with her best strength, she said within herself, "How tight and clean SHE will keep all when she takes

charge! I know she will, and comfort me up too, and learn me a deal more of **Heavenly things than I can** come at now!"

At **the** Hall, **Mercy** was up, before the lark had risen to chant **his first** glad song at Heaven's gate, and now she hastened down the misty road, with her bridesmaid's attire in a handkerchief on her arm, to help **her** grandmother **put all** things straight, and then to hasten **on** to stand beside the bride.

Mrs. Smith might have been up since midnight—for all the sun could tell when he first looked across the farm and glanced in radiance through its uncurtained window-panes. Rose was moving, working, speaking, as quick again as usual—as if all the labor of that day had to be completed before the day had well begun. Farmer Smith was out in the freshening morning air, giving directions **to his men; and** William was helping the yard-boy sweep the garden **walks, and** the path down the sloping greensward. And where **was** Patience—the faithful servant always at hand when work was **to** be done, the faithful servant through years of trial, sorrow, peace—where was Patience? Kneeling alone in her chamber, looking **up** through its small **window to** the rosy sky above her head, thinking on the past, the present, **and** the future, till tears overflowed her eyes, and she hid her face and wept; then enshrining all her thoughts and feelings in one fervent thanksgiving and prayer, she went down to the family below. This was her **wedding-day,** and she the affianced bride of **Jem.**

"There now, child, **we** don't want **you** standing about in the way!" exclaimed Mrs. Smith, as she saw Patience looking on, at **a** loss how to act without being told. " Go and be after any thing you may want to get done," added Mrs. Smith. So Patience had her time to herself. Rose at last went to put on her

bridesmaid's dress; and Mercy came down to the farm in her's—
and she dressed the bride; and William put on his Sunday suit,
for he was to walk by the side of the bride and give her away
in the Church—for she had no relative on Earth to stand beside
her there. But before they set out, Mrs. Smith said to Patience
alone, "Patience, girl, I know they say black should never be
worn at a wedding! but you won't be against my wearing that
black silk, as I always do on Sundays, for the sake of little Tim !
Not but what I know his robes are as white as the driven snow,
but I did not like for myself any other color in silk, and being
for him—it could not tell of any evil to come! I know you
won't mind, but I thought I would just name it beforehand."
Patience answered with a tear; for she too had been thinking
of the child, and how he had been her little comforter there,
and how he loved Jem! and she could not help wishing he could
be with them then, though still she knew it was better to
have entered Heaven—safe from all changes, and sorrow **and**
sin.

Widow Jones did not go to the church; nor would she consent to lock up the cottage and come to **the** wedding-feast at
the farm. She said she was wanted " to keep things straight at
home;" whether she knew some mischievous spider to be lurk-
ing in some hole or corner, all ready to disfigure the pattern of
neatness **she had** finished off within; or whether she wished to
be there to give Jem and his bride a motherly greeting at the
threshold of their home, she did not say; the only reason she
gave was the "keeping things straight," and this one word
"straight" with widow Jones admitted a meaning so full, and
application so endless, that it often might baffle the learning of
most to discover the precise point she had in view under this
word of universal use ! And it proved well that widow Jones
did keep her resolve to "bide in the house," for reasons far

more important than keeping dust or spiders at distance, with apron or broom.

A dependable man and boy were in waiting **at the** farm, and no sooner was the bridal party off for the church, than Mrs. Smith said to her husband, "Now, don't lose a minute, for things are quicker done than you would think for, and they will be back in no time!" So saying, Mrs. Smith hastened off with farmer Smith and the dependable man and boy to the further barn, where the wedding-gifts had been placed in readiness by William that morning. Mrs. Smith looked upon them with fresh satisfaction. She had said, "The girl has served me like a child, and she shall not be sent away like a stranger!" And no one who looked into the barn that morning, could doubt Mrs. Smith having kept her resolve. First stood the gift of her mistress to Patience, the prettiest of young cows, as black as a raven's wing, with one star **of white on** its broad forehead. Rose had named it "Black Beauty," after the favorite horse. Mrs. Smith said, that as a bit of meadow-land went with the cottage, there could be no reason why Patience should not have a cow of her own, and sell milk to the poor! which was a thing, **Mrs.** Smith said, that wanted to be more done than it was; she was thankful that for her part she could say, that never with her knowledge, had the poor been sent away with an empty can, when they came up to buy a little milk for their families! Mrs. Smith knew how to give generously when she did give, and beside the young cow, stood a new milk-pail, two milk-pans, a cream-pot, and skimmer; all these were the wedding-gifts of her mistress to Patience. But then Patience had been no common servant—the nurse and comforter of little Tim, her mistress's own devoted nurse—when infection and death were near, and in her service faithful in all things—this had Patience been, and her mistress was resolved to testify her sense of it.

Next stood the gift of Rose to Patience: a pair of hens of perfect whiteness, with a black cock, **all reared on** the farm. The fowls were in a basket, chiefly constructed by the hands of the sailor-boy, his mother bestowed on Patience, having another of a different kind herself; for she said, that to leave her sailor-boy out, would look as if he were no longer one of themselves! In a corner of the barn a little black pig was inclosed, waiting for his removal to fresh quarters—this was farmer Smith's gift to his servant Jem. Added to these was a new barrow, made at the village wheelwright's, a famous substitute for the one that Jem had used from a child, and which **the** largest nails would now hardly avail to hold together—this was William's present to his favorite farm-servant. But these were not all: Mrs. Smith had a maxim which she often used, applying it variously as occasion served, and this was the maxim, "There's no good in remembering one to forget another!" Accordingly Mrs. Smith said she was not going to overlook Jem, as if she had altogether forgotten the value to be set by his services. **What** she had saved by his care in eggs and young fowls when he **was** yard-boy, she said she knew pretty well by the loss when his master took him away to make him a shepherd—she had never been able to get up, or keep, such a poultry-yard since. But Jem should see his mistress had not forgotten him! And there, in demonstration of the fact, stood a small box containing household linen, all bleached and made by Mrs. Smith. In this same box was a shawl from Samson, chosen and bought by him in his uncle's shop, and sent down from London for Patience. While, from all the great city could offer, Joe had chosen for **Jem** an engraving of the Good Shepherd, with the sheep **gathered** near Him, when He said to Peter, "Feed my **Lambs:**" and having it put in a frame, with a glass before it, Joe sent it down to gleam from the cottage walls of the

village shepherd, with its light of holy and blessed remembrance.

No sooner did Mrs. Smith with hasty step arrive at the barn,
than the whole array of gifts began to receive their dismissal.
Farmer Smith haltered the young cow and led her himself;
while a tumbril received all the rest, as nicely adjusted as the
case admitted of—the boy down in the midst securing the little
black pig, the box in the barrow, and the fowls on the top of
the box, while the milk-pail with its bright rims, the dairy pans,
cream-pot, and skimmer, were all settled in; and the tumbril
drove off.

Farmer Smith arrived first with the young black cow—
widow Jones in the midst of her business within, was still looking from time to time from the window, to see what might be
happening without. **And now** she saw farmer Smith at the
stile with the cow. "Why, if there isn't our master himself,
and that handsome black **heifer!" said** widow Jones, with surprise; and making haste from the door, she got **down to the**
stile just as farmer Smith had succeeded in removing it to lead
in the cow. "Well, neighbor," said kind farmer Smith, in his
most cheerful, pleasant tone,—which tone always rose up as
by instinct when his words had to do with a gift or any token
of goodwill,—"Well, neighbor, I am sure I wish you joy of
to-day; though you will just please to remember that you are
growing rich by making us poorer! I don't mean because the
black heifer is to stay as yours, instead of ours—no, I don't
mean it of any thing money could have bought—but for her
who's your daughter by this time, if the Minister **kept to his**
hour at the church. I made her servant-girl to **my wife, who**
must choose for herself now—for I am sure I can**'t hope to**
please her so well any more!" Widow Jones stood in silent
surprise. The black heifer for them! Could it possibly be,

that farmer Smith had led down the handsomest of all his young
cows for **her** children! "Come, then," said farmer Smith, "there's
plenty more things on the way, let's make one safe at a time.
You tell Patience, her mistress has sent her this cow, with her
love and her blessing; and there's a milk-pail and pans, and a
cream-pot and skimmer, that Patience may sell milk to the
poor; for it's a fact in this village, that the poor often don't
know how to get half a pint, and I **wish** that some one would
name it to the Squire, that he might just speak to his tenants
about it!" O with what wondering eyes **of** delight and of joy
poor old widow Jones looked **on, while** her **master, as** she
always called farmer Smith, led up the black heifer and made
her fast in the warmly-thatched shed! But there **was** no time
allowed for expressing her feeling; farmer Smith hastened
back to the stile where the tumbril was waiting, and widow
Jones hastened after, and then she stood by while its stores
were unloaded. Out tumbled the little black pig, and the **boy**
jumped down just in time to secure him: then the **milk-pail**
and milk-pans, the cream-pot and skimmer; **the** box tied
round with a cord and directed; the handsome white and black
fowls; and, last of all, the new barrow **for** Jem. Farmer Smith
gave the messages one by one to widow Jones, who stood listening beside him in **the midst of** the things; there she stood in
her short-sleeved, **half-length,** large-flowered, print bedgown,
bought new for the wedding occasion, and put on first by her
that day, her snow-white kerchief beneath it with its thick folds
in front, and her single-crimped bordered cap with a scarlet
ribbon pinned round it—saving all need of strings, and **her**
white apron tied on, all ready for whatever on that summer-day
might befall; there she stood wiping away with the corner of
her apron her fast-starting tears, as she listened to farmer Smith
and looked on the gifts—all telling the praises, so sweet to her,

of her Jem and his bride ! "The box," said farmer Smith, "will speak for itself when it's opened, which need not be done till your children return. The fowls are from Rose, her present to Patience ; my wife says Patience will know who **made the** basket, and she **is** to keep it for our poor sailor boy's sake. My son William had the barrow made on purpose for Jem : he says **Jem is** not to think too much about him in the gift, for he had it made as much in remembrance of our poor little Tim, who always took such a fancy to Jem : my son had a wish that Jem should have something to serve him through life, in remembrance of the child. But I must be off, for my wife entirely set her mind on my being and knowing the things safe here, before **they** returned from the church." **So** farmer Smith saw the little black **pig** secure **in** the stye ; and then leaving the man and **the boy to help** in with the rest, he hastened back again to the farm.

Mrs. Smith was impatiently waiting her husband's return, and losing more time by her looks from window and door than she gained by her haste in all things beside. But now seeing him ascending the hill, she was satisfied ; she heard of the safe bestow-ment of all, the messages delivered as she had given them in charge ; and then bringing out farmer Smith's Sunday coat, she waited in something more like quiet expectation for the bridal **party's return** from the church.

And now in the distance the party came in sight. Jem led his bride, Rose and Mercy followed after, and William beside them. Mrs. Smith gave one hasty glance into her parlor to be assured all was right there, then hastened to the **door-step** to receive them. Farmer Smith held open the **small garden-**gate, and gave them his hand, and blessed them as they **entered ;** then smiled on Rose and Mercy, and shut the gate after them **all.** There stood Mrs. Smith, in her Sunday gown of black silk, upright on the' door-step, but when Jem led up his bride, she stooped her tall figure, and kissed the cheek of Patience, and led her in herself, as with a mother's feeling. The water was boiling, so the tea was soon made; the coffee was ready beforehand; and full of gentlest cheerfulness they all sat down to the wedding-breakfast. Mrs. Smith poured out the tea, and Rose the coffee; Jem and his bride sat on one side of the table; and **Mercy** between farmer **Smith** and William on the other. No pains had been spared in preparing the **feast: a** plum-cake, **black with** richness, **was placed in the center;** it was **not frosted** over with **snow, which the art** of the confectioners alone can accomplish — such borrowed skill was **not** needed at their wedding-feast, nor would Mrs. Smith have seen the merit of crusting a cake with a coating of ice for a table, round which only affection could gather. Ornaments they had —nature's own, and not wanting in taste of arrangement. Rose had gathered white lilies, and laid them all over and in a circle round the large cake which her mother had made; and strewn on the white table-cloth, in long winding lines, lay the flowers of the season reposing; **while round** the plate of the bridegroom and bride bloomed **a circle** of nothing **but heart's-**ease. Among **the** frail flowers **stood** the solid mass of the dishes—a great **pie** filled with rabbits, a ham dressed for the occasion, a **fresh-cut** cheese from the dairy, with butter made **into swans that** floated **in a** lake of water, or reposed on green borders of **parsley.** Each corner-dish was a large shining loaf, with a circle of smallest loaves in the plate round it. Cakes of every description—all home-made, with fruits from the garden; sweet wine in glass decanters; and a tankard for ale. While the faces around looked down on those smiling flowers, and the fingers **of** tenderest care still on all sides removed them—when any change of the dishes might have pressed on their forms: for

the recklessness **that** can **gather** together the fairest flowers of
the Earth, to please the eye of those **who** will take no care to
preserve their frail Heaven-given loveliness, is not found in the
poor man's **home,** nor in the dwellings of those who **sow** and
reap the ground.

Meanwhile, at the cottage, widow Jones had scarcely marked
the progress of time, intent on the interests of her newly arrived
charge. "Pretty creatures!" said widow Jones, "sure enough I
must find them **some** food!" So stooping **down her** aged
figure, she cut up some grass and mixed it with such leaves as a
cow, she well **knew,** would like, and **then** strewed it before
the black heifer, who licked the old woman's hand before feeding, as she used to do the hand of Patience—who had brought
her up from **a** calf: then, having no corn of any description,
widow Jones crumbled up a **small** piece of bread for the fowls,
though she said **at she showered it over** them, that it would
have been a shame on any other **day to** give them such food!
And, finally, she cut up a few vegetables for the pig. The
creatures all liking their food, and the notice bestowed on them
in their strange **quarters,** called after the dear old woman, **till**
she heard such **a** lowing, and cackling, **and** grunting, that she
hastened back **to see** after them again; but at last, quite **fa-**
tigued, she told them **all,** gravely, that they must think she had
something else to do than to see after them! and having ventured so far in a reproof for **their persevering** demands, **she**
returned to the house, and **putting the small kettle on** the little
back-kitchen fire, made herself a quiet cup of tea, which greatly
refreshed her, so much **so that** after the toil and excitement of
the morning she **at** last fell asleep in her arm-chair. She slept
quietly there for some half-hour or **more,** when a sudden sharp
tap at the door aroused her. "They **are** come!" thought widow
Jones, as she started up from sleep; **but no,** it was not her son

who opened the door and looked in, it was a **stranger.** " Is this Roode's plot ?" asked the man. " Yes," replied **widow** Jones, rather in alarm at sight of the stranger. " I suppose you are the mother of the man who lives here ?" " Yes," said **widow** Jones, still more uneasy. " Then **you** will please to give **your** son that letter, from Madam Clifford **at** the Hall, and be **so** good as to show us where to set **up** this eight-day clock !" Widow Jones looked out, and there at the stile stood a light cart with another man in it, and the eight-day **clock.** But before she had time to consider, the **men** were in **with** the clock, and soon **fixed on the best** place to put it in themselves, and, finding the old woman had no objection to their choice of situation, they set it up at once, observing **as** they did so, that it **was** one of the best time-keepers ever put together ; and before widow Jones had recovered enough from her surprise to do more than look at the outside of the letter in her hand, from that to the clock, and then back again to the sealed letter, **the** men were gone, and the cart, and all out of sight **like a dream** —except that there stood **the** clock, ticking each **moment of** time, and over the bright hands **at** the top of **the face a** colored picture of a shepherd-lad **with a lamb** on one arm, and his sheep feeding at **his** feet. It **was** well widow Jones had had her cup of tea and her refreshing sleep, for most surely neither would **have been thought of** after the arrival of the clock. " Then it's **from** Madam herself, for my Jem on his wedding-day !" at last said widow Jones, as she once more looked at the letter. " Well !" she added, " if all this is not wonderful, I don't know what **is** !" and lifting a thankful look upward, old widow Jones sat down again in her arm-chair, to consider all things over before her children's arrival.

But when Patience at the farm **at** last turned to take leave, Mrs. Smith's pleasant smile was gone, her lip quivered, and **her** strong firm voice faltered. Patience could not tell her own feeling in words, but none needed to hear it spoken, her years of faithful service left no doubt of that—the moments passed, and the maid and her mistress had parted, the record of her years in that place of service was finished, and nothing of the past could be altered. How often does that solemn moment come and go unheeded—a service ended, a place left, and the past is supposed to be done with; but the record of that past— what is written there? that moment of parting has sealed it, and it lies from that time in the hand of the Judge, till the day, that bringeth all secret things to light—must see it unfolded. In the hands of the Judge lie the records of the past years of all; and not one created being can unfold or read them, still less alter a single word they contain. But there is One, and only One, to whom they still lie open—even Jesus, the Saviour of sinners; and earnest prayer to Him may still avail to get all the hand-writing against us blotted out in his blood; only let us not go thoughtlessly forward—as if those records of the past contained no sentence against us! For Patience the record was blessed; and she knew the secret of prayer to that Saviour, whose blood cleanseth from all sin—blotteth out all His people's transgression, and maketh their imperfection perfect. So Patience had parted in peace, beneath the blessing of Heaven and of Earth, and was now descending the hill. Mrs. Smith waited a few moments looking out of the window, in the effort to recover composure; then turning to Rose, who was watching beside her, she said, "I wish you would run after Patience with that," taking a book done up in paper from her pocket, "you know what it is, I did not feel able to speak about it when she went, as I meant to have done. You can tell her it's for the sake of little Tim!" Rose took the book, and her swift steps soon overtook Patience, who, leaning on Jem, was ascend-

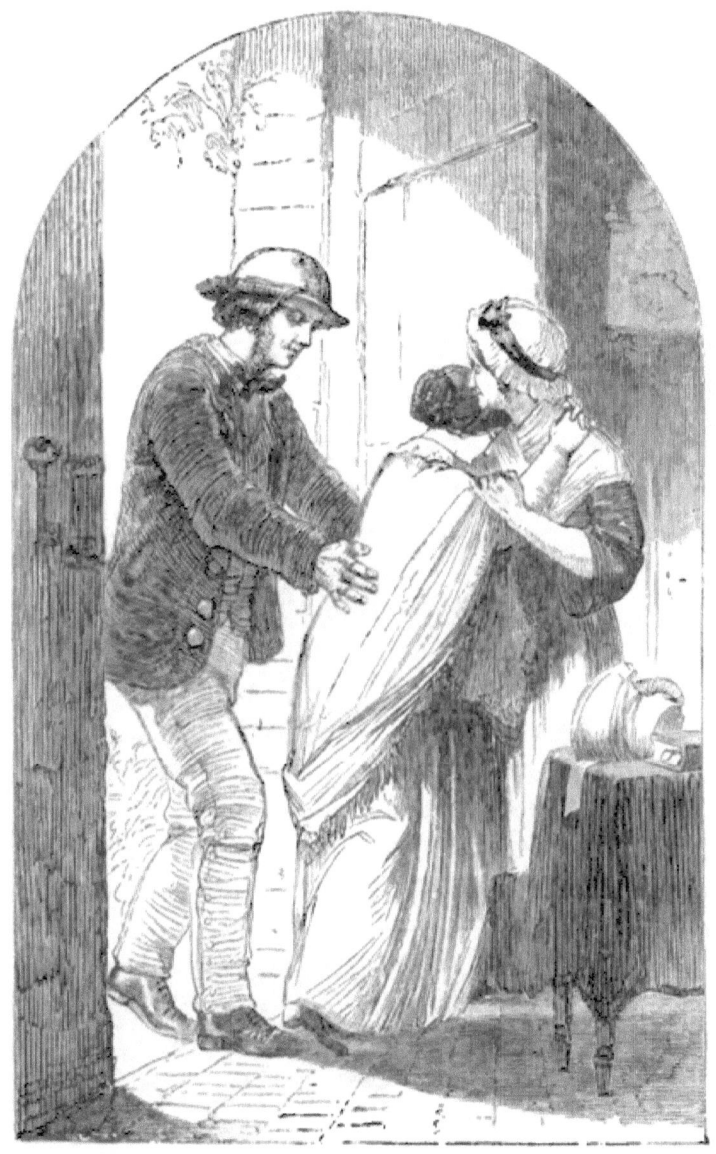

ing the opposite hill. "Patience, mother sends you this, it 's a book of family prayer, like the one my aunt **gave her**; she wishes you to keep it for the sake of little Tim; **she** meant to have given it you herself, only she was so overcome **at** your going!" Patience took the small parcel, and looking back **at** the farm, sent a message by Rose of her duty and her thanks **to** her mistress, with the assurance that they would take it into use every day.

Mercy stayed at the farm to assist Mrs. Smith and **Rose, in** the clearing **away;** and **to** make things more cheerful **there** where she **was** a favorite with all. And **now** at length widow Jones looking out from above the bright geraniums in the window, saw Jem and his bride at the stile. Then she opened wide the cottage door, and stood just within—where the sheltering vine on one side, and the drooping honeysuckle on the other, softly shaded the view of her now feeble figure. Patience walked up the path first, and Jem followed close after, and the old **woman** stretched out both her arms and clasped them round **Patience,** and Patience threw her's round the old woman's neck, **and felt** for the first time **in** life, that she **too had a mother!** Then as Patience unlocked that close embrace, **the old woman** turning to her son, said, "God bless **you, my** Jem, and bless us all here together, **for I am sure 't is his** goodness that brings such things to pass!" and **Jem** looked on as if he felt the sight he then saw was the best sight of all. But just then, Jem started and stared, for a loud-striking clock told the hour, with a slow decided call upon the attention of all.

"Why, mother! a clock! where did it come from!"

"Ah! never mind that!" replied widow Jones, **"look** here in **this** drawer, here's a letter in Madam Clifford's own hand if that don't tell you all about it I am sure that I can't!"

Jem took up the letter.

17

" But now, child, come, sit down," said the old woman, turning
to Patience.   " Why, to think that you have never been inside
the door, and yet all these months you have known the place
was just waiting for you !"

Jem had opened the letter, but finding it not easy to read in
a moment of time, he folded it up for a better opportunity, and
turned again to his bride, and then leaning on the back of her
chair, told his aged mother, who **was** seated **before him,** of the
feast their good mistress had made at the farm.   While Patience
held closely that treasured book of prayer, and looked round on
her new abode.   What comfort beamed upon her from every
corner : and there lay the large Bible, dear old Willy's own Bible,
of which Jem had so often told her !   She longed to look on its
pages where the old man had read, but she said nothing then !
and Jem seemed to wish to give her time to look round ; and
poor old widow Jones looked so happy on the two, that she
seemed in no hurry either to move or to speak.

" Well," at last Jem asked with his own cheerful smile, " do
you think it looks any thing like what you fancied, and as if you
could content yourself here ?"

" Not like what I fancied !" said Patience, looking up, "you
never told me how beautiful it all was inside, I never saw such a
home as it is for any like us !"

" **Ah,** that was all our young Squire's doing," said Jem, " and
I don't know, but somehow a blessing seems to bide with it all,
for it always looks as beautiful and cheerful as can be, just as you
see it **looks now !"**

" But what a clock that is !" said Patience, " do yo see that
shepherd with the lamb in his arms ? and the clock is so like
ours at the farm, it seems quite natural to look at it !"

" Yes," replied Jem, " I never was more taken by surprise in
my life then when **it set up** striking just as we had come in at

the door! it seemed as if it must have a word to say to us also! but I don't seem to have thought about it yet. I can't think," added Jem, "what that kind of grunting is I hear, I could almost have thought my poor little pig that I lost had come to life again, to welcome you here!"

Then old widow Jones rose up from her chair, and said, "I advise you to go and see what it is, **and** settle your mind about it at once!" so Jem opened the door **into the** back kitchen when a loud shrill crow from a cock burst on the **ear** of Patience.

"You come and all!" said Jem to Patience, **who** hastened after him, the aged mother following—to the pig-stye; there looked up the little black pig, grunting eagerly again as if quite sure now of a feast; and then turning away from Jem and Patience, looked up at widow Jones, as soon as she, his kind feeder, arrived as the stye.

"Why, mother! what a beauty of a pig!" exclaimed **Jem,** "how ever in the world did you get it? Why, it **'s just** like **one** of master's at the farm!"

"I am not going to tell you every thing in a **moment!"** said widow Jones, decidedly; while **the cock,** at the sound of pleasant voices, crowed forth a further announcement of his presence on the premises. Jem stepped on to the shed and opened the door, then holding it back, said in amaze, "Patience, only you look in here!" Patience looked in; there stood the black heifer, who at sight of Patience pulled hard at the rope, by **which** she was tied, to get to her side; there stood the new barrow; the **hens** and the cock—in the basket made **by** the sailor-boy **Ted. "Now** you just listen," said widow Jones, " **and** I 'll tell you **all."** So Jem stood there and listened, still all in amaze, and Patience beside him—while the black heifer was happy with her hand, which it licked on both sides.

"I was nere in the house then," said widow Jones, "keeping all straight within; when, who should I see but our master leading up the young cow! Out I went; and he told me he had brought it from our mistress, a present for Patience—for her very **own, and** he said she was to have it and sell milk to the poor; and it seemed to me wholly a beautiful thing, that she who had been altogether a comfort up there, should come here **to a** home and sell milk to the poor! But that was just what our master said; and if you will believe, there's the whole concern for the milking **come too! It's** all set out in the **dairy**; just you come and look." Back widow Jones hurried, and Patience and Jem followed after, to see the milk-pail with its bright rims, the milk-pans, and cream-pot, and skimmer, all set out in the dairy. Then, returning again, widow Jones went on to tell all the history, not shortened the least by her remarks in between the matters **of** fact that she **had** to relate: how the fowls were from Rose; the basket the sailor-boy's work, and all that their master had said about it; and the barrow for Jem, to serve him for life, in remembrance of the love of little Tim. Then followed the box and all its contents—quite new to widow Jones; the house-**linen,** the shawl, and the picture: till Patience could bear up no longer against such tokens of affection and kindness, and, tying **on** her bonnet, she said, "I tell you what, Jem, before we do any thing more I must go down to the farm, and you with me, and **speak** about what we found here!" So Patience and Jem re-**turned again to** the farm, and going in by the back-door, found **Mrs.** Smith still busy clearing away: Patience sat down on the low-backed kitchen chair, where she sat in tears the day little Tim first **took** notice of her; she could not now speak a word, but, quite overcome, **she hid** her face and wept, while Jem stood silent beside her. "Why, Patience, child!" said Mrs. Smith, stopping short with a cloth in her hand, with which she was rubbing up the tankard; "come back so soon! why, child, what's the matter?"

"It's only your goodness, and master's too," said Jem; " indeed it's all over too much for us both!"

"Well now, if that's all," replied Mrs. Smith, "you have done and said quite enough, so never let me hear another word about that, nor your master either—here he is close by to say the same."

"But the black heifer!" said Patience, without looking up; "I am sure I never could of thought it! **I thought** I was leaving all the creatures behind, and then, when I got up there —why they seemed all up there before me!"

"And where could they have been better, child, I should like **to** know?" replied Mrs. Smith. "Haven't you and Jem just tended them all with that care that nothing seemed to be lost that was under your hand? You know that very well; **and** though it's just what every one who has a right principle **would** do, yet I was not going to seem as if I did not know **it, for I** did, and your master no less! And I do **say,** if there's one in the village who has more of a right **than another** to sell milk for the poor, it's just you and Jem! **I know** I always have taken a pleasure in that, and I **am** pretty sure you will no less; and such a fancy we all had for the black heifer—what could we wish better for her than to live for serving the poor with her milk! **Why I** am sure I little thought you would not get over the day without being down here again! But it's just your way for all that, and you may be sure I shall soon come up and look after you; so not a word more about any thing—you re- member I have said it!" And with that Mrs. Smith made **an** end of her reply.

And now in looked Rose and Mercy, both ready for a walk, all surprise at sight of Patience and Jem.

"Why, here's Rose and Mercy coming off up to you, and you not at home to receive them! There now, be satisfied, and don't shed another tear over that which comes only as a blessing!" said Mrs. Smith, and then adding, "Good-by to you, my good girl, I don't think any the worse of you for coming so soon down!" and with fresh and livelier parting words than before, Patience again hastened back to her cottage-home with Jem.

The good mother had set out the tea all in readiness—the picture of comfort. Rose and Mercy followed after, Rose bearing the round wedding-cake, her mother's own making; and Mercy carrying all the white lilies in an open farm-basket on her arm, and a nosegay of the flowers in her hand. The cake was set down in the middle of the table, and Rose would do and look at nothing till she had covered it again with its lilies —to the admiration and delight of widow Jones. Then visiting all the creatures with Patience and Mercy and Jem, she hastened back again to the farm; while Jem and his bride, and his mother and Mercy, sat down at the round cottage table. Then Mrs. Clifford's letter was brought out again; and Mercy knew her mistress's handwriting, and was able to read it every word to the pleasure of the whole party.

Now Jem began to consider how he could get his duty and his thanks to Madam Clifford; he consulted with Mercy whether she thought he might make bold and step up that evening and ask to speak to the young Squire; or whether he ought to wait till the next day. Jem's grateful heart did not like to pass the day over without offering his thanks; he was dressed also in his best, which seemed suitable for going up to the Hall on such an occasion; but still more than this, Jem had a feeling of not liking to pass his wedding-day over without so much as a sight of the young Squire: he seemed to think that all could not go so well with him .f he went over the day without a sight of him; so it was decided that after tea he should walk up. But while they were still seated round at the table, (the cottage-door wide open,) in that summer afternoon, and Jem seated in full view of the road, he suddenly started up, saying, "There's our young Squire himself at the stile!" So Jem hastened out; there Herbert stood, with a noble dog waiting beside him. "Well, Jem," said the young Squire, "I could not be the only one not to wish you well in a friendly greeting to-day, so I walked down this way, expecting now I should find you at home." Then Jem sent his best message of duty and gratitude to Madam Clifford for the handsomest clock, Jem said, he ever had seen! And he asked the young Squire if he would please to walk in and see how it stood. Herbert went in with Jem, and there he saw that dwelling of comfort and peace; the tall clock with the shepherd-lad and the young lamb on his arm painted on it; the lily-covered cake; the aged mother in her new array; and Patience **and** Mercy beside her. The young **Squire sat down,** and the dog sat at his feet and looked **up in his face.** Then Herbert said, "Jem, now you are a rich **man, and** I thought you might manage to keep a good dog. I had this from some distance for you, the best of his kind, I believe; he is a huge fellow, but he won't cost you more, I fancy, than you will be willing **to spend on** him. What do you say to having him for a helper?"

"Well, sir," replied Jem, **"to** my thinking, he **looks to have** sense enough to **keep** sheep by himself!"

At Jem's **wit they all** laughed, **and the young Squire** was quite satisfied; **but he said,** "You **must take a little** notice of him at first, or I am afraid **he will run off to** me, for I have made a great favorite of him; we must tie him up for to-night. **And see here, I have** brought a cord, for I remembered that

you only engaged for a pair of hands—when I came to you supposing you furnished with ropes for drawing up the log from the
ditch!" The young Squire went with Jem to fasten up the dog,
and then Jem showed him the presents received that day ; and
to be able to show them to him seemed to double the joy Jem
felt in them all : and if the black heifer was a treasure to Patience, what was not the noble shepherd's dog to Jem—the
young Squire's own gift! Then the Squire heard how Patience
was to sell milk to the poor, and this led him to inquire why
there should be occasion for that, and then he found from Jem
that all the farmers made their milk into cheese, and so had none
to sell, except farmer Smith ; and the Squire made a note in his
book of the fact, and remembered it in years to come. Then he
left honest Jem with his bride and his mother in old Willy's
cottage—and returned to the Hall.

After tea, while **Patience and** Mercy cleared away, Jem went
after food for the creatures ; he longed to take his dog with him,
but he could not venture so soon. Then the sun went down in
the sky ; and when all the live creatures were provided for—
before Mercy returned to the Hall—Jem opened old Willy's
Bible, and while they all sat around, he read the 103d Psalm,
and then they knelt down, and he offered up the evening prayer
from the book Mrs. Smith had given in remembrance of little
Tim. And so closed that bright summer day.

CHAPTER XXVI.

" When the ear heard, then it blessed me; and when the eye saw, it gave witness to
me: because I delivered the poor that cried, and the fatherless and him that had none
to help him. The blessing of him that was ready to perish came upon me; and I
caused the widow's heart to sing for joy."—Job xxix. 11–13.

SOON after the young Squire came of age, it was necessary to
appoint a fresh steward **for the estate on** which he resided, to
watch over and receive the rents of the farms, and for all such
affairs as belong to the office of a farm-steward. He had looked
forward to this change, and made his own choice as to who
should fill this office—so important in the manner of its exercise
to the comfort **as well** as to the integrity of **those over whom**
the **steward is** appointed to watch. **No sooner was** the office
vacant than William was sent for **to the Hall, and it** was offered
to him. Farmer Smith's **farm was not large, and it** would be
easy for William still to **live with his** parents, **assist his** father on
the farm, and **yet accomplish all** that this new employment
would **require of him: while the** yearly salary received would
make **the circumstances of his** family all he could desire—for it
was only **the** difficulty of always being ready with his rent that
kept farmer Smith's mind harassed by his business. So William
gratefully accepted the offer, and was appointed farm-**steward** of
the estate.

A year passed peacefully over **Patience in her new abode;**
and when the summer came again—with **its** long days and
refreshing fruits, **she** received **a** visit from her first master's

family; they all came over to spend a day, to the joy of Patience and the delight of all the children—but especially of little Esther, who was left for a month's visit with Patience, till she became so fond of all country sights and sounds—of the black cow with its brimming pail of white-frothed milk; the poor women and children coming to buy of Patience; the white hens, and little chickens who flew upon her shoulders; the shepherd's dog and the sheep; and even of feeding the pig with all that Patience put by in a plate for its food, of vegetables and apple-peels—that she returned to her home in the town, fully resolved on being a farm-house servant, and living with Mrs. Smith—if she would receive her when her age was sufficient.

Mrs. Smith had had a trying year with her servants, three times in the course of the year she had been obliged to make a change; she tried to be patient and not to expect too much, but it was all of no use; she said, she found all the servant-girls of one mind —and that was idleness and finery, instead of real honest work! So thoughtless girls came and left a situation where Patience had stayed to earn the favor of all. Mrs. Smith was quite in despair, and said she saw no help for it but doing the work herself with Rose, for such servants were more trial than all their service was worth. Patience often came down to the farm on baking-days, or churning-days, or washing-days, and stayed for some hours to help; and these were pleasant times both to her mistress and herself. One day while Patience was busy taking out the bread from the large brick oven at the farm, Mrs. Smith being then without a servant, a pleasant-looking woman came up to the door and asked if Mrs. Smith was within.

"Yes," said Patience, and she went to let her mistress know.

"I daresay it's only a girl after the place!" said Mrs. Smith.

"No, she looks over age to be after that," replied Patience.

So Mrs. Smith came down as soon as she was ready, to the back-kitchen where the young woman waited. Mrs. Smith looked at her for a moment as she stood there before her, then exclaimed, " Why, Molly ! is it you ?"

" Yes, that it is," replied Molly, " I heard you were unsettled, and I thought perhaps you would not be against my coming back to you again, for I have never felt at home, or stayed long in any place since I left **you**, and I think if I could but get back here, I should feel settled again. I am sure I have often repent-ed that I gave up as I did, instead of trying on a little longer ; but I hope I should be wiser for the future !"

" Well, Molly," said Mrs. Smith, " I always felt I was to blame **for** your leaving ; but I hope things are better now in some re-spects, than they were : though the child is gone !—you know that, I suppose ?"

" Yes," replied Molly, " I vexed sadly for him ! it cut me up more than any thing to have left him ; but I hope it was all for the best for him, by what I heard."

" Well, Molly, I know you, and you know the place, and if your mind is to come back, I am sure my mind is the same, and your master's I can answer for as **well** as my own, and therefore there's no need to say any more words about it." So Molly came back to the farm, a more patient servant, to find a more patient mistress ; and comfort was once more restored to **Mrs.** Smith's household arrangements.

Another pleasant event of this summer was the return of the sailor-boy from his first long voyage. Full of spirits and bodily **vigor**, sun-burnt, and laden with his gifts **of** love—he came to gladden the hearts of all ; to shake heartily every friendly hand —and none were foes with him ; to visit every familiar spot ; to hold discourse with all the men of village-trade on the use he had made, or was likely to make, of their **arts**—though he had yet known no shipwreck; to learn again from the lips of the Minister—to tell him what he had seen and heard and done, and to listen to his advice for the future. He made no little stir both in the farm and village; and then, having formed a strong friendship with Jem's noble dog; comforted his mother; and satisfied his father and William, he went off again—light and swift as a bird of passage, to be tossed once more on the free-crested waves.

Another year passed by, and when the next Autumn came, the young Squire had completed his college life, and satisfied the best hopes of his boyhood's tutor, and it was understood in the village that he was going abroad again with his mother. These tidings gave great disappointment to the hopes of those who had looked to the comfort of his residence among them; but having assembled his tenantry, he told them that he believed his absence would not be for more than six months, and then he hoped to return and live among them for the future. He had no sooner left than repairs and alterations were begun at the Hall; and the mansion, far from looking desolate and deserted as before, was a scene of perpetual life and activity.

Two years of unclouded comfort Patience had enjoyed in her cottage home. Jem's aged mother, relieved from all care and toil, had regained fresh vigor and spirits—she was always busy in little ways, always at hand, always reflecting the brightness of that bright cottage-home. But the winter of the Squire's absence proved a severe one, and the sudden cold seemed suddenly to snap the old woman's feeble stem of life, and she lay down on her bed to die! Patience could not believe, when the doctor told her that her mother's death was near. "Why it was but a week ago," she said, "my mother was up and as cheerful and well as ever I have known her to be!" The doctor re-

plied, " It might be so, but her hours are numbered now !" Still
Patience could not believe ; she thought **it must be** a sudden
chill, and that warmth and care would restore her. She lighted
and kept up, day and night, a bright little fire in the small **grate**
up stairs ; she made cordials, and Mrs. Smith came up more
than once in the day ; but the old woman smiled on them, and
said, " It 's just sweet to my old heart to feel you all bent to
keep me still, if you could ! but I am going where I shall be far
better off even than here—though my last days have been my
best days !" Then, looking up at Patience, she said, " You
have just been my evening star, lighting **me** Home—for I have
gathered more knowledge these two years with you, than I had
in my whole life before—let the thought of that comfort you as
long as you live ! Jem, **my son**," she added, turning to him, " you
have been your mother's staff all through the weariest of her
way—which lay on this side your poor father's grave. **God**
grant your mother's blessing may fall upon you in the hour **of**
your need !   I know you will take care of Mercy ; she is not fit
to stand in this rough world alone, it **would** soon break her
down ; but the God of the orphan will not **let his** promise fail.
It is not darkness to me ; the light that has but glimmered before me so long, shines all bright round me now ; and I hear
the voice of Him who says, ' Come unto me and I will give you
rest !' " **So the widow** departed, and her children mourned for
her.   Mercy was far away with Mrs. Clifford in a foreign land.
but tears were shed for old widow Jones by the eyes of those
who owned no tie of kindred with her. **The** snow lay deep
upon the ground, and Patience, ill from the anxiety of nursing
and the shock of so sudden a loss—having also her infant child
to tend—was little fit to venture **to the grave.** Jem earnestly
persuaded her not to go, but Patience would not be persuaded ;
she said it was the only respect she could now show to one who

had been all a mother could be to her; and to have lost her so suddenly—was a trial she had never so much as thought upon ! Jem gave way, and Patience followed their aged mother to the grave by his side.   But she took cold, as might have been expected, and was soon confined to her bed.   Rose now came and tended Patience and the infant, day by day, with gentlest care; and Mrs. Smith was continually contriving in every way to minister to her comfort: but, notwithstanding all this care, and Jem's ceaseless anxiety, the spring was approaching before Patience was able to leave her bed and sit down stairs in old Willy's . arm-chair.

But the cheerful spring advanced—the frost gave way before the sun's warm beams, the flowers raised their heads above their wintery graves, the birds looked down from tree and hedge and sang a welcome to them ; new life and vigor came slowly back to Patience, and hope and comfort to the heart of Jem. Patience had not yet milked the cow since her illness, nor stood in her dairy to help the poor people who came, nor walked down once to the farm; but the spring had set foot on the Earth, and the Earth was rejoicing at his presence, and Patience felt that her life was reviving.   And now all her anxiety was to go to the church for the Sunday's service ; she said she knew when she had once been there she should seem to be well again, and able to milk her cow and attend to all her home work.   But Jem was firm now, he had sorely repented having suffered Patience to attend their mother's funeral, and he now was resolved to act prudently.   At length as May was giving place to June, the very last Sunday in the month dawned as soft and lovely a day as the spring-time ever beheld.   Jem could not refuse Patience her wish on such a day ; so, wrapped up and leaning on the arm of her husband, with steps more feeble than she had expected them to be, while Rose kept house with the infan

In the cottage, Patience went to the afternoon-service in the church.

The Minister—their own Minister, preached a missionary sermon: and when he told of the poor heathen without God—because without Christ, and therefore without hope in the world, Patience thought she could feel something of what it must be to live, and sicken, and die, without one glimpse of Heaven, one hope of entering there! She thought of her dying mother's peace, she thought of her husband's Christian life, she thought of their child baptized in her Saviour's Name, she thought of her own faith and hope—and she longed to do something for the poor heathen as a token of her thankfulness to God, and her pity for them. But what could she do? Their mother's funeral, and the doctor's long attendance on her, had taken all Jem's savings. Jem's last week's wages were all spent on the Saturday except one shilling, which he had in his pocket, and that she would not ask him for, because perhaps he might be thinking of giving it himself. If Patience had known of the collection she would have tried to save something back for it on the Saturday; but Jem had not told her—most likely he had forgotten it himself. What could she do? Patience had still one treasure, a possession in money that she always kept with her. She had kept it through want and distress, through trouble and sickness, through prosperity and comfort; she had thought to keep it through life, and that nothing would ever win it from her—it was the Lady's half-crown, the first gift she had ever received from the hand of love; her first knowledge of tenderness was bound up with that gift; and she had kept it, as her treasured possession, through all her life's changes. But now the call to part with it entered her heart—it seemed to come from Heaven, and Earth seemed to repeat the same call—"Is it too much for you to give up, to send the Name of your Saviour to those who never heard the blessed sound of pardon and Heaven through Jesus Christ?" Patience felt the question deep within her heart, and she resolved—" No, I will part with it for that !" But now a trial of her resolution came: Jem crossed from the men. benches, after service, to her, and slipped their remaining shilling into her hand, saying, " It's all we have, so you must give it !"

"**No,**" replied Patience, "I have something besides, you must give that !" Jem looked at her, as if thinking she must be mistaken, but seeing her decided, he took the shilling and put it himself into the plate as he passed out. Patience followed slowly, and dropped her half-crown into the same plate, then, as if in a moment, her heart seemed lightened and her steps strengthened. Her husband was waiting **for** her outside the door, and she walked home by his side.

The sky that Sabbath afternoon was beautiful before them as they descended the hill. **When they** reached their peaceful cottage the door stood partly open, and they **heard** the voice of Rose singing to their infant; the kettle was boiling on the wood-fire, the tea was set ready on the round table, and all looked the picture of repose. Rose hastened back to the farm, and Jem, with lighter heart and brighter face than he had had **for** many a day—sat down with Patience to their cheerful tea. **No cloud of** troubled feeling hung over Patience—no, her personal sacrifice was made **to** Him who gives a present as well as a future reward: and Jem could scarcely believe the change for the better he saw in her. It seemed as if the Lady's piece of money—that gift of tenderness, true to the feeling which bestowed it, was not **only** to possess a power to soothe through years of trial, but, **when** at last parted from, was to yield more present comfort and peace, even than when possessed; while the endless **future** alone can make manifest the results of what

is so given, as this treasured possession of Patience—in love, and faith, and prayer! From that first Sabbath at church, Patience improved daily in health. Their infant, little Peace by name, grew strong and merry when more with its mother in the open air; and though Patience could not at once recover her strength and her look of health, yet the home of Jem again wore its cheerful aspect, and the voice of joy was again heard within it.

When May had given place to June, the preparations at the Hall were completed. All that was the work of the builder's art had been renewed, or fresh adorned: only one room had been left unentered by the repairer's step—it was the room that had been his sister's, which Herbert had made his own; affection invested the faded adornment of that room with more attraction than any power of art could have imparted. Around the mansion the stately trees and verdant slopes wore as fresh an aspect as when they first put on the emerald brightness of the spring. Tidings had arrived in **the** village of the Squire having been married abroad: and **now** the **day** was fixed for his return, with his bride and mother, to the **Hall.**

The appointed day arrived: and the early stir of preparation was general. No gifts had been ordered by the Squire to celebrate the event; well he knew that his presence—his heart and mind, his eye and voice—would be a gift more prized than any, by villagers whose affections had grown around him from his boyhood. But orders were given by him for all the **park-**gates to be opened, that those who wished might receive him, on his return to reside `among them there, **where he** first had parted from them at his father's side. None were slow to go forth to the welcome—all dressed **in** festal garments, with the look of expectant gladness, they waited and watched. The **tenantry** had gone forward on horseback, a few miles. While

William, steward of the farms, mounted on Black Beauty,
stood at the grand entrance gate. Four had been named as
the hour; and now it struck from the great stable clock.
Then the scattered groups stood up from the greensward; and
children took their parents' hands in questioning excitement.
William rode on Black Beauty—who chafed at his long holding
in—once down the broad walks of the park, and shouted a
request that all would stand off **at the** arrival, then back again
quickly to his post at the great entrance gate. Ringers had
been stationed by William in the first village church where the
Squire had property, and as soon as the long line of tenantry
returning and escorting the Squire were seen from that village
steeple, the bells were to strike up a peal. A watcher was set
on the tower of the next village church—and as soon as he
heard the signal of approach, the solitary bell in that tower
was to send on the tidings—over hill and valley, over the
green waving corn and the yet unmown grass—to a watcher
on the tower of their own village church, then were their own
bells to ring out the welcome heard from afar. All hushed
their breath to listen for the first distant sound—too impatient
to wait for nearer tidings, trusting to catch from their friendly
hills **an** echo to the first joyous peal. And who could wonder!
Had not he, who now drew near, made their sorrows and joys,
their welfare and happiness, his own?—not by general dispen-
sations of kindness, but by that frank and personal intercourse,
which binds the heart with the tie of devoted affection—a tie
far stronger, far higher, and deeper, than that of mere personal
gratitude for favors received. Had they not seen his warm
feeling gush forth, seen his active sympathy spring to the
surface at the sight or hearing of trouble or sorrow of theirs?
Was not the quick glance of his boyhood-eye, his generous
utterance, familiar to many assembled there? Who would

not come forth to receive in his manhood, the boy who had toiled in the ditch over old Willy's log; who had climbed the thatcher's ladder to lay in an armful of straw, in the eager gladness of his heart at effacing the neglect of the poor man's oppressor! The whole village might have received gifts on some stately occasion, in some stately manner by the boy provided with the means for the large bestowment; but it would not have bound the heart of the village to that boy like one free spontaneous effort—such as Herbert's had been, bearing witness to his self-forgetfulness in the poor man's distress. And was he not the brother of her who, to them, had seemed an angel upon earth? When once aroused to a sense of their blessedness, had he not followed in her gentler steps with his manly power, and had not the light of her life shone reflected in him? Then might the deep well-spring of feeling that had followed her to Heaven break forth again to welcome his return to his home! True loyalty is happily a contagious emotion, and many a heart beat quicker, and many a cheek glowed with feeling that day, in those who did but estimate the event by the expectation of others.

The servants had now gathered to the door; the men, in their livery of dark blue and white, stood in two lines extending one on each side the steps; while the maids stood assembled in the entrance-hall. Again and again some eager listener said, "I heard the bells strike up—I am pretty sure I did!" But, no, it could not have been, for their own village tower still stood silent. At length William, the farm-steward, turned Black Beauty's head round, and facing the people and the servants, waved his hat above his head, then replacing it, turned instantly back again, standing sideways by the gate— he had caught the sound of the distant peal: breathlessly the people now listened, and in a few minutes more their own vil-

lage chime struck full on the ear: then the throng pressed side
by side, as near as might be to the broad carriage sweep, while
on pealed the bells; till the sound of many tramphng hoofs
was heard along the road. Still on they rang, till full in sight
came the traveling-carriage, with its four horses and its blue
postillions; then the people raised a shout, and the tenantry
who followed lifted their hats and joined the welcome cheers;
through the great gate the carriage dashed, and William held
his hat above his head, scarcely able to restrain **Black Beauty's**
excited spirit; and his eye glanced up from his master's face,
to where young Mercy sat behind on the carriage—the village
maiden back from the foreign land, pale with her own deep
feeling, and the sound of that thrilling welcome. The carriage
stopped **at** the Hall-door, and the tenantry dismounted and held
their horses in hand. The **Squire** stepped from the carriage
and led his mother **in** to the care of her faithful servants; then
returning handed out his Lady, and waving his hand to the
people, led her within. William riding up, dismounted, and
slipping Black Beauty's bridle over his arm, took down the
orphan Mercy from the carriage with a brother's softened welcome—for she wore mourning for the grandmother lost in her
absence, who had filled the place of both parents to her, and
her eyes were filled with the tears of mingled feelings. Then
a servant brought a message to William from the Hall, and he
instantly mounted Black Beauty again, and riding down the
walks shouted, "The Squire begs you will be seated on the
grass." Servants quickly appeared bearing between them trays
of cake, and baskets filled with bottles of wine, all prepared by
the Squire's orders in readiness beforehand. Then rising, the
people breathed—not with a shout—but in a low murmur, a
blessing on the head they had seen from its childhood uncovered beneath their roofs and among them; a blessing on the

Squire's Lady; and a blessing on his mother. The Squire stood at an open window looking down upon them and hearing the thrice-repeated blessing; and his Lady at his side; and his heart filled with thankfulness that his tenants and dependants were his friends. Then the Squire turned away from the window, and the people took their refreshment all seated on the grass, till the Squire came out, and his Lady on his arm; they stood on the first Hall step, and the people rose in silence, and he said in a voice not loud but clear—a voice whose tones were all familiar, "God bless you, my friends, and enable us to retain your affection. We thank you for your welcome." And then he came down with his Lady; and he passed slowly among the people, with his friendly greeting, and his Lady at his side—and all the time the village bells rang out the same glad peal.

The eye of the Squire sought out Jem: well he knew his heart would be among the first to welcome him there, but he could nowhere discover his figure. At last he saw him, with his dog close beside him, his infant on his arm, and Patience at his side, at the further edge of the assembly, so he made his way up to him. The dog knew the Squire, and sprang forward to greet him, and leaping up licked his hand, and the Squire caressed him as he passed on to Jem, and said, in his kind cheerful tone, "Well, Jem; do you pretend to be the last to welcome home your friend!" and that beautiful Lady stood beside the Squire, and said with a smile, "I know the name of Jem! Is this your wife and child?" When Patience heard her speak she looked up at her face, then falling on her knee, she caught hold of that Lady's dress, and pressing it to her lips, looked up again into her face, exclaiming, "O dearest Lady!"—It was the Lady Gertrude! And—faint from long standing and overcome with feeling—poor Patience fell back upon the arm of Jem, who laid her gently on the grass, and knelt beside her. The Squire said, "Bring water! and fetch the gamekeeper's light cart to carry her home!" and Jem looked up and said, "She has been ill for months, and was but just getting over it, only I persuaded her to come with me to-day, —but it's been all over too much for her!" And the Lady Gertrude looked on the pale face of Patience—pale with her late long illness, but she saw no trace there of that early misery that had left its impression so strongly on her heart—she did not know her to have been that child! Women had gathered round, Mrs. Smith and Rose were by this time with Patience, and the Squire and his Lady passed on; but as they returned toward the Hall, the Lady Gertrude said to the Squire, "They are still there, let us ask how Jem's wife is now!" so they stopped, and **the** little **close-gathered circle** opened, and the Lady Gertrude said, "How is **she now?**" Patience was still seated on the grass, leaning on the arm of Jem, but she had revived, and now seeing their Lady again, she said, "O, Jem, she is not gone! ask if I may speak to her?" And the Lady Gertrude heard the words, and saw the flush suffuse the cheek of Patience, and kneeling on one knee upon the grass, beside her, she laid her hand upon the clasped hands of Patience, and said, "You are better now, you will soon recover this!" But Patience **looking** up, said, "O, forgive me, dearest Lady! I was that poor child you comforted in ——! it was you that put feeling into my froze-up heart! and I thought I should never have seen you again, and then to see you stand there—it wholly overcame me!" Tears came to that Lady's eyes, as she said, "Are you indeed the same? then I am come to live near you now, and as I saw you in sorrow, so I hope I shall often see you in joy! You may be sure I shall soon come to your cottage!"

Jem had heard all about the love of Patience for that heavenly child that had come to her in her misery, and he looked upon that beautiful Lady kneeling there, with eyes of reverence and wonder; and tears were in the Squire's eyes as he stood there—but he did not speak a word; and Mrs. Smith, and Rose with little Peace in her arms, and the women standing round—looked on astonished; but the light cart drove up, and **the** Squire returned with his Lady to the Hall, and Patience was taken back to her home, and so her heart's long desire was fulfilled—beyond all she had ever hoped or thought; and she quickly recovered strength; and the voice of joy and health was heard within her dwelling.

Wagons and carts carried home the rejoicing people; and **those** near at hand returned on foot. And now the sun went down, and the long shadows fell over lawn and wood. Mrs. Clifford stood at the window with her children, and gazed on the slopes where the welcoming throng had been, and said, "It was too much for me to look upon, but not too much to feel the deepest thankfulness for!" and her son looked on her in answering tenderness. And then the Squire asked his Lady, if she missed the mountains from the landscape that she had been used to from her childhood! And she replied, "O, human hearts are better than the hills, and stronger too in their encircling power! **I know not where on Earth I** could be so happy as here. **And meeting, the** first thing, with that poor child, **whom** I have thought of in **her** sorrow through **so** many years, **seems** to me a bright earnest of good." The sun went down, **and the** fervent feelings of that day reposed in the **quiet** of night's **restful** hours.

And now we must take leave of our **ministering** children,—who have all outgrown their childhood;—to write of and for childhood **being all** that we promised from the beginning. We have only to ask the children who read this story, whether they also are ministering children? This story has been written to show, as in a picture, what ministering children are. There is no child upon Earth who may not be a ministering child; because the Holy Spirit of God, even the blessed Comforter Himself, will come to every child of God who asks that blessed Spirit to teach him how to comfort others. Even the beloved Son of God, when He came down from Heaven to Earth, came to minister to those who were in need—He Himself tells us so. And God sends His holy angels down to Earth to be ministering spirits here. The youngest child of God, who is able to understand any thing, can learn to be a ministering child; therefore, all who pray to God as their Heavenly Father, must try in every way they can to minister to others: and then one day they will go where there is no want, and no sorrow, and no sin, but only fullness of joy and pleasure for evermore, in their Heavenly Father's presence in glory; and there they will see those whom they comforted and taught to know the love of God their Saviour upon earth. "And so shall they ever be with the Lord;" "and God shall wipe away all tears from their eyes; and there shall be no more death, neither sorrow, nor crying, neither shall there be any more pain; for the former things will be passed away."—Rev. xxi. 4.

THE END.

www.ingramcontent.com/pod-product-compliance
Lightning Source LLC
Chambersburg PA
CBHW020858130726
47900CB00014B/1019